— PRAISE FOR —
~SLIPPER

"*Slipper* is the most engaging novel I have read in a long time. Part romantic love story, part fairy tale, part feminist commentary, this is a wonderful, old fashioned novel to be savored. It is as if a graduate student had stumbled upon a handwritten, 19th century manuscript in the British Library, read it, and declared, 'There was a fourth Bronte sister—and she was the most talented of the brood!'"

> — Daniel Klein, best-selling author of
> *Travels with Epicurus* and *Plato and Platypus Walk into a Bar*

"An unexpectedly honest modern novel clothed in the traditional tropes of historical romance. As a bildungsroman the story is refreshingly authentic in the growth of the heroine from an unfettered idealist to a nearly-perfected realist. ...The charm of the protagonist is more than potent enough to draw the reader along through a story that both pointedly charges us with taking command of our own fate, and tasks us with deciding for ourselves what the moral of our own story should be."

> — Thomas A. Peters, *Readers' Favorite*

"Although this novel pays specific homage to Cinderella, Velmans laces the book with references to the other tales. She builds this network with remarkable care, and although the resulting novel is a complex web of influences, it's never a confounding one. Furthermore, she writes in a delicate, ornate prose style that has a transporting effect, bringing readers back to Perrault's time and nestling them in a thoroughly alluring narrative. A satisfying blend of history and myth that breathes new life into Cinderella."

> — *Kirkus Reviews*

SLIPPER

Hester Velmans

V H B

ISBN 978-0-9994756-0-7

Cover design by Ben Hillman, adapted from Bathsheba at her Bath by Veronese (1575)

Book design by Jessika Hazelton • thetroybookmakers.com

"Fairy-tale motifs are not neurotic symptoms..."
Bruno Bettelheim, *The Uses of Enchantment*

"Human beings never enjoy complete happiness in this world. I was not born for a different destiny to the rest of my species; to imagine such a lot befalling me is a fairy tale—a daydream."
— Charlotte Brontë, *Jane Eyre*

"I might have made my tales more agreeable by adding some titillating elements with which it is customary to enliven them. But I have never been so tempted by the desire to please as to break a rule I have set for myself never to write anything that might offend either modesty or propriety."
— Charles Perrault

CONTENTS

PART TWO

PART THREE

BIOGRAPHY AND MYTHOLOGY

AUTHOR'S NOTE

Asked what this novel was about, I would tell people it was the story of a woman whose life was the inspiration for one of Charles Perrault's tales. *Charles who?* they'd say. The name almost never rang a bell.

It seems I could not have been more deluded in thinking "Perrault" was a household name, like Shakespeare, Tolstoy, the brothers Grimm, or Hans Christian Andersen. No one I spoke to seemed to be aware that a seventeenth-century Frenchman named Charles Perrault was the author of our culture's most famous fairy tales. Who knew that the author of Sleeping Beauty, Puss in Boots, Tom Thumb, Little Red Riding Hood and Cinderella lived a full century before the brothers Grimm and almost two hundred years before Hans Christian Andersen? It was Perrault who invented the clear, straightforward prose of the fairy tale as we know it, at a time when his peers were writing in ornate, flowery verse. Shouldn't that be enough to give him a place in the literary pantheon?

Once I began investigating, I found out there wasn't much information about his life, either. A patient librarian at the Bibliothèque Nationale in Paris was unable to dig up a significant biography of Perrault for me. There are plenty of studies of the fairy tales, to be sure, but very little about the author himself. Literary historians have shunned the poor man, it seems, leaving him to linger in obscurity for over three hundred years.

Perrault did leave a short but engaging memoir, *l'Histoire de ma vie*. His life was far from uninteresting: he may not have achieved great acclaim as a poet, but he was a man of many other talents and achievements. As an important functionary in the glittering court of Louis the Fourteenth, he oversaw the decoration of Versailles;

hobnobbed with fellow members of the French Academy including Racine, Molière, and La Fontaine; was involved in a famous literary feud; and helped his brother Claude design the colonnaded façade of the Louvre after conniving to have the great sculptor Bernini thrown off the project.

It wasn't until the end of his life, hoping to find favor with the ladies of the court, that he wrote the simple, appealing tales that embody our most basic yearnings and dreams. The fact that his stories are universally known but his name is forgotten is an irony that would surely have struck the father of Mother Goose as a fate that (as a fawning subject of the great Sun King) was entirely to be expected.

Charles Perrault

PERRAULT'S WORLD

Aman—a gentleman once considerably richer, less corpulent and more important than he is now, retires to his closet, sits down at a table, and picks up his quill. The rays of the late afternoon sun, plumped by dust on the windowpane, give the man's brocade coat and bulbous nose a ruddy glow. He rereads the last lines of the poem he began some days ago, a paean to his sovereign, the great Louis the Fourteenth, then puts down his quill.

For what is the use? His work will only be met with sneers by his colleagues in the Academy, chiefly Boileau and his little coterie—Racine, La Fontaine, and all the rest. They accuse him of being a sycophant, an untalented hack who owes his sinecure to favoritism and graft. Years ago, when he was Comptroller-General of the King's Buildings, Gardens, Arts and Manufactories, he wielded considerable influence, and they have never forgiven him for it. Everything he writes is twisted around and flung back in his face. If he expresses reverence for a patron, or even the king himself, he is excoriated as a hypocrite or a toady. Show a little enthusiasm for modern artistic endeavor, and he is deemed a traitor to antiquity. Every triumph is turned by his enemies into yet further proof of his mediocrity.

He groans softly to himself, fiddling with the lace emerging from his sleeve. Who in this scheming world has been as much maligned as he?

His mind strays to the young Englishwoman whom he once helped when he was in a position to do so, Madame Sunderland, a talented painter whose spirit captured his imagination. The story she told him of her misfortunate origins, her unwise choices, the tricks fate played on her, would break your heart. Once upon a time she asked him to write down her history, as a cautionary tale for other naïve damsels. He loved her dearly, this aristocratic orphan—as a sister, a friend, a daughter. But his enemies, naturally, found a way to turn even that harmless liaison into a tawdry scandal.

Charles thumbs through a stack of papers on his desk, a collection of tales he is readying for publication. It is a late-life hobby, a mere bagatelle, which his learned confrères will no doubt take as further proof of his frivolity. Stories to amuse the court at Versailles; instructive, yet at the same time entertaining. He hopes they will find favor with the ladies; perhaps they will even help him return into the king's good graces. In order to disarm his critics, he muses, he will probably attribute them to Madame Sunderland's old nurse, la mère l'Oie—mother Goose. Or perhaps he'll just call them 'Tales and Stories of the Past, with Morals'; he hasn't quite settled on a title. The setting, however, is one he knows well—a world of scheming courtiers, capricious kings, opulent palaces and cruel stepmothers. The difference is that in his stories, beauty, patience and virtue are rewarded in the end, and the wicked always receive their just deserts.

This is the world according to Charles Perrault.

PART ONE

1

ONCE UPON A BED

Once upon a bed and long ago, there lay a maid. And the maid had to huff and to puff, and to puff and to huff, until finally she gave birth to a small bundle of child.

"Go to sleep now," the midwife told the maid who was now a mother, "You must rest, you're so exhausted, lamb."

But the mother was too elated to sleep. "Bring her to me, please, please nurse, I just want to hold her again," she pleaded.

She spent the next seventy-two hours staring into the new infant's eyes and playing with the tiny fingers when it was awake, or nuzzling the downy head and sniffing the honey smell when it was asleep. She even experimented with crooning lullabies of love into the translucent shell of its dainty ear. The enormity of what had just occurred dazzled her: the idea of a baby, a new human being, had never seemed real when it was still inside her. Now that it was out, and wrapped in its own separate package of broody skin, it was so tangibly, deliciously real, that the thought of her previous indifference blurred her eyes with tears. She surrendered abjectly to this new and terrible tenderness. It pounded through her veins, and surged from her to the child and back again. For even though the cord had long been cut, there was clearly a connecting thread still between her battered womb and the infant's taut belly; both felt it achingly.

In the midst of this ecstasy, a blood clot no bigger than the tip of your thumb dislodged itself from one of the mother's blood vessels and began to wend its way along the passages of her bloodstream. Skirting the liver and the spleen, it clambered upward, bulldozing legions of blood cells out of its way. Nonchalantly it rolled and floated along, bumping into walls and trailing along avenues, until it flipped into the right-hand chambers of the heart and, somersaulting out again, reached the spongy region of the lung. There, in narrowing corridors, it finally stuck fast, unable to move forward or backward, causing a fatal gridlock. And the young mother, on her way to answering a call of nature, fell down on the chill cobbled stones of the bedroom floor.

They said she died of a broken heart.

2

A SILVER SPOON

To ward off evil fairies and a lifetime of bad luck, it is customary to place a coin on the infant's tongue at birth. Sensible godmothers, however, mindful that the lucky coin presents its own hazard, since infants are inclined to choke to death on it, advise that the coin be replaced with a spoon—preferably a silver spoon, if the family can afford it; an item, in short, that is more difficult to swallow.

The midwife made the decision to take care of the nursling until the young woman's relatives showed up to claim her. A good soul of no fixed abode, she made herself indispensable whenever called for, as midwife, wet nurse or even, in happier days, as temporary occupant of the master's bed. Her full name was Elizabeth Sarah Goose, but being a humble person, she always referred to herself as Bessie.

Despite a somewhat questionable reputation, her services were always much in demand, for she had what was called the Touch. This meant she was one of that rare breed who can give a woman in labor a shot of relief by resting a finger just so on the exact spot where pain or panic are at work, filling the bewildered mother with renewed strength and resolve.

But now Bessie found herself saddled with a newborn in an empty gentleman's house on the Thames west of London. Summoned there to deliver a maiden too young to be a mother of an infant about to become an orphan, she had found no one in the house besides the young lady moaning on the bed. Later a charwoman had come in to clean and make the fires, but she too knew nothing about her employer and told Bessie she'd stop coming if she weren't paid for the extra days.

On the day following her patient's death, Bessie took it upon herself to notify the parson's wife, Mrs. Dunes. Mrs. Dunes often found work for Bessie in Chiswick; she was the person you first thought of if you had a wedding, a funeral or a lying-in to arrange. She was a large woman who sighed frequently out of a loose, wet mouth, helplessly out of breath at the thought of all the busy things expected of her.

Bessie had found a family crest embroidered on the pouch containing the young mother's personal knife and spoon.

"This should not be too difficult to trace," wheezed Mrs. Dunes, twisting her head around to make out the emblem. "Two boars rampant on a field of lilies, and the motto *Pecuniae Fiducia.* Let me have this, and I shall see what I can find out. She died of the fever, then?"

"No, no sign of the childbed fever, nor tearing, either," said Bessie eagerly. "It was an easy birth, and she was mending nicely. It came up very sudden-like. From one moment to the next, no life in her. But the poor thing had been grieving, and then the baby filled her with such joy. With such a confusion of humors, no wonder her little heart cracked..."

Mrs. Dunes snorted. "Just retribution more like, if you ask me. Delivered of the child all alone, and neither husband nor relative in sight? Come now. Don't tell me all was well and proper." She smacked her lips wetly, reproachfully, and turned her attention to the bundle in Bessie's arms. "Now, Bessie—the nursling. Are you able to, er, *provide*, or shall I ask Brandy Nuthatch...?"

"Ah, no thank you, ma'am," said Bessie, "the milk is still in, I make sure of that. It must be, oh, a good twelve-month since my little Jonas passed, God rest his soul..." she piously wiped away a tear..."But the milk's the more precious for it, so I tell my ladies. A glass of ale at bedtime does wonders for the flow, old Annie Coles used to swear by it. 'Bessie,' she used to say, 'a glass of dark ale—dark, mind you—that's the way to increase the flush'..."

She gathered that this subject was not one upon which Mrs. Dunes was eager to have her elaborate further, since that lady now closed her eyes and, taking in another rattling breath, heaved herself to her feet.

Bessie hastily tried another gambit. "Poor soul. Must be quite the fancy folks, wouldn't you say? The little miss spoke so prettily, I thought she must be well born, with her heavy knife and spoon—real silver, they are—and you should feel the silk of her niddy-hose..."

There being no hint from Mrs. Dune that she was interested in examining the aforementioned undergarments for herself, Bessie took her leave, wedging the wellborn infant between her abundant side and the shell of her rough woolen cloak.

The baby brooded over its loss, trying to find the thread that had connected it with its mother. It did not cry much, but waved its little fists, rooting with its mouth for the missing link.

"Don't fret, my lamb," whispered Bessie as she stopped the searching mouth with her own breast. "We'll take good care of you, I promise." It occurred to her that the baby did not yet have a name. "Lucinda we'll call you," she said solemnly—a name that to her epitomized everything that was grand, noble and expensive. "And you'll be a lady," she promised, "just like your mama." Then, underscoring each point with a touch of her forefinger to the tip of the baby's nose, she chanted,

"And you'll be rich, and you'll be famous, and you'll be loved-loved-loved..."

As it turned out, it soon became clear that if Bessie Goose wanted this baby to be loved-loved-loved, it would be entirely up to her.

Within a week, the parson's wife sent word that the deceased girl's family had been found. Bessie was to take the infant by stage and hired coach to Wriggin Hall, in Hampshire. This was the country seat of William Steppys, Earl of Hempstead. He was the child's grandfather.

The midwife duly set out for that destination dreaming of a world she had never seen first-hand (a world of silver soup tureens and ladies in taffeta dresses), the aristocratic Lucinda tightly wrapped in her muslin shawl.

"Oh my Lord!" exclaimed Bessie, who had fallen asleep during the last leg of the journey and had to be jogged awake by the coachman. "Are we here, then?"

She could not believe her eyes. It was just as she had pictured it, only grander. Reverently she peered up at the mansion before her.

What Bessie saw was an imposing stone structure three stories high. Spaced out along the façade was a line of stone pillars, which upon closer inspection turned out to be statues of beautiful ladies with vacant eyes and indecently draped undergarments. There were heavy carved doors rich with brass, sumptuous stone urns brimming with petrified fruit, and wide steps leading to gardens crisscrossed with meticulously shorn hedges. Bessie had never seen the likes of it.

Nor did the interiors disappoint. The servants' quarters were vast. The kitchen ceiling was at least two stories high, she reckoned, and filled to the rafters with foodstuffs—braces of pheasants nicely decomposing, several hams drying, pigs' bladders, a pair of freshly slaughtered geese, bunches of herbs, sacks of meal, turnips and onions, a rack of cheeses pungently ripening. Not one, but two fireplaces, each large enough to roast an ox, their spits turned by a team of dogs on a treadmill; and even a stove made of bricks along one wall. (Bessie had heard of this new-fangled contraption—it meant you could stir soups and sauces with scarce any risk of burning yourself—but she had never before today seen one firsthand.) There were also a staggering number of windows—Bessie counted at least six— each glazed with real glass.

Even this magnificence, however, did not prepare her for the gala grandeur of the main house. She gaped at gilded panels on walls and ceilings depicting glorious scenes of a place she took to be heaven, since the elegant people in them were being fawned over by cherubs; dark portraits of grim men and women glowering into old-fashioned ruffled collars; sparkling chandeliers; gleaming floors that echoed impressively underfoot; the most ornately carved chairs lined up against the walls.

"Do you like it, pet?" she whispered to her charge. "This is where you belong. This is how the fine sirs and madams live. Nothing but the finest for you, my lamb."

* * *

The interview with the lady who was the lamb's grandmother was brief.

"So this is the child," she said distastefully. The child had chosen the moment to let out her most piercing wail.

"Yes my lady, madam," said Bessie. She kept her lips compressed in a tight circle, in an effort to sound elegant. "Our Lucinda is such a good girl usually, she just..."

"Lucinda?"

"So I've been calling her, milady, but..."

"Lucinda will do."

Lady Hempstead indicated that she could not bear the noise any longer and flicked her illegitimate granddaughter out of the room with a flip of a bejeweled hand.

It was sitting by the servants' hall fire that Bessie heard the juicy details of the scandal. The infant's mother was Olivia, Lord and Lady Hempstead's fifth daughter. Lady Olivia had always been an obedient child and was perhaps less closely watched than her older sisters. Her innocence, however, had landed her in trouble when she'd made eyes at a debt-ridden baron who had allegedly had her in the bushes while her sisters were dancing the gavotte.

"And it was five months before milady found out, when anyone could see she was with child. Although it isn't as if some of us didn't have our suspicions, what with her secretive ways and feeling so poorly..."

Bessie nodded, and in doing so caught the eye of a footman who had a delicious crease running from the side of his mouth all the way up his cheek.

"Well, as you can imagine, Milord declared she would never be allowed back in this house. Milady had a family friend arrange for a place..."

"In Chiswick," Bessie supplied.

"No, that may be where she died, but that is not where she was sent. And all the trouble milady went through, too, to make the arrangements! She was to board with a person who takes in ladies in her condition, up at Aldringham, I think it was, wasn't it, Nell? We heard she never arrived, but if you ask us, there was some as was relieved to be rid of her."

Bessie raised her eyebrows.

"Well, you know, the shame of it, the good family name and all."

And so Bessie never did discover how Lady Olivia had wound up in the house in Chiswick, but she had other things on her mind just then, including the footman's creased cheek. It occurred to her that she could not possibly leave her little Lucinda, her lamb, her pet, with these indifferent, although clearly very wealthy people. For Bessie, who had seen not one of her own offspring live this long, was beginning to feel she had a legitimate claim to the infant. After all, after having delivered the little sprite, hadn't she been the one to christen her too? She, Bessie Goose, had chosen Lucinda's name, and milady had approved it. And then, in the absence of a godmother, it was Bessie who had placed the silver spoon upon Lucy's tongue for good luck—none other!

Bessie decided she would go to Lucinda's grandparents and offer her services as the child's nurse. It was the right thing to do.

Of course the crease in the footman's cheek may have been another factor in her calculations.

"Very well," said Lady Hempstead, probing beneath her curved finger-nails with an ivory implement. "That will do, I suppose." Bessie's application saved her the effort of having to find some other candidate. It really was better for her health if she did not trouble herself any further with that pitiful token of her youngest daughter's shame.

And so Bessie Goose and her pet-lamb became members of the Hempstead household. They were assigned a garret in the top of the west wing where the servants lived, and had nothing to do with the elegant folks living below for a good long while.

3

THE ART OF LOVE

Once the question of her staying at Wriggin Hall was settled, Bessie set about winning over the household staff. With her midwifery background, Bessie had picked up a fair deal of expertise in simples, salves and other remedies, and was always ready to provide a medical opinion, whether called for or not. Her enthusiasm came as much from a need to mother everyone as from a desire to impress people with her knowledge. But here was the unfortunate thing: Bessie had yet to master the art of holding her audience's attention. Not that what she had to say wasn't interesting; it was her voice that let her down. It was not a voice to inspire confidence; it was a tentative, chirpy thing. Her sentences tended to end on an upward note, seeking approval, asserting a good-natured willingness to be contradicted or overruled. And so people usually became bored with her chatter, and, since they assumed she did not know what she was talking about, seldom heard her out.

Winning over the footman, however, was an easier matter. Although she was at the end of her childbearing years, Bessie was blessed with certain attributes that still made a man look twice. For whereas some women in their prime are unappealingly pulpy, Bessie Goose was dimply, twinkly and eminently kissable. Weather and age had given her face the beauty marks that only the true connoisseur will appreciate, but none the less precious for that: a pleasant sunburst of lines at the outer edge of the eye, giving her a look of perpetual merriment. Under her pretty plump face, the neck and freckled shoulders spread out soft as a featherbed, and from there the eye traveled down to an ample, although not immodest, bosom, an uncomfortably cinched waist over full hips and rump, and brisk little feet peeping out beneath her petticoat.

It had been some time since Bessie had buried her last husband, and the odd romp in the hay or the master's library no longer satisfied her. Bessie longed for a companion with whom she could gossip and share her wages, a mate who would like to be pampered and cuddled on a more permanent basis.

The footman with the creased cheek was, she lost no time in discovering, unattached. He had a wide-eyed, almost puzzled gaze, a nose flattened in boyhood games, and delectable little curls at the nape of his neck.

At first Bessie worried that the attraction might not be mutual, and lost two nights' sleep fretting over that possibility. But sitting herself down calmly and going over the facts one by one, she concluded her fears were groundless. For did he not turn up wherever she happened to be with greater frequency than could be mere coincidence? Were his cheerful efforts at making himself useful not met, by the others, with arched eyebrows and glances in her direction? Did he not studiously avoid looking at her, feigning an indifference that his bright-eyed interest in everything else, including the dogs and the cook's doddering mother, left open to reasonable doubt? And what were his self-conscious swagger and sheepish grin whenever he did have to address her directly, if not the very earmarks of an infatuation?

Turning these facts over in her mind, Bessie decided the footman would not be able to resist her subtle encouragement.

"Thomas," she murmured, prying loose Lucinda from her breast, and neatly tucking everything back into her corselet, "Thomas, could you assist me with something?"

Thomas, staring straight ahead, mumbled, "Ah—Mum..."

"It's the babe's cot, I want to move it over by the window upstairs, you see the sun's the best thing for an infant's constitution, much better than the elixir, I've always told my ladies a dose of sun and a sip of mother's milk is worth any bottle of Daffy's..." She gazed up at him, helpless. "But I cannot manage it myself."

His Adam's apple bobbed up.

"So I was wondering, Thomas, if you wouldn't mind..."

"When—now?"

"Are you needed elsewheres?" Lord and Lady Hempstead had left the previous day for Newmarket, and the household was taking it easy.

"No, I suppose..."

She swayed up the stairs ahead of him. Thomas practiced looking nonchalant, aware of the eyes following the two of them out of the hall.

They worked up quite a sweat pushing the furniture about. For to make room for the cot by the window, the chest had to be moved next to the bed, and the bed had to be angled into a corner. Finally Bessie flopped onto the pallet, as if to try it out, fanning herself. Thomas looked enquiringly at the door. Bessie sighed heavily.

Thomas suddenly noticed a splinter in his thumb. He examined it intently.

"Thomas..."

"Mum?"

"No—Never mind."

Thomas looked up from his thumb and saw that her eyes were cast down and her shoulders hunched.

"Is there...?"

"No, nothing. Please, please...Just go away. Really."

She turned her face to the wall.

It now dawned on Thomas that this performance might very well have something to do with him.

"You want me to go?" he asked, incredulous.

"Yes, just go. *Go*, I said!"

She had snapped at him! It was so unjust and so unexpected that Thomas now found himself at a loss. He clenched his teeth, dug his nails into his palms and stepped back toward the door, eyes on the ground. But as he lifted the latch, he could not resist one last glance at the bed.

What he saw was that she was holding herself very still, as if listening for his next move.

Experimentally, he took a step forward again. "But..." he began.

She spun around to face him. Her grey eyes locked defiantly with his.

He swallowed. But he stood his ground like a man. It was she who had to look away first, her chin trembling—with confusion or excitement, it was hard to tell which.

Thomas approached her with new resolve.

He reached down and touched her waist, clumsily slipped his arm around her back and pulled her up to him.

"No, Thomas," she whimpered, struggling deliciously against him. "No, you mustn't..."

And there we will leave the couple for now, the ardent seducer and his willing prey, and the infant quietly asleep under the window.

4

THE UGLY STEPPYS SISTER

Whereas Lady Hempstead was an established member of the aristocracy, a granddaughter of the Marquess of Stornton, her husband's credentials were of more recent vintage. He had been born Willie Stepps the sail-maker's son: humble origins he was glad to put behind him. Willie's grandfather had amassed a fortune before the boy was born by landing a monopoly on the manufacture of sails for the Royal Fleet during Queen Elizabeth's reign. The judicious application of that fortune, and some adroit maneuverings during the Civil War period, had enabled his heirs to add a "y" to the family name and to switch their allegiance from Whig to Tory just in time to qualify for a title when a grateful King Charles was restored to the throne.

Suffice it to say that the Steppyses had long since ceased to trouble themselves with canvas or hemp. They had moved from Newcastle-upon-Tyne to an area southwest of London, allied themselves with the nobility by means of generous marriage contracts, and taken on the monotone accent and distinctive pursuits of England's upper classes.

The Earl of Hempstead's pursuit was politics: he could often be found meddling in internal affairs at Westminster when his social or hunting engagements allowed. Let it be noted for the record that he was at this time suffering from a touch of the pox. Happily, he had acquired that disease some years after Lady Hempstead's bedroom door had been shut to him—happily, that is, for that good lady, who knew nothing of such sordid matters as venereal diseases. No one had ever considered clouding the countess's perfumed universe with the stench of the gutter, and she lived in Elysian ignorance. For her own life's calling, she had focused largely on dress and outward appearance, and had seen to it that fourteen confinements, or *accouchements*, as she called them (only half a dozen offspring, all but one female, survived childhood), had not significantly spoiled her looks. She did not take much interest in her children, except in tracking down good matches for her daughters. It must be said, however, that she was extremely fond of her spaniels.

Three of the daughters had made very satisfactory marriages indeed and were suitably installed in mansions of their own, with the requisite number of servants and bedchambers. The spirit of sibling rivalry, however, was not left behind: the sisters were in the habit of scrutinizing each other's porcelain, plate and tapestries as shrewdly as a milliner examining a knot of ribbons.

The last Steppys sister—if, that is, you discount the disgraced and deceased Olivia, whose name was now taboo—was not married, and her mother despaired of ever pairing her, whether suitably or not. Her face was, if you wanted to be kind, homely, or, if you wanted to be blunt—*"A kitchen-maid's face, by Jove!"* according to her insensitive father, *"and a figure to match!"* And it must be admitted that Lady Arabella's eyebrows did grow in dark tufts over the bridge of her nose, and that there was a patch of scaly skin around her mouth that no amount of powder could conceal. Her wrists were crawling with black hairs, and it was distressingly clear that her waist was not made for corsets. But most off-putting of all to even the most hardened dowry-hunter was the squint—the legacy of a childhood infection that had left her with a milky left eye.

It would be nice to be able to report that the disfigured maiden had a heart of gold and that a compassionate prince was eventually found for her, but alas, even her personality contained no redeeming feature. Her wit was loaded with tactlessness, her sense of humor was distressingly underdeveloped, and, having been cheated of affection at too early an age, she had perfected an annoying whine and snide temper that made all who knew her avoid her like the pox.

Now it eventually occurred to Lady Hempstead that her unmarriageable daughter could be turned into an asset if she were given the responsibility of running the household—a task necessitated by the death of Barking, the last housekeeper.

Arabella took on the job with touching enthusiasm. Delighted with the opportunity of venting her spleen on hapless inferiors, she made pernicious lists of finicky tasks for the cleaning staff, snooped in pantry cupboards to catch culinary misdemeanors, and set impossible standards for all who fell under her exacting command. She became the scourge of Wriggin Hall, and her high-pitched outrage rang from garret to cellar. Where none of her class had bothered to tread before, Lady Arabella now roamed obsessively, leaving nowhere for a loyal retainer to find respite from her eagle eye or vicious tongue.

Arabella's promotion did not happen until the fifth year of Bessie's employment at Wriggin Hall, long after Lucinda had become the entire household staff's pet. For Lucy, life was one long round of treats and surprises. All she had to do was to act winsome, and to reward the adults from time to time with her coveted dimpled smile.

Meanwhile Bessie and Thomas had set up house within the larger house. Thomas had been more than happy to give up his pallet in the stables, and had moved into Bessie's room without delay. She prepared special little meals for him at times when the kitchen was not busy, and made an art out of concocting salves and tonics for him that would "make him feel better".

Thomas felt so much better most of the time, and the effect of his wellbeing was so noticeable in the glowing contentment of his companion, that Bessie soon found a market for her potions among the household staff. Who, it must be said, became slightly more respectful of Bessie's arts, although they still quickly changed the subject whenever someone accidentally set her off on one of her perorations.

Lady Arabella, in her new role, examined the wages ledger for Wriggin Hall.

"What is this Elizabeth Goose person, nursemaid, who is costing us ten shillings every quarter?" she asked her mother.

"I have no idea, my dear," replied her mother vaguely, "I thought you were taking care of these things now, Arabella. Do not trouble me with such matters."

Arabella took her quest to Tucker, the steward.

"Bessie has been taking care of our Lucinda," said Tucker, surprised at Lady Arabella's ignorance.

"And *who*, may I ask, is *our* Lucinda?" said Arabella spitefully.

"Uh, if I may, ma'am, she is…is…your niece. The child. The Lady Olivia's baby," he explained, embarrassed.

"Olivia's baby! Aha!" exclaimed Arabella, who had until this moment not realized that her sister's peccadillo had had any consequence other than banishment from the parental home and a sorry death.

Arabella stomped down to the kitchen and after grilling the head cook, sent for Bessie.

"Now, I have reviewed your service here," she said peevishly, "and it appears that your only function has been to look after—the child. Is that so?"

"Indeed, milady, it is so," said Bessie brightly.

"And Cook tells me that you peddle potions and salves and such. Have you, or have you not, used the kitchen's commodities in preparing your little remedies?"

"No, milady! I would never…that is…I go out and pick my own, that's what I…"

"Ah! Then it is true!" interrupted Arabella triumphantly. "You pick your own! To concoct your diabolical preparations!" As she stood up, her chair scraped harshly against the stone floor. Bessie flinched.

Arabella leaned forward over the table, blasting Bessie with her vinegar breath. "I am amazed, madam. Simply amazed! Did you think the kitchen was an apothecary? Look at it! Does this look like an apothecary shop, or perhaps an alchemist's laboratory?"

Bessie shook her head abjectly.

"No, no, but I don't understand! Are you telling me that although you *know* that the kitchen is not an apothecary, yet you *continue* to pursue your…dark arts here?"

Bessie opened her mouth to say something, then thought better of it and bowed her head again.

"Pah! I don't understand, I'm sure. You have a perfectly enviable position here. Forty shillings a year! And yet you abuse your position, you abuse my mother's generous nature...Fortunately *I* am now in charge, and we shan't have any more of this nonsense. Is that clear? I will not have it. You will reimburse the kitchen for what is missing. It comes to eighteen shillings and thruppence. Understood?"

Bessie inclined her head a fraction lower. Her neck ached. It was an enormous sum.

"And if I catch you taking a single clove from the pantry again..."

"No, mum."

"Now this—this child. Bring her to me. I wish to see her."

Bessie slunk from the room. She had a notion that Lady Arabella was not planning to bounce Lucinda on her knee.

Bessie was right. Arabella did not have a soft spot for children, and her impulse to see Lucinda owed more to diligence than a sentimental nature.

What Arabella saw was a little doll with porcelain skin, dark brown curls, large, limpid eyes and not a single blemish except for the blubbery nose. For Lucinda had burst into tears quite early on in the interview, having never in her short life faced an adult who did not smile at her besottedly, pinch her cheeks, or generally dote.

Arabella glared.

"How old are you?"

Lucinda sniffled.

"Can you recite the Lord's Prayer?"

A hiccup.

"Can you count to a hundred? Have you any French? Do you sew?"

Arabella was not familiar with children. This was the first child she had ever been called upon to cross-examine, and she was quite disgusted with the girl's performance. She called for Bessie.

"This child is appallingly ignorant. Have you taught her nothing?"

"Oh, but ma'am, she's so young yet, there's plenty of time for lessons..." Bessie herself could neither read nor write—not an uncommon circumstance for a woman of her class, and certainly not something to be ashamed of.

"How *dare* you argue with me! Take her away! I shall have to think about what to do with the pair of you..."

Upon consultation with her sisters, Lady Arabella decided that the best place for her deceased sister's bastard was a household where provisions were already in place for the rearing of children—that is, one with a proper complement of tutors, music teachers, dancing instructors and governesses, each charged with conducting a healthily disciplined regimen in an atmosphere of suitably obsequious indoctrination.

Lady Clarissa, the eldest of the Steppys sisters, was living wealthily among the rolling hills of Dorset. Her husband, Sir Edmund Nayerdell, was considered the best fox and stag hunter in the county. Edmund and Clarissa had already produced five children, and in addition to their own brood they were also raising Clarissa's only brother—young Robert, Viscount Swyndhurst.

The infant Robert's unforeseen arrival into the world seven years earlier had come as a nasty shock. To assuage Lady Hempstead's dismay at finding herself saddled with yet another child at this late stage, when she thought she was done with all that, the infant Viscount had been bundled off to board with Clarissa and Edmund, who were only too happy to have some influence over the old earl's sole male offspring, the boy who would one day control the Steppys fortune.

"Of *course* she must come to us," Clarissa told Arabella, with a smirk. Fancy that—Olivia's brat living at Wriggin Hall for more than four years without anyone being aware of her existence! "We'll treat the poor little thing just like one of our own, shan't we, Edmund?"

Edmund grunted. He was not interested in children, let alone a bastard sired by someone else.

Clarissa turned back to Arabella. "As for the nurse. You say that she also cooks?"

"I told you!" said Arabella evenly. "Don't you listen? I would rather not have to tell you everything twice, Clarissa. She helped herself whenever she felt like it, Widow Ben swears to it."

"What I was thinking was, our kitchen could use another set of hands...Wait—let me speak! I know you are upset, dear, I know *you* would throw her out. But *I* could find it in my heart, I *do* think, to overlook her trespass. It is a shame, of course, a crying shame, the creature simply delving into the larder without permission. Still, Arabella, one must forgive. It is our Christian duty."

She sighed, overcome by her own magnanimity. A glance at her husband revealed that he was not attending. She stared in the gigantic gilt mirror opposite. Some day he would realize how lucky he was. After all, how many men had wives endowed with such a pleasant disposition, such kind instincts and such...*womanly* attributes as she?

Bessie was heartbroken. She had no choice but to take the kitchen job in Dorset, for she had become so attached to the child that even an inferior post was better than being parted from her lamb. But Thomas...poor Thomas would be left behind.

Poor Thomas had in fact found the courage to ask Arabella if there might possibly be a position for himself in her sister's house. But the very intimation (raised by his impudent suggestion that Bessie and he might "stay together") that these servants had been mating, right here under her nose, while she—the Lady Arabella Steppys—was doomed to spend her life as a maid, albeit not in the domestic sense of course, sent her into such an apoplexy that Thomas considered himself lucky to have held on to his post at all.

5

THE CUCKOO IN THE NEST

"Lucy-doosy, quack-quack goosy..."

Lucinda had had it with her mean cousins. Blinking away tears, she stormed out of the nursery and stomped down the back stairs, three at a time and avoiding the cracks. She had meant to go for a walk outside, but when she opened the door and saw the snow coming down, the desire for fresh air left her. She pushed open the door to the hot and steamy kitchen instead. A dozen pairs of concerned eyes looked up.

"Lucy, lamb, what's the matter?" Bessie exclaimed, bustling over to her.

"Nothing. I just came down to see what smells so good." Lucinda was not about to confess to her unpopularity in the nursery. "What's that? Quaking pudding?"

"Yes, my pet. Marchpane too. Company tonight. And we haven't forgotten you. Whitepot for the nursery—your favorite!"

"Lucy, Lucy!" Two pint-sized urchins ran up to her: Tom, whose job it was to tend the fire and turn the spit, and who was so small for his age that they called him Tom Thumb; and Audrey, scarce any bigger, who had been employed in the kitchen as bottle washer since the age of five.

Lucinda's spirits lifted. It was hard to say which was worse—to be ignored by her cousins, or to be the butt of their jokes. From the time she had arrived here as a little girl, the pestering had been fairly relentless. But down here she was special, the brightest star of the universe. Here they were overjoyed to see her and overflowing with love for her. Her own love surged in return.

"Bread pudding? What are you doing, Bessie, trying to fatten me up for market?" To the little tykes tugging at her skirts, she whispered, "You two will have my portion, I shall see to it."

Bessie shook her head and pursed her lips. "I just *wish* you would put on some weight, lamb." Turning to the others, she sighed, "She's really much too thin, if you ask me. One of these days she'll blow away in a west wind…"

"Lucinda laughed. "The things you say, Bess! Anyway, do we really want to be like one of your jellies, all blubbery—boing! boing! boing!—when we walk…?" The two tiny kitchen helpers giggled. There was no danger either of them would ever grow plump, even with Lucinda's habit of slipping them tidbits when no one was looking.

"You look fine to me, sweetheart," purred Mrs. Kettle, the head cook.

"A lovely young lady!" said Lena the laundress.

The entire kitchen staff agreed.

And Lucinda was able to skip upstairs to face her cousins with a fresh dose of pluck.

"We are having company tonight," she announced importantly.

"What do you mean, *We?*" sneered Sarah, closest in age to Lucinda. Sarah had taken it upon herself never to let Lucy forget who was legitimate and who was not. "*Your* parents are having company tonight, are they?"

"Perhaps she means the cook-maids are receiving the chimney sweep," remarked Robert. Even though Robert, the Viscount, was treated with greater deference than the other cousins, he could be just as childish and mean as the rest of them.

"Or a turnspit," giggled Catherine, one of the twins.

"The swineherd!" gleamed little Samuel.

Quick and easy retorts were never readily available to Lucinda. A shrug of the shoulders and a lame "*You'll* see…" were all she could muster.

It was only when she had retreated, crestfallen, to her little footstool by the window that it came to her: she should have let on that *she* knew what was for pudding, then refused to tell. She opened her mouth. But it was too late: the moment had passed. With a sigh she picked up her charcoal and opened her little sketchbook.

"*Lucy-cinder, sitting by the wind-er,*" she heard one of them whisper, followed by snorts of laughter.

But it didn't matter, because she was already drifting into another world, a world where they'd all be sorry they had made fun of her; a world where a pair of strong arms caught her by the waist, lifted her onto his steed and galloped away...

"Let's go!" said Mrs. Limpid sharply, "Lucinda! That means you too! They are expecting you downstairs."

Lucinda got up from the footstool and smoothed out her crumpled skirt, suddenly conscious of her drab smock. The others had changed into better finery. They had no reason to resent playing the part of model children on show for the visitors. Lucinda, however, had refused to get up from her post by the window. She had gone on staring at the drifting snowflakes and daydreaming about her handsome knight and his daring rescue. She had been planning to avoid the evening's embarrassing ritual altogether by sneaking out just before Mrs. Limpid arrived to round them up, but she had been so engrossed in that other world that she was trapped now in this.

"Children!" exclaimed Lady Clarissa, as if the appearance of eight children in her dining room were a startling surprise. "Let me present the children to you, Captain," she chirruped, turning to one of the visitors, "They did *so* wish to meet you."

There were six guests for the children to make their curtsies and bows to. The Blandys, Henrietta and Samuel—neighbors and frequent visitors to the manor; next, the children's two married aunts and one uncle; and, last, a stranger.

"This, my dears, is Captain Henry Beaupree, my *very* favorite soldier," crooned their mother.

The captain looked sternly at the young faces staring up at him. He was not a connoisseur of children and, examining the dwarfish crew, wondered what all the fuss was about. Here there were mouths slightly open with tongues protruding; a fair number of missing or rabbity front teeth; freckles, pockmarks and blemishes, skinny shoulders, pudgy little hands with dimples instead of knuckles, daft grins, protruding ears and, Lord! even a runny nose.

"Nice, very nice," he finally muttered in recognition of something rather more appealing: two young maidens, one blonde and rosy-cheeked, the other dark-haired with skin as white as snow.

The audience was over before the children had had a chance to take in all the glittering sights of the dining room. Their mother had even forgotten to invite them to approach the sideboard piled with sweetmeats and nuts—ordinarily the best part of the ritual.

"Now run along, dear ones," said Clarissa, catching in the reflecting glass the tender picture of a mother kissing each child warmly on the forehead, even Lucinda, that cuckoo in her nest.

"He's a captain, he wears a sword, and he said I looked very nice," boasted Sarah to Mrs. Limpid.

Lucinda looked at Sarah. She had been so mesmerized that she had forgotten for a moment Sarah's presence beside her. Could it have been Sarah the stranger had been looking at with those piercing eyes? It could have been. Sarah's hair hung loose and fair, and little pillows of round flesh were beginning to show at the top of her tightly corseted bodice. Her mouth was a rosebud, and matched in color her satiny cheeks. Her eyebrows were thick and downy, and the eyes underneath, although somewhat colorless and close-set, held a perfectly benign expression. Sarah was her father's favorite. She reeked of lavender-water and self-possession.

It must have been Sarah.

In bed, Lucinda's head pounded and she felt the same searing sensations that usually accompanied her daydreams. Only this time it was the stranger she was thinking of. Was it he? He had seemed so...so stern, and so disdainful. And yet...No matter how hard she tried to change the subject and conjure up her other dream-world knights, she could not banish him from her sleepy mind.

* * *

In Lady Clarissa's bedchamber, a battle was in full swing. The good lady was screaming at her husband.

"It is not true! I have *not* been making eyes at him! All I ever have from you is accusations! This is so unjust! Of course the captain had to sit next to me—he *was* the guest of honor. Would you have me banish him to the foot of the table? Don't laugh! Edmund! I *forbid* you to laugh! Just because there are some men who *do* appreciate me..."

She caught sight of herself in her looking glass, and wished Edmund were the sort of man who said, "Begad, but you are beautiful when you are angry..." But the reality was that she no longer appealed to him, now that her skin was no longer smooth as snow, now that the outline of her form was rumpled with fat, each layer the badge of yet another pregnancy. It infuriated her.

"And you! How dare you complain! Don't you think I know about your nasty habits? Take that—Annie, for instance. There goes *another* chambermaid. What, do you think it is easy to find good help? I cannot go on like this, spending half my days engaging new maids. The *trollop*! I knew she was a bad egg, another bun in the oven, and the yeast yours, I have no doubt..."

Edmund grinned. He rather enjoyed his wife's culinary euphemisms, and was hardly ashamed of his own robust appetites. He was a full-blooded male, and he liked to spread his seed around. All he was trying to do was point out to the woman that she'd made a fool of herself tonight.

"Clarissa-a-a-" he drawled, "will you quiet down like a good gel, or shall I be obliged to return to my chamber and make some other arrangement...?"

He had to admit it was not the most tactful approach, but he enjoyed needling her when she was like this.

"'S-truth, and to accuse *me* of making eyes at men!" she brayed. "And you, sir? You...you...I have seen you ogling that little minx Lucinda. You were ogling her tonight. Were you not! She is just your cup of tea, isn't she! All lanky and no flesh on her. Don't think I hadn't noticed. Well, sir, you shall not have her. She is *my* poor sister's child. I shall see to it that you lay not a finger on her—it's the least I can do for Olivia. If only—I wish now that I had never taken her in! There's gratitude for you, a child

I have raised as my very own...I should have seen it coming, I should have known she would repay me thus!"

Edmund closed his eyes. It was painful to have to listen to more of this ranting. But damn if she hadn't just put an interesting notion into his head. The child in question—what was her name, Lucinda, was it?—had grown into an attractive little proposition. And whereas he would never tamper with his own flesh and blood, this one was no relation—at least no *blood* relation, was she? His deceased sister-in-law's bastard. Fair game, then.

"Clarissa-a-a," he repeated. And yawned. "Enough! Half a minute and I shall be asleep..."

Clarissa sniffed, dried her eyes, and snuggled down beside him, like a good gel.

6

WHO'S THE FAIREST

If Sir Edmund had been a crony of Henry Beaupree's, which he was not, the two men would have found that they shared something in common: namely, the opinion that illicit dalliances were far more satisfying than those sanctioned by matrimony. Where they differed, however, was that Edmund had a wife to be faithless to, while Henry had the bachelor's perk (some might call it duty) of dallying with the faithless wives of others.

In accepting Lady Clarissa's invitation to a week of hunting in Dorset, extended over the basset-table in the Duchess of Ricksborough's salon, Henry thought that the lady's offer was intended to make her husband jealous, so that a little gallantry was all that was required of him. It was disconcerting, therefore, to find himself surrounded that first evening in Dorset by not one, but three married women vying for his attention. It was clear from the family resemblance—a disproportionately long expanse of upper lip drawn tightly over the front teeth—that they were related to each other.

How was Henry to know that the ladies Clarissa, Edwina and Margaret enjoyed one another's company largely for the opportunity to establish which sister was to be envied most? On this occasion, Clarissa's desire to make her husband take notice of her was superseded by the challenge of making her sisters jealous.

Thus Margaret and Edwina, on arriving at the manor, had been greeted with the breathless news that Clarissa had made a conquest in London, a dashing military man no less, and that he had followed her here, hoping to break down her iron resistance in her very home! This was news indeed, and a triumphant Clarissa discerned a tinge of envy around her sisters' pursed lips. Clarissa was not a clever strategist, however, or she would have foreseen the outcome of this move: now Edwina and Margaret had no choice but to join in the game, and try to coax the captain away from their sister.

And so Henry had found himself the target of a heavily perfumed firing line after the meal had been consumed, the sack-posset had been swilled, and the ladies had repaired their toilette.

"Pray tell, Captain," wheedled Lady Margaret, "How is it that you serve the *French* king? Does England not need protection too?"

"Madam," said the gallant captain, "if ever an enemy were to threaten such fair company"—his eyes flitted diplomatically over each lady without resting on any one in particular—"I assure you, not even the King of France himself could stay me from rushing to your defense."

"Is it true," asked Lady Clarissa, "that the French officers dine better than they do at the French court, what's it called, Saint-Germain?"

"No, Clarissa, you mean that new place everyone's talking about, you know, Versayles!" Lady Edwina corrected her.

"*Versailles,* dear Edwina," said Margaret, "is how it is pronounced."

"Nothing, madam, compares to what I have sampled at your table." Henry said smoothly. He could not help a wistful glance at the adjoining room, where card tables had been set up.

"But," Edwina said with a pretty pout, planting herself squarely in his line of vision, "you have not given an explanation, sir. Why must you go overseas?"

"Ladies, ladies," Henry replied with a sigh. "As you know, we are in alliance with France. His Majesty King Charles has ordered that his French cousin be provided with as many able-bodied Englishmen as he needs to help him vanquish Holland. But believe me, my fealty is to England first."

"I understand that son-of-a-whore Louis has been paying a fair rogue's ransom for his fealty, too," Edmund mouthed to his brother-in-law Sherworth.

"Certainly more than our poor Charles can squeeze out of those penny-pinchers at Westminster," murmured the other.

"Oh, Captain! But aren't those Hollanders or Spaniards or whatever they are, *animals*? We hear such stories! Is it very dangerous? I should be *so* frightened!" Clarissa looked ready to swoon.

Henry decided that if he was going to have a tryst at all during this hunting week, it might as well be the tall one, Lady Margaret. She had the freshest face and the tautest breasts; and her husband did not seem to be of the company. Happy to have solved his little problem, and to cover up his stratagem, he turned his back on the chosen one and oozed his charms at her sisters, the ladies Clarissa and Edwina.

The highlight of hunting week at the manor was a ball to be held on Saturday, and Sarah was to be allowed downstairs for it.

"My lady deems you are old enough," said Mrs. Limpid over breakfast. "And she says you will wear the new dove-taffeta."

"What about me?"

Mrs. Limpid and Sarah turned to Lucinda with identical expressions of annoyance.

"What *about* you, Lucinda?" Mrs. Limpid said.

"May I go to the ball too? I'm the same age as Sarah."

Mrs. Limpid thought the question was a fair one and, since she had always tried to be even-handed and even felt a little sorry for the girl, she took it to Lady Clarissa in her dressing room. She already knew the answer, however.

"Lucinda? Certainly not." Clarissa spoke to the governess hovering over her shoulder in the looking glass without taking her eyes off her own reflection. "It isn't suitable. I mean, considering her origins, it will not do to..." The sentence trailed off, as Clarissa remembered with whom it was that she was sharing this confidence. It was better to be vague with the servants. She sat back a little, digging a knuckle into her cheek in the spot where a dimple would have been so becoming.

"And anyway," she chided, "what would the poor girl have done for a gown?"

7

THE KISS

Lucinda decided the sketch was no good. She couldn't help brooding about the injustice of not being allowed to go to the ball, and it made her heavy-handed, too clumsy for the light touch the snowy landscape demanded. She had been sitting on the frozen ground so long that her right leg had begun to fall asleep, but was too intent on capturing the stooped silhouette of a willow tree to shift her weight under her board.

"Ah, if it isn't one of the little Nayerdells," she heard, and looked around. When she saw who it was, she tried to scramble to her feet, but crashed inelegantly into the snow when her numb leg refused to bear her weight.

"Let me help you up," he said, smirking.

"I can manage, thank you," she panted. "I am not, actually," she stammered, stamping her foot to get rid of the pins and needles.

"You are not what?"

"I'm not one of the little Nayerdells—I mean, I am not a Nayerdell."

"I do beg your pardon. I thought we met...?"

"Yes, I came down the other night, with the others. Only, I am their cousin." She felt a little sick, and her breathing was unnaturally ragged.

Henry Beaupree was well enough versed in the behavior of young women to know that this one was ripe for the plucking.

He shook out the cloak she had been sitting on and led her to a bench, then motioned her to sit down, all in a manner devastatingly chivalrous.

"Are you not cold?" He carefully draped the cloak around her shoulders.

Lucinda shook her head no, at a loss for words. She thought guiltily of the role he had played in the night, in her head, and wondered if he could have read her mind. She quickly tried to think of something pure, something irreproachable, to blot out the fantasies.

"You have been drawing, I see," he said. "That is admirable. I cannot for the life of me draw anything—a child of three sketches better than I." He smiled, and Lucinda couldn't help smiling back. Then jerked her head down, flustered at having been caught gazing into his eyes.

Henry drew closer, and very deliberately let his eyes skim her entire person—up and down. Gently, he picked up her hand.

Lucinda sat frozen still. Something told her that he was taking a liberty with her, and that she should not let him. But she could not move. It seemed terribly important just then to let not a quiver, not a movement, not even a breath escape her, lest he notice that her heart was performing cartwheels inside her ribcage, and that her lungs were suddenly, inexplicably, bursting with superfluous air.

"My sweet girl." He did not remember her name (if he had been told it), hence the endearment. "Such soft, soft skin," he continued, teasingly raising her hand to his lips.

A shock wrenched her lower abdomen. Her eyes slid out of focus.

"And so cold, too," he deplored, and started chafing her icy hand between his two large warm ones.

The spell was abruptly broken, and she pulled her hand away. From close by, someone was calling the captain.

They both looked up guiltily. It was Sir Edmund who had come striding around the corner of the building, with a stable hand leading two saddled horses.

Edmund flashed Henry a warning scowl. All he had caught was the guilty look, but that was enough to draw his own conclusions.

"Ah, there you are! Come, man, the hounds are already on the scent."

"Sorry, old man. I was looking for the stables and got lost. Your niece was very kindly showing me the way."

The niece in question, mortified and bewildered, clutched her cloak at her neck and ran.

* * *

The hunt had returned. Lucinda heard the commotion in the courtyard, and dashed outside with the other children who, as custom allowed at the manor, were clamoring to see the spoils and pet the hounds.

She hung back a bit, aware that a lady kept a certain composure and did not scream *"Let's see him! Let's see him!"* as the twins were doing when the carcass of the slain stag was lowered to the ground.

She did not glance at the captain, not even in his direction. She just tried looking happy and interested. Her gown this afternoon was impeccable, her hair prettily braided and tied up in satin. She wondered how she looked to him.

She heard him bark directions at the servants. His voice sounded a little crabby, normal, bored. It was not the voice of a man who had lost his heart that morning, here, on a bench behind the very building he was about to enter. He disappeared into the stable, surrounded by the other riders.

Crestfallen, she walked around the back to the kitchen door. Bessie was churning butter on the snow-covered stoop. Her cheeks were flushed, for it was hot work, even in this bracing weather.

"Look at you!" exclaimed Bessie, "A little lady! A right gentlewoman! I do wish you would take such care every day, my pet. You look so pretty!"

"Why should I?" muttered Lucinda. "Nobody notices anyway." Her hand went up to her head to yank out the hair ribbons.

Bessie did not protest, because her attention was on something happening a few yards behind Lucinda.

"Sir. May I be of service...?" She bustled to her feet.

Lucinda swung around.

He was leaning over a low brick wall. He did not say anything. He had a quizzical smile on his lips. And he was staring fixedly at Lucinda.

"Oh...Ah, Bessie, this is Captain Beaupree. My old nurse," she introduced them, her face aflame.

He smiled vaguely, politely, but kept his eyes on Lucinda. "I seem never able to find my way around here. Would you be so kind as to show me the way to the grooms' quarters? My man has disappeared and I need him to pull off these boots."

Lucinda was at his side in a flash. She did not look back at Bessie. He offered her his arm, and she slipped her hand under it. How firm, how cool his flesh felt, through the stuff of his coat! They walked down the snow-crusted garden path arm in arm. Like walking down the aisle, she thought, elated.

The captain's man was not in his room. Henry entered it just the same. He kept Lucinda's arm in his. He looked around, shrugged and said,

"Well, you see now? The fellow is not even here. Although I don't know why I should be surprised. They're never to be found when needed, are they!"

Lucinda nodded, flattered that he assumed she belonged to his world, that she shared with him the burden of having to put up with insubordinate personal servants.

"Hmmm...?" he teased, looking down at her with a knowing grin. She could feel him slip his arm around her back.

And then, the kiss. But it was disconcerting, that kiss. It wasn't anything like the softly melting lip-touching of her fervid imaginings. A little rough, a little cruel. And rude, too: his tongue—what did he think he was doing? She drew back. Her lips stung.

"Oh," she complained, twisting her head away.

He let go of her abruptly, causing her to stumble and grab at him for support. With a delicate gesture he pried himself loose.

"Well. Come, let's see if we can't find this rogue eye-servant of mine. I must get out of these boots..."

He strode down the stairs ahead of her. She had to take a few running steps to catch up.

What had she done? She had frightened him away. And now he didn't like her anymore. Wait, wait, she wanted to shout. Give me another chance...

Lucinda wiggled her freezing toes. Under her woolen cloak she had on nothing but her linen nightgown and a pair of flimsy slippers. When the other children had started making the sounds of sleep, she had slunk out of the nursery, padded along the corridor and clambered out the window at the far end, where a wide parapet afforded a view of a slice of the ballroom below.

It was one of those crisp winter nights when everything seems crystal clear and new. The shapes of hedges and trees were outlined in pristine white. She sniffed deeply. The freshness of the night stung her nostrils. The stars sparkled as if newly minted, and the moon, half-full and reclining lazily on its back, provided a blaze of white light that made the snow glitter as gaily as the sky.

Through the wavy glass of tall windows, hundreds of candles lit up satins and silks of every hue. Sounds wafted up to her ears clear as the night—a clatter of dishes, the heavily accented dance music, a baritone guffaw here, a trill of feminine laughter there. She felt a thousand miles away from the throng below—the initiated, the privileged, the glamorous denizens of the ballroom, who moved with such confidence in and out of her field of vision, and who excluded her so ruthlessly from their sensational secrets and brazen delights.

Every once in a while she would catch a glimpse of the captain, unmistakable in his red officer's coat, sweeping past in a long line of bowing, tapping, and twirling people. She smiled when she saw the dignified skill with which he evaded Monsieur Piétain, the dance instructor, who was prancing around the dancers singing out directions in an obsequious falsetto. She saw the captain holding now this, now that lady's hand: he had already danced with each of her aunts.

She hoped he was disappointed not to see her. She had not told him she would not be at the ball. He must be wondering where she was. So far, he had not yet appeared with Sarah. Lucinda prayed. She prayed and prayed that Sarah would be left fluttering her sandy eyelashes at him in vain.

She closed her eyes and for the umpteenth time replayed the scene of that afternoon. The kiss that had dismayed her a few hours earlier had already undergone a transformation and become a passionate embrace.

When they had arrived back at the main house, the captain had solemnly bowed over her hand—a mark of respect Lucinda had not before enjoyed in her life—and said wryly, "You see, there was nothing to worry about—I have delivered you safe."

Lucinda had nodded. She'd even ventured a saucy retort.

"I am grateful, sir. But weren't *you* the one who needed a guide...?"

The sentence ended in a mortifying squeak.

Henry laughed out loud. "Funny child," he said. And winked at her, and left.

She had been craning her neck for close to two hours when the dancing below stopped, and the guests disappeared to partake of the midnight feast prepared by Mrs. Kettle, Bessie and their helpers in the dining hall. Lucinda turned and made her way along the parapet to the window, slid open the casing and slipped inside. She brushed some telltale snow off the windowsill, and was about to sneak back to the nursery when she froze.

At the far end of the intersecting hallway, where the guest chambers began, she made out two figures struggling a little and bumping into the walls. The woman was trying to stifle giggles, and the man had a hand awkwardly pressed into the top of her gown. In the tall figure of the woman, Lucinda recognized her Aunt Margaret. The man was wearing a red officer's coat.

Before she knew where her bolting legs were taking her, she was running, almost tumbling down the narrow circular staircase, out the back door and into the biting night. She ran past the barren kitchen garden, along dark paths sheltered by ghostly hedges, to the spot behind the stables where they had met that morning. There she stopped, panting and sobbing. The bench still showed the imprint where they had sat side by side. The print of two ludicrous human bottoms resting on a snowy bench while their owners were playing out some scene above that was suddenly too painful to recall...

Her breath came in raw, angry gasps. Running had not helped—the pain inside her ribcage was sharper than before. Her chest was being crushed by an awful, humiliating weight. Helplessly she lifted her fists high above her head and spun around and around, like a crazy spinning top, faster and faster, until dizziness made her totter and sway. She lost her footing and found herself sprawled on the ground in a heap. The brutal sting of the snow was a welcome diversion. She tore at her cloak, flinging it as far away from her as she could, and continued to roll and writhe until she was drenched to the skin.

The cold finally penetrated her madness and made her come to her senses. She sat up, panting, her hair dripping. She looked around anxiously, sick with embarrassment. Had anyone seen her? The silhouetted trees drooped lugubriously, their branches bowed down with ice. What on earth had possessed her? She got up and, as quietly as she could, slunk back to the house.

8

AFTER THE BALL

From her earliest childhood, Lucinda had shared every delight and every setback with the woman who had taken her mother's place. Bessie had consoled her through umpteen disappointments, mended her torn gowns, bandaged her scraped knees, and helped her weave nests of straw and wool for all the injured frogs, insects and birds Lucy was in the habit of rescuing. From the very start of her stay at the manor, when Lucinda's sunny little world was first darkened by the realization that her cousins were never going to stop shunning her, Bessie had provided her with the ammunition to hold her head high. It had been Bessie's whispered tales of princesses masquerading as paupers and of goodness triumphing over evil that first introduced Lucinda to the world of her own imagination, that great healer of blows to the ego.

But now for the first time there was something Lucinda felt she had to hide: a disturbing, dark thing that could not be shared. Which meant that she was suddenly unable to talk to Bessie about anything at all, in case she involuntarily betrayed the one thing that was uppermost in her mind.

"What's come over our little Lucy?" asked Lena, the laundress. "I swear she's been avoiding us. Too good for us now, is she?"

"Oh, no, no," Bessie told her. "She's just growing up. Wanting to stand on her own two feet, you know. She'll be back soon enough."

But Lucinda wasn't back. She avoided the kitchen and tried harder than ever to fit in upstairs.

On the day after the ball, she had woken up with a fever and sore throat.

"Tsk, tsk," Mrs. Limpid fussed. "All that traipsing about outside will be the death of you yet, I warrant."

She heaped an extra featherbed on top of Lucinda's blankets.

"But Mrs. Limpid, I'm so hot..." complained the patient.

"Mind those covers stay put, young lady, do you hear? Do you want Doctor Garth to come with his leeches?" said Mrs. Limpid spitefully. "Ah, I didn't think so. We'll sweat that fever right out of you."

She closed the heavy drapes of the nursery, shutting out the sunlight, and called for the maid to stoke the fire with more wood. Mrs. Limpid, an enthusiastic advocate of preventive medicine (the dreaded elixir and weekly wormings), prided herself on having lost only two of her charges to illness in her sixteen years of service at Belweather Manor.

"Could I...do you know if Sarah enjoyed the ball last night? I should so much like to hear all about it," Lucinda said in a small voice.

"You will have to ask her yourself. I hear it was a great success."

With that, Mrs. Limpid swept out of the room, leaving Lucinda to decide if she had meant the ball or Sarah's debut.

Sarah condescended to visit her ailing cousin that afternoon. She needed an audience, and here was a captive one.

"You should have seen me. Everyone said I was beautiful, a *beautiful* young lady. They all fussed over me. You should have seen it!"

Sarah had stars in her eyes. She was gratified to see that Lucinda had tears in hers.

"Mother says I may accompany her to London next month. I am old enough, she says. I shouldn't wonder," she whispered, looking over her shoulder to see if Mrs. Limpid was out of earshot, "if they weren't planning my marriage. I heard Aunt Edwina say she could help arrange a good match, given our family and my settlement."

"Settlement?" asked Lucinda.

"I have five thousand pounds when I marry," boasted Sarah.

"Really?" said Lucinda. "How do you know?"

"Robert told me, he read a letter from Grandfather to Father. That's my portion."

"Do *I* have a portion?" asked Lucinda.

"You? I shouldn't think so. Ask Robert. You should have seen it when I led off the Branlé. I didn't put a foot wrong. Monsieur Piétain was very pleased."

She got up and demonstrated.

Lucinda propped herself up on an elbow. "How about the captain? Did you dance with him?"

"Of course I did!" Sarah started to giggle. "I think Mother is wild about him. And so are Aunt Margaret and Aunt Edwina." Looking down modestly, she added, "He could not keep his eyes off me. Remember how he looked at us when we went down to be presented? Just like that, only even more intense. Like this." She squinted and pressed her face close to Lucinda's. "He said he hoped he would see more of us," she added.

"*Us*—you mean—you and me?" Lucinda said, clearing her throat.

"No, what..."

"You just said '*us*'!"

"Well ...he did ask, did I not have a cousin, and why was she not at the ball—"

"What did you say? What did you say?" squealed the cousin.

"Oh, I don't really remember. I told him you weren't a *real* cousin—not a legitimate one, anyway."

"Thank you very, very much," cried Lucinda, losing her self-control. She had been trying so hard to be pleasant. "You are despicable, do you know that? No wonder we can't be friends. You—you never think of anyone but of yourself. I don't *ever* want to speak to you again."

Gathering the blankets around her, she clamped her eyelids shut and turned her face to the wall.

As soon as Mrs. Limpid allowed her out of the suffocating sickroom, Lucinda sought out Robert.

As the old earl's only son, Viscount Swyndhurst was treated with a certain measure of respect by the other children. They knew that some day Robert would hold the purse strings for the entire family. It was he who would inherit their grandfather's title and estates. It was Robert they would have to turn to for their support, grateful for whatever the heir chose to dole out to them.

Viscount Swyndhurst, conscious of his future responsibilities, was different from the other children. A tall, slightly hunched adolescent, his pale face splotched with burgundy blemishes and the sparse bristles of an embryonic beard, he actually paid some attention to his tutors, and attended to his daily prayers dutifully.

It was outside the chapel, a small paneled space furnished with some pews that was tucked away at the end of the long gallery, that Lucinda found him.

"My lord!"

His lordship had just closed the door behind him and the vacant gaze of peaceful meditation had not yet left his face. He looked up and, seeing Lucinda, blushed a slow, vermilion blush.

Lucinda had no way of knowing that Robert was much troubled by certain natural yearnings which he felt it his duty to suppress, and that his morning's devotion had been dedicated to the cleansing of those shameful thoughts. Nor could she guess that they featured a damsel who looked suspiciously like herself. Robert and the others had so drummed into her their low opinion of her that she ascribed the flush now spreading down his neck to annoyance.

"Forgive me. I wanted to ask you something. But it can wait."

"What do you want? I wasn't going riding this morning anyway," he lied.

He strode ahead of her down the corridor to give himself time to think, and for his blush to subside. Casually, he opened one of the doors and glanced in. It was a small waiting room for unimportant guests, sparsely furnished. It was empty.

"Shall we talk in here?" he suggested. It occurred to him that God had deliberately sent her as a temptation, but he pushed the thought from his mind.

Lucinda followed him inside.

"So! What is it you want to know?" he said, carefully shutting the door behind her prettily arched, slender back. He forced himself to look away, walking over to the window, whose height and dustiness prohibited a pleasant view of the garden outside. He stared out intently nevertheless, his eyes seeing not the grimy glass but the symmetry of the female form as he imagined it under the layers of skirts and bodices: two round breasts in front, two round buttocks behind, a narrow waist the axis.

Lucinda decided she had better get to the point, before he lost interest.

"It's about our...settlements. Sarah told me that you know what Grandfather and Sir Edmund have—planned, you know, for us. I just wanted to know...just in case, you know..."

Robert turned around, astonished. "Are you telling me you have—marriage plans? You?"

"Not exactly, I should just like to know..."

Robert threw back his head and laughed, a forced, bleating laugh. His voice sometimes played tricks on him, especially when he most wanted to sound like a man.

"Well, all I can tell you is that *we*"—he stressed the word importantly, having regained control of the deeper registers—"have nothing planned for you. You should be grateful for the roof over your head and the food on your plate. As for your father—whoever that may be—let *him* come forward and offer a portion. You are his responsibility, after all."

"But that's not fair!" exclaimed Lucinda. "I am Grandfather's grand-daughter just as much as Sarah or Catherine or Belinda! Why won't he...?"

"You know that as far as Lord Hempstead is concerned, you do not exist," said Robert gravely. "Your existence greatly displeases him." Now that she was the supplicant he felt strong enough to face her, although he continued to avoid her eyes. "But," he went on, frowning intently at her left shoulder, "I myself am of course sympathetic to your unfortunate situation." His breath started to come a little faster. "You must under-stand my position. I would see what I could do if, ah, that is if..."

In a split second, Lucinda understood what was about to happen. As he lunged, she ducked under his arm and darted out of the room. Backing down the hall, she stammered, "Thank you, my lord, you are too kind..." and fled.

* * *

Clarissa had expected the ball to be a triumph. Her husband, her sisters, and guests were to see what a brilliant hostess she was, how she glittered in company, still able to enchant men with her considerable charms.

Instead, the evening had ended with Lady Clarissa receiving her guests' compassionate good-byes standing conspicuously alone, Sir Edmund having disappeared for a good portion of the evening with some as-yet undetermined person. There was nothing unusual in that, and would not have assumed great importance if her own appointed swain had stayed by her side. But the captain, too, had vanished shortly after the dancing. It was this that had turned the evening into a nightmarish duty, the strain on her face reflected in the sympathetic and not-so-sympathetic glances of her guests. She had been humiliated, abandoned, betrayed, dismissed, left out of all the fun.

"And to think that it was Margaret...!" she muttered.

It was not hard to link her sister Margaret with the captain's disappearance. Margaret had left the ball early, pleading the headache—her cheeks flushed with excitement and wine, *hah!* Margaret had been unnecessarily smug and loving to her sisters when they had reconvened late in the afternoon of the next day—*pfff!* And then Margaret had had the nerve to suggest that the captain escort her back to London, where she said she was suddenly urgently needed, thus cutting short his visit. Oh, the utter, utter *strumpet!*

Clarissa had taken to her bed, pleading exhaustion. And consoled herself with the leftover candied walnuts, despite the pain they caused her decayed teeth. And plotted sweet revenge.

"What do you think of our Captain Beaupree?" she said casually to Sir Edmund a night or so later.

It was here, in her chamber, before the conjugal act was consummated, that all of Lady Clarissa's other business with her husband was transacted. It was the only time that she had him at her mercy and that he was forced to listen to her.

"That favorite of yours?" He sniggered. "Seems to be a favorite of all you Steppys sisters, that one!"

She stiffened, and bit her bottom lip, casting around for another way to broach the subject. But Edmund had begun to yawn theatrically—"Aawnnnn!" (stretching his torso) "...Aawn!..." (pounding his fist on the bedpost) "...Aaarh!" He shook his head, blinked his eyes rapidly, and dabbed at the ghost of a tear. That done, he sat down heavily on the bed, and pointed at his feet. Clarissa stooped, and, one by one, pulled off his shoes.

"I was thinking," she finally said, "Sarah is getting to be of an age—I should like to see her settled. You saw how she comported herself at the ball."

"Charmingly. Everyone can see she takes after you, my dear." He was anxious to hurry her up. It was getting late. Bedding a woman was the best way he knew to assure himself of a sound night's sleep.

"Well then, do you agree that we should start to make arrangements?"

"Now that you mention it, I was thinking of having a word with Lord Bortroyd. I hear his second son has been left an estate by an uncle that is quite adequate. They tell me it's teeming with game..."

"I thought," she interrupted tactfully, "that the young captain was rather taken with her."

"The young captain?" he laughed. "Beaupree, you mean? That rake was rather taken with every pair of loins in the vicinity, young *and* old."

Clarissa's pleasant expression did not change. She was determined not to let revenge escape her by losing her temper.

"I am sure that he was. And she had eyes only for him. Did you not notice?"

"Silly nonsense. Since when do we take such things into account? She'll marry whom I pick out for her, and no mush. You know how I feel about this *billey-doo* business, Clarissa. I will not stand for it. Not in my family."

But truth be told, Edmund did have a soft spot in his heart for his eldest daughter. If this was what his Sarah liked in a fellow, and come to think of it, if this was what his wife had been after all along with that fop...Well, perhaps he had been a little unfair. He asked bluntly, "What does he have? Who are his people?"

Clarissa had done her homework. "He is a cousin of the Duke of Corot. A second son, but that will make him all the more ready to hear our proposal. He does have an income from his soldiering. His command is worth close to four thousand, so I'm told. The family has a large estate on the Isle of Wight, and some holdings near Salisbury. His brother is the heir, but unmarried, no children."

She paused, and looked at him expectantly.

"We might look into it, I suppose," he said.

Clarissa struggled to tamp down the excitement creeping into her voice.

"Shall I—will you invite him to go hunting with you again? You could propose it to him then."

"I'll think about it," he muttered. An image had just flashed through his mind. A picture of Beaupree and the pretty little bastard, Olivia's child, seated on a bench together. The girl had looked quite flushed. The rake reminded him of himself. He had acquitted himself well in the hunt, too. The rascal had been on the prey before Edmund on two separate occasions. It was quite possible that he had already beaten Edmund to this one too.

9

POTIONS

In a certain way, Lucinda was now happier than she had ever been before. She was also unhappier, naturally, since almost immediately upon finding love, it had slipped out of her reach. But as we know, simply being in love, even hopelessly, impossibly so, can be a thrilling experience in itself. If Lucinda told herself that she wished she were dead, or even that she had never been born, it was her way of underlining the exquisite pain which she was in her heart of hearts very much enjoying. The crystallization of her yearnings was in itself a fulfillment. Her fantasies were so much better, now that she could focus on an actual face.

She spent countless hours recreating the smallest nuance of each moment she had spent in the captain's company, analyzing every gesture, dissecting every repartee. In the end, it was easy enough to come to the conclusion that it was she who had driven him into her aunt's arms by pushing him away when he had tried to kiss her, and she convinced herself that he was pining for her, contrite and repentant, just as she was longing for him. She imagined she could feel what he was feeling, and sent him silent messages in return.

Even though she was now fully aware of the implications of her station, recently confirmed to her by Robert—namely, that the lack of a dowry, compounded by her questionable parentage, was a serious obstacle to her marriage prospects—it only added to the excitement: a hurdle to be overcome by true love, providing endless fodder for romantic speculation.

She spent hours examining her face in the looking glass, twisting her head this way and that so as to capture herself in a moment of inattention, hoping to catch a sidelong glimpse of herself as she might appear to him. Whereas in the past she had never paid much attention to her appearance, she now preened and experimented, pinning her unruly hair up in the back, and twirling ringlets in the front for an impression of studied dishevelment. She pouted her lips at the mirror, stretched her mouth into a grin to reveal her dimples, frowned, and opened her eyes wide. And yet no matter how she stared and leered, gazed and ogled, she could not tell whether she was pretty or not, or what exactly it was in her face or form that had started to make men look at her with such a funny, surprised attentiveness, when before she had not warranted a single glance.

She sat back and considered the image before her. The eyes—she really could not judge them. In the process of staring at themselves, the eyes assumed an astonished expression. She saw that they were large, certainly, and dark. She wasn't sure if that was a good feature or not. It looked a little common. The swivel-gazed beauties in the paintings that hung in the reception rooms downstairs had softer, lighter, more protruding eyes and rather more placid expressions. Her mouth was a wide slash in her face, not the tight little pout Sarah was so proud to own. She puckered her lips, but they were too plump for a perfect cupid's bow.

She looked down at her chest. It looked childishly meager in her low-cut gown—a hand-me-down from Sarah. She leaned over the dressing table and squeezed her arms tightly against her sides, pushing what flesh there was into view. But as soon as she sat back again, the cleavage disappeared. She did it again; imagined a man's hand pressed into the top of her bodice...

Her mind clamped firmly shut on the unladylike thought. She turned her attention back to her face. Her cheeks and her jaw line were not round and soft as she'd have liked; the bones underlying them were clearly visible if you stared at them head-on. She pressed her chin back and down toward her neck, puffing out her cheeks to see if she could make herself look like Sarah and Aunt Clarissa. A frightened hog stared back at her. She burst out laughing, the air in her cheeks exploding in a loud squelch.

"And what, may I ask, is so funny?"

It was Uncle Edmund, standing in the doorway. Lucinda jumped to her feet. She could not imagine what he was doing here. So far as she knew, he never set foot in the children's quarters. As always, Uncle Edmund made her feel as if he had caught her doing something she should not have been doing.

"I was just..."—she wiped her mouth on the back of her hand—"just arranging my hair."

He grunted, but made no move to leave. To her dismay, he hitched up his tight-fitting breeches and carefully perched on the side of the bed. Lucinda looked down guiltily. She'd been staring. She had never seen Uncle Edmund's ruddy face and blue beard stubble up close before.

He was whistling tunelessly through his teeth and looking around with his aloof stare. His eyes came to rest on a pile of soiled female linens. It was not the sort of thing gentlemen were supposed to see. He turned his gaze slowly back to Lucinda. Who herself was turning crimson.

"Well," he said, knowingly, with raised eyebrows.

All sorts of thoughts raced through her brain. She could not imagine what he wanted with her. Yet his continued presence implied that he wished to speak with her. She thought guiltily of the fateful morning when he had surprised her sitting on a bench with the captain.

"Well, well," he repeated, relishing her unease.

Lucinda's knees began to quiver. She sat back down on the stool, with her back to the dressing table.

"How old are you now, gel?" he asked.

"Fourteen," she said, swallowing, quickly adding, "almost fifteen."

"Fifteen," he echoed. "Aha."

He continued to look her over.

"You are not a wicked gel, are you?" he finally asked. Even though his voice was not unkind, to Lucinda this sounded menacing. "I mean," he said, scooting over toward the foot of the bed, causing the feather-bed to billow incongruously around his hefty thighs, "the kind who would commit a *sin*, with a stranger?"

The blood pounded in her ears.

"I don't understand..." she began.

"Of course not. It's just as well," he continued, "because you do know what happens to wicked gels, don't you?"

She nodded guiltily. The gallows...the executioner and his bloody axe. Being a wicked girl meant losing your maidenhead; everyone knew that. Lucinda always assumed that losing your maidenhead meant having your head chopped off.

His tone turned fatherly, concerned. "Wicked gels are used goods. No one wants them. They are disgraced. And they die old maids."

"Oh," she said. It was almost a disappointment. That particular fate held no new dread; it had been pounded into her head by Mrs. Limpid often enough. But she did see an opportunity, and seized it.

"I understand," she said, "that penniless maids *also* die old maids."

Edmund's head jerked up. He had not expected her to talk back. "Eh?"

"I mean...no one wants a maiden without a portion either."

Edmund was on his feet. He towered over her menacingly. "What's this about a portion? What in damnation are you talking about, gel?"

"Robert told me—he told me there was no settlement for me, sir," she whispered, regretting too late her impulse to stand up to him. Now she had really done it.

"You hussy! How *dare* you speak of matters that are not of your concern! A settlement! A settlement, eh? The impudence!" he hissed. "I...I...I'll settle you, baggage, I'll give you a portion right here and now, I'll give you a portion you'll not soon forget!"

He lunged, grabbing her by the wrist and throwing her onto the bed, expertly tossing her skirts over her head so that everything below the waist was exposed while all above was gagged and muffled under the weight of her clothes. A heavy knee pressed down on hers, prying her legs apart. She gasped, struggling for air.

Suddenly he let go. The unexpected chill on her thighs gave her goose bumps. The coarse cloth chafing her skin was abruptly gone, leaving her legs exposed to the cold air.

It took her a few seconds to fight her way out of the tangle of her petticoats. Dazed, she bounced off the bed and ran to the door. Uncle Edmund had already disappeared down the back stairs as her cousins came bearing down upon her from the opposite direction. Their father had heard their approach; she had not. She smiled at them foolishly.

"Lucinda! Your hair!" Mrs. Limpid railed. "How many times must I tell you that a young lady does not slouch about like Drowsy Dot late risen from her bed! Stay there, Mistress Slovenly, and do not leave this room. I will send down to the kitchen for that nurse of yours. Perhaps *she* can do something with that rat's nest. It's a disgrace!"

Bessie was not in the kitchen. She was in Lady Clarissa's dressing room, earnestly conferring with her employer.

"But milady," she was saying, "I don't know, I simply..."

"You do not have to *know* anything," Clarissa interrupted. "I am *commanding* you to prepare it. It is your *duty* to obey me." She looked rather put out. Bessie was usually more enthusiastic when it came to her potions. "It really is too bad of you to deny me. I thought we always had a good understanding..."

"I know, madam, I am always more than happy to oblige, but this...I just don't know enough..."

"That will do," Clarissa said with finality. "I expect you to have it ready for me. This night." She turned back to her dressing table, and that meant there was no more to be said.

Bessie curtsied to Clarissa's broad back and quietly let herself out of the room.

Clarissa had offered Bessie a place in her kitchen ten years earlier not because she felt sorry for her, but because she was eager to avail herself of Bessie's salves and potions.

From the start of her service at Belweather Manor, Bessie had been frequently called upstairs for secret conferences. She was charged with supplying remedies for Lady Clarissa's many complaints: willow-bark and violet for the headache, fennel for dyspepsia, and groundsel for constipation. She had also discreetly supplied her lady with abortifacients—hellebore and pennyroyal—to "bring down the flowers," for Clarissa considered her childbearing duties to be over now that she had produced a sufficient number of male heirs. Moreover, a variety of aphrodisiacs—Bessie's avowed specialty—had been pressed on Sir Edmund, which he swallowed obediently in the belief they were preventatives for the gout. These seemed to be doing the job most effectively; the problem was that her ladyship was never, alas, the first or indeed the last beneficiary of Edmund's appetites.

Of late, however, Clarissa had changed her tactics. Having to face the fact that pumping her husband full of love-potions had done little to make him more devoted to her, she had now decided to tackle matters from the opposite end, namely, her own person.

She had thus begun asking Bessie for salves to soften the skin, scents distilled from the glands of animals that would bring out the animal in a man, and poultices to melt some of the excess flesh off her frame. This area was not one in which Bessie was particularly expert, and since the whole operation was based on trial and error, it made her a little nervous.

Clarissa's latest idea had been to dose herself with the extract of the deadly nightshade, which was supposed to improve the complexion and make the eyes brighter and more beautiful. Bessie had been careful to dispense the belladonna in exceedingly small doses, since she assumed it wasn't called "deadly" for nothing. But Clarissa, pleased with the results, and finding considerable pleasure in the herb's narcotic side effects (she claimed it "eased the humors"), was now insisting on stronger, more frequent dosages.

Troubled, Bessie shuffled back down to the kitchen, where she found Mrs. Limpid's message. She immediately put her other worries from her mind. How gratifying to be needed by her dear lamb, who was too, too independent these days and rarely requested Bessie's help anymore! She scurried up the back stairs as fast as her legs would carry her.

She found the disgracefully coiffed Lucinda in the nursery, staring into the fire in the hearth, impervious to the noisy jostle of the younger children around her.

"Come, pet, let's do something about that mop-head of yours," clucked Bessie. She sensed immediately that something was very wrong.

"Bessie," said Lucinda blankly. "Bess, will you stay with me a while?"

"Of course, my lamb," Bessie crooned. "Now, now, sit still and let old Bessie untangle your hair."

Lucinda grabbed her arm.

"Stay with me, Bessie. Don't leave me here alone."

10

THE WOLF

If a young maiden on her way to her grandmother's house comes across a wolf in the forest, and the wolf devours her for his breakfast, one expects there to be a great hue and cry.

And yet one can't help wondering what sort of girl prances about dressed in red from head to toe. Or indeed what she was doing alone in the forest in the first place.

In the weeks that followed, Lucinda acted uncharacteristically silent and demure. If Mrs. Limpid or one of the tutors gave her an order, she promptly obeyed; there was no sign of the contrariness she had exhibited since the start of adolescence. When her cousins teased her, she smiled and did not protest; they soon found a more rewarding target in Monsieur Padutou, the shy new French instructor. Instead of wandering off by herself, Lucinda stayed close to the others, dogging their footsteps even when she was not wanted. She paid determined attention to the communal lessons and clenched her hands and eyes tightly in prayer when prayers were required.

Mrs. Limpid was, on the whole, pleased with her. "Now *this* is the way we expect you to comport yourself, Lucinda," she told her one morning. "You are showing the proper behavior for a maiden of your station. I shall inform your uncle of this improvement in your demeanor."

Her comment alarmed Lucinda. "Oh please, Mrs. Limpid, don't say anything to him about me—please don't," she pleaded.

"We'll see," said the governess, marveling at her pupil's new humility.

* * *

But it was too late for Lucinda to save herself. On the day after this ex-change, a footman knocked on the door of the schoolroom, where the older boys were at their Latin and the girls at their needlework. Lucinda's aunt wished to see her.

Lucinda started for the central staircase.

"Not in her chamber," the footman called. "Come with me."

He led her by the back stairs down to one of the smaller sitting rooms. "In here," he said, opening the door.

She sensed even before the footman had shut the door behind her that she had been tricked. The room smelled not of rosewater and powder, but of damp wool, wine, horses, sweat. She stood rooted to the spot.

Sir Edmund turned to face her. "Well, baggage! Never did finish our little business, did we?"

Somehow she found her voice—a whisper. "Sir, I regret what I said—about my settlement."

"Ah?" he growled. It was disappointing. One would rather see the wench defiant.

She bowed her head. "That decision is yours. I should not have questioned it."

"Decision?" he snorted. "I have not made any decision. Yet."

"Oh?" She ventured a hopeful glance at him.

He cleared his throat.

"What I mean is, if you did your best to please me, I might look upon you more favorably..."

She nodded demurely.

Edmund frowned. The girl was a little too compliant. He preferred a little spunk. Although if she was as untried as he hoped, she might not have understood the subtext of his speech.

"A man and a woman—do you know about that?"

She stood perfectly still. She did. She had been kissed, and knew all about it—the probing tongue, everything. She blushed. She hoped he could not read her mind. She shook her head no, her eyes cast down.

"I see." He decided to be a little more brutal. "And this?"

She knew he wanted her to look at something. Reluctantly, she lifted her eyes from the rug.

Oh horror! In that one split second she had seen something blue, something lurid, which should not have been there! She sprang back, and lunged for the door. But with one hand he grabbed her by the shoulder and twisted her around, pushing her down onto a settee. The other hand was a pinion around her wrist, wrenching, forcing her hand to where it came into contact with the fleshy thing...

"There! Feel it. Do you want to know what it's used for?"

"No, no," she begged, "please, please..."

Edmund was enjoying himself now. This was how he liked them: unripe, innocent. And terrified. He put a hand inside her bodice and pulled hard, snapping some of the ties.

"Edmund!"

Neither had heard Clarissa enter. Her face was puce, blown up like a frog's.

"How dare you! Let go of her this instant!"

Edmund hastily tucked the offending appendage inside his breeches, like a little boy hiding a filched apple from his angry mother.

11

RUIN

Lucinda was being sent back to Wriggin Hall, the home of her widowed grandfather. "Until," said Clarissa sternly, "we can decide just what to do with you."

Lucinda thought of her unforgiving grandfather and the malevolent Aunt Arabella. Terrifying as the last fortnight had been, it was not a happy prospect.

"But I didn't do anything...?" she attempted.

A blast of anger snapped Clarissa's carefully composed compassion into bits. "Young lady. *I* know what you have been up to. We *all* know what you have been up to."

"I haven't, I haven't, please, please believe me!" sobbed Lucinda. "I didn't know what he wanted—I thought it was you who sent for me..."

Actually, Clarissa knew this to be the truth, for Bessie had come running to alert her. Bessie had overheard Bert, the footman, snigger to his mate about the sneaky task he had been given by his master. But that fact only served to fuel her anger.

"Men—you have much to learn about men, hussy. They cannot help themselves sometimes. It is our duty to help them, by our proper behavior, to control their urges."

Lucinda rubbed at her tears. Her aunt was confirming something she had suspected all along. She was a wicked, wicked girl, and it was all her fault.

"Believe me," sighed Clarissa, "no woman is ever ruined against her will. And you, mistress, are embarked upon a course that will lead you to damnation. Mark my words. We shall do our very best for you, of course. I'll pray for your soul, and your Aunt Arabella has some other ideas as well..."

And with that ominous news, she swept out of the room.

* * *

Lucinda, sitting at Bessie's feet, had her head in her nurse's lap. She had even let Bessie cover her head with her apron and gently massage her back, as she used to do when Lucinda was a little child.

That was why her voice sounded muffled.

"Bess, oh Bess, I can't...I can't go without you! What will I do without you?" she keened.

"I have to stay here, pet. Lady Clarissa needs me, she will not let me go."

"I'm so frightened..."

"I know, I know," said Bessie, choking on a sob.

"It was horrible..."

"I know," Bessie repeated, rocking back and forth.

In fact, Bessie did not know exactly what had transpired between Master and her pet, and although she was just as curious to find out as the rest of the tittering household, delicacy forbade her from probing. She just hoped that her Ladyship had interrupted the proceedings in time and that the girl was not with child. What she did know, however, was that Lucinda had been compromised, and that was tantamount to ruin for a young lady. She sighed.

"You'll see, this will all blow over in the end. It will come out all right, my lamb."

This was too much for Lucinda. She jumped up.

"That's what you always say, Bess! And how has it ever come out all right? Things just keep going from bad to worse for me!"

"Pet, pet," shushed Bessie. "Surely they won't hold it against you forever..."

"It's not just that! If only it were! Don't you see? It doesn't even matter what—what Uncle Edmund did. I'll never be happy...I'll be an old maid all my life—"

"What...?" Bessie said.

"Because they—Grandfather and Uncle Edmund—won't provide me with a portion. No portion—no marriage. *I* know that. Everyone knows that. Because I'm a bastard. You hear? A *bastard*. See? I've said it. It's what everybody thinks when they see me. They never say it to my face, but it's what they're all thinking. Because no one knows who my father is. Because my father doesn't care if I'm alive or dead..."

The last sentence came out as a braying wail, and Bessie had quite a time of it trying to calm Lucinda down. When the wails had quieted to sobs and hiccups, she said,

"Just because we have never heard from him, pet, doesn't mean he doesn't care for you. He probably doesn't even know you exist."

She paused, thinking of her own offspring. Had they lived, they would certainly have been in a similar situation. "Look at me," she said, cupping her lamb's chin in her hand, "No, really look at me. I promise you—I swear on the souls of my poor babes—that I will try to find out who your father is. Or was," she added.

"But you can't, I know you can't," Lucinda whimpered.

"How do you know that? I never tried. I should have, but I never did."

Bessie paused. Why had she not tried to find out who the poor child's father was? It wouldn't have been all that difficult, at the time. Was it because she had been afraid of uncovering a messy tangle of grief? Bessie liked things to be pleasant and tidy.

What if she *had* found the baby's father at the outset? What if he had then claimed her? He might not have been as indifferent as the child's maternal relatives. He might have wanted to keep the child. And he might have had a wife or a mother who'd likely, yes, who would almost certainly have sent Bessie packing.

She knew, in her heart of hearts, that she had preferred to keep things as they were, happy in the self-imposed task of raising an aristocratic child who was unwanted and unloved by her own kind.

But now? Now Lucinda was nearly grown, and everything was different. She should have seen it coming. Lucinda no longer needed someone to bandage her knee or tuck her in at night. Lucinda needed the friendship of important relatives, people of her own class who could protect her from disasters such as the one that had just befallen her; relatives who could provide her with the cold hard coin a damsel needed to assure herself of a decent future.

"Go," she whispered. "I hear the coach. Be good, and stay out of your aunt's way if you can. Thomas will look after you. He will help us find your father. And remember that I love you, and always will."

Lucinda gazed into the older woman's crinkled eyes, now watery and blurred with sentiment. And reflected sadly that this might be the closest thing to a declaration of love that she could ever expect to have in her life.

12

QUICKSILVER

Lucinda gripped the window ledge on either side of her with out-stretched arms, trying to anticipate the bumps, to ride the coach as if it were a horse. But unlike horse riding, this form of transportation was irregular, without any particular rhythm to it, so that the random jolts and stumbles caught her unawares. Her sit bones were being pummeled to a bruising pulp, her jaw kept snapping shut, and her neck ached with tension. To make matters worse, she felt an urgent need to relieve herself. She gazed out of the window in despair. They had only been on the road for a few hours; the journey was to take over two days. She did not know if she could take much more of this.

Luckily she did not have to. The coach drew to a halt in the middle of a beech tree wood.

"Hoi there, Missy, time for old Giles to stretch his legs." The gruff voice of the coachman wafted into her window, along with his rather sour smell. Lucinda, not wanting to offend such a nice old man, tried not to draw back, but reached inside her cloak for the scented pomander that Lena the laundress had made for her.

"I'll be going this way," he called over his shoulder. "If the young lady wishes to take a little jaunt herself, I think she'll find it very pleas-ant up yonder."

The hint was not lost on Lucinda. Gathering her heavy skirts in one hand, she jumped out and skipped up the path he had indicated. Behind a stand of saplings she availed herself of the opportunity so considerately offered.

When she returned to the road, she found a group of youngsters—cottagers' children—gathered around the coach, peering in through the windows and trying to climb up on the roof. Old Giles was grumbling at them, swatting at them like so many pesky flies.

"Off, off you go, then," he chided, "that's enough, that's enough, make way for the lady."

The smudged, red-cheeked faces turned and stared at Lucinda. She tried not to laugh, but a giggle bubbled up from her throat nevertheless. They looked so solemn, so awestruck. One of them timidly approached to touch the lace-encrusted flounce of her petticoat. Suddenly overcome with shyness, the little thing turned and ran back to hide behind her brothers.

"Don't be afraid, I won't eat you!" Lucinda said. In an impulse, she pulled out the pomander, and held it out to the little mite. "Here. For you," she offered. The child darted forward, and took it from her reverently.

An unexpected flush of pride pushed out Lucinda's feeling of worthlessness. No matter how humiliating the last few days had been, no matter how gloomy her prospects, one thing was certain: she was no longer a child, and she was not a guttersnipe. She was a lady, a young lady. The awe of these children was most gratifying. Little did they know that her richly embroidered gown was a hand-me-down, and certainly not this season's fashion.

She lifted her head high and with mincing step made her way to Giles' side. The old man bowed low, and, beautifully playing along with her, gallantly helped her back into the coach.

To say that Arabella welcomed Lucinda to Wriggin Hall with open arms would be an overstatement. It is true that when the coach pulled up, she came bustling outside to receive her niece in person; she did so, however, not out of courtesy, but to forestall the servants, who could not be trusted not to gossip.

"Come, Lucinda, this way, this way. His lordship wishes to see you immediately. Hurry along now, come."

Lucinda, aching and stiff from the long ride, stumbled along behind her aunt. Her numbed brain was trying to make sense of the news that the grandfather who had never acknowledged her existence was now requesting her presence. In trying to keep up with Arabella, she skidded on the gleaming marble and only just managed not to crash into a chair.

Arabella looked back at her, annoyed. "In here," she snapped. "And watch your step," she added snidely.

Lucinda tiptoed into the library's gloom. An odor of sickness enveloped her. Her grandfather was sitting in the far corner of the paneled space, huddled before a flickering fire. He was sitting not in a chair, but in a hipbath. A tall man in a black coat hovered in the background, stepping forward now to rearrange the linens draped over the old man's shoulders and across his chest.

"Child," said the old man hoarsely, and motioned the reluctant girl to come closer.

She approached him, trying not to stare at the red, watery eyes and the contorted, drooling mouth. A lop-sided periwig drew attention to his papery skull. Something dreadful had happened to his nose: the nostrils were gaping holes. Lucinda had never smelled or seen such sickness before. She gagged a little.

"You have been a wicked girl," he stated.

She bowed her head.

"Turn around," he commanded.

Obediently, she shuffled around in a complete circle.

He said nothing more, but made a suppressed sound. It could have been a sneeze, or maybe it was a snigger—an old man's titter.

Lucinda caught a glimpse of the retainer in the black coat bending over her grandfather as she obeyed her aunt's hiss to leave the room at once.

In the seventeenth century, to cure the pox was an impossible goal. This fact did not, however, stop physicians, apothecaries and quacks from experimenting on their patients in hopes of stumbling upon a palliative that might bring them fame and riches.

Lord Hempstead had been undergoing the quicksilver cure under the supervision of a Dr. Hoogschotel, from the Spanish Netherlands, who had brought with him the latest ideas from the Continent. When he had first arrived, Dr. Hoogschotel had laughed heartily upon hearing that the local surgeon's idea of therapy had been to wrap his lordship's syphilitic genitals in the innards of a freshly slaughtered chicken.

"No, no. No, no!" he exclaimed at last, wiping away a tear, "Dese English barbers! Poor deffils, dey'll belief *any*sing!"

The consensus nowadays within the *enlightened* medical community, he went on to explain soberly to Lady Arabella, was that the *morbus gallicus,* or French disease (as it was known in England), was best persuaded to leave the body via the secretions. One could swaddle the patient in heavy blankets and make him sweat it out; emetics and purgatives were often administered, and of course therapeutic bloodletting was always helpful. There was lately also a school of thought that proposed that the best channel for ridding the body of the pox was the mouth. And the quicksilver, amongst its many other miraculous properties, causes great quantities of saliva to well up under the tongue. Quicksilver had already proven itself the most effective treatment for the localized lesions of the pox, so it was fair to conclude that the wholesale administration of this heavy metal was the way to go.

(Privately, some advocates of the mercury therapy would admit, if pressed, that there were some unpleasant side effects. You could expect to see mouth-ulcers and abscesses in your patients, loss of teeth and hair, rotting of the gut, and kidney failure. In fact, most patients did not survive the cure. But since death could be attributed to so many other causes, and since the quick-silver was so very expensive, the victim's family was usually left satisfied that everything humanly possible had been done to save the departed one.)

So it came about that Lord Hempstead spent several hours a day drooling copiously from the mouth whilst seated in a bath of quicksilver. It was in this posture that Lucinda had found him on her arrival at Wriggin.

Little did she know that her grandfather, incorrigible to the end, was—how to put it delicately—stimulated by the thought of a young maiden discovered in the company of an older man with, to be blunt, his pants down. If his lordship was no longer, alas, in any physical shape to indulge his appetites, he felt he should at least be allowed to enjoy the simple pleasures left to him by the vestiges of a lewd imagination.

Happily Lady Hempstead, being no longer of this world, was spared the sight of her husband reduced to such a sorry state. She had been carried off some years earlier by the *small* pox—an irreproachable, if very nasty, disease quite unrelated to the venereal version.

Her mother's death had left Arabella more firmly in control of the house than ever. She was determined, however, not to let her father's life slip through her hands, and was doing everything in her power to keep him alive. This she did not out of love, but out of fear of what would happen to her after he died. There was no reason to think that Robert would keep his spinster sister in charge of the household once he came into his inheritance. Consequently, upon their father's death, Arabella's role would change overnight from the tyrant of Wriggin Hall to that of poor relation, dependent on the hospitality of others for her room and board. Since the waspish Arabella was not considered an asset to have around—and even she knew this to be true—it was not a happy prospect.

If the shame that currently clung to Lucinda was a secret source of pleasure to Lord Hempstead, it was doubly so to Arabella. Not only did her niece's arrival provide her with the opportunity of licking a fresh new victim into shape; it was also so very gratifying to have a taste of another's downfall, another who was, it had to be admitted, considerably younger and lovelier than herself. And to top it all, the little slattern was the lovechild of a sister whose own ruin had been the result of those exact same unfair advantages!

Lucinda's shame just proved to Arabella once again that Beauty and Virtue were irreconcilable, and she thanked the Lord devoutly for having made her own person so perfectly Chaste, Pure and Undefiled.

"Now then," she said sternly to the girl, "what *are* we to do with you?"

It was a rhetorical question. Arabella already knew exactly what she was going to do with her.

"I have decided that in order to improve your character, we must put you to work."

Lucinda nodded.

"And I don't mean needlework, either."

A response was expected, so Lucinda shook her head no.

"Labor, undertaken with godly devotion, cleanses the impurities from the soul," Arabella explained. "You, madam, have always had it too easy. My sister has been much too indulgent." She sniffed. "In my opinion, you youngsters have always had far too much leisure, far too little supervision and in your case, far, *far* too little discipline. I have always maintained that one such as yourself, being the Issue of Scandal, ought to have been more closely watched and guided. Clarissa has never listened to me, but now she admits she was wrong," casting her eyes upwards to heaven, "poor, poor Clarissa. Leisure and Freedom, Leisure and Freedom, they are the Poisons of Virtue."

She stopped to catch her breath.

"Now. We shall start with"—she fixed her good eye on Lucinda's garments contemptuously—"your appearance. You will change out of those clothes at once. They are indecent, and unfitting of your station. My maid has laid out a more suitable gown. You will pin your hair back, away from your face—" here she inclined her head, to demonstrate on her own sparse skull a tightly pinned knot, "...so, and you will wear the bonnet I have picked out for you. At all times, do you understand?"

She threw the stricken Lucinda a sickening look of sympathy. It was a thousand times harder to take than the more usual tight-lipped malice. Her voice even climbed an octave, and in an uncharacteristic falsetto, she added, "You may go now, dear. Supper has been laid out for you in your chamber. Go! Tomorrow we begin."

Lucinda looked around the dank little room to which she had been assigned. A bed, a chest of an inferior quality reserved for servants, and on it, a cracked wash-bowl, a candle and a bible; a low table set with a bowl of cold porridge and a tumbler of water; a small shuttered window. Nothing more, except for the bundle containing her personal possessions—her knife and spoon, comb and nightshirt—and the somber-looking clothes laid out on the bed.

Lucinda did not sleep very well that night. She tossed and turned in the unfamiliar bed until daybreak, when she fell into a deep, desperate slumber.

She awoke with a start, afraid it must be later than Arabella would consider decent. At home there had always been someone to wake her and keep her on schedule. The place where her face had been pressed into the pillow was damp: a round, wet spot attesting to the heaviness of her troubled sleep. She wiped her mouth and shuddered, remembering her drooling grandfather. In an instant she was out of bed.

Fortunately, dressing herself without assistance did not pose a problem, since she had never rated a personal maid. Her early training in self-sufficiency had made her limber, double-jointed almost, and, arching her back and twisting her elbows behind her, she managed to reach every little hook and lacing-hole.

Her new clothes were certainly not new, and judging from their sobriety, possibly hand-me-downs from Arabella herself. A shift and petticoat of a much coarser linen than she was used to, and not a scrap of lace on them; a dark gown so decently cut that only the chin and hands protruded; a drab apron (she had to wrap the ties twice around her waist to take in the slack); and, to complete her toilette, some pins for her hair and a pleated bonnet which at first made her very self-conscious, since it was the sort governesses and spinsters wore. There was no glass, so she could not inspect herself. But she knew that if the cottagers' children who had gaped at her yesterday were to see her today, they would take her for a domestic of no consequence. She squared her shoulders and headed for the dining room, where she expected to find Arabella triumphantly waiting.

13

CINDERSWEEP

The penance Lady Arabella had planned for her wayward niece was a practical one. She was a frugal housekeeper, and closely watched every penny spent on domestic help. She therefore extracted as much labor as possible from her servants, often going to the trouble of making extra work for them, just so that they would not have to sit around with nothing to do. Now the unexpected arrival of the disgraced Lucinda provided her with a golden opportunity: if the girl could be set to work, and proved adept at it, then Arabella might dispense with one of the maids and send her packing. The wages thus saved could be diverted into Arabella's little nest-egg—a secret stash nurtured by just this kind of economy, which was the spinster's insurance against a bleak future.

A description of the tasks awaiting poor Lucinda is hardly necessary. We have all had to do housework at one time or another, and the least said about it the better—the boredom, the drudgery, the despair of knowing it has to be done all over again the next day; not to mention the thick taste of ashes and dust, the sting of lye, the numbness, the rawness, the cramp. Bear in mind, however, that these tasks were doubly degrading and unpleasant in an age without running water, flushable toilets or disposable articles of personal hygiene.

To say that Lucinda tackled her work with good cheer, or that her pure young voice was heard ringing in happy song throughout Wriggin Hall, would be a lie. It was a terrible humiliation for her, a dreadful, dreadful comedown in a world where servants had always discreetly taken care of such matters, where "work" meant needlework and young ladies otherwise never lifted a finger except to pick up a comb or strum a lute.

Thomas the footman found Lucinda in the scullery, washing out slimy washbasins.

"Is it...? It must be!" said Thomas shyly. He had, of course, heard all about Lucinda's arrival and her reassignment to menial labor.

Lucinda looked up. "Thomas! Oh, you're Thomas, I remember you! Bessie told me to look for you...Oh, Thomas!"

She was in his startled but gratified arms, sobbing her little heart out.

"There, there!" he said, giving her fatherly pats on the back. At last he gingerly pried her arms off his neck and held her at arm's length.

"Let me look at you! The last time old Thomas saw you, you were just a little lass. How you've grown! A lady, a beautiful young lady!"

At that, the sobs redoubled. He decided to change the subject.

"And Bess—how is she? Do you have any word for me from her?"

Thomas and his Bess had kept up a correspondence all these years, as Lucinda well knew, since she had often acted as Bessie's scribe.

"There wasn't time to write it down. She sends her love, and hopes you'll look after me here."

"Of course I will," promised Thomas. "I'll see to it the other servants treat you proper, and do what I can"—he wasn't sure if this was very much—"to make you feel at home. It's a shame, a shame, a fine young lady like you, scrubbing basins..."

Lucinda cringed. Whenever she thought of the shameful thing that had happened to her, now made so public by her debasing punishment, she wished she could shrink into a ball, like a hedgehog, and roll away out of sight. Since early that morning, she had been casting about for ways to escape. But where would she go? She had no money, no friends, no relations to save her from this awful fate.

Except, perhaps, one.

"She also—she also said you might help me find my father."

"Your father?" It took a while to sink in, as Thomas' mind groped about for the ramifications of that label. "Ah," he said at last, "You mean your real...*father!*"

Thomas' reaction showed Lucinda how far-fetched the idea was. She went back to her scrubbing, her face closed.

"Of course, miss, er, Lucinda—that's a notion," Thomas added quickly. "Why not? Your father!" He laughed. "That would show them, wouldn't it? Her ladyship, she'd have a fit...ah, I beg your pardon..."

Lucinda shuddered. She suddenly had a vision of this mysterious father as he might well turn out to be in real life: a red-faced, blue-bearded, strong-smelling creature like her Uncle Edmund. Sir Edmund had also had a lovechild—more than one, in fact. Everybody knew that. Was it not likely that her father would be like him? Finding him could mean even greater trouble...

"Never mind, Thomas," she said. "Please forget that I ever mentioned it."

But Thomas did not let the matter drop. He was glad of the opportunity to do something for his beloved Bessie. Thomas was ashamed that he had not tried harder to keep Bessie by his side. Should he not have taken a chance and followed her to Dorset, trusting in God or Fortune to provide him with a way of making a living? Would that not have been the devoted, the dashing, the daring thing to do? No, anything he could do to be of assistance to Bess would make him feel a lot better.

Thomas had aged noticeably in the time Lucinda and Bessie had been gone. His tight curls were grey now, especially above the temples, and his forehead had grown higher and shinier where the hairline had receded. The crease in his cheek had become a groove and was flanked by many other creases, most of them vertical and all of them permanent. His shoulders had narrowed, his arms had sinewed, and if you'd had a measuring tape with you and cared to use it, you'd have found that his hands hung a few notches lower by his sides than before.

But if the years had dulled his looks, they had not dampened his character. His eyes still radiated a quizzical openness that spelled trust, and his grin was even more impish, ingratiating and childlike than before. For Thomas had found that a manly swagger and stern expression only landed you in trouble, whereas boyish charm, laid on with an expert hand, opened doors, mended quarrels, and deflected criticism in the most ingenious way. Even Arabella, in all her viperish spite, was disarmed by that frank innocence and genuine bewilderment, so that Thomas was the only one of the household staff who was routinely let off with a mild reproach instead of a screaming tirade.

The first person Thomas approached in his new role of sleuth was Mistress Spudding, head cook at Wriggin, and incorrigible gossip.

"Missus S.," he said, springing to her aid as she tried to tip a large cauldron filled with broth, "—here, dear, let me help you, that's much too heavy for you—Missus S., do you remember that girl—what's her name—Lady Olivia's personal maid, you know, who ran off when her mistress was sent away?"

"Josie. Josie Davenport, was her name. Ah, she was a piece of work, I remember her! One day, I catch her wearing paint. On the lips! And a patch, too. Mind you, this was when patches was not as common as you see 'em nowadays. I say to her, 'Well, mum,' I says, 'what do I see, is that paint? And where do you think you're going, all tarted up like that?'" Mistress Spudding dipped her ladle into the broth and thrust it into Thomas' face for a taste; at his approving "Mmmm!" she continued in the same wheezing breath. "'Do you think Our Lord meant us to bepaint and besmirch His Image,' I says, 'I mean that form which He created in His Own Likeness?' 'Out,' she says. 'Out?' I says, 'looking like a harlot? Off you go to the scullery, my girl,' I says, 'and scrub that paint off your face before you go mucking up the good name of Wriggin Hall—'" (here Mrs. Spudding wiped her own glistening face smartly on her bespattered apron) "— but I can't tell you if it did any good. And then she left, running after poor Lady Olivia, and her disgraced and all. I shouldn't be surprised if she'd taken to bad ways..."

"Yes, Josie Davenport," said Thomas dreamily, "that was her name."

"What's come over you, thinking about *her*?" asked Mistress Spudding, suddenly suspicious. "I tell you Thomas, that wench was no good. No good at-all. You oughter be ashamed of yourself."

"Me? Oh no, never a fear," Thomas said brightly. "You know your poor Thomas better than that, now, Missus! No, I was just wondering what happened to her, is all. But don't let me keep you, dear, there's supper to be fixed, I'll just run upstairs and fetch Master's tray..."

* * *

There was one good thing about living among the servants, Lucinda decided, and that was that they called a spade a spade. No beating about the bush for them: none of the vagueness and euphemisms that had kept Lucinda and her cousins in the dark about life's major mysteries. Lucinda had always been a quick study. Now she was picking up the meanings of words she had never heard before, and was able to piece together a good deal of information normally hidden from females of her class.

And so she learned that her grandfather, far from suffering from the gout, as she had been led to believe, was actually stricken with the pox. She gathered, too, that one caught the pox by doing wicked things, things that were too shameful to mention, things of which God did not approve.

This knowledge led her to consider in a new light her grandfather's erstwhile understandable refusal to acknowledge her existence.

"Thomas," she said, as they sat side by side, he polishing plate, she scouring copper pots, "if Grandfather has the pox, then he must have been awfully wicked, mustn't he?"

Thomas smirked and looked around at the others. "His lordship has never been what you might call a pillar of virtue."

"Tell me, please. What did he do?"

"Please, ma'am. I don't think this is a fit subject for a lady..."

"I am not a lady!" Lucinda exclaimed. "Can't you get that through your head? I am no better off than any of us down here. Worse off, actually. Look at me! Am I a lady? Am I?"

"No, no," Thomas placated. "Don't take on so, please, Miss Lucinda. All right, all right, I'll tell you. He—he had a thing, you see, for young boys, your grandfather."

"Young boys? What did he want with young boys?"

Thomas immediately regretted having responded so freely.

"Well ma'am, some men—so I'm told—" He looked around apologetically. He hoped none of the others would assume he was speaking from personal experience. "...They have their pleasure, you know, lying with their own sex..."

"I see," said Lucinda, although she didn't quite see. At Belweather Manor, in the nursery, all the girls had shared one bed and all the boys another. Lying with your own sex was what you were supposed to do. But she was willing to let up a little on poor Thomas, whose brow was now glistening with sweat. "So is that—is that how you contract the pox?"

"No, no, ma'am. 'Tis a life of wickedness, so they say, leads to the pox. Whoring, debauchery, the like."

"Whoring." Lucinda sighed. There were so many new concepts to grasp. "Is that—young boys?"

A titter went around the kitchen. Thomas was growing more and more uncomfortable.

"No. Whoring, now, that's when a man does it with a woman, for instance, who isn't his wife. The whore—she does it for profit. Do you see now?"

"I see," said Lucinda, and bowed her head over the pot she was scrubbing. She mulled over this new information.

"Thomas," she finally whispered fiercely, "how can a man, like Grandfather, who does whoring and debauchery and such, who has the pox, how can he be so ashamed of me? Whatever my mother did, it can't have been more wicked than that, can it?"

Thomas pursed his lips noncommittally. "Ah, but that's different, ma'am," he said.

"Different? How? Tell me!"

"Well, because—it's different, that's all. Your mother was a lady, and ladies are expected to..."

"I know," Lucinda interrupted impatiently. "*Ladies* must protect their *Virtue*. Can the men just do as they please, then?"

Take her Uncle Edmund, she thought to herself. He was just as bad as her grandfather. Everyone knew he chased every petticoat in sight. And then what did he do? He accused *her* of being a wicked girl, and used that as an excuse to ruin her! (Actually, Lucinda wasn't sure if her "ruin" was what Thomas was talking about: she suspected there was more to this debauchery, this whoring, this lying with, than a stolen kiss, or seeing an uncle's naked part, as she had done.)

"Well," she said, tossing her head back and rolling her shoulders to loosen them, "that's men for you, isn't it? That's men for you." It was an expression she had heard many times from Bessie.

Thomas swallowed. He could not for the life of him understand why suddenly he felt so sad.

14

THE SLEUTHS

A few months into this new life, Lucinda felt as if she had never known any other. The daily drudgery, performed for the most part in silence, was now second nature to her: her body functioned in automatic response to the demands made upon it, and pushed itself to its physical limit. Meantime her mind was far away.

Never had she spent so much time in that imaginary realm where anything was possible, and where she was the most enviable, the most important, the most beautiful and the most beloved damsel in all the world. Where everyone sang her praises, where ladies fainted with envy when they beheld her, where men fought deadly duels over her, and where Henry Beaupree was the hero who swept her off her feet and saved her from fate after terrifying fate. And kissed her, kept kissing her. Gently, softly, tenderly; and sometimes, too, passionately, roughly, uncontrollably. If you were to creep up on our poor Lucinda sweeping out a sooty fireplace so that she did not hear your approach, and you noticed through the grime on her face that her eyelids were momentarily closed, her mouth drawn into puckish grin, you would be right in assuming that at that very moment, just such a kiss was being rehearsed.

Oh, Henry, she sighed to herself. Where was he? Why had he not come to rescue her from her aunt's evil clutches? But she would catch herself and quickly take it back, deciding that no, it was better if he did not see her in this posture, her unwashed hair falling stringily in her face, her face gleaming with sweat, her unbecoming clothes reeking of the same. Better that he not find out about the shameful episode for which she was being punished, better wait until it had all blown over, as Bessie had suggested it would. Better that he continue to think of

her as a poised, fresh, untouched maiden. A beautiful young lady. For
that was what she was!

But it was hard to retain that image of herself in the face of such
odds. There were no looking glasses in the house; Arabella did not enjoy
being reminded of her own disappointing appearance, and the first thing
she'd done upon her mother's death had been to order all the mirrors
taken down. It had proved not only a valuable lesson for the servants (on
the Folly of Vanity) but a lucrative one as well. Selling the looking glasses
had brought a nice little sum into Arabella's secret coffers, for Wriggin
Hall had had many splendid mirrors in Lady Hempstead's day.

As time went by, Lucinda barely remembered what she looked like,
and she did not like, nor did she identify with, what she saw when she
caught a glimpse of herself in the wavery window-glass—a bowed, common, wispy-looking creature in drab, threadbare clothes. Meanwhile, as
the novelty of her presence wore off, the other servants began paying less
attention to her too. And so she became, in her own perception as well
as theirs, just another faceless drudge.

Thomas, however, had not given up on the quest for her father. He
was determined to find out more about the circumstances of Lucinda's
birth by hunting down Josie Davenport, but none of his peers at Wriggin
had heard from Josie since she left.

"Hmmm, yes now, let me see," said Mr. Tucker, the steward, when
Thomas screwed up the courage to ask him. Tucker's florid color had
deepened somewhat at the sound of the girl's name: he had had quite a
crush on her at the time. Josie had been a sassy young wench, and very
popular with the stable hands. But she had turned Tucker down rather
cruelly. All he'd done was to offer her a ride to church, in front of him on
his nag, one Sunday! As if he'd had any unlawful intentions!

"If I remember right," he told Thomas wistfully, "she came to me the
day after they sent poor Lady Olivia away, and said she was leaving, because she was afraid she'd be put into Lady Arabella's service, and she
couldn't bear to work for *her*. Said she didn't care about references. And
that was that. She left without her wages, and without a word to milady,
God rest her soul."

"Do you know where she went?" asked Thomas.

"No. But I think she was friendly with one of the cottagers' wives. What do you want with her?"

"Actually," confided Thomas, "I am trying to trace our Lucinda's father—her real father, I mean. Doing it as a favor for Bess."

"Ah yes, Bessie," smiled Tucker. "How fares our Bessie?"

"Well enough," said Thomas. "Well enough. And she has asked me to do this for Miss Lucinda. You know how fond she is of the child."

"Poor little wench," sighed Tucker. "But it isn't surprising, what happened to her, is it? Her reaching an age, and well, being such a little peach, and no one to protect her. Her uncle—those fine sirs, if you ask me, there's not a one among them as has any morals at all. Not a one."

"And they call themselves our betters," said Thomas, then looked around in alarm, in case any of the aforementioned betters were within earshot.

"The rake who fathered Miss Lucinda, eh? Now there's another one for you," Tucker continued. "I hope he rots in hell, for what he did to poor Lady Olivia. *There* was an angel for you. And Miss Lucinda her spitting image, if you ask me."

"Help me find her father, Tucker. It's the least we can do," said Thomas.

Tucker coughed, suddenly aware of the excessive familiarity with which the footman was addressing him. Thomas Boothby was a servant born-and-bred; he, Will Tucker, the youngest son of a clergyman, had gone into service because he had not the stomach for soldiering, the only other course open to him. "Good," he said haughtily, turning away. "If you discover anything, I trust you will let me know."

On his next afternoon off, three weeks later, Thomas began making the rounds of the cottagers.

Mrs. Pennyroyal, who with her husband tilled the hayfields on the northern edge of the estate, remembered Josie.

"Josie? There's one we didn't see much of once she got her job up at t' big house. Too good for the likes of us, all-a-sudden. Fanny Bryar was her cousin. Why don't you ask her? She lives up at t' cobble, the little hut on t'other side of the lake."

Fanny Bryar lived by herself. When, years ago, she had proven unable to produce children, her husband had left her for a more fertile woman. She had a mat of prematurely white hair poking out of her kerchief, a deeply grooved, sun-browned face, and gnarled, stubby hands. She got by in the winter by gathering firewood and bartering it for food. In the summer, Mr. Lockjaw, the head gardener, employed her in the kitchen garden.

"She's my cousin, is Josie Davenport," she told Thomas. "Our fathers was brothers. When she was sixteen, she come here, looking for employment. Mr. Lockjaw got her a position up at t' house. She come and visit me when she could. She was plenty of laughs, that girl. She brang me leavings—bones and suchlike—from t' kitchen." She sighed wistfully.

"But what I'd like to find out," pursued Thomas, "is what happened to her after she left. Is she still alive?"

"I don't know," said Fanny. "Her people is from Simmins-Hollow. They'd be t' ones as I'd ask."

And so Thomas took his leave, though not without a promise to procure some leavings from the kitchen for Fanny.

Simmins-Hollow was less than a day's ride from Wriggin Hall, but for Thomas it might as well have been the Indies. For rest and recreation, Thomas was granted one free afternoon a month; he had never been away, not in the thirty-odd years he had lived there. How was he to pursue the search?

He wrote to Bessie of his predicament.

"Bless me," said Bessie, when Kitty, Lady Clarissa's chambermaid, had finished reading Thomas's letter to her. How clever of him! Thomas's quest put her own apathy to shame.

It wasn't long before Bessie came up with a scheme of her own. If she told Lady Clarissa that she had heard of a woman in Hampshire who was growing a new kind of plant with rejuvenating properties, she was fairly certain that her lady would authorize a trip—nay, fund it, even.

Clarissa took the bait.

"What does it do, then?" she asked excitedly. "Does it erase wrinkles, or lighten the complexion? Is it something to swallow, or does one rub it into the skin?"

"I don't rightly know, milady," said Bessie. "But I shall find it out. The stagecoach stops at Stilmouth, so I have been told, and I can go on foot from there."

"Very well," said Clarissa, counting out some coins. "But you must be back by the Lord's Day."

Bessie accepted the coins reverently. Outwardly, she was calm and composed. Inwardly, she was dancing a jig.

Two days later, Bessie found herself regretting her adventurous impulse as she slowly picked her way along the track between Stilmouth and Simmins-Hollow, avoiding, as best she could, the puddles, the horse dung and scattered rocks. Her legs ached, and her best petticoat was covered in mud. She toddled up to a stile along the side of the road, and carefully set herself down on one of the rails.

"Oh my Lord," she sighed to herself, "Lordy-Lord," and peered down the road. She had been walking for close to two hours, and was growing rather discouraged, for at the end of every stretch of road, instead of the promise of a village around the next bend, another interminable hedgerow came into view. Bessie was not used to so much exercise. Nor was she built for it, her upper body being proportionally too heavy for her short legs and little feet, giving her a side-to-side waddle that was ultimately very tiring.

Just as she was considering turning back, she heard footsteps and the grinding of wheels.

"Hoy!" It was a young lad pulling an empty cart down the road. He stopped when he noticed her sitting there all forlorn.

Bessie mustered her most charming smile. "Young man. Could you tell me please, how far it is to Simmins-Hollow?"

"Not far, Mississ," said the young man, wiping his brow. "Just round yon copse, past Master Herrin's fields, and then up Simmins Hill. Hollow's just t' other side."

Bessie looked down at her painful feet, which she had slipped out of her brogues. She sighed.

"Well, Mississ, me cart's empty. Jump in, why not. I'll get 'ee there in half a tic."

She did not have to be asked twice.

By the time they got to the village, Jeremiah, for that was his name, was beginning to regret his kind offer. It wasn't that the woman was a heavy load, it was just that she hadn't stopped talking, and having to turn his head to reply made him stumble and curse himself under his breath. He set her down at the edge of the green.

"Here you are then, Mississ."

"Thank you, Jeremiah," she said, clambering out. "So that will be the cottage? That one, on the far side of the green?"

"That be it, Mississ," said Jeremiah, and hurried off in the opposite direction.

"Mrs. Davenport?" asked Bessie of the woman who was draping some grubby wet linens over the bushes in front of the cottage.

"Who are you?" she replied, suspiciously.

"Elizabeth Goose—Bessie," she hastened to explain, "and I am looking for one Josie Davenport, employed at Wriggin Hall some sixteen years ago as a lady's maid. Your daughter, perhaps?"

The woman laughed a toothless laugh. Her hands were twisted with arthritis, her skin was slack and her hair was a dull grey.

"I am herself. Josie I mean. Mother's been dead these five years. What do you want?"

Bessie looked down at her feet, embarrassed. "I'm sorry...I didn't mean to offend you. Then it is you I was hoping to find. I was taken into service at Wriggin soon after you left."

Josie smiled wryly. "Wriggin, eh? Now back then, back then I were a beauty. Yes, a beauty."

Bessie smiled. "Weren't we all, weren't we all."

"Well, come in, come in. I see that you're tired. We'll have a cup of cowslip."

Bessie gratefully followed her into the sooty cottage.

What Bessie found out was, at first, a good deal about Josie Davenport, and nothing whatsoever about Olivia Steppys, because Josie was delighted to have a visitor, a real visitor who had come especially to see her—

Josie—thrilled, really, she was! It reminded her of her lady's maid days, when she had vicariously lived the life of the wealthy, seeing her ladies, dressed to the nines, spend their afternoons paying calls on other ladies, giggling, gossiping and drinking that fancy new brew, China tea.

Josie had no tea in her larder—where would she have obtained the money for such a luxury?—but the cowslip wine was an acceptable substitute. She spiked her own cup with the last dregs of a jug of ale. They sat at the rough table, sipping genteelly.

"And so," Josie finished her personal history, "after just a year of the life, in London, I found myself with child. When I begun to show, madam turned me out in the street. Said I'd scare away the customers. Said I were a poor tart to get into such a fix. And though I'd made a good living—some of my gentlemen was most kind—all that was spent, or lost in the Great Fire, and I hadn't a farthing to my name. So I quit London and come home, and had the child, and six more since. There's not a one willing to marry such as me, but they're not aversed to beddin' me. Leaving me with another mouth to feed..."—she glanced around the filthy cottage—"and then I think, I wisht to God I'd never left service at the big Hall."

Josie, having poured out her story, was silent. Bessie looked down at her feet. A bundle of rags lying in a dough box—Bessie had assumed it was some bread rising—had suddenly begun to wail. She hadn't realized it was a baby. She picked it up expertly, cradled it to her bosom and sniffed its bald head. It was pitifully scrawny. She could tell from the smell—not that soft milky sweetness but something more sour and pungent—that it was not thriving. She threw Josie a questioning look.

Josie shrugged. "It won't take the pap, and I use good ale in it too, nought's good enough for it, that one, it just spits everything out."

Bessie began rubbing the flaky skin gently. The little thing was all skin and bone, born before its time. "You should keep it warm," she said, automatically dispensing unsolicited advice, "close to your heart, see, and give it a good rub—like this—from time to time. That might make its appetite come back. Don't let your milk dry up, for goodness sake! A sip of mother's milk does more good than a gallon of ale-pap, I always say."

Josie did not reply. It was not the first time she had found herself saddled with a dying child. Mentally she had already sealed herself off, withdrawn her love. It was easier that way. She changed the subject.

"I often think of those times, up at t' big house. How is Tucker? Did he ever take a wife? And Lady Olivia, what happened to her, after she had the baby? Did she ever come back?"

"Lady Olivia," said Bessie, "never came back. She died giving birth. It was a girl," she added, "I was her nurse."

"Poor soul," said Josie. Then she grinned, showing empty gums. "I were the go-between, you know, between my lady and the baron."

"The baron." Bessie caught her breath. Now they were getting somewhere.

"Yes, *you* know. The one she were in love with. Couldn't right blame her, either. A dream, a right dream, he was. Could have welcomed him into me own bed, I could."

"That's—that is precisely what I've come about," said Bessie. "Lady Olivia's daughter is my charge. I raised her, actually," she added. "Now she wants to know who her father is."

"My lord and lady was set against it. The match, I mean. They had someone else picked out for her. This one was naught but bad debts. The family lost everything, in the wars." She shook her head. "Lady Olivia told me. But Lady Olivia, she was so taken with him, she would not listen to no reason. Late at night, I'd help her sneak out into the garden. They used to meet in the pavilion, you know, by the lake."

She paused, and wiped her forehead.

"Poor lady. So in love, they were. I wisht I was in her shoes, I did. Thought she had it all. But now look what happened. Her sent away in disgrace like that. Now me own mam, she didn't like what I did. But she never sent me away neither. Let me come back when I had nowheres else to go. Poor, poor lady."

Human nature being what it is, speculating on the troubles of those more fortunate than us is often the best way to forget our own. It was thus not an unnatural digression for Josie and her guest to start swapping satisfyingly shocking stories about their betters, and to find examples of decent kindness in ordinary folk like themselves. There was the old duke, for instance, whose daughter, a beauty, had hanged herself the day after her wedding to a wealthy beast almost forty years her senior. Or old king Harry, that bearded blueblood whose excuse for killing six wives (this was Josie's version; Bessie thought there might have been eight) was that they were all faithless and he a six-fold cuckold; and then Bessie told the story she had heard about a kind cobbler's widow who was raising a dozen children not her own, even though it meant near-starvation for all.

She finally brought the subject tactfully back to where they had left it.

"Now tell me, who is this baron?"

"Lord...Sunningham? No Sunderland, that's the name. He were a visitor at Bissenden, staying with Lord and Lady Doughby. They first saw each other at a ball, up at Bissenden. I tell you, it was love at first sight, it was..."

"Can you describe him to me?"

"My lady called him Gillyam. 'Sweet Gillyam', she'd say. Fine figure of a man he were, too. Dark hair, and a lovely smile he had." Josie sighed wistfully. "I wonder what's become of him."

"So do I," said Bessie grimly. "I am going to find him. And when I do find him, I will give him such a piece of my mind..."

She was silent a while, absently rocking the dying infant lying across her knees. From the rigid set of her back and the firm set of her mouth you could tell she was already preparing for the scene, in her mind.

15

WILLIAM

It was clear to Thomas, when he read Bessie's report, what had to be done next: he would have to sneak off to Bissenden on a quiet afternoon in order to ask Lady Doughby about that guest of hers. He could not think of any way to request an interview with a high-born lady other than pretending to be seeking employment.

Bissenden was a great house about seven miles from Wriggin Hall. Lady Doughby, a widow, was living out her days on the estate that now belonged to her son. Lord Doughby was too busy cavorting about London to tend to his inheritance, so that Lady Doughby continued as absolute monarch of Bissenden. Unlike most of her neighbors, she used no intermediary in hiring household help.

One of her serving men had recently died of the gangrene resulting from an ingrown toenail, and she agreed to see Thomas as an applicant for the job so sadly left vacant.

"Well, er, Boothby, is it? Thomas, yes of course, Thomas. Well, Thomas, Graves tell me you are not happy in your present employ."

Thomas opened his mouth to explain, then thought better of it, and nodded.

"I know Arabella Steppys." She paused, and raised an eyebrow. "I suspect she must be hard on her servants." She smiled at him encouragingly. "We have not spoken since Lady Hempstead's death, God rest her soul. Well...?" She was dying for some good gossip about her elusive neighbors. "What makes you seek to terminate your employment?"

"Actually, ma'am," said Thomas, pulling little balls of wool off the cap he was clutching, "It's not...it's not...you see—"

"Don't be shy, don't be shy. I promise you I shall not betray any confidence."

"Well, madam, for myself, I have no complaints."

"No?" she probed.

"For myself, ma'am, no, only it's the way she treats our poor Miss Lucinda..."

"Lucinda. Ah. Who is that?"

"Miss Lucinda—she's Master's grandchild, Lady Olivia's little girl."

"Olivia...Olivia? Well! That's the first I've heard of it! Olivia had a child? Well I never. I always thought she had died a maid..."

"She had the baby, uh, out of wedlock, ma'am, begging your pardon, of course."

"And the child's name is Lucinda? Well, well, Lettice certainly kept that one under her hat," she muttered to herself.

"Yes, ma'am. Lucinda. And, you see, now her aunt—her aunt the Lady Arabella, she has been giving the poor girl a very hard time, put her to work like a servant, she has, sweeping out fireplaces and the like. And, well, it's a crying shame—"

"It certainly is, Thomas. A cinder sweep? My, my."

"Yes, ma'am. So—so that's why I come to you, ma'am..."

"I don't see...."

"Begging your pardon, milady, I was hoping..."

"I cannot do anything for that poor girl. I think you must know that. It is not my place."

"No, I know, but...It's her father. You see, we thought, if only we could have her father come forward, to have him recognize her..."

Lady Doughby lost all the color in her round little face.

"Her father? How do you mean? If you are implying that my son..."

"Oh no, oh no, ma'am, not to worry! Not Lord Doughby, oh my Lord, no." Thomas was aghast at having given this nice lady such a fright. "Not him, not him at all. No, it was another, a young gentleman visiting here—Lord Sunderland, we think was his name—er, he..."

"William! Of course!" Lady Doughby's expression softened. "Yes, of course. I knew that he wanted to marry one of those Steppys sisters.

I made him confess it to me. He had nothing to bring to the table, of course. I don't blame 'em for turning him down. So William was the one—what a rogue, eh?" she joked.

Thomas flushed. He liked this lady, who was so straightforward and pleasant. She spoke to him almost as an equal. He smiled at her. "Well milady, seeing as you know him, we thought that maybe, well, maybe you could direct us to him…"

Lady Doughby looked grave again. "I am sorry. He died years ago. A duel. His mother, my dear, dear friend"—she sighed deeply, and her lips briefly relaxed into a sorry droop before snapping smartly to again— "never got over it. She died a year later. Broken heart. Her only son."

"Oh," said Thomas. That was it, then. Poor Lucinda. Still an orphan, this last hope dashed. "Well then. I must go. I am sorry to have given you so much trouble…"

"No! Don't go yet!" Lady Doughby had taken a liking to this serving man with the boyish charm and the kind heart. He looked ready to cry. He would do. He would do very well. And Lady Doughby was used to getting what she wanted. If she could not persuade him to desert Wriggin for Bissenden—well, then she had lost her touch.

"I shall write to the estate's executor. Sir Matthew Chancrey, I know him well. It is unlikely, in view of the family's debts, but perhaps—you never know, there might be something that poor young girl can claim. Now come here, and sit down—" she patted a chair across from hers—" and tell me more about her."

And that was how Lucinda found her origins and Thomas a new employer.

16

THE BEADED SLIPPERS

My Dear Lady Doughby,

As regards her Ladyship's enquiry to me, viz. the Sunderland Estate, it is my Sad Duty to inform her that we were fain to sell all Holdings left at the time of My Lady Sunderland's death, to Wit, the House in London & My Lady's personal Effects, in order to defray remaining Debts, wherefore the young person in question is indeed left penniless. I am entrusting to her Ladyship's care, however, a personal Memento, one pair of lady's Slippers, which Lord Sunderland had asked his Mother to embroider for his Bride and which, sadly, were left Unfinished upon news of his Death.

I write "Bride" because I must further advise that despite the Family's refusal to sanction the union, Lord Sunderland and his Lady were conjoined in Matrimony upon their Elopement, on the twenty-eighth day of October of the year of Our Lord 1657 & I have as proof of this a Letter written by his Lordship to his Mother informing her of the Same. The young Lady in question, if indeed Born as she claims in February of the year 1658, is thus the Honorable Miss Sunderland & Sadly the Sole surviving Heir of that Line, since his Lordship was killed in a Duel by a Jealous Suitor of the Lady Olivia shortly after the Marriage. I do not think that his Lordship's Mother was apprised that the Marriage had borne Fruit, otherwise I am persuaded She would have shown Greater Perseverance in trying to find her Daughter-in-law & might even have put aside the Notion that that poor Lady was responsible for Lord Sunderland's Death.

Her Ladyship's most devoted, obedient and humble Servant &c.
Matthew Chancrey.

Lucinda carefully smoothed out the stiff paper and rolled it back into a neat cylinder, tying the blue ribbon around it. She had read it at least twenty times since that morning, when Thomas had given her the package. She looked down at her feet, and rotated them slowly, pointing first one foot, then the other. The ivory leather sparkled with glass beads and intricate embroidery done in metallic thread. The heel of the left foot was not quite finished; there were pencil markings in lieu of silver and beads, but it did not matter. Never had she owned anything so lovely. They were a perfect fit, too. Apparently she had inherited her mother's narrow little feet. Her heart was bursting with pride. The glass-beaded slippers defined her at last! Finally she had an identity, an assurance of being someone real, someone with a real father and a real mother, two real living beings who had fallen in love and run away together. He had died defending her honor; she had died of a broken heart. She, Lucinda, was both the proof and the product of this most glamorous, if tragic, love story.

Her own two feet suddenly acquired a fascination of their own. This, then, was where it all began, in these dainty little toes! How had she never noticed them before? Because they really were too exquisite. The Hon. Lucinda Sunderland, she was. Not just a *young* lady: a *real* lady, daughter of a lord! Her feet were her mother's; that much was obvious. But what had she inherited from her father? The hair, perhaps? Reverently, she freed the curly mass from the fetters of the bonnet. She patted it apologetically, regretting her frequent complaints about its unruliness. Henry would not find it so; Henry would love running his fingers through that aristocratic mop. As for the feet—surely he had noticed them, and deemed them the prettiest, most elegant, most precious little feet he had ever seen...

"*What* have we here?"

A sigh of happiness stuck fast in Lucinda's throat. Planted wide apart in front of her were two alien feet, thick and graceless, jammed into heavy brown leather.

"Well, well!" snarled Arabella. "If it isn't little Miss Cinder-face, neglecting her duty! Get up, you filthy swash-bucket, and put that bonnet back on. At once!"

Lucinda scrambled to her feet, nervously wiping her hands on her apron. She had to swallow a few times before she could speak.

"Forgive me, Aunt Arabella, I was just..."

"What's this?" Arabella had noticed the rolled-up letter, and snatched it out of her hands. "A letter? Are you plotting something, young lady?"

"No, no, give it back to me! It's mine!" Lucinda shrieked, grabbing her aunt's arm.

Arabella calmly swung her arm free, sending her niece flying into a corner. "We shall see about that," she said, and, tearing off the ribbon, quickly scanned the neat lines.

"Well, well," she repeated at last. "That's it, then. It seems that we have an *Honorable* here now. Ha! An honorable gutterslut!" She seemed to find it supremely comical. "Oh, and quite the inheritance too! A pair of unfinished slippers! My, my. Such riches! Such power! May I humbly beg your forgiveness, my *lady*, for mistaking you for a common trull."

Arabella paused, gathering up her ire, her amusement giving way to great snorts of indignation. Lucinda cringed.

"And what, may I ask, does Lady Doughby know of all this? Fancy her sticking her nose into our family's affairs without so much as a by-your-leave! That woman is a scandalous gossip. How did she find out about you? How? Tell me, you little rat! You viper! You...you...*Honorable,* by God! How *dare* she! How dare *you*! You had better confess at once, or I'll give you such a thrashing you'll wish you had never been born!" She crumpled up the letter and hurled it at her niece's head.

Lucinda was four years old again, facing terrifying adult disapproval. Incapable of standing up for herself, all she could do was to deny the blame.

"I didn't know...it had nothing to do with me..." she whimpered.

"You conniving little bitch. Go! Get out of my sight! I cannot stand the sight of you! *Out!*"

And Arabella, in her fury at learning that her sister Olivia might not have been quite as ruined as she had supposed, and that Olivia's daughter was not some wretched bastard but the legitimate offspring of a lord, could not resist a vicious kick at those "honorable" legs—and, with a running leap, again, there! right in the shins!—before slamming the door shut, with a mighty crash, behind her.

Lucinda, shaking all over, sat perched on the edge of her bed, rubbing the bruises on her leg. She did not know what to think. On the one hand, she was now legitimate. Not a bastard. They could no longer hold her mother's supposed sin against her. She had proof, right here, in the crumpled letter that she was smoothing back into readable shape. So that was one thing, one very, very good thing.

She stopped, and sighed. Her head was spinning.

On the other hand, she was still penniless. And it was clear from Aunt Arabella's reaction that she would have to contend with the same level of ill-will; she was still the poor relation, and would have to continue to sing for her supper.

She shuffled over to the chest at the foot of the bed. She shook out the voluminous gown she had worn on the day of her arrival, Sarah's hand-me-down; it was a little creased, and musty-smelling, but glamorous compared to the grimy garments she now ripped off and kicked into a corner. She dipped her kerchief into the stale water in her washbowl and dabbed at her hands, her arms, her neck, and face, wiping them dry with a corner of the bed sheet. She pulled on the smock and lace-edged petticoat which Arabella had condemned as excessively frivolous. Next, she stepped into the gown, pulling it up to her chest and wriggling first one arm, then the other, into the sleeves. With great care she laced up the boned front. Last came the embroidered stomacher, an inverted triangle designed to lengthen the torso and whittle the waist. She had no pins, so she pulled two ribbons out of the tiered sleeves of her smock and used them to belt the stomacher in place.

She pulled the hairpins out of her aching topknot, and shook her curls loose. Having no mirror, it was not easy to fashion a hairstyle, but, working by touch, she managed to pull the hair back from her face and twist it into a loose bun with a few pins at the crown. She pulled some shorter strands free at the hairline and along the temples; these sprang by themselves into the little corkscrew-curls ladies' maids spent hours coaxing into shape with hot tongs. Licking her fingers, she tried to slick them down into what she hoped was a more deliberate pattern. She bit her lips and pinched her cheeks, as she had seen Sarah do. Lastly, she shook out her skirts, and, bending over, pushed each breast up into the very top of the décolleté, creating two small mounds separated by a faint shadow that could almost pass for a cleavage. Her legacy, the glass slippers, peeked out from beneath her skirts. It would have to do.

She let herself out of the room quietly.

"Grandfather..."

"Err?" A bubble of spittle popped out of a corner of Lord Hempstead's mouth. "Wha...whazzit?" He had to shake himself, to rid himself of the dream in which he had been a nursling, slippery, fresh and new.

"What *is* it?" he intoned imperiously, through the permanent film of catarrh clogging his throat.

"It's just me, Lucinda..."

Lucinda? Before him stood a lean little thing, quivering. Had he sent for him? Her? He sent the feelers of his memory fumbling about in the region of his breeches, to see what was going on down there.

Alas, there was no enthusiastic response from the nether parts. Ah yes, of course. The reality of his illness spilled into his consciousness in a flood of sourness. He fixed the futile apparition before him with a peevish stare. "Well?"

"Grandfather, please read this..."

Grandfather. A relation, then, not an assignation. He sighed, and took the creased paper from her hand.

When Arabella received word that her father wished to see her, she knew it was not a good sign. She had intercepted the slut Lucinda on her way back to her room, dressed in a manner expressly forbidden. Arabella had taken great pleasure in ripping the girl's gown to shreds, but she now regretted her momentary loss of control. (There had been some good lace and expensive embroidery; Mistress Wapping would surely have paid a handsome sum for it.) She had also given the minx a sound beating until she confessed that she had been to see Lord Hempstead; had then beaten her some more, for good measure. Now Arabella's wrist hurt, and it was all Lucinda's fault. She stomped into the library.

"Ah. There you are." Lord Hempstead averted his eyes. He could not bear ugliness, which was why Arabella's presence was seldom required.

"Yes, Father?" she asked sullenly. Her arms were crossed in front, over her midriff, an awkward stance that emphasized the bulges she was trying to hide.

"Send word to Edmund. Today. I wish to consult with him on a matter concerning my granddaughter Lucinda. It appears—it appears an injustice has been done." Turning away from her, he muttered the rest at the embers in the grate. "My little Olivia, she was such a—sugar-plum, that one! I had high hopes for her. She'd have made quite a stir at court. Fool, wretched little fool, she was. Ah, well." He tapped the stem of his pipe absently against a lone front tooth. "But now her child—the baggage from Dorset—it seems she's all right, legitimate enough. Without my consent, of course, but born under the Law. Fresh little thing too, just like her mother." He chuckled. "She'll do quite nicely. With *her* looks,"— Arabella stiffened—"we shan't be long drumming up a husband. But we need bait. A modest sum will do." He drew himself up a little higher against the pillows. Scowling at his hopelessly unmarriageable daughter, he ordered, "Have Edmund come here at once. Remind him I do not like to be kept waiting. And Robert too. What are you waiting for, woman? Go!" he scowled.

"But Father..." Arabella began.

"I am tired now. Send in Hoogschotel."

"But Father..."

"Did you not hear me?" He waved the back of his hand at her, shooing her out of the room.

Arabella dutifully sent a groom to Belweather Manor with the message that Lord Hempstead requested the attendance of Sir Edmund and the viscount at their earliest convenience. She also gave Dr. Hoogschotel

permission to step up the quick-silver cure, which she had ordered suspended some weeks earlier, having observed—correctly, as it turned
out—that the treatment was sapping the old man's remaining strength.

Sir Edmund and Robert arrived at Wriggin five days later, just in
time to witness Lord Hempstead's final delirium. They decided it was
a good thing that none of the ladies of the family had been present at
his death-bed, because at the end he had thrown off the sheet, arched
his back, grabbed his withered part through his shirt and snorted something no one could understand. And as the solemn group around the
bed stared in disbelief, he fell back onto the pillow, a miraculous erection
in his hand, his face frozen in wide-eyed, open-mouthed ecstasy.

17

A PROPOSITION

Consider the proposition that Love Is Blind. Even the sagest of women and wisest of men may find that it is possible to be so blinded by love that all common sense, alas, flies clear out the window. Which is why the great moralists maintain that Love is governed not by Goodness or Grace, but is led around by the nose by Folly.

Lord Hempstead's death provided Sir Edmund with the opportunity to bring his young niece back to Dorset. Sadly, he was obliged to invite his sister-in-law as well, since he could not have Arabella staying on at Wriggin Hall; he did not trust her. The steward, Tucker, a good fellow, was to take care of the place until a wife was found for Robert, the new earl.

Both men had been shocked by Lucinda's pallor and gauntness (enhanced, to be sure, by the unflattering shade and shape of Lady Arabella's cast-offs), at the bruise marks on her skin and at the sooty greyness embedded in the pores around her nostrils. "Really, Arabella," Edmund complained, "the gel's all skin and bones. And those bruises, how'd she get those?"

"I thought you liked them lean, Edmund," Arabella said snidely. "Just like father, you are. You don't like a woman to look womanly. I don't know how she got those bruises. She is a clumsy thing, very, very clumsy. And wicked, too. I haven't any notion how Clarissa put up with her for all these years."

"Well, she'll have to put up with her again for a while," Edmund said.

Lucinda looked at them dully when they told her she was going home. She'd be happy to see Bessie again; that was all. Grandfather had died before making good on his promise to her; it was no use raising the question of a marriage portion now. Uncle Edmund and Robert would never allow her to encroach, however modestly, on their own shares of the Steppys fortune. As for Sir Matthew's letter, they were not impressed.

"So you see," Robert said patronizingly, waving the letter at her, "you should be grateful for the roof over your head. This makes it plain that your *father* is not going to do anything for you. You should be *more* than thankful to us." His voice rose to a triumphant bleat. "Do you have any idea how much it costs to..."

"Enough, my lord," said his brother-in-law. "I am sure the young lady is grateful, and cognizant of her obligations toward us." He leered at her behind the new earl's back. "Eh, my dear?"

Lucinda kept her eyes on the floor—at least, that's what it looked like. It was actually the tips of her beaded slippers she was scrutinizing.

"Fine," Edmund said. "You will come home with us, my dear. You are our charge, after all. Belweather Manor is where you belong," he added sentimentally.

"Sir," Lucinda mumbled, confused. How had her Uncle Edmund, who'd been such an ogre to her, metamorphosed into this well-meaning gentleman who winked at her conspiratorially, as if to ally himself with her, against the world?

"Well! We shall see what *Clarissa* has to say about that," muttered Arabella under her breath.

"What did you say, Aunt?" asked Robert.

"I? Say something? No, my lord," fluted Arabella, trying out some feminine meekness on her younger brother, the brand-new master of Wriggin Hall.

Clarissa was in no state to protest the return of her disgraced niece. She was lounging in front of her dressing table, appraising the effect of a dose of the belladonna cordial on her languid eyes. She noted that one of her breasts was lolling, exposed, across the lace of her half-open dressing-gown. She smiled at it lovingly; imagined her lord and master coming in at that very moment and being transfixed...

It so happened that Edmund did enter her closet at that very moment. But he was not transfixed. In fact, he looked away, annoyed. She sat up. How, she wondered indignantly, how could he *not* be transfixed, when she presented such an alluring sight? She had seen the portrait of the Duchess of Cleveland, the king's mistress, when she was in Sir Peter Lely's studio to have her own portrait done, and had studied it intently for clues. The painter had captured the duchess in a similar artless *déshabillé*. Clarissa was convinced that her own skin was whiter, her lips droopier, her eyelids heavier than the king's favorite. For Heaven's sake! How could Edmund avert his eyes from this vision, this presentation of all that was womanly?

"Good God, woman, cover yourself! Have you no shame?"

Shame? He was a fine one to talk. But the belladonna had got her tongue, and she found she was unable to recriminate. With great dignity, she drew the lace across her chest.

"I came to tell you the earl is dead."

Father dead. Ah well. She sat forward a little and peered at her reflection, curious to see the effect of tears in those limpid eyes.

He was saying something else, explaining the arrangements, the necessity of having someone stay at the manor. He was needling her, demanding a response. Challenging her. "You haven't heard a word I've said!"

"Of course I have," she protested, wrapping the words with difficulty around her relaxed tongue.

"And...?"

"F—fine," she pronounced airily. She'd had enough of him. She wanted him to leave her alone so she could ponder her bereavement in peace and practice a suitably distraught demeanor. And she might need another nip of the cordial, for her nerves...

It was not her intention, but not an hour had gone by before Lucinda had told Bessie about her uncle's renewed attentions. She had meant to keep quiet about the whole thing, but somehow, as soon as she found herself in Bessie's comforting presence, it came tumbling out.

"So..." Bessie had purred, after the hugging and the exclaiming and the tears were done, "so you see, everything's all right again, pet, all's forgotten and forgiven."

It was only because Lucinda was so thoroughly in the habit of disagreeing with Bessie that she couldn't help sighing, "What? *Nothing's* forgotten."

"Oh, lamb. Your uncle and aunt have decided to take you back: surely that means..."

"It doesn't mean it's forgotten. *He* hasn't forgotten."

"Who, 'he'? You mean your uncle?"

Lucinda nodded.

"What do you mean, *he* hasn't forgotten?"

"Oh, nothing."

"Nothing? No, tell me, what did you mean?"

"I meant nothing."

"No, my young lady, I know you better than that. I know you meant *some*thing by that. Tell me. Now."

"Well, Bess, *you* know."

"Know what? I know nothing. I am waiting for you to tell me."

"*You* know, I just meant that Sir Edmund didn't bring me back here because all has been forgiven and forgotten. He brought me back because he wants to..."

"Wants to finish what he started?"

"..."

"Wants to finish what he started, is that it?"

"...."

"Oh my pet...oh my pet! Lord. Did he say as much?"

Still no answer.

"He did, eh? And what did you say?"

"Nothing."

Was it only fifteen short years since Bessie had carried this little bundle in her arms, had been able to rock her to sleep at will, had been in control of every taste that passed her lips, had encouraged her to take her first steps, had taught her her first words, had made her believe in fairies and in God and in miracles; indeed, had had the conceit to think that every thought in the child's head had been put there by her? And yet here they were but a few years later—where *had* the time gone?—and Bessie, who had groomed Lucinda to believe she was special, could not understand why, just when it was established she was not illegitimate after all, and would now have to be accepted by her peers, the girl suddenly seemed willing to throw it all away for a life of shame.

"But you haven't...you didn't agree!" she cried.

"It's too late, Bess," Lucinda sulked. "Don't you see...?"

"I don't see! I *don't* see!" Bessie's voice was shaking with fury. "He can't! You can't! I won't have it!"

"Oh, come on, Bess. Where do you expect me to go? What do you expect me to do? At least this way, I stand a chance. He has promised me an income, you know, if I will be, you know, his—"

"An income!" snorted Bessie, outraged.

"Yes, an income. Fifty guineas a year. If I am discreet about—it." Lucinda knew that by giving Bessie the details, she was only making it worse, but she pressed on, as if explaining the thing reasonably could make it seem a reasonable thing to do. "I could save it up, for my portion. In five years, when I am twenty, I'll have over two hundred and fifty pounds, and with that..."

"In five years nobody will have you! No matter how rich you are! Don't fool yourself, girl. You'll be used goods in the eyes of every decent gentleman. No, no, that's no future for a lady. Oh please, please lamb. I know, we'll run away. Perhaps that nice lady Thomas is working for now, she'll take us in, and..."

"No Bessie," Lucinda said firmly. "You know we can't do that. We have no right to expect charity from anyone, least of all from someone who is no relation." She turned to look out the window, avoiding Bessie's eyes. "Anyway," she said dramatically, "this is where I belong."

Since it is impossible to read another person's mind, there is really no point speculating about their motives. It is hard enough to understand our own motives sometimes. Given the fact that Bessie was ignorant of her pet's secret crush on Captain Beaupree, and that she had no idea how very little Lucinda understood about the true nature of sex, there was no way Bessie could make sense of Lucinda's puzzling capitulation.

The clue lies, simply, in a chance remark overheard by Lucinda on the journey home to Dorset in the claustrophobic carriage. The men were sitting on one bench, the two women on the other. It was very hard to avoid knee contact with the person sitting opposite you; Lucinda's thighs and calves ached with cramp. Aunt Arabella had fallen asleep, snoring, her mouth wide open. Lucinda was also pretending to be asleep in order to escape the men's probing glances.

"I don't think, Sir, that my sister Clarissa will be very pleased about this," the new Lord Hempstead was saying.

"About what? The old earl? Nah."

"No, I mean—the girl. Returning to the manor. After..."

"Oh, that. Don't worry about that. I am not afraid of her tongue, my lord, although I will admit she can be trying."

Robert grunted.

"And besides, my wife's all a-twitter about that Beaupree fellow she's trying to reel in for Sarah. I doubt she'll even notice the gel's back, what with the captain's upcoming visit to explore a possible arrangement."

Lucinda's eyes had snapped open wide. Then, seeing Edmund and Robert looking at her, she'd pretended a jolt of the carriage had woken her up, and sank back into the seat with an exaggerated yawn.

Meanwhile her uncle's words were rattling around inside her head. The captain! Beaupree! He was talking about Henry. There was a scheme to snare Henry for Sarah! But—he was coming to Belweather Manor! He was not coming for Sarah. No, no. He was coming for *her*. Surely? Yes, surely! It was a ruse. A ruse on his part to see her again. Yes, that was it. He was doing it all for her, Lucinda, because he sensed his true love was in distress. He had heard her secret call! Nothing, nothing, *nothing* bad could happen to her now!

That had been her conviction when Uncle Edmund had furtively whispered his proposal to her when they were alone in the idle coach during a rest stop. And his proposition, instead of revolting her—as it should have done, of course—only served to fan the flurry of excitement in her ribcage. Yes, yes, Henry would rescue her in the nick of time from her uncle's lewd clutches! The fact that another man desired her and wished to press his advances on her—surely this could only increase her desirability in Henry's eyes, and confirm to him that he had made the right choice!

"Well, lamb, I just cannot make you out. At all." Bessie was shaking her head sadly. "Don't you see..."

"Leave me alone!" Lucinda snapped.

"If that's what you want," said Bessie, hurt.

"It's what I want!" she shouted. "All you ever do is meddle, meddle, meddle! I'm not your baby anymore, you know!"

And to erase the reproachful sight of Bessie shuffling out the door, she took a deep breath, closed her eyes, and pictured herself in Henry's adoring arms.

18

A WITCH

It was extremely fortunate for Lucinda that Uncle Edmund and Robert had to leave the very next day for London. A host of distant relatives and illegitimate offspring were expected to come clamoring for their piece of the Steppys pie; the trick was to forestall those claims, to nip them in the bud, by the ruthless wielding of one's influence at court and in Chancery. In the order of things, this was a more pressing matter for Edmund—and a more thrilling sport—than the deflowering of a dependent virgin. So his niece was given a reprieve and left to resume her place, albeit temporarily, in the nursery.

A fresh, nose-tingling breeze awoke her, promising a brilliant day. After all those months of being cooped up indoors with Aunt Arabella breathing down her neck, it was a joy to steal outside without being seen. She found her charcoals and drawing board where she had left them, in a chest in the nursery.

She climbed the hill behind the manor and sat down under a tree overlooking the valley. The shimmering landscape was dotted with amiable old trees, every one planted in its own perfect puddle of shade. The horses and sheep had their heads lowered, all facing the same direction: a perfect composition. She began to sketch, but before long her attention was drawn by a hawk looping high above.

She let her drawing board slide off her lap and leaned back, her elbows digging into the prickly turf. Minuscule insects hopscotched hypnotically before her half-closed eyes, spark-specks in the sun. Lulled by the sleepy air, she let her mind drift.

She was standing in the manor's ballroom. There was a wild dance going on, a country dance—a contredanse, Monsieur Piétain would have cor-

rected her. Everyone she knew was there, laughing, perspiring, panting. She looked down at her dress: it was her kitchen uniform, ragged and dirty. She shrank against the wall, hoping no one would notice her.

Suddenly her heart skipped a beat. That attractive couple leading the dance—they were looking straight at her! Shyly, she tried to melt into the shadows, but the dazzling man and woman beckoned to her. Come! They caught her by the hand and then she was whirling around between them, wings on her feet, her skirts billowing behind her. On the other side of the circle, she saw Henry Beaupree staring at her in amazement and pride. And there were her aunts and uncles, and all the neighbors too, beaming encouragement. Only Sarah, Robert, and the rest of her cousins were scowling. They started bickering and hitting each other, and were expelled from the circle...

A bee zoomed past her ear, jolting her out of the reverie.

An immense tower of white had materialized overhead, thick cauliflower clouds stacked atop one another precariously. Seen from this angle, the whole pile appeared dangerously top-heavy. She let her head hang back, enjoying the dizziness. A prickly blade of grass scratched at her nose. She slapped it away, but it sprang back impertinently. She sneezed, never taking her eyes off the clouds overhead. Even if they did topple, what harm could they do? She waved at the clouds, inviting them to smother her in softness. *Her* clouds. *Her* sky. When she was a little girl she had been convinced that the sky was hers, that no one else saw it as *she* saw it. She gazed at it with proprietary awe.

A shout came wafting up from the kitchen garden at the foot of the hill, answered by a scolding complaint. She sat up. It was two squabbling servants, thinking themselves unobserved.

She rubbed her palms together to wipe off the grit and twigs, then picked up the charcoal and paper beside her.

Winning over Sarah, whose disdain for her cousin had grown even more scathing since the "scandal," was out of the question. But even if there was no prospect of sisterly confidences, it was easy enough to extract information from Sarah by provoking her.

They were sitting at their needlework in adjoining window nooks, their backs to the glass in order to catch the last slanted light of day. Their faces were hidden from each other by the pillar between them; each could just see the other's swinging feet.

Lucinda sighed. "So. Nothing came of it, then, I gather?" she said.

"Of what?" Sarah's voice came back.

"Oh, of your betrothal. It's been eight months since I've been away, and here you still are."

"That shows what you know of it," said Sarah snidely. "It's still a secret."

"Hmm."

Sarah bent forward, peering around the column to catch a glimpse of her interlocutor. Lucinda was intent on her needle. She showed not a flicker of interest. Sarah leaned back into her alcove again.

"Wouldn't you like to know..." she taunted.

No reply.

"Well, I'm not telling, anyway."

"So? I don't want to know. I'm not interested."

Lucinda watched her cousin's feet freeze, the toes in an upward position. Then they began to swing again. The heels banged on the paneling.

"Actually, it's a fine match. Everyone says so." There was a pause. "He's *sooo* handsome!"

From Lucinda's niche a snort could be heard. It put Sarah on the defensive.

"Yes he is. Who would want an ill-favored husband? *I* certainly would not."

Lucinda sighed pityingly.

Now Sarah was really mad.

"Well, little Miss know-it-all, it's someone you know. Someone you've been sweet on yourself."

"I have never been sweet on anyone," came the calm reply.

"Oh no? What about Captain Beaupree? You...you quizzed me about him after the ball, last winter, didn't you. Yes you did. I could *tell* that you liked him."

"So?" asked Lucinda.

"So? So the point is, he's the one I am to marry."

"Oh," said Lucinda. "You thought...? I...? *That* man? Oh, no. You are *quite* welcome to him. Thank you very much."

Sarah was quiet for some moments, wrestling with Lucinda's intimation that Sarah was pursuing the captain as a matrimonial prospect only because she believed that Lucinda had once been attracted to him!

Seething, Sarah now took the offensive.

"Of course. I forgot. You cannot *afford* to be sweet on anyone. Without a portion, no one will want you, will they!"

"When I marry," said Lucinda with great dignity, "it will be for love. Not for money."

"Then you will die an old maid," Sarah said primly.

"If I must."

"But just wait until *I* am married." Sarah's voice was charged with as much dreaminess as she could muster. "There will be *such* a feast. I am certain the king will attend—and the entire court too."

"If there *is* a wedding. It's a secret, you say? Why?"

"It's almost settled. They just don't want me to say anything about it yet..."

"Come, Sarah, you just told *me* about it, didn't you? You did!" Lucinda was aware of the sharp edge of triumph in her voice, and she wasn't proud of it. "So *you* must want it known, because you just told me and I *said* I did not want to know! Did I not! Therefore it must be Hen—I mean the captain—who wants it kept quiet. And what do you suppose *that* means? Are you *quite*, quite sure he is as keen on this union as you are?"

"*I* don't want it at all! I mean..." Sarah was close to tears now. She jumped off the window ledge and patted her skirts, front and back. "I mean I *do*, I do want it. It's a good match, everybody says so."

"Who's 'everybody'?" taunted Lucinda.

"Everybody!" shouted Sarah. "Mother. Aunt Edwina. Mrs. Limpid."

"Just as I thought," said Lucinda.

"What?"

"As usual, Sarah," Lucinda explained patiently, her head bent low over the needle stabbing efficiently at the canvas, "you are allowing others to make your decisions for you. How do you know what this captain is like? Have they arranged a meeting between you, so that you can find out for yourself what sort of a husband he will make?"

"Well," Sarah began doubtfully.

"You mean you only met him when he was here that one time last winter? Surely you will not allow them to push you into a marriage with a man you saw but twice?"

"Three times," Sarah lied sullenly. "And besides, he is coming back next week, to arrange it with Father. At least he was, before Grandfather died."

"Next week?" repeated Lucinda carefully.

"Yes."

"Well, I hope your father will consider the captain's suit carefully. I mean, it's not even as if he's a duke, or a count, or anything..."

Having planted a suitable crop of doubts in her cousin's head, Lucinda folded her needlework and skipped out of the room.

There was something the matter with Lady Clarissa, and Bessie was troubled. The other servants too had begun to notice that their mistress had withdrawn almost completely, and spent day after day cooped up in her closet. When you tiptoed in, you would find her sitting at her dressing table, staring vacantly at her reflection. It took several *ahems* to coax her into acknowledging your presence, and even then she seemed to have difficulty rousing herself to formulate an order, or even to respond to a respectful query. Even less characteristically, she paid little heed to her husband, barely seeming to care whether he was home or not. The nights in particular were strangely silent, for the corridors no longer echoed with the sound of Clarissa's nagging protests and conjugal sighs.

One afternoon Kitty, ordinarily calm and competent, came running into to the kitchen in a panic, looking for Bessie. She was very upset.

"Bess, could you—could you come and have a look at milady? She's making funny movements with her hands, and she's trying to speak, but no words come out! Eerie, it is! She's given me *such* a turn! Please, please come!"

Bessie hurried after Kitty to milady's chamber. Milady was obviously not well. She was shaking all over. Her bonnet had slipped down her neck, revealing hair that was matted and unkempt, her skin was strangely flushed under a very thick layer of white powder, and she was making jerky movements with her hands and torso, bending over at the waist and then straightening again with difficulty. There was a startling resemblance to the puppets that entertained the village children on market day.

"Madam, what's the matter?" Bessie exclaimed in alarm.

Clarissa opened her mouth to speak, but no words came out. A beaded line of spittle spanned the space between her top and her bottom lip. The rouge was smeared right down to her chin.

"Rrahrrrr," she rattled.

"Come, now, dear," Bessie fussed, forgetting for a moment, in her shock, how one should address one's lady, "let's get you into bed now, pet, there's a dear. That's right, that's right, *there* we go. Now isn't that better? Don't try to speak, love, quiet now, just rest."

She turned back to the appalled Kitty. "Don't just stand there, girl! Fetch some warm water to sponge her face. And change her into a clean gown. There's Lord-knows-what all over the front of this one."

"But...but what's the matter with her?"

"I don't know!" exclaimed Bessie impatiently. "I am not a physician!" She turned back to the dressing table. An alarming thought had just occurred to her.

Sure enough, there was the vial of belladonna that Bessie had supplied her with yesterday. As usual, she had tried to impress upon her lady the danger of taking more than two drops at a time. The vial was half empty.

"Oh my Lord!" said Bessie, and then, for good measure, "*Oh*, my Lord."

"What?" quavered Kitty, and, "What?" said Mrs. Limpid, who had been alerted, from the doorway.

"It's the deadly nightshade," Bessie said. "I think she's gone and poisoned herself."

"Poison!" exclaimed Mrs. Limpid. "Poison! How can that be? In this house!"

"It's not really, in small doses," Bessie began defensively, but Mrs. Limpid had already started a tirade.

"I've told you, woman, your quackery is not to be tolerated! Now look what you've done! If she dies, it will be your fault!"

"Mnnaahrr?" came a quavering sound from the bed.

They all turned and stared at Clarissa, who had been forgotten.

"No, no, milady," Bessie clucked, rushing over to her, "Of course not. You are not going to die. What an idea!" She busily tugged at the bed-covers, so the others would not notice how her hands were shaking.

In the absence of Sir Edmund, Lady Arabella took it upon herself to send for Dr. Hoogschotel, who happened to be staying nearby in hopes of collecting his outstanding fee. The Flemish doctor was of the opinion that a cure of purging and bleeding would very soon restore Lady Clarissa's health. As for her speech, he ventured that it was witchcraft that had struck her dumb.

"Dis is de furrist time I haff seen de fiend's work wrought on a lady off de—iff I may be zo bold—qvality," he told Arabella in his carefully articulated English. "But de signs are de same as in de commonvolk. You see, de deffil is at vork here. You see dis fit, how she moves like dat. Dis is de deffil acting upon de yuman body by natural means, dat is to say, by sturring up de superabundant yumors, egciting dose yumors."

Everyone looked at Clarissa, who had grown even more agitated since the doctor had started speaking.

"Tell me, has she—pardon me vor asking—vomited anysing out of de ordinary? Pins, for instance?"

"Vomited? Pins?" asked Mrs. Limpid, aghast.

"Yes. Crooked pins and such. Or nails. Any phlegum?"

"Only phlegm," said Kitty, uncertainly.

"Well, it may yet come. De phlegum, already, iss a symptom. And see her mouss? How she tries to speak. Satan has robbed her off de power of speech." He suppressed an unprofessional smirk. "It is a good lesson, iss it not..."—here he winked in the direction of Mrs. Limpid and Kitty—"for wives to heed deir husbands when dey tell dem to hold deir tongue?"

Kitty giggled. Mrs. Limpid pursed her lips and said nothing. Arabella threw the good doctor a venomous look.

He put his hands together piously, and nodded. "Yes, it iss a most interesting case, yes. Tell me, is dere anyone whom you suspect might vish to hex dis poor lady?"

Mrs. Limpid shook her head. "But see here. Witchcraft—I cannot imagine such a thing...Can't it just have been the poison? That's what Bessie thinks. There is the bottle. She drank too much of it, you see."

Dr. Hoogschotel reverently took the flask from Mrs. Limpid's hand and rolled it around in his joined open palms.

"Well. Vat iss in it?"

"I think she said the deadly nightshade."

"For the complexion," added Kitty.

"I see. It iss possible, yes. Who is dis Bessie?"

"One of our cooks. She dabbles in plants and remedies and such, and she..."

"I see. I sink vee must interview dis cook. She may be de sorceress vee are looking for."

"Sorceress?" repeated Arabella.

"Yes. De deadly nightshade, madam, you see, is one of de hexes' favorite brews. Dey drink it, so I am informed, during deir fiendish ceremonies. Dey anoint deir bodies wis it too."

"What are you saying, Doctor?" demanded Arabella.

"My dear lady. Let me be clear. We have before us de victim of poison and witchcraft." So Dr. Hoogschotel wrapped up his snap yet learned diagnosis.

19

THE CURE AND THE CURSE

After Lady Doughby heard from Thomas that Lucinda had been removed from Wriggin Hall and sent back to Belweather Manor, she could not help agreeing that the girl's future was at stake.

"You are afraid the poor girl's uncle will prey upon her virtue, are you not?" she asked her new footman and confidant.

Thomas, who had fed the good lady enough hints about Sir Edmund's lecherous activities and his previous conduct toward his niece to lead her to this conclusion, cast his eyes down.

"Don't be afraid. I share your suspicions."

Thomas looked up gratefully. "It's not just for myself, you understand ma'am, but for my Bess's sake. She'd take it so hard if anything happened to that girl. Raised her as her very own, she did."

"Of course she would take it hard," said Lady Doughby, "of course she would." She was touched by the footman's fondness for his Bess, whom he had described in tender detail, and the young girl who had been her charge. It occurred to Lady Doughby, not for the first time, that servants' affections were so much more straightforward than those of her own class, where other considerations, primarily monetary, took precedence over sentimental attachments. In her world, it was hammered into one from the youngest possible age that such attachments were precarious at best, and that it was unwise to set store by them. It was a world where arranged marriages wiped out romantic dreams, where excessive maternal doting was nipped in the bud by the custom of handing the baby over to a wet-nurse until it was safely past the dependent stage, and where filial love (and this was what Lady Doughby regretted most of all) found a substitute, at best, in correct filial duty.

"But Thomas," she said, with a sigh. "You know that I cannot intervene directly. I have no connection with the family."

"You see if I—I would never ask this otherwise, milady, but..." he tried, "if you will give me leave to go to Dorset, then I might be able to help in some fashion." Seeing that there was no negative response, he continued, "To protect her, perhaps, from..."

The ingenuous Thomas was taking advantage of Lady Doughby's sympathetic nature, and they both knew it. But since she was the one who had encouraged from the very start of their association this cozy familiarity, and had extracted confidences from Thomas which were not ordinarily a part of a footman's job description, it was a little late for her to draw back now.

And so it came about that Thomas found himself on the open highway, savoring the unfamiliar taste of freedom.

He made his way to Dorset in record time, considering that he'd set out on foot. Fortunately, there was ample opportunity for hitchhiking. Despite the threat of footpads and highwaymen, few of the coachmen or farmers who overtook him along the road refused to stop for him, for the fellow's evident delight in his unexpected adventure was infectious to behold. Beaming excitedly like a schoolboy on an outing, he had no trouble convincing fellow travelers that he was harmless and would provide them with good company if invited to hop on.

Arriving at Belweather Manor, however, Thomas found very little to be delighted about.

Belweather Manor was a squat, vine-covered structure at the foot of a tall hill dotted with grazing sheep and horses. It looked, thought Thomas as he strolled up the drive, as if the animals were nibbling at the roof's chimneystacks and drinking from the gutters. An afternoon rainstorm had washed away every trace of haze, making what was left of the day bright and brisk. As he drew near the house, he had to stop himself from breaking into little skips of excitement.

Beaming with anticipation, he walked around to the back, noting with approval the neatly swept stone yard and the tidy chicken run. He twisted an iron ring and pushed open a door—made of heavy wood, like the doors at the front, only single and uncarved— and recognized, by the tiles on the floor and the smell of cooking, that he had come to the right place.

The servants seated at their supper looked up, surprised to see a stranger.

"Where's Bess?" he asked.

"Bess?" repeated Mrs. Kettle, her mouth open.

"Yes. Bessie Goose. I'm her Thomas. Thomas Boothby. She must have told you about me. Hasn't she?"

His voice faltered because everywhere he looked, he saw only expressions of dismay.

"Thomas. Yes, of course, Thomas," Mrs. Kettle stalled. "Here, sit down, you've had a long journey, haven't you..."

"Something has happened to Bess. Tell me!" As there was no answer, Thomas panicked. "She's not—she can't be...?"

"No, of course not—!" cried Mrs. Kettle.

"As good as," muttered Brackthorn, one of the gardeners.

Thomas swung around toward the source of this alarming comment. He heard himself croak, "What's happened to her? Lord, what's happened to her?"

"Oh, dear," Mrs. Kettle blubbered. Tears came to her easily. "She's gone and got herself accused of witchcraft. Can you believe that? Our Bessie!"

"Witchcraft!" The news knocked him off his feet and he collapsed onto a stool. "Oh God!"

"Satan, you mean," said Brackthorn darkly. "Are you in league with her?"

"What are you saying, what are you saying!" cried Mrs. Kettle. "Brackthorn, watch your tongue! She hasn't even been tried yet!"

"Beg pardon," Brackthorn sneered at Thomas. "But I know she's a witch. Don't tell me she is not. I know witches. I always recognize 'em."

"Oh yes?" Lena the laundress yelled at him. "And why didn't you ever say something, all these years? All these years she's been rubbing you with poultices for the ague, and you couldn't get enough of it, 'Rub me aching shoulders,' you used to beg her, 'There's none but you, Bessie, can make old Walter feel better'..."

"See, it's what I'm telling you, woman, she had me bewitched, same as Mistress," Brackthorn insisted. "Anyhow, it's she as laid t' ague on me shoulders in the first place."

"How do you know that..." began Mrs. Kettle. Thomas interrupted them.

"Where is she now? Can I see her?"

"Oh no, you can't do that," said Mrs. Kettle. "They have her locked up. There's a witch-finder, Master Boulderdash, don't worry, they say he's ever so good, he's with her now..."

"Where?" asked Thomas grimly.

"In the jail at Bitterbury, but..." It was the nearest town, some five miles away.

"Right," said Thomas, and turned toward the door.

"Where are you going?" asked Mrs. Kettle, alarmed.

"To find her," he snapped.

"Oh dear, oh dear," she keened as he strode out the door, "he shouldn't go, he shouldn't go, he'll have himself accused of witchcraft same as her..."

But Thomas was already out of earshot.

In Bessie Goose's time, witchcraft was a serious business. A primitive superstition that should have vanished with the Middle Ages, the belief in witches retained its popularity in England thanks largely to King James the First, who used his personal crusade against the devil to polish his public image. (During his rule, one confessed witch testified that she had heard the devil swear James was the greatest enemy he had ever faced. What sane politician would refute such a brilliant endorsement?) By the time the witch-hunt mania began to wane at the century's end, some forty thousand people had been executed as witches in England alone.

The majority of the accused were old, poor, and female, and were often easily persuaded, through torture and their own credulity, that they were indeed witches, thereby contributing to the popular belief with their own fanciful confessions. Even if they maintained their innocence, their guilt was easy enough to prove. A common test was "swimming": the accused was bound hand and foot into an awkward bundle—the right hand tied to the left foot, and vice versa—before being lowered backwards into a body of water. If you sank (and drowned) you were declared innocent; if you floated, you were a witch, and were executed. Another foolproof test involved being tied cross-legged to a chair or table and left to sit there without food or water for twenty-four hours under constant watch. A door or window was left ajar, so that one of your imps (creatures assigned by the devil to serve you) could come in and suck your blood. Since an imp could take the shape of an insect, any fly or mosquito that came into the room was suspect. If it evaded the guards' attempts to catch or kill it, it was declared to be an imp, and your chance of being found innocent was not good.

Fortunately, Bessie had not yet been subjected to these ordeals, since Dr. Hoogschotel maintained that such methods were hopelessly unscientific. Pricking, he said, was the only *medically correct* way to determine guilt. A diligent search with long needles would eventually turn up the devil's mark on the witch's body—a place where there was no sensitivity, where a needle would draw no blood. Arabella, upon receiving instruction in the technique from the good doctor, had undertaken this investigation, assisted by the equally assiduous Mrs. Limpid. Poor Mrs. Limpid had had quite a time of it holding Bessie down during the examination. They had finally found a spot in the right calf that did not bleed; but since repeated jabs drew howls from Bessie, the evidence was inconclusive. And so it was decided that they would defer to the opinion of the expert, Matthias Boulderdash, who was duly sent for.

Personally, Dr. Hoogschotel told Arabella, he was quite convinced the woman was a creature of the devil. He had heard reports of Bessie's amateur medical practice; and for a lay-person, and a woman at that, one who had not the benefit of years of study in Europe's various seats of learning, for such a person to gain the expertise and the modest successes attributed to her, was impossible, he swore, without the devil's help.

Now of course this was most unfair to Bessie, whose apprenticeship
in midwifery had been thoroughly practical, if not academic. She had
made the study of plants her life's hobby, and it so happened that she
knew more about their properties than most apothecaries of her day.
Until Lady Clarissa's illness, her ministrations had always been harmless
at worst, successful at best; she genuinely cared about her patients, and
had a motherly instinct for healing that was fundamentally altruistic as
well as sensibly lucrative.

On the other hand, is it fair to criticize Hoogschotel for defending
his turf? After all, physicians have always put their faith in the gospel of
rigorous scientific proof. Who can blame them for jealously guarding
the Hippocratic secrets that are theirs to keep only after an expensive
and grueling education?

Arabella, who was not stupid, had challenged Hoogschotel at first.

"But Doctor. Why would the devil, if he is indeed her master, aid her
in *curing* people? Why not employ her for his most evil deeds?"

"Ah, dere, lady, dere you have it. You see, de deffil is a cunning fellow.
Diss is how he vorks. First, to gain de volks' trust, de good cures. And
den, as ve have seen here in de poor lady your sister, de curse."

For most of her thirty-odd years, Arabella's life had been lacking in
any form of excitement. Here, finally, was a riveting drama, playing itself
out in her own family. It was an opportunity that came along but once
in a lifetime—the thrill of the hunt, the commitment to a cause, the ex-
hilaration of ferreting out evil and the prospect, possibly, of a heavenly
reward. Pricking the alleged witch had provided her with an even greater
sense of accomplishment than she usually derived from beating the servants; she had performed the task devoutly, happy in the knowledge that
in this, she was performing a service for the Lord, a service which He
would appreciate and which He would no doubt take into consideration
when tallying the Heavenly Accounts.

20

PLUCK

"Psst—Bess!"

Bessie lifted her head from the bundle of rags she was using for a pillow. It was black with filth and blood.

"Bessie!"

Bessie lay rigid with fear on her pile of straw, her head and neck straining upward, the rest of her sore body paralyzed. Her eyes were bulging, her nostrils wide with terror.

"Bess! It's me! Thomas! Don't you recognize my voice?"

A moan came from her throat. "Art thou—the devil?"

"The devil? What nonsense! Don't you know me? It's your Thomas!"

"Thomas?" she whispered into the darkness. "Is that really you?"

"Yes, Thomas, my sweet. Himself. Who else would I be?"

"The devil. I am expecting the devil."

"Oh, come on now, Bess..."

"He assumes many guises."

"Oh stop your foolishness, Bess! I am no devil. Surely you can tell the difference! "

The cell in which Bessie was being held was really a cellar: a pit with steep sides dug into the ground, divided into two by a stockade down the middle. The ceiling was a wooden platform with a trap door in it. Above the platform there was a one-room hut that protected the jail keeper from the elements. The only way in and out of the dungeon was by ladder; it was lowered from above when needed. The floor and sides of the pit were bare earth, propped up with a smattering of wooden supports; the hygienic facilities consisted of a hole dug into the floor at one end of the cell. When the stench became unbearable, the occupant was handed a shovel, and told to throw a few spadefuls of earth into the hole. A colder, damper, smellier, muddier, nastier place is impossible to imagine.

This dungeon, situated in the central square behind the pillory, was what passed for a prison in the town of Bitterbury, whose citizens believed in fiscal responsibility and poured all available resources into churches and bridges and fortifications of one sort or another. A decent prison was not high on the list of priorities, since most of the accused who were detained there were as good as dead anyway, and there was no point in throwing good coin after bad carrion.

Thomas, relying on his natural charm (although it was rather strained at this point, evident from the glint of sweat on his upper lip) had had no trouble finding out where Bessie was being held. The constable on duty had told him that there was one witch in the jail at present. This piece of information was leaked over a tankard of ale at The Worm, where the constable spent most evenings, as he confided to this friendly stranger, since not a single felon had ever succeeded in escaping from that pit, not even with Satan's help.

Now, under cover of darkness, Thomas was lying flat on his stomach on the floor of the hut and calling to Bessie through the chinks in the platform.

"Up here! Look up!" he hissed. Bessie looked up; saw nothing but darkness; and started shaking again.

"How do I know you are what you say you are?" she yammered. "My Thomas—you can't be Thomas, Thomas lives in Hampshire ..."

"Believe me, Bess!" Thomas pleaded, and hastily whispered how he had managed to obtain leave from Lady Doughby.

"If it is really you, then..."

"Then what, love?"

"Then—go away."

"No."

"Yes!"

"Not before I obtain your release."

"Please, please go. I don't want you here. Just go!"

"I can't go back now, Bess, you know I can't."

"But...what if the devil...what if he should find you here...?"

"By all that's blessed, Bess, what's all this talk of the devil! Have you seen him, then?"

The question hung in the air a while. Then she burst out, "I don't know, I don't know! It's what they keep asking me. I tell you I don't know!"

Thomas interrupted her. "The rack! They've had you on the rack, haven't they!"

"So?" said Bessie defensively.

"Oh my poor soul!" Thomas had met an escaped felon once, a chicken-thief, who had told him of the agonies of that apparatus. "And they told you the devil would come...?"

"Yes. They say the deadly nightshade proves that I am a witch, and a child has seen me flying through the air, and they want me to say who my familiars are." Her voice rose to a whispered wail. "And I tell them I don't know, I don't know anything, I call on God to be my witness, that I know not of what you speak, and they say I am sure to remember soon enough, that Beelzebub will appear to me in person if I don't confess soon, and then...It's all for my own good, they say. My confession will be my salvation, and..."

"Oh, Bess, you don't believe them, do you? *I* know you're no witch! By God's truth, Bess, all you have ever done has been to care for people, you've never meant anyone harm. And I know you say the Lord's Prayer at every turn, and..."

"That I do," said Bessie, swallowing a sob, "that I do—"

"And all this talk of the devil, it's nonsense, you know that, Bess, he won't come to one such as you, they are just hoping to frighten you into thinking that he will. Oh, Bess! And then, when finally you do confess, do you know what this salvation is they're speaking of?"

Bessie gave no reply in the darkness.

"You know that you will be burned at the stake, or hanged, and there's not a one can save you then, not even your poor Thomas."

* * *

Thomas had no practical plan to free Bessie, only impractical ones. There was Lady Doughby—but he doubted her word would carry, since she did not know Bessie personally, and appealing to her meant a week or more in lost traveling time, during which...He shuddered. He considered enlisting the help of some of the other servants at the manor to break open the jail and set Bessie free; but from the gardener's reaction he knew it was unlikely that they would be prepared to risk their own lives or livelihood. Lady Clarissa might have spoken up for Bessie, but that, too, was out of the question, since her voice had not come back. Sir Edmund and Lord Hempstead were away in London. This left only Lady Arabella.

Bessie had told Thomas about Arabella's part in the pricking, and his eyes had stung with hatred. It was so like her! Still—she had always been rather lenient with him, and perhaps he could turn on the charm once more, and make her see the injustice of this accusation...

Here we can see that Thomas was not in full possession of his faculties, otherwise he would not have overlooked the fact that he had but recently resigned from Arabella's employ to take up a post with one of her neighbors. This was an unforgivable affront to Arabella, and if you had innocently mentioned Thomas' name to her in passing, it would have been plain that she was not at all favorably disposed toward this heinous, this odious, this treacherous creature who had once dared to call himself her servant.

"Thomas!" Her good eye narrowed as he closed the doors behind him; the other stared in outrage at a spot on the wall some twenty degrees to his left. "Well, well. That did not last long, did it? That Doughby woman, the nerve of her! What are you doing here? If you thought that I would take you back, you are much deceived..."

"My lady. It is - uh, a pleasure to see you again..."

"Idiot!" Arabella snapped, her head projecting forward, like a turtle's, then jamming back against her neck.

Thomas's heart sank. This was not going to be easy. He had to steel himself, bite back tears.

"I am not asking you to take me back, madam, I..."

"I shall see to it that you never—do you understand me?—never have a place again..."

He had to interrupt her before his courage gave out. "But ma'am—I came about Bess. She..."

"The witch! Your lady love! Aha!" Her mouth puckered in a travesty of amorous smooching. "How sweet! Of course! You want me to have her set free!"

"Madam, please. She has served your family well for fifteen years, and does, I think, deserve a fair..."

"Ha! *You* are asking *me*! Ha!" The suggestion struck Arabella as so funny that she brayed with jeering laughter.

At this, something in Thomas snapped. Years of resentment spilled out of every capillary in his body, drowning him in hatred for this nasty, this domineering, this bullying creature.

"My lady," he said in a low voice, the pauses between the words indicating a pressing need for self-control. "Hear—me—now. If you won't help us—the Lord help me—"

"A threat!" she interrupted him gaily. "Well, well!"

"So help me God—then I shall tell all who will listen—"

"Tell what?" jeered Arabella. She was a little shaken; not once in her life had a servant ever spoken to her like this.

"...tell all who will listen," he continued haltingly, "that you - *YOU!* Are a witch. Yourself."

The threat that had come out of his mouth was just as appalling to Thomas as it was to Arabella. He swallowed, and looked around in a daze, to see if someone else could have uttered those preposterous words. Lord!

And yet—it wasn't totally off the mark, was it? Was it now? Just look at her. Wasn't she unspeakably nasty? Wasn't it the first thing you thought of when you saw her face and had to listen to her ranting and raving? Not only Thomas; the other servants felt it as well. Hadn't he heard "ugly old witch" whispered behind her back a thousand times?

The blood drained from Arabella's face and collected in patches all along her neck. It took her a good minute to think of her next retort. She coughed lengthily, raspily, to give herself time.

"Well then," she finally said, "As God is my witness. I shall accuse you of the same. In turn."

They stared at each other a long moment in blank amazement.

"And then we shall see," she continued, her voice cracking ever so slightly, "whom they believe. The mistress or the servant."

In a flash, Thomas realized he had just done something truly heroic. And, like most heroes, realized that there is a very fine line between a hero and a fool.

Yet—unaccountably—he found in himself some remaining shreds of courage. A few tattered shreds of pluck and the remnants of a just and roaring indignation that made him stand his ground.

"Yes, we'll see, won't we?" he said, trying to inject some cool amusement into his wobbly voice. "We shall see."

21

A TIDY CATCH

Arabella did not wait to see if Thomas would make good his threat. At the conclusion of their confrontation she ordered Thomas to be locked up in the scullery at once.

When Matthias Boulderdash rode up to the manor, he found Lady Arabella anxiously waiting outside, on the front steps.

"I did not expect to return here so soon, my lady," the witch-finder said, suppressing a satisfied smirk.

"No indeed, Mr. Boulderdash," she replied primly.

"You wished me to examine another suspect?"

"If you will," said Arabella. "The man in question is Bessie Goose's—uh—erstwhile paramour."

"Yes?" he asked, discretion glinting in his respectful smile.

"They were not joined before God, you understand..."

"Witches seldom are, my lady," said Master Boulderdash. "They revel in their unholy lusting."

Arabella cleared her throat, a hint that she should perhaps be spared a subject so far removed from her own experience. She cast about for the best way of conveying what she had to say.

"Well, shall we...?" Matthias was anxious to get a look at his new victim.

"But first, sir...I must warn you. He has threatened to—to..." She threw him a sidelong appeal for sympathy, her voice rising to a tight, unpleasant whine, "to tell evil lies about myself, to cast aspersions on my person. It is understandable, of course, he wishes to take his revenge on me, being the instrument of his arrest, but I felt I must bring it to your attention..."

"Of course. You did well, my lady." Matthias remained calmly polite and reassuring. But he was excited, very, very excited to hear it. Matthias could sniff a cull here, a tidy catch: a member of the nobility, perhaps, thrown in for good measure. The lady in question fit the bill perfectly, both in looks and in reputed temperament. Yes, what a masterstroke, if he reeled in such a prize!

"If my lady will lead me to this warlock," he said smoothly, "she may of course rest assured that I will use the full force of my influence and authority to defend her august name against such a patent absurdity."

The only positive outcome from Thomas' heroism was that he and Bessie were finally reunited. They appreciated that for what it was worth, considering that the reunion took place in the coal-black jail pit, with a wall of wooden stakes between them.

"Oh Thomas!" moaned Bessie. "How did this happen? How *could* you let it happen? Now we're both in the same pickle, with no hope, no hope at all..."

Thomas had tried to explain to her what had happened, but the scene between him and Lady Arabella lost something in the retelling. Since Thomas felt it necessary to put as positive a spin on it as possible, it sounded as if he had been uncharacteristically bold; provocative, even. While he had in fact approached Arabella with his usual deference, and this appalling outcome had been the farthest thing from his mind.

"Why?" Bessie moaned. "Why, why, oh why? It's bad enough they think I'm a witch—but you...? I *told* you to be careful, how could you *do* something like that, talking back to Lady Arabella, you know how vicious she can be..."

"Bess!" he interrupted at last. "Bess. I'm not sorry for what I've done."

"You're not?"

"No. Because without you—"

"Oh Thomas..."

"No, without you I..."

There was a crack between two of the dividing boards, and Thomas managed to squeeze two of his fingers through to Bessie's side. She held those fingers lightly, and they concentrated a while on the throbbing, warm-blood feeling.

"You know what I wish, Bess?"

"What?"

"I wish you had never left."

A long wistful sigh caught in her throat. "It *was* nice, wasn't it—"

"Yes, but I mean..."

"I *know* what you mean, Thomas."

There was no need for further explanation.

22

WISH COME TRUE

Be careful what you wish for! If ever Jupiter, or a magic fish, should come along and grant you three wishes or your heart's desire, you are well advised to step back and consider the offer for a while. For there is almost always a catch. Instead of a golden carriage, a kingdom, or happiness beyond your wildest dreams, you could find yourself saddled with a sausage stuck on the end of your nose—in other words, worse off than you were before.

A brown day. Lucinda was kneeling at the window of the nursery, her nose pressed to the cold pane. She turned around. Spots danced before her eyes, her nose was numb and her dry eyes stung. A smoldering fire was doing very little to dispel the chill. An urge came over her to escape the thick air and inhale some freshness. Without a word, she jumped down and ran out the door.

Downstairs, she pushed against the heavy outer door with her hip and shoulder, shaking her hair to rid it of the acrid odor. Even out here the air smelled of chimney-smoke, although somewhat diluted by the wind and rustling trees. She pushed out her chest and took some deep gulps.

Anguish clung to her like the smoke. There was no one to turn to now. There was nothing she could do for Bessie. Thomas had tried to do something, and what good had that done? Poor Thomas. Poor, dear, sweet-natured Thomas. And Aunt Arabella, too! Locked up in her chamber, with a guard outside the door and all the servants and children whispering, hugging each other with excitement...

The only thing she could do now was pray. To God, desperately. And to the king, in case he could hear her. To her parents in heaven. And of course to Henry—

Where *was* Henry? Why wasn't he here? He was the one who would clear up this mess, and she ached, ached for him. He was her hero; he would come to the rescue. She wished, she willed, she begged him to come. She *ordered* him to. Come, Henry! Now! At once!

Of course Lucinda did not seriously believe that fervent prayer can make a wish come true. She knew perfectly well that if a wish ever *does* come true, sensible people attribute it to luck, not to supernatural intervention. And yet, despite being an eminently sensible young woman, Lucinda often found herself in silent communion with God, or Fortune, or the stars, appealing to them, bargaining with them, hoping against hope for some signal that her mind had—nevertheless—been read and that her wish would—nevertheless—be granted.

So what was she to make of it when, standing in the side yard, she suddenly heard a clatter of hooves? And when, moments later, she spied three profiles bobbing along the top of the hedge—Uncle Edmund's, Robert's, and...Henry's?

She did not stop to debate whether it was coincidence or destiny. She ran. She flew. She streaked along the gravel path, through the archway, tripping on some stone steps and almost tumbling headlong into the forecourt.

There she stopped short, panting. Three male faces whipped around toward her as if they had been caught in some secret act; but they were merely dismounting.

"Uncle Edmund! My lord!" She could not risk looking at Henry, nor acknowledge him. "You—you have returned!"

"We are back." Uncle Edmund was smirking at her.

"You haven't heard—" she stated breathlessly.

"Heard what, my dear?"

"The news—"

"What news?"

"Oh, the...It..." Her throat would not stay open long enough to let the words out. She swallowed a few times, but her mouth stayed dry and thick. She chanced a glance in Henry's direction. He was giving the reins of his steed to a groom, staring at her dolefully.

She tried again. "There..." But choked on a sob, and burst into wrenching, ugly, shameful tears. Because it wasn't supposed to be like this. She was supposed to fall into Henry's arms. Instead, here she was talking to her wicked uncle as if to a friend—a *friend*! And Henry looking on like a disinterested stranger...

Wait! He was saying something. She stifled her sobs in order to hear what Henry was muttering.

"...tell blacksmith to be careful with her. She may have pulled her fetlock..."

The tears came even more profusely now.

"What *is* it?" asked her uncle, impatient now.

But she could not make herself understood, and it was her cousin Sebastian (he had raced downstairs when he'd heard the horses) who gave them the news, shouting excitedly as he scrambled down the steps.

"It's Mother! She's—she's sick. She's gone dumb!"

"Who. Your mother?" demanded his father, disbelieving.

"Yes. It was witchcraft, and Bessie, you know, *her* old nurse," (waving at the sobbing Lucinda) "she's been arrested, and some other fellow as well, and Aunt Arabella. She's a witch too. We've got her locked up, she can't escape, come look!"

"Wait a minute. Wait!" said his father sternly. "Sebastian. You too, my lord. Inside, please. And call Fields and Mrs. Limpid. They will have to explain what this nonsense is all about. And you, gel. Stop your sniveling." Turning to his guest, he smiled urbanely. "Domestic trouble. It's always the same thing, isn't it. One crisis after another..."

"Indeed," said Henry, following his host up the steps.

The wind starched Lucinda's wet cheeks. She threw her head back and noted with despair that her sky had lost its arc.

The sky hung low overhead, flat and heavy as a slab.

* * *

Just as Bitterbury's jail was a primitive one, so too was its panoply of torture. Sophisticated mechanisms such as the thumbscrew or leg-vise had recently been introduced to England from the Continent, but the townspeople of Bitterbury had never heard of such contraptions. The method they employed for extracting confessions was the time-honored one of binding the ankles and wrists of the accused with ropes and tying him, hands stretched overhead, to a rack—in this case, an ordinary ladder. All the interrogator had to do was to keep twisting the rope a few notches tighter around some pegs or a cleat, like trimming a ship's sails, except that in this case, it was the human body that was being stretched bit by bit.

Bessie's stints on the rack did not last long, since the humiliation of being exposed naked to her tormentors made her cave in after the first turns of the tourniquet. Breathlessly, tearfully, she agreed to whatever they coached her to say, upon which they untied her, allowing her to put her disgracefully soiled garments back on.

The problem was that in order for the confession to be valid, it had to be repeated by the witch freely in a court of law, without resort to torture. But when Bessie, fully clothed once again, was tested on the validity of her admissions, she always found the courage, or rather the outrage, to recant, tearfully invoking every prayer she knew, scolding her torturers and vaunting her innocence before God. And so time and time again her confession had to be declared invalid. Matthias Boulderdash was not wholly discouraged, however; even if a confession could not be extracted, it did not much matter in this case. The woman had freely confessed to supplying Lady Clarissa with the belladonna confiscated by Dr. Hoogschotel; it was sufficient to condemn her. The only reason Matthias was persevering with her was that a confession of witchcraft would net him an additional eighteen shillings.

The newly accused warlock, Thomas Boothby, was another matter altogether. The evidence in his case was thin—the only accusation against him having been made by Lady Arabella Steppys, who was herself a suspect. And since this man was a stranger in town, it was hard to find any past mischief to pin on him. Not only that: the fellow seemed better able to withstand the torture, and underwent the procedure with a silly, determined grin on his face. To every question, he gave the same infuriating answer.

Matthias: *Thou art a creature of the devil, art thou not!*

Thomas (ingratiating, entreating): *The Lord preserve me?*

Matthias: *In what form hath Satan appeared to thee?*

Thomas (through gritted teeth): *The Lord preserve me.*

Matthias: *What are the names of thy familiars? Tell us the names of thy familiars.*

Thomas (groaning):...**Lord!** *preserve me.*

Matthias: *We have reason to believe thou wert seen at a witches' sab-bath in Hampshire last May, supping in fiendish company.*

Thomas (almost unintelligibly):...*Lord...pre...ser...vme.*

Matthias: *And there didst drink thy fill of the blood of innocent babes. What sayst-thou to that?*

Thomas (howling): *Lord **p...fff** me!*

As you can see, Matthias was getting nowhere with this one. What was particularly galling was the warlock's fawning expression—as if he truly wished to help Matthias out, and was chagrined at not being able to do so. To make matters worse, the fellow had the cheek to faint at inopportune times, thus wasting any momentum gained.

It was during the eighth or ninth interrogation—even Matthias was starting to lose count—that he decided more drastic measures were in order. And so he suggested to Robert Fetshank, the town's butcher and part-time executioner who was assisting him in these exercises, that the next time the accused said the words, "The Lord preserve me," he should take the cudgel to him.

"An excellent idea, sir," said Robert, who was beginning to feel a little peckish, and was thinking of the capon his wife had promised to roast for his supper.

"Thomas Boothby," the witch-finder intoned. "Thou art a witch, a warlock, a wizard, and a wretch. Thou hast indulged in lewd couplings with thy fellow-witches and hast even—yea, hast even been buggered by Satan himself!"

"*Lord* preserve me!" gasped Thomas, who had been holding his tongue tightly between his front teeth after hearing Matthias' threat, but whose outrage at this most unjust and shameful accusation was not to be muzzled.

"Right!" crowed Robert Fetshank, and swung his cudgel.

The blow hit Thomas below the belt (although he was not wearing a belt or any other item of clothing). And it was the fearful shock of seeing the cudgel's trajectory aimed at his very manhood that now caused in Thomas a massive, fatal coronary.

Matthias Boulderdash, noting that untying the accused and employing the usual revival techniques did nothing to arrest the grey pallor seeping into Thomas's face and spreading silently along his limbs, had finally, regretfully, to pronounce him dead.

In his report to the magistrate, he wrote:

"As to the demise of Thomas Boothby, it must be concluded that Satan was Determined not to let His servant reveal the Magnitude of his Sins & so, making himself invisible to All except the Aforesaid, came into this Place in Person to Wring his Creature's Neck."

23

FOND, FOOLISH, WANTON

By the time her husband returned home, Lady Clarissa had recovered sufficiently to milk her indisposition for all it was worth. A prolonged course of purging and bleeding had left her somewhat wan and gaunt, which, granted, rather suited her. She had not yet recovered the power of speech, but she had been able to pull herself together, so that anyone entering her chamber was met with a most piteous sight: the Lady Clarissa in creamy low-cut satin, draped tastefully against the pillows in her own hair, which was allowed to cascade loosely to one side, drawing attention away from the double chin; skin pallid as snow, the mouth rouged so artfully that one hardly suspected paint; beckoning one to come closer, indicating with fluttering gestures that even if she could not converse, she would be happy—grateful, even—to hear what one had to say. It was a spectacle designed to move a man to tears; but of course her husband was a man difficult to move.

After receiving an account from his steward and the governess, Sir Edmund paid his ailing wife a visit. This was their conversation.

"So! How fare you, wife?"

The eyelids were lowered, then opened in wide helplessness.

"I am sure that you will mend in no time, no time at all."

A brave little smile of reassurance trailed into a look of worried sympathy for *him.*

"No need to concern yourself. I know what I must do."

Adoring gratitude, accompanied by a languid sweep of the leg.

"Not now, Clarissa. "

A pout.

"Heavens, woman! Where is your shame?"

The head was cocked to one side in defensive surprise.

"No really, Clarissa, *really*! 'S-truth. Are you really such a fool that you don't even realize the havoc you have caused...?"

Wounded outrage.

"Don't look at me like that. I am only stating the truth. If you hadn't been so...Christ! And now it's up to me to sort it out, isn't it? Or we'll have a full-scale witch hunt on our hands, and who knows where that may end!"

A sullen shrug.

"You have no idea, do you woman? You simply have no idea what kind of damage this can do. They already have that sister of yours locked up."

She assented sadly.

"She has you to thank for it, has she not! And now you probably expect *me* to plead for her release! Well, there is nothing I can do to save her, I'm afraid. She is worse than you are—her mind is quite addled. I don't know where you Steppys sisters get it from. She's been screaming threats and insults and frightening the servants out of their wits. And quite frankly, I don't even know if I *should* save her. No sane man would, in my place." He slammed his fist on the table. "Do you know what that viper—" now his tone suddenly flipped, turning high-pitched, plaintive, "—that *Gorgon* has done? Stealing from us, on the sly! Selling the family furnishings, mirrors, silver and such, and pocketing the proceeds."

He saw her struggling with the automatic reflex to console him, to apologize. "Your father's man Tucker has provided us with a list. It's been going on for years. Did you know about it? Bitch! I wouldn't put it past you, to hide something like that from me!"

Furious, hurt denial.

He snorted loudly. "And what do you think our fine *suitor* is going to say about all this?"

Her hand went up to her mouth.

"Yes, your *dear* Captain Beaupree. We came down from London together. Forgotten about him, had you? A mind like a sieve, you have. I don't know what to tell him. What would *my lady* tell him?"

A sad shake of the head.

"Oh, we are sorry now, aren't we, when it is too late! You hadn't considered, had you, what this scandal would do to our plans for Sarah. Let's hope the captain is not easily daunted. Or that he is in serious need of money."

Contrite now, his wife bowed her head in shame.

"But—Gad, Clarissa, I don't see, I still don't see, how you could have put yourself into the hands of one of the *cooks*—"

She shrugged.

"I am truly disappointed in your...judgment."

His stern mirth was met by a blank gaze—like that of a naughty child given a dressing-down.

"Now this woman, this she-quack, ha! She's the gel's, er, I mean your niece's nurse, isn't that so?"

Clarissa remained icily uncommunicative.

"It was at your behest that she supplied you with the deadly nightshade. Do not deny it."

Clarissa did not deny it.

"Your maid seems to think that you took too much, and poisoned yourself."

Her nostrils flared slightly.

"Answer me!"

Clarissa now allowed herself a martyred sigh.

"Begad, woman! This is all your fault." He rolled his eyes. "I should count my blessings, I suppose. I hope—yes, I pray to God that that tongue of yours has stopped wagging for good. Christ only knows how I've put up with your scolding all these years."

Clarissa now turned her back on him. She lowered her head into her hands.

He snorted. "I don't feel sorry for you, I really don't, woman. Fie! I can read you like a book. Do you know that?" It was probably the first time in his married life that he could berate her without interruption, and it was beginning to excite him.

He moved around to the other side of the bed, planting himself squarely in his wife's line of sight.

"Oh, Clarissa, stop your sniveling. *Wehn, wehn, nah-nah na.* You females are all alike, aren't you. The old bishop was right about your sex, he nailed it right on the head..." Sprays of projectile spume landed on her averted cheek as he spat out as much as he could recall of his favorite sermon: "...*fond, foolish, wanton, flibbergib, tattlers, triflers, wavering, witless, feeble, eavesdroppers, rumor-raisers, evil-tongued, worse-minded, and in every way doltified with the dregs of the devil's dunghill!*"

He had already started unbuckling his girdle.

Later Sir Edmund sent for the witch-finder, and the witch-finder came to Sir Edmund hat in hand. Sweat poured forth from the perimeter of his cheap wig, for he was anticipating a mighty row.

"I am afraid, sir," Matthias ventured respectfully, "that we have too much evidence against the lady your sister to release her at present. There are some matters yet to be resolved, for there have been many accusations made against the dear lady, too numerous, unfortunately, for us to disregard..."

"I know, I know," interrupted Edmund. "A face like hers could curdle all the milk in the county, couldn't it!"

Matthias was not sure if Sir Edmund was jesting or not. Nor was he sure if a jest was appropriate at this point. "More serious allegations than that, sir. It seems she..."

"Spare me the allegations. I know you witch-*finders* never have any difficulty *finding* those." He sent Matthias a condescending wink. "Yes, and then there's a jolly hanging for the whole town to enjoy, and everyone's happy. When's the 'trial', man?"

Matthias replied with wounded dignity, "The magistrate has been sent for, sir. We expect him within the fortnight."

"Well." Sir Edmund's tone became business-like. "Let us hope this shameful affair does not drag on too long. The sooner it's over, the better. Now. As for the other case—Elizabeth Goose—we are withdrawing the charges against her. So that matter may be dropped."

"Sir?"

"I mean you may release her. My wife has admitted that the belladonna was her own doing; she took too much of it. Therefore there is no
further reason to persecute the woman."

"But sir!" Matthias could hardly contain his disappointment. "With
all due respect, the charge of witchcraft—we cannot simply turn a blind
eye! We have been gathering evidence, and we were about to..."

"Mr. Boulderdash. Let us speak man to man here. Let us see how we
may resolve this matter amicably. It means a great deal to a niece of mine,
a lovely young lady—" he winked at Matthias—"to have this woman
freed. She was the gel's nurse, you see..."

Matthias nodded. He had expected Sir Edmund to object to the ar-
raignment of his sister-in-law, but not to that of a mere servant. What
came next, however, surprised him even more.

"If I and my family were to pledge not to lodge a protest in the matter of our sister's indictment, nor appeal her conviction...might we then
come to an understanding with you about this cook?"

"But sir —" stammered Matthias, confused and suspicious.

"And if I were to say that there was no need to keep her—I mean the
lady our sister—here at the manor, and that you have my permission to
conduct her to a place where your investigations may proceed apace, will
that not make it less incumbent upon you to pursue your efforts with
regard to this good woman Goose...?"

"You are too good, sir, but..."

"I give you my word upon it, as a gentleman and a knight," Edmund
said firmly. "And a gold piece for you, my good man, to seal our bargain."

Matthias Boulderdash left clutching the gold sovereign in his fist.

Lucinda had been prowling about the gardens all afternoon despite the
fierce chill. She wanted to make it easy for Henry, who was surely hoping
to find her.

Returning from a stroll through the kitchen garden and around the
back of the stables—the location of their first encounter—she spotted
Mrs. Limpid, standing with her back to her in the box garden. She began
to retreat, but then heard a peal of laughter.

A hundred paces or so beyond Mrs. Limpid, half-hidden by a hedge, stood Henry...with Sarah. He was pressing Sarah's hand to his chest, as if to show her where his heart was beating, and she was giggling, struggling to free herself. Mrs. Limpid took one or two warning steps in their direction, and he dropped the hand with an apologetic smirk.

The smile froze on his face as he spotted the other maiden lurking by the yew hedge. Then he turned, and, offering Sarah his arm, led her through the wisteria arbor to the steps down to the stream.

Numbly, Lucinda sped back to the house.

24

DONKEY'S SKIN

Lucinda spent the rest of the afternoon soothing herself with plausible rationales. When they were finally alone together, Henry would mock her for her lack of faith in him. Of course he had to pretend to be wooing Sarah! How else to explain his presence at the manor?

By the time she sat down to supper with the others, she was able to face even the glowing Sarah with some composure.

Sarah was laying it on a bit thick, however.

"My poor loves," she said, addressing her siblings, "will you miss me?"

"What do you mean, Sarah?" said Sebastian. "Going to meet your maker, are you?"

"She's dying!" exclaimed Harry.

The others giggled, for they all knew about Sarah's impending betrothal, but family dynamics dictated that if someone flaunted some piece of good fortune, you had to make them pay for it.

"Leave *Dorset*, yes," said Sarah haughtily. "When I am married, I will live in London. If you are nice," she added, "I may invite some of you to stay."

"Oh, may *I*, may *I*?" asked Belinda breathlessly.

"You, and Catherine, and Robert, and Samuel, *may*be," said Sarah. "But not Harry, and not Sebastian." She glared at them.

Lucinda was too used to being left out to take the omission to heart; she just swallowed, telling herself that the tables would soon be turned on her cousin. She was sure it wouldn't be long now before Henry revealed his true intentions. She bit her lip, but could not suppress a little smile as she saw herself inviting Sarah to visit *her*, in London. She might even offer to help poor Sarah find a husband; wouldn't *that* be a magnanimous thing to do!

"What's *she* grinning about?" asked little Samuel.

They all looked at her. Lucinda concentrated on her soup.

At this moment Kitty burst into the nursery and tiptoed over to Mrs. Limpid. She whispered something in her ear.

Mrs. Limpid pursed her lips.

"Lucinda!" she ordered. "You may be excused. There's someone wants to see you. But mind you return in time for prayers."

Lucinda jumped up. Her spoon fell on the floor with a loud clang. Hastily she picked it up, blushing a bright red now, and ran out of the room after Kitty.

Kitty turned and hugged her in the corridor. "It's wonderful, isn't it!" she breathed. "She's back!"

Lucinda was momentarily confused by the feminine pronoun. "Who?" she said.

"Why Bessie of course! She's been released! She's not a witch. I knew it all along, of course, we all knew it, but it's ever such a relief, isn't it? Hurry now, she wants to see you, she has been asking after you."

Lucinda flew down the stairs. She felt very wicked for not having had Bessie uppermost in her thoughts. Bessie had been freed! She was not going to be hanged! Oh, but this meant that everything would come out all right after all! She was *sure* it was Henry's doing.

She found Bessie sitting wrapped in a blanket before the fire. Not the old Bessie: not comfortable, plump, red-cheeked Bessie, but a gaunt, bruised, unpleasant-smelling, sore-covered, anguished old woman.

All she could say when Lucinda threw her arms around her was, "Oh my pet, oh, oh, oh, my pet!" over and over again.

"Bessie! Bessie! They've let you come back!" moaned Lucinda, "I was so afraid..."

"Pet, pet!" panted Bessie. "Thank the Lord, thank the Lord. But poor Thomas, he— "

"What happened?"

"Thomas is with the good Lord now."

Lucinda's legs started shaking, and she had to sit down. "Dead? Oh, Bessie," she sobbed, "Thomas—dead? I should have...If only I had... Maybe I could have..."

"No, nothing," Bessie said. "Lamb, there's nothing you could have done."

When Lucinda returned red-eyed from the kitchen she found one of the footmen waiting outside the door to the schoolroom.

"Miss!" he whispered.

"Yes?" she answered.

"For you!" and he thrust a piece of paper into her hand.

Her heart leapt out of her chest and landed at the base of her throat. It beat there, wildly. She tucked the note into the waistband of her apron; but when she saw that the room was empty—the others were already in the adjoining bedchamber—she took it out and quickly scanned the words.

The handwriting was sprawling, manly. It had been written in haste. *"The library. Tonight. Midnight."*

She clenched her fists and looked up at the ceiling. "Oh *thank* you," she breathed fervently.

So Henry had just been *pretending* to ignore her! It was as she had suspected. How could she have doubted him? The visit, the betrothal to Sarah—all a charade. He had arrived just in time to save Bessie; he would have saved Thomas too, if only she'd had the chance to tell him about Thomas. And now he was going to save *her*.

She stuck the paper carefully under a burning log in the hearth and watched it until it caught. Then, her face glowing, she joined the others in the next room for prayers.

In bed, she lay awake, rigid with excitement, her feet cold with tension, her torso taut with anticipation. Her mouth was dry and her feet were icy, but she dared not move in case she woke Sarah, Catherine or Belinda, who shared her bed.

The intervals between the chiming of the clock were endless. Every hour stretched to at least three. It was agonizing, experiencing time this way.

Then, at last, the twelve. One. Two. Three. Or was it four? Nine. Ten. Eleven. Twelve. Silence.

Casually, as if stirring in her sleep, she rolled over onto her stomach. Moving by fractions, she drew her leg and hip away from Belinda's sleeping side. Once she was free, she began inching her way over to the edge, where the blanket stopped and the cold night air began. Experimentally she lowered one leg over the side; lifted her head a fraction, and listened. There was no movement from the bed. The girls' soft breathing was answered by grunts from the boys sleeping on the other side of the partition. In the alcove, Mrs. Limpid was snoring gutturally.

She slid down off the bed and onto the floor. For a minute or two she lay there, stifling the panting that accompanied her beating heart. No one stirred. On hands and knees, each movement deliberate and restrained, she crawled to the door and quietly, ever so quietly, let herself out of the room.

The hall was black as tar but her eyes were wide, wide open, drinking in the thick blackness, letting it sink deep into her eye sockets. Her arms were out in front, her fingers spread apart, like antennae feeling for obstacles. She stumbled forward, expecting at any moment to bump into something. But gradually the black turned to grey, and she began to perceive recognizable shapes.

Here was the cold stone of the staircase. She made her way down, feeling for each step with her bare toes before planting her foot. When she reached the bottom step she crept through the deserted outer drawing-room, which smelled faintly of mildew and wax. The carpets felt nice and soft to her cold feet. She was sorry it was too dark to make use of the looking glass over the mantel; she hoped she did not look too disheveled. At the far side of the room a set of doors led into a larger room, similarly furnished with ornate furniture stationed around the perimeter, the center open. And there, on the far side, were the doors to the library.

She touched the polished handles, hesitated a moment, then with silent resolve turned them and let herself in. Some candles were lit, and she gratefully felt the warmth of a fire. Too excited and flustered to look at him directly, she turned and carefully shut the doors behind her.

"So. You received the message."

The voice was not Henry's. It was Uncle Edmund's.

In her panic she tried to pivot on her bare heels but was glued to the spot, as in a nightmare. For Edmund had caught her neatly around the waist and held her in a firm grip.

Edmund was grinning. Smart, this gel. And quite the little actress into the bargain. She had read him correctly and—like the best-trained filly in Mrs. Bennett's stable of trollops, by God!—was ready to play the part that suited him best: the scared, the reluctant, the cornered damsel. Ah, there would be good sport tonight. He congratulated himself on having tolerated his wife's whim, a decade or so ago, in giving the bastard child a home. Here was ample reward indeed!

"Not so fast!" he said, his teeth gritted in a mock scowl. "Don't I deserve a kiss?"

Lucinda was paralyzed. The scope of her own stupidity had knocked all the strength out of her. It couldn't be. It couldn't! How could she have thought...It was the terrible news about Thomas—no, it was Henry's arrival that had put her off her guard...

"Don't I deserve a kiss, for pardoning your nurse?"

She stared at him, horrified.

"She'd have been hanged, you know, if I hadn't intervened," he said.

She cleared her throat and shook her head, as if to loosen it. "Thank you, uncle," she managed.

"Well?" he mooched.

She gave him a quick peck on the cheek. But still he did not let go. His grip tightened. "You owe me more than that, young lady," he said hoarsely.

"Please let me go," she stammered. "Please?"

She heard his rough panting and smelled his hot sweat. He was standing too close to her, much, much too close. She averted her face, turning as far away from him as possible.

"Ah, nn-nn-nnn!" he chided, chucking her under the chin, forcing her to face him. She shrugged loose with a sharp twist of the head, but he had already transferred his attention elsewhere. Her skin puckered to goose bumps—he had pulled the nightshirt up over her head. There was a brief tug-of-war as, giggling apologetically, she tried to recover her property. But the nightshirt was ripped out of her hands and tossed across the room. Now she was no longer giggling. She was gasping, close to tears. She tried to hug herself, to cover her nakedness with her arms, but he pried them off her chest and with little effort pinned them to her sides.

And now without any further ado or explanation he started on something that was all wrong, terribly, terribly wrong, taking her to the furthest reaches of alarm: something that was much, much too intimate to be subjected to at the hands of an uncle she loathed. Yes, she really really, *really* loathed him and—God, what was he *doing*?—he was forcing himself on her like a battering ram! No. Stop it. It couldn't be! What was she supposed to do? What would a lady do in this appalling situation? How could she register her refusal to participate in such a disgusting activity? She could not push him away, could not get a proper foothold—he was pressing her back against a cabinet; only the tips of her toes touched the floor. She attempted a scream, but he was squeezing her too tight; the scream came out as a strangled cough. She tried struggling, too, but when that elicited a playful snarl of approbation, she decided it was best to hold herself rigidly still and uncooperative instead.

Apparently whatever he was trying to do was not easy for him either, for now he was grunting with frustration. Again and again he rammed and again and again he was repulsed—five, six, seven times. She felt a little surge of hope. Maybe he'd have to give up? But he kept at it. She tried, desperately, to spit out a woolly thread of wig clinging to her nauseated tongue.

At last he broke through, and her eyes stung suddenly with stupefied tears. All her muscles ached with recoil. No! No, no! This could not be happening! It was the very center of her being he was invading, a place— a secret, a sacred, a *forbidden* place—a place she hadn't even known existed, until now! What was in it for him? Did he *like* it? She really didn't see what there was to like about it. It was like being poked and scraped by an icepick. Yet Uncle Edmund was making little snorting, grateful noises in her ear. The cabinet he had her pinned to answered him with loud creaking groans. What if someone walked by, and heard...?

It occurred to her there was another noise. It was loud too. It was even more mortifying. It was—Oh Lord, it was her. It was the worst thing of all. It was the breath being squeezed out of her lungs, rhythmically—*Uhnn, uhnn, uhnn.* As if she were condoning this depravity with grunts of approval. The hideous indignity of it almost choked her. She wanted to die. But she could not stop the sound, not even by holding her breath.

Did other men and women do this? Like this? Surely not. Surely it was her uncle's sick aberration. Surely no maid before her had ever been subjected to something so shameful. How could she have let it happen to her? For it was her fault. She should not have come here. Even if it had been Henry who had sent her that note, she should not have come. A proper lady wouldn't have. In her mind she heard her Aunt Clarissa's bitter words—men cannot help it, you know. It is up to us to help them control, through our proper behavior, their urges...

She peeled away the outer layer of her distress and tried to crawl under it, drawing it over her like an invisible cloak, or some comforting animal hide. A fleece, a donkey's skin. In the calm darkness she could finally focus on Henry. Henry was upstairs asleep, wasn't he? Henry could not, would not let this happen. Never. He was going to come bursting in—now, at any moment—and push this monster off her, restore everything to its proper order. No, better yet: Henry would kill her uncle. He was a soldier. He had a sword. He could do it. He loved her. He had kissed her once. He *had* to come, let him come, please, God, come and save her...

But Henry did not come. It was Edmund who came, noisily, perfunctorily. And then released her.

She sank to the floor. He fumbled with his clothes, not looking at her. He said, gruffly, his voice loud in the stillness, "You may go now."

Obediently she pulled herself to her feet and stumbled to the door.

"Don't forget this!" she heard behind her.

With a sweaty, chiding grin, he was holding out her nightshirt.

She snatched it from him, and fled.

25

RESCUE ME

Bessie was sitting on the edge of the bed.

"What's the matter, lamb? Are you ill?"

"I—I don't feel well this morning, that's all."

"Keep still now, let me feel your neck. A little warm, I think. I'll fetch you a nice cup of comfrey, that will make you feel better."

Bessie's eyes had taken on a new quality—a haunted, puzzled look, set in hollow sockets. Looking into them no longer gave you the confidence that no matter how bad things were, at least Bessie knew that everything would come out all right in the end. Looking into those eyes now, Lucinda could not help thinking about the night's ordeal, and—worse, much worse—Henry's apparent indifference...

"Ah, pet!" At the sight of Lucinda's tears, Bessie started crying too, and gathered her up in a big hug. They clung to each other, cheek to cheek, ear to ear, each facing out over the other's shoulder so that their tears might mingle but their eyes, thankfully, did not have to meet.

Bessie was crying about Thomas, and, naturally, she thought that Lucinda was crying about Thomas too. But what Lucinda was really crying about was a broken heart, the horror of the night before, and the shameful soreness between her legs; she knew that Bessie didn't know that, and that Bessie thought she was crying about Thomas. Which made Lucinda cry all the more, because it made her feel terribly selfish, a lousy friend to Bessie, a hypocrite too, and more lonely and miserable than ever.

When the sobs had dwindled to hiccups, they untangled themselves.

"Dear me!" said Bessie, and stood up. "I'll just go and fetch that comfrey now..."

Lucinda did not protest.

* * *

Later that afternoon she was allowed out of bed, after telling Mrs. Limpid she was just suffering from her monthly terms. She had barely set foot in the schoolroom when Sarah burst in through the opposite door.

"Children!" said Sarah breathlessly.

There was no time for the older children to object to this put-down, for right behind her, in stepped the visitor, Mrs. Limpid in tow. Sarah was proudly showing her betrothed around.

"My darlings! You do remember Captain Beaupree, don't you?" Sarah simpered. She sounded just like their mother.

"Hullo!" Henry muttered, grimacing like a bear forced to balance on a circus-ball before a rowdy audience.

Harry, aged twelve, immediately planted himself in front of Henry. "I am joining your regiment, sir, as soon as they'll let me. I'm an excellent horseman, ask anyone. Everyone says I'll make a topping officer..."

"Harry," Sarah snapped, "Don't talk nonsense. You're just a baby." She went on in a sweeter voice, "Captain, come, I want to show you the work I was telling you about..."

She dragged him off into a corner, by the window, so that he could examine by the best available light the little embroidered cap she had just completed.

Lucinda pressed her back into the wall and kept quite still, hoping to make herself invisible. But Henry looked up and saw her.

He gave her a rueful wink of recognition.

It was enough to make her hope again.

That night, a little after eleven o'clock, Henry Beaupree heard someone fumbling at his door. He sat up in bed, quickly pulled a shirt over his head, and struck the flint to light the lamp.

"Who is it?" he called.

"Me," came the trembling reply.

"Who?"

"Lucinda. I must speak to you..."

"Ah, the little cousin! You had better come in then!" he laughed. When she pushed open the door he swung his bare legs over the side of the bed and stood up. He motioned to her to come forward, and pulled out a stool for her to sit on.

As soon as she was installed on the little footstool, fidgeting with her nightshirt, pulling it tightly over her knees and down below her ankles, like a drum, the words came tumbling out.

"I'm sorry...I know I shouldn't, but I don't know what else to do, where else to turn, you've got to help me..." she stammered.

Without his wig, his head close-cropped, his ears exposed, he looked quite different—younger, more innocent, like a schoolboy. He said nothing to encourage her to continue, but gazed at her with a knowing smile. She had to look away. Glancing down, she saw the crumpled paper she had been clutching in her hand. She thrust it at him mutely.

"What's this?" Quickly he read the words. *Midnight. Same place.* He looked up at her, his eyebrows raised. "Is this for me?"

She shook her head.

"No, not for me? For you, then?"

She nodded with her head down.

"Who is it from?"

"Uncle," she whispered.

"Your uncle? Sir Edmund?"

"Yes."

"Ah," he said, not unkindly. "Your uncle desires an—assignation. With you."

She nodded.

"Tonight."

She nodded again.

"I see. And you do not wish to go."

She shook her head vehemently.

"And this has been going on—a long time?" Henry looked at her sternly.

She shook her head again. "No. It was last night—he tricked me...I didn't realize..." She started to cry.

With a tinge of sarcasm, he continued, "You do not wish to visit your uncle. At his request. At midnight. And yet—if I understand you right—you are not averse to visiting me, a strange man, in *my* rooms, at a similar hour?"

"Oh, but—" She swallowed. There was an unbearably hollow feeling in her chest. It wasn't pretense, then. She understood it now. "A strange man"—that was how he thought of himself in relation to her. As far as he was concerned, she had nothing to do with him. The daydreams, the mystical connection between them, all empty lies. No, not lies: foolish wishful thinking. That much was finally clear.

"I thought you could help me," she whispered.

"How can I help?" he asked reasonably. "What exactly did you have in mind?"

"Oh—I don't know..." It did seem a silly idea, all of a sudden.

She shuddered in the brutal silence that descended upon them. She watched the lamp's flame flicker, and followed the narrow curl of black smoke wavering and dissolving into the air.

Henry, watching her, sighed. Curse his creditors! It was true that his debts were considerable; that was the reason he was here. The bride on offer had an attractive portion, but her family was another matter altogether—one aunt, the lady Margaret, threatening to tell the world about their brief liaison if Henry went ahead with the marriage to her niece; another aunt, reputedly as ugly as sin, accused of witchcraft; the mother a foolish coquette mercifully struck dumb; and, it now appeared, a scoundrel of a father with no compunction about doing the dirty deed with his poor young ward in the dead of night...Truly, it would be best to cut one's losses and beat a hasty retreat. He sighed. Yes, surely that was the best, the decent, the only thing to do.

"So. How can I help?" he repeated.

Rescue me, she thought. Sweep me off my feet and carry me away on your galloping steed. Kill my uncle. "Oh, I don't know, I really don't know why I came," she whispered, and felt her eyes filling up and spilling over.

She looked very small and vulnerable, and he could not help feeling sorry for her. He placed a hand lightly on her head. The head turned up towards him in an affecting gesture of appeal, like a lapdog grateful for being petted.

"I love you," she gasped, desperately. "I'll do anything, only please, please...!" She bowed her head again, and rubbed angrily at her tears. "I am in love with you, that's all."

It made Henry laugh. "In love?" he said. "Do you realize what your uncle would do to me if he found out?"

"He doesn't have to. Find out, I mean."

Henry was not a man to resist temptation.

Gently, courteously, he led her to the bed.

It was well past one o'clock when Sir Edmund betook himself to his own bed, cursing. He was not going to humiliate himself by waiting for the little baggage any longer. But he had to confess to himself that the waif's reluctance made it all the more exciting. For if shocking a young maiden was all one was after, then one had but to betake oneself to Mrs. Bennett's in Whetstone Park, where a bevy of damsels stood by to be horribly scandalized and outraged, if that was what one ordered. Instead, here was the real thing, the pleasure enhanced by a tinge of incest and the fact that this was not a slut but a lady. The waiting and the anger would only increase the fun of it. Although one's patience did, of course, have its limits.

Tomorrow, he resolved, he would take measures to ensure himself of access to his prey.

26

LIFE'S GREAT SECRET

There were many things whirling through Lucinda's mind the next morning, but her failure to obey her uncle's summons was not one of them. She was sitting on her bed, carefully putting on her beaded slippers, when she heard shrieking next door.

"No! *No!* You're lying! It isn't true!"

She pushed two of her cousins out of the doorway to see what was going on. "What isn't true?" she whispered to Catherine, who, with the other children, was silently observing Sarah's spectacular tantrum.

"Hush, hush, my dear," Mrs. Limpid was saying, "these things happen, don't they. You will see, there are plenty of other..."

"Oh shut up! I hate you! Go away. I hate the lot of you! Leave me alone, can't you..." Wailing, Sarah ran blindly from the room.

"But Sarah my dear...Sarah!" Mrs. Limpid scurried after her pupil, pleading for decorum.

"*What* isn't true?" Lucinda repeated. There was a loud thumping in her ears.

"It's her captain, "crowed Sebastian. "He's bolted! He left a note for Father, he's broken off the betrothal!"

At first Lucinda felt only joy, her head spinning. Henry would not continue the pretense with Sarah! He could not do it! At last, *at last,* he had recognized the love that had been in his heart for Lucinda ever since the first time they'd met!

But there was a catch. The doubts and insecurities came hurtling back, whacking her with a mighty wallop between the ears: but how *could* he have left without some message for her, without taking her with him, without taking revenge on Uncle Edmund?

Reeling from these conflicting emotions, she crawled back into bed in order to review what had happened in the night, and sort it all out in her pounding head.

Henry had led her to the bed, and when she had seen where they were headed, she had drawn back a little.

"Actually," she had protested shyly, "That wasn't what I meant…"

What she wanted to say was that he had misunderstood her. She *had* told him she'd do anything, but surely not this, not the bed, for heaven's sake! At least, not now, not *right* now; eventually, yes of course—and gladly. But these things were supposed to happen only after a decent interval of courtship, after all the details were settled, the vows exchanged and the proprietary band of gold had found its way onto your finger! Surely he knew that a young lady wasn't allowed to lie abed with a man… It was a sin, wasn't it?

But how was she to convey this to him tactfully? It was her fault, she had blurted out the wrong thing, as usual. And of course her coming here in the dead of night might have given him the wrong idea.

She did not want to offend—no, no, that was not the right word— she did not want to hurt his feelings. For she might put him off, she knew he was easily put off, and this time she mustn't chase him away, as she had done that time in his valet's room, when he had tried to kiss her.

Already—as if there were nothing to it, as if he was sure she was expecting him to do this—he was busy removing her ankle-length night-shirt, only to find, underneath, the lace-trimmed corselet she had kept on tonight, partly out of vanity and partly out of modesty. And now he was looking her over, up and down, and grinning slyly at what he saw. Surely— yes, surely he liked what he saw, surely she looked fine, for would there not have been a different expression on his handsome face otherwise, as he untied first one ribbon, then another, and with a gallant gesture pulled them right out of the eyelets, instead of simply loosening them, as she would have done? And oh, she was charmed, as charmed and as flattered as she had been the first day, on the snowy bench. Joy tickled her skin where he ran his fingers over her arm, her neck, her breast, teasingly.

"Don't!" she squealed.

He pushed her down onto the bed. And, as she allowed herself to fall backward, the realization hit her that she could not, she really, *really* could not disappoint him. No, not now. However dire the consequences, she knew for certain she was not going to protest, to resist or—Lord!—to desist.

It did come as a surprise, however, to discover that after some quick pecks to her nose and lips, he turned his attention to the very body parts Uncle Edmund had so recently violated. Modesty and the memory of last night's nightmare made her want to push him away from that most shameful spot. But suddenly, with a shock, she understood that Henry was equipped with the same kind of appendage as Uncle Edmund...

And now finally, *finally*, it dawned on her that it was this—this pressing of flesh into flesh, not so unpleasant in itself, once you overcame your initial outrage—that constituted the act young ladies were so strictly admonished to avoid at any cost!

Here, then, was life's great secret! *Finally* she understood what was meant by *bedding*, by *lying with*; here at last was the explanation of that unspeakable mystery so often hinted at yet so strenuously kept hidden from her until now!

And with that discovery came the happy conviction that whatever the desire or the quest for pleasure that drives men to this strange and forbidden act, a woman seeks but to please. And she knew instinctively that it would please him very much if she stretched wide her legs and thrust forward her hips and hugged him tightly with her knees; in short, if she gamely did everything in her power to accommodate his probing. How proud, how happy it made her when she glimpsed the intentness on his face! And when, after not too long of this, he seemed able to contain himself no longer, and convulsively moaned and gasped on top of her as if she, and she alone, could catch him in his fall and save him from the demons of delight!

Then he was still, and she was still too, in respectful sympathy.

But he recovered remarkably quickly, and it was what happened next that was so hard for her to understand.

He rolled off her, smacked her on her bottom, and said, "You had better go now, little minx, before that wicked uncle of yours discovers what you have been up to."

The words pierced her euphoria and a lump rose in her throat.

"But..." she quavered.

"Ah! No buts, please!" Seeing her stricken face, he continued not unkindly, "Do as I say, my dear. All right? There's a girl. Or there will be hell to pay."

At the door, she turned around. But all she could see of him was the back of his dear bristly head.

"Er—then when will you...?" she began.

The question was cut short by a satisfied snore.

Sarah was already feeling a little better. Mrs. Limpid was summoned downstairs for a conference, and came back reporting that, while Sir Edmund was certainly furious about the captain's absconding, there was no blame whatsoever attached to Sarah.

"He said to tell you that the captain is a cad, and you are well rid of him," she said. "This little episode will not help his chances of preferment—your father will see to that."

Sarah sniffed.

"And he had better never show his face around here again..." began Sebastian.

"If he ever comes back," cried Harry, "I'll—I'll run him through with my rapier!"

"If he comes back," said Sarah haughtily, blowing her nose into a handkerchief she had embroidered with the letter S prettily entwined around an H, "I'll have none of him. He is a monster, and I shall tell him so."

"Well, now!" said Mrs. Limpid. "That's the spirit! Your father knew you would see it that way. He knows that I have always done my best to raise you children to be Obedient and not Proud." She took Sarah by the shoulders and turned her around so that she could grasp the long blond hair in the back and stroke it absently. "There really is no reason to be downhearted. Your father says he has another suitor in mind, one that he, not your mother, has picked out for you, a very *proper* gentleman."

"Does he have a title, or anything? I'd so much rather have a duke or a count or a..."

"Or a marquess, or an earl!" interrupted Catherine excitedly.

"Yes, I'd much rather have one of those than a plain old *captain*," said Sarah, giving a final, quiet sniff. The placidity that was so much a part of her makeup was settling on her once more.

"You'll be a countess! Or a duchess!" Harry cheered.

"Shall I, Mrs. Limpid?" asked Sarah, angelically.

"You will have to wait to find out, Sarah. Remember, Patience is a Virtue. But first, I have another lovely surprise for you."

"Yes?"

"Yes indeed. To show you that in his eyes you are now truly a grown young woman, your father has charged me with settling you into a chamber of your own..."

"A chamber of my own!" breathed Sarah. "Really?"

"Like Robert's?" exclaimed Samuel, awed.

"Just like His Lordship's," Mrs. Limpid assured him.

"Oh, please, *please* may I have a chamber of my own too?" whined Belinda.

"When you are of marriageable age, and as prettily behaved as your sister, I am sure that you will. Come, Sarah, come look at your new abode."

The new abode was a small paneled room on the other side of Mrs. Limpid's own alcove off the nursery. It had been used as a sitting room by the governess and the other instructors. The children all thronged in behind Sarah and Mrs. Limpid, oohing and aahing as if they had never seen it before. A carpenter was already at work assembling a four-poster bed in place, since the door was too narrow to allow this bulky piece of furniture to be installed in one piece.

Lucinda couldn't help feeling a pang of envy. "Oh, Sarah," she sighed, "You are *sooo* lucky!"

At this, Mrs. Limpid turned and peered at Lucinda. "Ah—Lucinda!" she announced, as if she had just been reminded of Lucinda's regrettable existence. "Yes. You...well now, Lucinda *is* the same age as Sarah, of course. We must not forget that. It would not be fair. Therefore she too must move out of the nursery."

Lucinda looked up from the pile of bed hangings she was examining. "You mean that I'm to share her chamber?"

"No!" wailed Sarah, "No! I don't want her in my chamber, she *always* has to copy me and spoil everything for me. It's not fair! After all, I've *deserved* it, she has done nothing..."

"No," said Mrs. Limpid, "Lucinda is to have her own quarters, in the east wing."

"But..." Lucinda began.

"It has been arranged," said Mrs. Limpid firmly, avoiding Lucinda's eyes. "Your uncle wishes it. "

The children had gone quiet, and examined Lucinda with unusual interest. It was obvious, from Mrs. Limpid's pursed lips, that there was more to this than met the eye. Sarah's removal from the nursery was an enviable thing; Lucinda's seemed more like a banishment.

Lucinda looked around at each one of them in turn, wildly. Her cheeks were burning. "I must—uh, tell Bessie," she muttered, and made her escape.

27

THE (ALMOST) TRUTH

It was time to come clean and tell Bessie everything. Or *almost* everything.

"Your uncle WHAT?" exclaimed Bessie, livid.

"*You* know. You warned me, Bessie, but I...I didn't understand. I had no idea what to expect. I'm sorry. I was a fool, I thought I could handle it. But—I couldn't. I couldn't stop him." She started to cry.

"No, lamb, of course you didn't understand. I should have—I should have explained these things to you..."

"It wasn't my fault!" wailed Lucinda. "What should I have done?"

"Nothing, there was nothing you could have done," whispered Bessie hoarsely. "No! You are not to blame."

"It was horrible..."

"Tell me, when? When did he...?"

"The night before last."

"But pet, why didn't you tell me straightaway?"

"I was so ashamed..."

"Don't be, don't be. Pet, my pet."

"But—it's not over," Lucinda sobbed. "Mrs. Limpid says I am to move out of the nursery, into the east wing. That means..."

"I *know* what that means," said Bessie. The east wing of the manor was where the guest quarters were located. No one went there unless the rooms were being readied for visitors. "Don't you think I know what that means? And we will not let it happen again. I shall not let it happen. No, lamb. We'll run away. This very day."

Lucinda sniffed gratefully. "Oh, Bessie! But how...?"

"Let's see. I have my savings, don't forget I have my savings. I've spent nary a penny all these years. Been keeping it for a rainy day. See? I always knew it would come in useful." She bustled over to her chest and rummaged around in it. Finally she came up with a worn leather pouch. "Twenty-eight shilling and tuppence," she said triumphantly. "I count it every Lord's day. Enough to pay for the stagecoach and lodgings, and much besides."

"But..."

"Yes, that's what we'll do. And we'll look up that nice lady of Thomas's in Hampshire, Lady Doughby, and she'll help us."

"No, Bessie."

"No? What do you mean, no?"

"We must go to London."

"To London? Why, that's no place for a young lady. No, lamb."

"We must go to London. We must!"

"But pet, what would we do there? Fall into sin, most likely. It's a wicked, wicked place, child," she fussed. "And filthy! Besides, we don't know a soul in London."

"I know someone, and he is expecting me."

Bessie stared at her open-mouthed.

Lucinda suddenly turned bashful. She bowed her head.

"Well?"

"Well, Bess, it's that visitor, the one who was supposed to marry Sarah, I mean, he..."

"What? The captain? What has he got to do with it?"

"Well, he—I—you know. We are in love," she whispered.

"In love? Oh, nonsense!" exclaimed Bessie. "How can that be?"

"It's true! It's true!" Lucinda said vehemently. "And it's because of *me* he's left, he couldn't go through with the betrothal because he loves *me, me, ME,* can't you get that through your head?"

Bessie was practically speechless. "Why, now, my pet, but..."

"And he wants to marry me! He told me that he would come back for me! And he said that if my uncle...Well, you know, if my uncle...he made me promise to be careful, he told me to come and find him if anything happened while he was away. I *promised* him! I did! And now—he doesn't know what happened, and he left before I could tell him..."

Honesty was one of Lucinda's most cherished virtues, and she made a habit of practicing it as often as she could. If she was bending the truth a little here, then, it was only because she deemed it necessary in order to persuade Bessie to agree to her plan. Surely it was expedience, not dishonesty, that made Lucinda ascribe certain sentiments to Henry which had not yet been expressed—not in so many words, anyway. For of course he had not yet made any mention to her of love, or of marriage, or even of coming back for her. But as soon as the words were out of her mouth, Lucinda was convinced they were fundamentally true. It was probably only just beginning to dawn on Henry that she was his one true love. Which would explain his abrupt, thoughtless, flight; confused about all the chaotic new emotions flaring up in his breast, he needed to put some distance between himself and the source of the conflagration. Once he had had some time to sort it all out, he would be ready, more than ready, to take her in his arms. She was sure of it.

"Where does he live?"

"What?"

"Your captain. Where does he live, in London?"

"I don't know."

"Pet. How is that possible, how can you say you don't know, when he told you to come find him? Surely you must have an address..."

"Wait! Oh yes, of course!" she laughed, slapping her forehead with the palm of her hand. "I do remember. York Buildings. Yes, York Buildings. Off the Strand, he said." It was as good a guess as any; it was the address written on Matthew Chancrey's letter, which she knew by heart.

"Well," said Bessie briskly, "London it is then. We must hurry. There is no time to lose. We'll pack up our things—just a few things, mind, only as much as we can hide under our petticoats, we don't want anyone thinking we're setting off on a journey. Not a word to anyone! I'll tell Mrs. Limpid that I am helping you settle into your new quarters. Take off that stomacher, pet—it's much too fancy, it will attract attention. Give it to me. I'll carry it for you. Here—wear my blue kerchief instead." She tied the neckerchief around Lucinda's shoulders. "And my calico apron—here, put it on. Good. And now tuck in your sleeves and hitch up your petticoat under your skirt—that's it—there, now the lace won't show. That's better, that's more common. We don't want you looking like a rich little runaway, do we! Where are your shoes? You can't go in those slippers, lamb. They won't do at all. I know you love them, but you can tuck them in your pocket. Let's hurry, pet, let's hurry—it's almost noon, and we must be long gone by suppertime. That's when they'll start missing us, let's hope they don't realize we're gone until then."

"Bessie!" A thought had just struck Lucinda. "How are we ever to make it to Bitterbury, where the stage coach stops? It's a long way—"

"That's a point, lamb. That's a very good point." Bessie remembered the trip to Simmins-Hollow. "My legs aren't what they used to be. My poor, poor legs. Oh dear." She faltered and let her hands fall to her sides, palms up. "Well. Perhaps it's best if I—"

"No, Bess, I won't go without you," Lucinda exclaimed. "I know! We'll persuade one of the grooms to let us have a horse."

"I don't ride, pet, you know that."

"No, but I do, and you'll sit behind me..."

Bessie was hesitant. She was afraid of horses.

"I'm very good, don't worry. You'll be safe with me." While she was speaking, Lucinda flipped through the roster of stable hands in her head, and came up with the tow-headed one—George, wasn't that his name? Yes, George. He was the one always staring at her with that peculiar gaze.

"I know, we'll ask George. I think he likes me."

Bessie compressed her lips. "Well, well. I trust he hasn't overstepped the bounds. I trust he knows his place."

But since this was neither the time nor the place for that sort of argument, and since Bessie could not come up with a better plan, Lucinda ran outside to find George.

In any large household there are undercurrents of love that may never play themselves out, but are present all the same. It was true that George the junior stable hand had been pining hopelessly for Miss Lucy for a while, just as the gardener, old Walter Brackthorn, had secretly fancied Bessie from time to time. Even Arabella Steppys had once had titillating thoughts about her servant Thomas Boothby, while Lord Robert had spent his adolescence lewdly fantasizing about Lucinda.

In George's case, the pining was hopeless, and he knew it. For Miss Lucinda belonged to the world of his masters, even though, being an orphan, she was more approachable than the other highborn children. She was always kind to the servants, and did not put on airs; she often came down to the servants' hall, and the best time George had ever had in his whole life was when they had all begged her to draw a picture of them, and he had watched from the other side of the table as she had rapidly captured likeness after likeness on paper—as if by magic! She had done one of George too: the little sketch of his head, in profile, his mouth foolishly open, was his most precious possession.

Still, there it was: she was a lady, and the tears he had seen her shed the other day (it was when Sir Edmund and the young earl had returned from London with that gentleman with the lame mare; George had been there to take the horses from them, and how it broke his heart to see her cry!)—those tears had had nothing to do with him.

The fact that she was seriously out of his reach, however, did not stop him from imagining all sorts of scenarios in which he, George, was called upon to perform heroic feats for her sake. And willingly give up his life for her. Ah, and then, when it was too late, you see, as she knelt in a pool of his loyal blood, finally she would come to understand the great, noble devotion she had lost, and shed bitter tears of sorrow and regret...

To be called, then, by the real Lucinda while he was watering the horses in the sun, was a tremendous shock.

"George!"

"Er, madam?" he stammered.

She was out of breath when she reached him.

"You—you like me, you have always liked me, haven't you?" she blurted out.

The shocking accuracy of the question made him blush bright red. He turned and busied himself with his bucket.

It was her turn to blush. "Forgive me, I just meant..." She stared at the burning neck under the mop of bleached hair, and considered a retreat.

George forced himself to turn around again. Fixing his eyes on the hem of her skirt, he began to whistle tunelessly.

She took a deep breath. "George!" she said again, as if to erase the false start. She was suddenly aware how fancy, how dignified her voice must sound to his ears. "George, I do so need your help. You are the only one I—"

At the word "help", his eyes shot up to meet hers. "'Elp!" he said. "Oh, pardon me, er, madam, but anything I can do to 'elp...to..." At the end of this speech, his tongue became all tied again, and he resumed his earnest survey of her skirt.

"I am *so* glad, because you are the only one I'd trust."

His heart was going to burst with pride! She came and stood closer to him, and he held himself very still and very erect. He hoped she wouldn't notice, as he did, that she was a bit taller than him.

She was speaking in a whisper now. "George, I am running away. I cannot stay here a day longer. Bessie is coming with me. Sir Edmund, you see, wants to—is trying to..."

"Lord! Really?" exclaimed George, indignantly. "What's 'e done?"

"It—it's not something I can talk about, George," she said, and real tears of self-pity came to her eyes.

"Lord, Miss! 'E never!" George began to blush again.

"Yes, so you see, I must go. As soon as possible. And we can't tell anyone, or he'll be after me..."

It dawned on George that he was being asked to help this angel of his to escape. Which meant that he might never see her again. He would have to give her up, just when it seemed that she was aware of his existence, and that she liked him too! She hadn't said as much, but she had said she trusted him. Wasn't that the same thing?

It was just the sort of terrible sacrifice he had always imagined he would be called upon to make one day. He swallowed resolutely. "My lady," he said as nobly as he could. "You was needing 'orses!"

"How did you know!" she exclaimed. "Just one horse will do, actually, for both of us. You *are* clever," she added.

"I don't know—I just guessed, is all," he replied. And, lest she think him conceited—he realized his earnest answer to her question had been unnecessary—went on, business-like, "Julia Sees-Her. Yes, Julia Sees-Her will do you best. 'E won't be missed, there's none as rides 'im much. 'E's a good 'orse and finds 'is own way home."

"I knew we could count on you! I'll never forget this, George. Never."

It wasn't much, but that vow was the closest George ever got to attaining his most fervent adolescent desire. There's no reason to feel sorry for him, however. He really had no right to expect even this much, and he certainly did not expect any more.

28

CIVIL LIBERTIES

George had chosen well. Julius Caesar turned out to be a thickset, heavy-footed gelding steady enough for two riders. He was unperturbed by the terrified squeals emerging from Bessie, or her thrashing legs on his flanks. Lucinda held on to the reins as best she could, although Bessie's panicked gyrations made it difficult, sending her into fits of laughter. George accompanied them for as long as he dared, to show them the way through the woods behind the manor. Since it was broad daylight, they thought it best to avoid the main roads.

They stopped at the edge of a large pasture. Before them stretched an expanse of grazed grass, with a church steeple in the distance.

"There you are. You'll find it from 'ere," he said reluctantly.

"Yes, there it is! Thank you *so* much, George." She was gazing at the hazy skyline, her eyes squinting excitedly in the harsh sunlight.

"Yes, thank you, young man," added Bessie. "You'd best get back now, dear, before they start wondering where you are. We'll manage from here. Somehow we'll manage."

"I..." George said.

"Come on, Bess. And *try* to sit still. Hang on tight!" Lucinda was gathering the reins in her fists, her back straight, her eyes on the horizon.

George felt there was more, much more to be said.

"Good-bye, milady—madam, and God-bless—" he began.

But they had already started moving away from him, Lucinda laughingly throwing words of encouragement over her shoulder at Bessie, who was hanging on for dear life.

George remained standing there a good while, staring after them. It was not until they were hidden by a stand of willows that he turned and slowly ambled back to face a good thrashing and the tedium of the rest of his life.

It took Lucinda and Bessie less than an hour to reach The Worm, Bitterbury's central inn.

"Lord!" Bessie panted as Lucinda helped her down off the horse. She plopped down on a bench inside the courtyard to rest her shaking legs, "I am too old for this! I'll never—Lucinda! Lamb! Where are you going!"

"Stay here, Bess. Just rest. I'll be right back. I'll just inquire when the coach is expected."

In the gloomy taproom that stank of stale ale, vomit and urine, she found the innkeeper pulling on a pipe.

"The stage for London? Three a-clock, Miss," he said. "It aye arrives three a-clock, or thereabouts. Be ye goin' to London, Miss?"

"No, Bath," Lucinda lied quickly. "To visit a relative who lives there."

"Bath? Ah, no. Ah no, no, no, you see, Miss, the stage does not stop at Bath. That would be the other way, see. No, ye'd best await tomorrow, there's the West Country stage, it..."

"No, this relative, I mean, he is to meet us at a crossroads, with his coach-and-six," Lucinda said a little crossly, and tried to change the subject. "Are there any refreshments to be had?"

"Mother!" the innkeeper roared into the back. "Vittels!" Turning to Lucinda, he leered, "Some bread and ale and a slice of porky-pie for the young lady?"

"Thank you *so* much," said Lucinda. She started for the door.

"His own coach-and-six, eh?" The innkeeper spoke loudly to her retreating back. "His own coach-and-six! Where did you say he was meeting you then?"

"Thank you *so* much," Lucinda repeated primly as if she hadn't heard the question, and slipped out into the sunlight.

She found Bessie sitting petrified on the bench where she had left her, staring open-mouthed at a portly middle-aged man who had one leg propped up on Bessie's bench.

"Aye," he was saying, "that was a kind thing your master did, a kind thing. I said to the wife, I said, 'It just goes to show you there's justice in this world, and fine gentlemen to uphold it too.'"

Spotting Lucinda, Bessie started fanning herself with her neckerchief. She looked uncomfortably hot.

"Bessie! There you are!" Lucinda said, and then turned to the stranger, as if she had just noticed him.

"Sir?" she asked.

"Ah!" he said heartily. "And you must be Bessie's daughter. Well now! Pleased to make your acquaintance, Miss. You have been holding back on me, Bess! My, my! Every bit as purty as her mam—"

"Aunt!" Bessie puffed, then resumed her apoplectic fanning.

"Beg pardon, aunt, ah, well, the resemblance's unmistakable. No, Miss, I was just saying to auntie here, I am so delighted to bump into her, we last met under less fortunate circumstances, you see..."

"Oh?" said Lucinda.

"Robert Fetshank. Butcher. At your service, ma'am. Bessie—well, she and I go a long way back. *Long* way back. Always one of my best customers, she was." Turning to Bessie, he beamed ingratiatingly, "You always did say none could dress a roast *a-la-modey-way* as well as old Fetshank, didn't you, Bess!"

Lucinda still could not understand why Bessie was being so unfriendly.

"I was just telling her how sorry I was about her being, er, taken for a witch, and all." He winked broadly. "Always thought she was a lovely sort of person. Never for a moment thought such a *fine-looking* person could be a-one of *them*. I told Master Boulderdash, I said, '*She's* not one of them, that one. Never!'"

Bessie was pursing her lips. Both Lucinda and Robert Fetshank assumed she was finally going to say something. But it was spit that came out. The gob landed right on top of Robert Fetshank's raised shoe.

Lucinda was shocked. "Bessie!"

"Ah, I see!" he said, straightening slowly with a pained laugh. "It's a grudge, is it? It's a grudge! Well, there you are. A man performs his duty for the common weal, and this is how he is thanked." He swung the foot with the minuscule patch of offending slime off the bench, and pivoted. "But I'm used to it, you see, Miss," he mumbled to Lucinda as he limped gingerly toward the tavern door. "Don't think I am not used to it."

"Bessie!" Lucinda repeated sternly. She was feeling terribly sorry for the fat butcher. "Whatever's come over you?"

"Oh, lamb," Bessie exhaled, "lamb—I'm sorry, I shouldn't have, it's not like me, not like me at all. But that man..." She had released her hands—she had been sitting on them—and was holding them up in front of her eyes. They were shaking visibly, and she stared at them vacantly, as if amazed at their independence. "That man saw me...with my clothes off!"

"No!" exclaimed Lucinda.

"Yes, lamb." She almost gagged, then swallowed painfully. "He was there when they questioned me. Oh my Lord. He was the one who tied me. On the rack. Naked. He touched me! And that man acting just like it's the most normal thing in the world, if you please! Oh the nerve, the nerve of the man!" She brought her hands up to her face and rubbed her eyes, nose and cheeks hard. "But you're right, lamb, I should not have done that, it was rude. Spitting. It's not like me. I don't know what came over me!"

"Oh, Bessie," Lucinda exclaimed, hugging her. "Don't fret. Soon you'll never have to see him again. We'll be far away."

"So we will," said Bessie, calming down. "Oh, you are *such* a comfort, my pet, what would I do without you..."

The incongruity of it suddenly struck Lucinda. When had this role-reversal occurred? Since when was it normal for her to comfort Bessie, and for a helpless, stricken Bessie to lean on her? Was this the way it was going to be from now on? It felt very strange. But it made her feel very grown-up, too.

Poor Bessie. She was suffering from an acute case of the affliction known as Blaming Oneself. All her life she had meant well, meant *more* than well. All her life she had tried to make herself useful, ignoring her own

needs in order to serve others. And what happened? Instead of helping those she loved, she had been the cause of their undoing! Bessie just
could not understand how all those good intentions could have led to
such a perplexing series of disasters. To wit:

First, Lady Clarissa's muteness. If only Bessie had not provided her
with the belladonna; if only she had not allowed herself to feel sorry for
the poor lady and help her try to seduce her husband; if only she had
never let on that she knew anything about herbal remedies and such...

Next, Thomas' death. If Bessie had never let on that she knew anything about herbal remedies, then Clarissa would not have overdosed
on the belladonna. And then she would not have had herself accused
of witchcraft. And then Thomas would not have been obliged to try to
rescue her. And then Thomas would still be alive...Here the tears welled
up again, and she had a good cry.

Sniffing, she went on, refusing to spare herself. And now here was
the worst mistake of all. Of all the stupid, stupid...! Here was her lamb,
her pet, her innocent girl. Faced with a ruin so obvious, so unavoidable,
that it had been staring them all in the face. She had feared it; so had
Thomas; even Mrs. Kettle and the others had speculated on it. Hadn't
they known what Sir Edmund was like?

If Lady Clarissa had been well, she might have kept her husband in
check. If Bessie had not been arrested for witchcraft, if she hadn't been so
weakened by her ordeal and so upset by Thomas's death, then she might
have paid more attention, and perhaps could have prevented the rape.
But even so—why had she never taught Lucinda the facts of life? Why
had she assumed, just because the girl acted so self-confident, so sure of
herself, that she would know how to defend herself? Why, at the very
least, had she not planned their escape earlier? Oh, she blamed herself,
she blamed herself, she really, truly, blamed herself!

While Bessie was thus castigating herself, Arabella, who had been
found guilty by everyone but could find nothing whatsoever to blame
herself for, was languishing in a stinking hole not fifty yards from where
Bessie and Lucinda were sitting. Prison conditions were far worse for
Arabella than they had been for Bessie and Thomas, because the guards

were so afraid of her that they did not dare descend into her lair. Her food and drink were thrown down to her from above, and since much of it spilled in the filthy mire before she could catch it, Arabella was starting to suffer from hunger and dehydration. It was becoming dreadfully clear to her that unless her unsympathetic brother-in-law had a sudden change of heart, she was doomed. Since in her looks she fit the popular image of a witch, there was no one in this bunch of simpletons who was going to give her the benefit of the doubt.

But was it Arabella's fault that she was born ugly? Imagine being unattractive in an age when the science of physiognomy was taken seriously by enlightened folks, even the king! Imagine going through life provoking negative responses in people who don't even know you; imagine the hurt of each recoil. Who could blame her for her bitterness and her peevish disposition? The worst that could be said of her, in the end, was that she had an unfortunate talent for making people squirm. It was true that she had often scolded and beaten her servants—but always in the conviction that she was improving their character and saving their souls. If she had stolen from her father (a father who, it must be said, never thought of making any provision for her future), it was only because she saw no other way to ensure herself of a living once he was gone. And although it can't be denied that she was responsible for Thomas Boothby's arrest, surely even that was done only in self-defense!

The truth is that Arabella did not deserve her sorry fate. She did not deserve to be tortured and degraded, then pilloried and jeered at, and finally hanged from the gallows, shamefully, like a common criminal, stinking of her own excrement, her eyes bulging like a frog's, her blackened tongue protruding, in death the very image of a witch. For this is what happened to Arabella Steppys in the end. Not one tear was shed for her, not one voice was raised in protest, not one gallant knight came galloping up on a white steed to snatch her from the jaws of death.

It was an age when life was cheap and justice hard to come by. An age when the phrase "civil liberties" meant "polite impertinence," and most humans had no rights at all.

29

THE RUNAWAYS

It did not take Robert long to overtake the runaways. The innkeeper was eager to share his suspicions with his lordship.

"The young lady said they were on their way to Bath, but I'd not believe a word of it, my lord. I'd look for her on the road to London, that's where they be gone, I'll warrant."

"Pardon me, yer Honor." It was the butcher, Robert Fetshank, slurring his words self-importantly, "I am acquainted with the other woman. She was charged, you know, with witchcraft. I'll never understand why she was released—she was the paramour of an affirmed warlock. A right bawd too. A base slut. I'd be happy to help, my lord, in any way..."

"That will not be necessary," said Robert coldly, and, having moistened his lips with the complimentary ale, slapped it down on the table, shouting, "Fellow! My horse!"

The London stagecoach put up for the night in Stow-on-the-Wold, at the Merry Maypole. When Lucinda and Bessie came downstairs in the morning, ready to resume their journey, they found Robert leaning on the banister.

"Where are you going, coz?" he asked pleasantly.

"Robert!" She grabbed Bessie's hand. "We...we...we were just..."

"Yes, I know. You were just absconding, were you not? Sir Edmund sent me after you. He wants you to come home."

Lucinda sat down heavily on the stairs. She started to cry.

"Lamb! Pet!" Bessie fussed. She turned to Robert. "Oh, sir! Don't you see she can't go back with you? She can't!"

"She can't?" asked Robert, reasonably.

Lucinda raised her head and gazed at him squarely through tear-filled eyes. Robert made a show of extracting a snuffbox from his tightly-cut coat pocket.

"No I can't, my lord," Lucinda whispered. "And you'll understand, once I explain—"

"No need to explain, coz," he said airily. He opened the box and carefully pinched a few grains of snuff between forefinger and thumb, threw his head back and sniffed, very debonair. It was a trick he'd been practicing since his return from London. The two women watched the entire proceeding in silence. There was a loud, messy sneeze. Tactfully, both looked away while his lordship made some adjustments with a large, ornate handkerchief.

"I said," he went on, "that your uncle sent me after you. I did not say that I would do his bidding."

"No?' said Lucinda.

"Ah!" said Bessie.

"No. If you wish to go to London—by all means. But please allow me to accompany you. It is not safe for two females to travel alone."

"I don't understand.You mean...?" said Lucinda.

"There is nothing to explain. If you don't wish to return to the manor, there is nothing I can do about it, is there."

"No?" said Lucinda.

"Of course not!" said Bessie.

"So. That's settled, then. Allow me," said Robert. And he bowed, offered Lucinda his arm, and walked her out into the courtyard, where a hired coach was waiting.

Coming into his inheritance had done wonders for Robert. Even though he was still a pimply, gangly youth, the sudden respect of those around him, the bowing and the scraping, had worked miracles on him. Instead of camouflaging his awkward length, he now held himself erect and looked down at you superciliously along his blemished nose. He was haughty. He was superior. His raised left eyebrow had become a weapon. It was clear that he was perfecting the stances that were to cover up his insecurities once and for all. Already, when he walked into a room, there was no doubt in anyone's mind that here was a young person of import, a person of standing, a person whom, if you were so inclined, you might wish to suck up to.

Since he was now an earl, while Sir Edmund was a mere baronet, Robert felt he no longer had to obey his guardian. Here was an opportunity to test his newfound independence: his niece, Lucinda. She was a sly little thing. She'd been taunting him far too long, hadn't she, with those flashing eyes, that glib mouth and mobile waist. Apparently Sir Edmund had pegged her for his own little plaything. The rake! Robert seethed at the thought. Sir Edmund was a greedy bounder. He had already had more, far more than his fair share. Robert gripped his silver-tipped walking-cane, and watched his knuckles grow white.

It was Lucinda who broke the silence.

"My lord," she began. "It is certainly very kind of you to accompany us to London, and we are ever so grateful, but you see, we do not need..."

"Lucinda." He coughed in order to suppress an impending squeak in his throat. "You are running away, are you not?"

The girl cast her eyes down.

"I am offering to help you."

"But..." she said again.

"London is a dreadful place, no place for a young lady," he continued. "But you may count on me to protect you. I have taken it upon myself to rent some lodgings for you. The arrangements are being made at this very instant. At considerable expense to myself, of course. I trust that you will find them comfortable. And if you wish to retain this person—" he nodded at Bessie, "as your servant, I shall see to it that she is paid."

"But..." said Lucinda, for the third time.

"All I ask of you is that you do not show yourself abroad. Our...uh, arrangement requires the utmost discretion. Do you understand?"

Lucinda nodded mutely. She understood only too well. She noticed Robert's eyes on her chest, and pulled Bessie's blue kerchief up around her neck. She sensed, rather than saw, Bessie's open mouth and rising indignation.

Bessie felt a sharp jab in her ribs, and kept her mouth shut.

30

LONDON

Lucinda looked out the window, aghast. Surely this could not be London, the London she had heard so much about, the London of all the fine society! The coach was lurching through narrow, stinking streets crammed with people, very common persons they were, who stared at her rudely through her window. Lucinda shrank back. There was a mood of aggression she did not understand. An unkempt young woman had just screeched something at her. There had been cackles of laughter from those close enough to hear. She could not understand the woman's accent, but she knew, from Bessie's stiffening beside her, that it had not been polite.

Look at these streets! Just look at them! They simply went on and on. Peering through the stream of hackney-carriages, sedan chairs, water-carriers, hawkers pushing their barrows, waddling washerwomen with their bundles, dung carts and herds of cattle, she could make out intersecting streets and alleyways, each as congested as the main avenue along which they were now proceeding at a snail's pace. Never in her wildest dreams had she imagined a place so vast, so smelly, so crowded with people. How was she ever, *ever* to find Henry in this maze?

She felt a sharp blow over her head. It made her jump. A pedestrian, angry at having to cede space to the carriage, had banged on the back of their vehicle with his stick. She clung to Bessie's arm.

"How does London agree with you, coz?" shouted Robert gleefully over the din.

"Well enough, my lord. Well enough," she said, trying to smile.

"Not to worry. Not long now," he said, turning his head to peer through the little window above his head.

"Oh—I don't mind it. I mean, I like it," she said quickly. "Where are we going?"

"Locket's. My preferred tavern, in Charing Cross. That is where I have arranged to meet Klepton. My valet, you know. I have a valet now."

"Oh?" said Lucinda, respectfully. The valet had been a matter of common knowledge and much gossip at the manor ever since Robert's return from London, but Lucinda pretended this was the first she had heard of any such thing.

"Yes, I charged him with riding ahead and finding suitable lodgings. Klepton's a good fellow, knows how to see to a man's arrangements." He frowned. "He is discreet and *very* loyal to me, I must say."

"Indeed," said Lucinda.

The coach swerved into a courtyard. "Here we are then, ladies," said Robert. "Please wait here. I shall return with Klepton."

"Come on!" hissed Bessie, as they watched Robert strut into the building. "This is our chance! Let's make a run for it!"

"Not yet, Bessie," said Lucinda. "Don't worry. I have a plan."

"But don't you realize what his intentions are, lamb?"

"I do, I do. But I can handle him. Watch me. It's a *great* plan. Don't look so worried!"

There was no time for further discussion, for Robert had returned, his valet in tow.

"Now then!" said Robert, climbing back into the carriage. The valet climbed up front. "Ladies, my man Klepton tells me he has found just the place, in Lincoln's Inn Fields. We shall proceed there directly."

The ladies smiled at him innocently.

The coach lurched off again. Someone close by was shouting a cheerful but deafening *"Dumplins diddle, diddle, dumplins ho! Dumplins six-a-penny!"* A beggar with no arms was ululating for alms. At the corner of a side street a crowd was gathered around a coach that had overturned in the mud; a foppishly dressed man was being pulled out of the wreckage, screeching and berating the driver. Some street urchins ran alongside their carriage for a while, grinning at them through the window and making faces. Robert put an end to that by poking his cane out at them, hitting one neatly in the nose. Some obscenities were shouted after them. Robert tut-tutted; the two women looked down at their laps.

They were now in a more fashionable street, and passed several carriages crammed with fluttering fans and beautiful gowns.

Lucinda pointed at a long building mobbed by elegant people. "Where are they going?" she breathed. "Is it a ball?"

Robert blinked his eyes rapidly with affected amusement. "A ball! A *ball*? At this time of day? No, it's New Exchange," he said. "Shops, you know. It's the place one goes for one's necessities. I bought my cane there, at Caversham's. They charge a fortune, but one must look one's best, doesn't one, to cut a figure at court..."

Bessie and Lucinda looked obediently at Robert's shiny new cane, and then out at the market.

"My, my," Bessie exclaimed politely. "Look at that hat!"

"Some of them look ridiculous," Lucinda decided.

Robert fixed her with a stare. He let his eyes travel slowly over her person.

"Not exactly the picture of a London lady, are you, coz?" he observed. She flashed him an indignant but insecure look.

"Don't worry, my dear. I'll put you into the hands of my tailor. I'm sure his people will be able to do—*something* with you." He laughed softly to himself, folding his hands over his cane.

Lucinda tossed her hair back, and looked down at her hands, composing her face. She couldn't wait any longer to unleash her plan.

"My lord," she began sweetly. "Are you not..." She left the sentence dangling.

"What?"

"Oh, nothing."

"What, coz?"

"Well, seeing that you are now in London, and that man, Captain Beaupree, who broke off the betrothal with Sarah, resides here too, I just thought..."

Robert looked taken aback. Lucinda noticed the hop-skip-and-jump of a gangly Adam's apple under the thin irritated skin above his cravat.

"Well...?" she said.

"Well what?"

"Don't you have to go and—well, call on him, or anything?" she asked lightly. "I thought it was the usual thing to do..."

"Call on him?"

"I mean, he *has* slighted Sarah, hasn't he, and offended our family..."

"He has, yes."

"Well, I thought..."

"I certainly do not condone his actions."

"Oh."

Robert was looking out of the window intently. He said nothing more. He was chewing the inside of his lip.

Lucinda let him stew a few more moments, then coughed discreetly.

"I thought—I assumed that was why you proposed to accompany us to London. I thought you had affairs—that sort of affairs—to attend to, I mean."

"If I did, do you think I would tell *you*?"

"No, of course not!" She fanned herself, then leaned forward, and continued in an urgent tone. "I only hope you will consider—well, consider your own safety. I hope you don't think yourself obliged to challenge him to a duel! He is an officer, after all, experienced in battle. Please be careful, my lord."

"Enough!" he burst out.

"I'm sorry, I—

"That is a man's business," he barked. "It does not concern you!"

"Forgive me. I should never have mentioned it. Please don't be angry with me, my lord." She was sitting up straight again, twiddling with the ends of her kerchief. "Whatever you must do, it must be done discreetly. I understand. As far as we are concerned, the subject has not been discussed. Right, Bessie?"

"Right," said Bessie firmly.

Robert's face was ashen now; little droplets of perspiration clung to the sparse whiskers on his upper lip.

Lucinda prattled on. "But believe me, I *am* grateful for the offer of a dressmaker, honestly I am. His lordship is too good. How many gowns may I order? What do you think, Bessie? How many do I need? Two, or three? And what of the shoes? I rather fancy that I'll need some footwear..."

"Not now," he groaned abruptly, shifting uncomfortably in his seat, from side to side, "Later!"

The carriage had now arrived in another courtyard, and Lord Hempstead almost fell out the door in his haste. Lucinda and Bessie were also grateful to get out, for the air inside the carriage was not fresh. The valet ushered them into a hallway; his lordship was already running up the stairs.

The rooms were not large, and not very nicely furnished. It was obvious that the nervously pacing Robert was disappointed, and felt he had been swindled by the valet, or the landlord, or both. He had handed over a rather large sum. Apparently he did not yet have the hang of intimidating people sufficiently to make them leery of cheating him.

But he could not afford to start complaining now. He needed to see to his exploding bowels. He groaned something to Klepton, and hobbled after him down the corridor.

"We can't stay here!" whispered Bessie in the dusty drawing-room.

"Patience, Bess," Lucinda reassured her. "Don't you see he is going to lead me straight to Henry?"

"I thought you knew where Henry lived—"Bessie began.

"Bess. *I* don't know my way in London. Do you?"

"No, but—well, a duel! How could you..."

"There will not be a duel," said Lucinda firmly, "if I can get to Henry first, somehow."

It was a rather big if, but she put that from her mind, and concentrated instead on what she would say to Henry when he opened the door and saw her standing there.

After an interval of about an hour, in which the valet had served the ladies a repast of cold meats and dumplings, bought from a street vendor since a cook had not yet been hired, they heard Robert stomping in the hall.

"Where are you going, my lord?" Lucinda asked, peeking around the door. He was fussing with his broad-brimmed hat, stooping in order to see himself in a speckled looking glass. A rapier stuck out ostentatiously from beneath his tight salmon coat.

"Out," he said brusquely. He was still looking a little pale, but managed a wan smile. "Has Klepton seen to your needs?"

"Yes, very well, very well indeed, thank you very much," simpered Lucinda. "Well —fare well, my lord," she added lamely. "God be with you."

"Adieu," he muttered, tugging at his cravat.

Closing the drawing room doors carefully behind her back, she whispered to Bessie, "Stay here. I am going to follow him."

"No, lamb!" exclaimed Bessie. "Over my dead body! You are *not* going out alone in this wicked place!"

"I must, Bessie!" she pleaded. "Don't you see? Robert will show me the way to Captain Beaupree's whereabouts."

"No. Stay. I'll go. York Buildings, wasn't it? I can ask people in the street to direct me."

"But London's such a big place, Bessie!"

"I am not afraid for myself, only for you, lamb."

"But it won't do for you to go, don't you see? Robert is going to challenge him to a duel! How are *you* going to stop them? Only *I* can do that! I must!"

This argument threw Bessie for a loop, and before she could think of another good reason why Lucinda should not go, they heard the front door slam shut.

"Stay here!" Lucinda said in as bossy a voice as Bessie had ever heard from her. Grabbing Bessie's large rough shawl from the table, she darted out of the room.

"Lamb! Oh, Lord!" exclaimed Bessie, puffing and panting in her impotence.

"How do I look?" Lucinda stuck her head around the door one last time. Bessie's shawl was now pulled up over her head like a hood. "Don't worry! No one will recognize me!"

By the time Bessie had heaved herself from her chair, the girl was gone.

31

THE QUALITY OF MERCY

Klepton had stepped outside with his master to call a carriage, and so Lucinda was able to slip out without being noticed. She hid inside a portal, waited until the hackney rattled out of the courtyard, then ran after it.

The carriage turned right and, conveniently, was immediately caught in one of the endless traffic jams London was famous for. Lucinda, strolling along at a reasonable pace, was able to keep it in sight.

Ughh! She looked down at her feet. She had just stepped into an enormous mud puddle. Except that it wasn't mud, it was dung. She had noticed that the other women walking in the street were tottering on wooden platform-shoes, and now she saw why. It was lucky Bessie had insisted she keep her beaded slippers in her pocket. She pulled the hem of her skirts a notch higher—to hell with decency!—and gallantly struggled on.

The carriage turned left into another busy street, and Lucinda suddenly realized she had better memorize some landmarks, in case she had to find her own way back to Bessie. She looked up, and saw an enormous sign hanging over her head. *Russell Street Mercers*, it said.

The carriage turned another corner, and halted. Lucinda stopped too, pretending to be interested in a fruit-seller's wares. She saw Robert getting out of the carriage and climbing some stairs to an establishment. It did not look like a residence. It did not seem to be a residential street—not for gentlefolk, at any rate. She was disappointed. Was this where Henry lived? She started forward.

"Heyyy! Ow, Miss! As touches me oranges, buys em! Fair as square!" The fruit-seller had caught her by the hem of her apron, and was yanking her backward.

"I'm sorry..." she stammered. "I haven't any money..."

"Nohw money? Nauhww *money* ?" he bellowed. Some passers-by slowed down and looked at the object of his wrath with hostile curiosity. "And it touches my wares, an' no money in's pockets? I'll teach you a lesson, jade, wench...bitch!"

In a panic, Lucinda fumbled behind her back, and ran across the street, leaving the open-mouthed fruit-seller holding Bessie's apron.

When she had determined that the man was not coming after her—he was fingering the calico to see if it was worth anything—she cautiously approached the establishment Robert had entered. She tiptoed up the steps.

"Sorry, Miss," said a doorkeeper, "Ladies not allowed, you know."

"Oh, I was just—" she fluttered, "just looking for someone."

"This is a coffee-house, my dear," he said kindly. "No ladies in here." He winked. "Nor maids, nor wives, nor widows neither."

"I see," she said. "I'll just wait, for him then."

"You may wait down there," he said graciously, pointing to the area beside the steps that led to a basement door.

"Thank you *so* much," she said.

She secured the shawl around her head and shoulders, and, leaning against the wall, examined her shoes. They were ruined. She tried scraping off some of the dung on the side of the building. God bless Bessie, who had made her take off the glass-beaded slippers before setting out on her adventure! The slippers were in her pocket, and when she arrived at Henry's house, she would kick off these disgusting clogs and slip them on...She patted the pocket containing the slippers. And realized they weren't there—

Fool! Fool! The slippers were in the pocket of Bessie's apron! Panicked, she charged back across the street. The fruit vendor was very much surprised to see her. He put on a hurt, defensive pout.

She gritted her teeth. "Sir, please!" she begged. "I *must* have my apron back, please may I have it?"

He turned around to spit discreetly, then spun back with a sheepish grin. "Oh, I cannat do that. I promised it to the wife. I cannat disappoint her, you know. It's mine now. You left it here, di-inn't you?"

"Here!" she said, and, bending over, pulled her petticoat down from beneath her top skirt, revealing the lace that had been hidden. "It's real Brussels. She'll like it much better. It's worth much more than the apron." She started tearing at the lace.

"Heyy, not so fast! Let's examine the mer-chi-andaiys first," he leered, and made a grab at her legs under her skirt.

She sprang back and shot him her severest expression. "Sir!" she scowled. "It is my final offer. The lace or the calico. Take your pick."

"The lai-ice, I s'pose," he grinned, and watched, humming lewdly, his head almost between his knees, as she completed the operation of ripping the lace off the hem of the petticoat.

Her face burning, both with embarrassment and with the physical effort (she had to crouch down in order to prevent the hawker and the gawkers who had gathered from catching a glimpse of her legs), she finally stood up. "Now give me the apron," she said sternly.

With a laugh, he held it above his head. "The lai-ice, first," he teased.

"On the count of three," she compromised.

To her great relief, the exchange was made without further mishap.

"Heeyyh! Look what I got!" he crowed to his mates across the street, waving the lace over his head, "Laiydee dun giv' me a pre-sent! In-nn't she *naiice* !"

Back at her post under the coffee-house steps, she found that she was trembling with rage and humiliation. But at least she had her slippers back.

"Lamb! What's happened to you! You look a sight!"

"No time to explain now—Robert's on his way. I ran—" she paused to catch her breath "— all the way, so he wouldn't find me gone."

"Here, give me those!" Bessie took the telltale muddy shoes and hid them under a table, while Lucinda put on her slippers and re-tied her apron neatly. Bessie tried to smooth her pet's wind-tousled hair. They heard the front door open, and his lordship bellowing for his valet.

Moments later he appeared in the drawing room. Lucinda had composed herself somewhat, although her cheeks were still flushed.

Robert raised an eyebrow.

"Ready for supper yet, ladies?" he asked. "I am ravenous!"

The ladies said nothing. They were confused by his good spirits.

"I have something I must attend to," he said. "Back in a trice."

"My lord!" exclaimed Lucinda.

"Yes, coz?"

"I...I am happy to see you back so soon, and—looking so well," she said lamely.

"Of course I am well!" He grinned. "Should I not be?"

"Of course you should!" But when he was at the door, she blurted, "Did you find him in?"

"Who, pray?"

"You know."

"If it's that *cad* Beaupree you mean, I can inform you that he will have to answer to me eventually."

"Oh?"

"But the knave's gone, don't you know."

"Gone?" repeated Lucinda, open-mouthed.

"Flown the coop. Back to his regiment. In France."

"Gone! Really!" exclaimed Bessie, tut-tutting in a relieved sort of way.

"*Really*," he echoed. "But it was to be expected, of a person of his breeding. It takes a *noble* man to stand and face the consequences."

"How—do you know?" It came out as a whisper.

"My dear girl. It's all over town. They've all gone—the Duke of Monmouth, Arlington, Villiers, the Marquis of Huntly, my Lord Rockingham's sons, Churchill. They say the King of France is preparing to lead his army against the Dutch. In person! I suppose they are all hoping to curry favor with him. It seems,"— he dabbed at his nose in exaggerated amusement—"it seems Sarah's suitor arrived here, found everyone gone, and took off after them in haste. Worried he might be missing out on some of the glory. Poor devil. Ha! Ha, ha, ha, ha!"

Lucinda found it hard to look sincerely amused.

"Well then. I shall tell Klepton to prepare a feast." He rubbed his hands. Turning to Bessie, he said sternly, "*You*, mistress, are henceforth to take your meals in the kitchen. And see to it that we are not disturbed."

He caught Lucinda's indignant glare and, blushing, backed out the door.

Lucinda and Bessie found lodgings that night in Clerkenwell, on the other side of London Bridge. By the time they arrived at the inn, they were exhausted and cross, and their clothes and footwear were spattered with filth. Bessie was trying to scrub the worst of it off, tsk-tsking about the loss of Lucinda's lace.

"We *are* going to France," Lucinda said stubbornly for the fifth time.

"No, pet! The journey! Think of it! We might drown at sea, or be stolen by pirates, or set upon by Frenchmen, or..."

Lucinda couldn't help giggling. The image of Bessie set upon by Frenchmen struck her as very funny. She couldn't help herself. The giggles turned into tearful, uncontrollable laughter. It was infectious, and Bessie had to laugh too. Soon they were both rolling around the narrow little room, gasping for air.

Other images came to mind that had not seemed funny at the time, but now struck them as hilarious.

"His lordship!" Lucinda shrieked, "and his rapier!"

"Oh, cruel, cruel!" gasped Bessie, "You wicked girl, he all but soiled his breeches!"

"He may well have, for all we know!" Lucinda choked.

"I wonder if he's enjoying his 'feast'..." Bessie snorted, for the tears were rolling down her cheeks and irrigating her nose.

"Yes, I hope he enjoys his feast," screeched Lucinda, "and his lodgings, and his valet, and his coffee-house, and his tavern, and his shops, and his tailor." She was holding on to the bedpost, her belly sore with laughter. "The only thing missing is his harlot; the concubine his lordship had picked out was no good. Flown the *coop*, don't you know." Her last sentence came out as a whoop.

"Lord!" panted Bessie, recovering. "Lord!" She gave a few last gasps. Then, disappointingly, she composed herself. She started shaking her head in an all-too-familiar way, and Lucinda, who was still laughing, but less energetically now, braced herself for what was coming. "Poor Lord Hempstead. Poor, poor boy. I can't help feeling sorry for him. And us running out on him like that, without so much as a by-your-leave. We are wicked to make fun of him. He can't help it."

Given Bessie's sudden change of heart, it was impossible for Lucinda to keep laughing. She too turned sober. Stone cold.

She let herself fall spread-eagled on the bed. "*Sorry* for him," she mimicked, exasperated. "Good God, Bessie! That's what you always tell me, you're always telling me we have to feel *sorry* for people. That they can't help the way they are. But do they ever return the favor? They don't! They make you feel soiled! They are mean! They are disgusting! They are...cruel!"

"Yes, dear, but we can..." Bessie began.

Lucinda slapped angrily at the ripped hem of her petticoat, which was hanging over a bedpost to dry. "Why should it be *our* responsibility to be nice, to be forgiving, to feel sorry for them, to see things their way? I'm sick and tired of it! I should like to be *mean* for a change!"

Bessie, who had totally forgotten the impulse that had made her spit at Robert Fetshank in Bitterbury, shook her head earnestly. "Christ the Lord, my lamb, teaches us to forgive, to be merciful—" she intoned.

"Oh, Bessie!" groaned Lucinda, "don't start! Please don't start on that!" And to forestall a long and boring sermon, she pulled the covers up over her head and then stuffed her head under a pillow for good measure.

PART TWO

32

THE KING'S NEW CLOTHES

The year was 1673. The place was Courtrai, in French Flanders, where a magnificent army was drawn up awaiting the much de-layed arrival of the king.

The king in this case was "le roi" if you were French, or "the French king" if you were English; to his contemporaries, there was no need for further identification. But in the history books he is identified as Louis the Fourteenth—not to be confused with Louis the Sixteenth, who was to be guillotined a century later. This Louis was the Sun King, builder of Versailles—the most magnificent, the most pompous, and arguably the most outrageous monarch ever to rule France. He was said to have paraded around his palace naked as the day he was born, on the pretense that he was wearing breeches of a special fabric that could be detected only by those who truly loved their king. There exists only one eyewitness account of this incident, in the memoirs of the Danish ambassador, but—what a story! Is this not characteristic behavior from a monarch who also made his top sycophants vie for the privilege of attending him as he defecated on that other throne? Do we need more proof that the man was not only a narcissistic show-off, but a sick exhibitionist as well?

The king had announced his intention of leading the upcoming mili-tary campaign against the Dutch Republic in person. He deemed it necessary to teach these ingrates, these republican peasants, a lesson. But now the army was twiddling its thumbs, with the king still held up at Tournai. He had set up a court there for the queen and two of his mistresses, and had gallantly sworn not to leave the ladies' side until Mme de Montespan, who was near the end of her term, was delivered of the royal bastard.

John Prynce, regimental chirurgeon to the Royal English, grumbled to himself about the utter idiocy of this plan, the daftness of an entire army awaiting a woman's pains, giving the Dutch all the time in the world to prepare themselves for the impending attack. What kind of a monarch was this, to bring his women so close to the theater of war? An *English* king would never dream of doing such a thing. Louis wanted to show off to his womenfolk, of course, but didn't anyone have the guts to tell His Royal Highness that this was not a *game*?

Lieutenant Prynce had just finished bandaging a foot soldier's festering blisters, and was on his way to one of the canteens, run by an Italian sutler named Marino, to inspect the latter's field kitchen. This was not ordinarily a task that fell within the surgeon's jurisdiction, but a number of English soldiers had come to him within the past two days with nausea and the flux, and the one thing they had in common was that they had all eaten at Marino's. He had made the usual report to the *Intendant*, but since that was unlikely to produce any result, and since he had nothing better to do, he decided to take on Marino himself.

He crossed the narrow creek that separated the orderly rows of army tents from the chaos of the camp followers' encampment: carts and wagons drawn up every which way, laundry hanging out to dry, women kneading dough and chopping vegetables, barking dogs, hawkers waving merchandise about, children playing outside closed-up tents, groups of soldiers drinking ale and playing cards. There was a game of skittles going on here; a cockfight over there. A provocatively dressed and powdered woman leaned down out of a wagon and brushed John's head with her scented shawl.

"*J'vous plais?*" she moaned, huskily. "I please you?"

He slapped the shawl out of his face, but could not suppress a grin at her pretty pout. "*Madame me fait fort plaisir,*" he said smoothly. It was true, she was a looker. Riddled with the clap, most likely. He did not stop.

Ah, there was Marino's. Marino's operation consisted of a flat cart that functioned as a table, several barrels of ale stacked up behind it, and two women cooking over an open fire. His was one of the more popular canteens, especially with the English. This was because the voluble Marino spoke a few words of their language.

"Ah! Eenglesich *Dottore* !" he now called out to the surgeon, "Eenglesich! Comma here! *Guarda!* Da Eenglesiche *donne* !"

Lieutenant Prynce saw that Marino had his arms draped around two shabbily dressed women. They shrank from him; the Italian's enthusiastic stranglehold did not sit well with them, apparently

"What is it, Marino?" Prynce said sternly. "*Assez!* Enough, let go of them!"

"Eesa Eenglesich, *Signore Dottore*," fawned Marino, bowing low. "A lookeeng a fora da Eenglesiche offeecers..."

The younger woman walked briskly over to him. "Sir," she began. "I wonder if you could help us..."

Prynce, for a moment, was stunned. Had they met? Something in her manner reminded him of someone. Perhaps it was the voice—

"We have just arrived from England. I am here to meet my betrothed..."

He shook himself. Nonsense—when was he going to learn not to fall for their little tricks? He smiled sarcastically. "Betrothed, eh? Got yourself knocked up, eh?"

"Sir!" gasped the girl. It was a fair imitation of ladylike sensitivity, offended.

"Yes, sir!" exclaimed the older one, "I mean, no, no, no, no! You've got it all wrong. We're not..."

"Marino," said Prynce coolly to the Italian, who had turned to go. "A moment, my man. I desire a word with you." He turned back to the fluttering women. It was his duty to tell them what was on his mind. But he felt uncomfortable looking into the younger one's eyes, and consequently found himself brusquely addressing her companion. "I wish you ladies good luck in your enterprise. I am sure that you'll do well here, our men are sorely starved for English females. But it was still very foolish of you to come, a very foolhardy thing to do. I hope you understand the risk. This is no place for women. You could get yourselves killed. This is war, you know."

"But we—" the older one began.

"I am sorry. *I* cannot help you. *I* do not get involved with that sort of thing. Find yourselves another pimp."

That shut them up. They both shrank from him, looking passably outraged, and as he sauntered after Marino, he could not help reflecting with amusement that here was a pair unlikely to have any trouble conning some poor English soldier—or an officer, why not?—into providing them with food, ale, and a base of operations.

"But *why* can't we cross?" cried Lucinda. She was fighting back tears. "We have had a horrible journey to get here, and we MUST see Captain Beaupree! He is expecting us!"

"Expecting you, ma'am?" twinkled the English corporal, who had been fetched by his French colleague and was now blocking their way into the military sector. "I don't think so, no. Not the captain. He never said nothing to me about no ladies."

"But that is because he doesn't know...!" Lucinda stammered. "Please believe me! If he knew I was standing here, he would..."

"Rules is rules, you see, Miss. And rules is, no unaccompanied ladies in the camp. Else what would this place look like? It would be overrun, a giant brothel, wouldn't it, ladies. I don't make the rules, you know; I don't even *like* the rules. But what our officers like, what the duke likes, what the French king likes, is discipline. We can't have people like you just coming here any time of day or night, see, flouting the rules as you please."

"I understand," Lucinda pleaded. "Please. I do not wish to make trouble for you. But if you could just..."

"See here, sir," Bessie broke in. She had fished a piece of silver out of the pouch that was tied beneath her petticoat, and brandished it under his mustachio. "This is for you. If you would let the gentleman, er, the captain, know that his lady is here..."

"Well!" puffed the corporal, "Well, well! *His lady*, eh?" He stole another doubtful look at Lucinda. "I'll see what I can do." He pocketed the écu discreetly, then turned to the French guard. *"Veillez à c'qu'elles ne bougent pas,* make them stay here,"* he instructed, and leapt nimbly back across the creek.

"Lucinda!" Lucinda shouted after him, "Lucinda! That's my name! Sir Edmund Nayerdell's niece, from Dorset!" Then she caught herself, and snapped, *"What*, Bess?"

Her defiance did nothing to dispel the anxious look of sudden comprehension on Bessie's dust-streaked face.

33

LOVE IS

"I'm sure we'll be very comfortable here," said Lucinda brightly the next morning. She was looking around the tent procured for them by the captain's adjutant. There was a tin bucket, some fresh straw for their pallets, and a pile of neatly folded horse blankets embroidered with Henry's crest. They had not been touched. She had found Bessie seated stiffly on the hard floor, her back against one of the tent poles. She didn't look as if she had slept.

"Mmm," came the noncommittal reply.

"Henry said, anything we need, we can ask Cornet Stickling. Is there anything?"

"Not that I can think of."

In the ensuing silence, Lucinda stretched demonstratively. She yawned. She swung her arms around, first in one direction, then the other.

Finally she pouted, "Oh Bessie, don't look so glum! Aren't you happy for me? You should be happy for me."

"Of course I am happy, pet."

"Oh. Good!"

"I'm happy if *you* are happy."

"And so I am! I am!"

"Well, that's good, then."

To give herself something to do while Bessie came up with a positive way to express her negative emotions, Lucinda knelt down and started unfolding the blankets, inspecting them for lice.

"Pet," Bessie began at last.

"Yes, Bessie."

There was another pause.

"I know you *think* you are happy. And Lord knows that is what I want for you, above all else in the world, lamb. But I wish..."

"What?"

"I wish—I only wish you had been a little more honest with me."

"What should I have told you?" Lucinda sat back on her haunches and put her hands on her hips defensively. "That the captain did not actually tell me, in so many words, that I should come after him? But I had to, don't you see? If I hadn't, you *know* you'd never have let me come!"

Bessie was shaking her head.

"I'd have come anyway, Bess, I just would have—I just would have come without you."

This threat gave Bessie pause. "Well, lamb," she said, grudgingly. "I'm glad you did not go without me."

"Oh, Bessie! You know I would never leave you!" Lucinda put her arms around her from behind, and squeezed. She was hoping that would be the end of it. But Bessie did not return the hug.

"The reason I am glad that I came is that *you* seem to have so little..."

"So little *what*?"

"Sense."

"Oh, Bess! Can't you see how happy I am?"

"Pet, I don't think you have the sense to see that Captain Beaupree really might not be quite as..."

"You mean because he seemed surprised to see me here? Well, that was only because..."

"Surprised? Yes, and—well, pet, not particularly pleased."

"But you don't understand! As a matter of fact he *was* pleased—later, in his tent, I mean. After he got over the surprise. I mean, that's why he laughed so. It was only because he was so surprised to see me here. If only I could make you understand how..."

"I do understand, lamb. I understand very well. You needn't describe it to me," Bessie said quickly. Then she let out a deep breath. "But you are so young! There is so much for you to learn!"

"What, for instance?" said Lucinda, with a certain amount of belligerence.

"About men, for instance."

"Oh please, Bessie, don't start."

"I mean—you are convinced that he loves you, don't you, because of—what you two did last night, in his tent…"

Lucinda blushed, and looked down at her hands.

"But has he acted like a gentleman? Has he proposed marriage? Has he—respected your virtue?"

"…"

"I didn't think so. No, you see, pet, gentlemen don't usually behave like gentlemen with the women they…why, the women who want them, who run after them, who make it easy for them."

"But Bessie! This is different! You don't understand!"

"Yes, pet."

"No, really, this really is different! I know it is!"

"Every woman who has ever been in love thinks that, lamb."

"But it is! It is!" Her voice rang out a little too loudly with jubilant conviction. "Because I am going to *make* him love me, don't you see? I can make him, I *know* that I can!"

"Pet," said Bessie, getting to her feet. "Pet. Listen to me. Love is not made. You know that? You cannot *make* love. Love—is. It just *is.*"

"That's what *you* think. But I know better. Just watch me!" Lucinda cried.

But it came out as a rather half-hearted crow, an anticlimactic cheer.

Their tent was located on the outer ring of the baggage train. Bessie and Lucinda had expected to find only men here, and were surprised to find hundreds of women in their sector. Most of the women made no bones about their calling. Their petticoats were red; their cheeks were rouged. Their nipples were rouged too: you could tell because their breasts often spilled over the tops of their fashionably pinched bodices.

There was another category of woman as well, more soberly dressed. They were the businesswomen—sutlers who ran some of the canteens; dungwomen who shoveled manure; laundresses who fought over the privilege of washing the officers' linens; and gypsies who made fortunes telling nervous soldiers they were born under a lucky star. And then of course there were the faithful soldiers' wives, to whom the prospects of mud, rape and death were less fearful than the perils of staying home alone.

Bessie decided she had to make it clear that she did not belong to the first category of camp follower. "I think I'll have to take up laundering or some such occupation," she sighed to Lucinda the next day, "else they'll take me for a bawd, as that unpleasant English officer did when we arrived. I do have to find a way to make some money, there's not much left, that wicked, wicked ship's captain charging us twice what we'd agreed in Dover, and not letting us off the boat until I'd paid..."

"You could cook, Bess!" suggested Lucinda. "Cooks make a fortune here."

"Where would I get the provisions, lamb?" said Bessie. "From what I can see, these sutlers survive by stealing pullets and hogs, and pulling up cabbages in the dead of night. That's not for me, pet. I just couldn't. These poor people—is it not enough that they have their fields trampled into mud, their crops ruined, their hay and grain confiscated..."

"True," said Lucinda. "It is a shame."

"But," Bessie went on suddenly, "what I *could* do, lamb, is sell my salves. I can gather my herbs and roots in the wild, and I am sure the soldiers will need healing..."

"What a *super* idea!" said Lucinda, suppressing a yawn. Because she really had not been getting much sleep these past two days, and even though she was concerned for Bessie, she could not help feeling smug about the fact that she herself had nothing to worry about. As the captain's woman, she had a legitimate position here.

The captain. She let out a contented sigh. His men adored him—he had a company of five hundred men who had sworn to lay down their lives for him. And he was so dashing! His legs were legendary in the Regiment. He had pretty, velvet lips and a fine, narrow nose. But the lower half of his face was seductively shaded with stubble, his eyebrows were bushy enough to be called manly, and he had a lopsided grin that was quite irresistible. Every woman who laid eyes on him desired him— Aunt Margaret, Sarah, possibly even Aunt Clarissa; and now she saw that it was the same among the women in this camp. She had already caught a few envious glances. What wouldn't the other women give to be in her shoes! And they were for the most part older than Lucinda too, and dressed in dazzling garments. But it was Lucinda, Lucinda who had won him! He could not get enough of her, he said. He kept comparing her to the French harlots, and saying what a breath of fresh air she was. His English primrose, he called her. He boasted about her to the other officers. He paraded her before them, and whispered nonsense in her ear just to make them jealous. He had made a great show of retiring to his tent with her. Oh, she was in heaven!

"That really is a super idea, Bessie," she repeated, patting her chafed cheeks and lips with the back of her hand.

Bessie looked more cheerful than she had in days. "I'll have to see about finding some sort of kettle, and a pestle and mortar."

"And I can help you gathering herbs."

"You will, lamb?"

"I will. At least, until the captain sends for me."

"So! I see that you have taken up with that little English harlot, Captain," John Prynce casually said to Henry Beaupree that evening. The officers of the English contingent were hanging around outside the Duke of Monmouth's tent, waiting to be briefed.

"Ha! The little English piece. Yes indeed I have," laughed Henry. "Only you know, my dear fellow, she's not really a *harlot*."

"No?" said John.

Henry made a wry face. "She's a *lady*, don't you know. Met her on a hunting party in the country. She threw herself at me. She's a runaway; followed me all the way here. What could I do?"

"You could have sent her back," said John mildly.

"Ah no, old fellow! She is wild about me! Absolutely besotted! Besides, she has nowhere to go. A poor relation, don't you know. And despoiled. Seems her guardian had already enjoyed her. Well, there it is, she prefers me, and now she's here. I truly have no control over the situation."

"That's exactly what ails you, man," interrupted Edmund Mayne, a lieutenant-captain in Henry's regiment. "No control, no control at all."

"Sirrah!" exclaimed Henry, jumping to his feet and unsheathing his sword with a flourish. "Watch your tongue!" He swished his sword back and forth under Mayne's chin. Mayne leaned back, laughing.

"Let me know when you're finished with her," he winked. "I don't mind used goods myself."

"Sirrah!" Henry threatened again, waving his sword in the air. Mayne grabbed Captain John Churchill, who was standing next to him, to use him as his shield.

"Nay, spare me, sir, I beg you!" he mocked.

"Aargh...enough of your childish pranks!" Churchill irritably shook himself loose. He was approximately the same age as Mayne and Beaupree, but cultivated an air of gravity.

"Hullo, Churchill," clucked Henry. "What's the matter? Can I help it if the lady in question doesn't fancy *you*?"

"You know I have no time for your nonsense," said Churchill primly, "womanizing and playing the infatuated fool, when there is work to be done."

"Ha!" exclaimed Henry. "Work—is that what you call it? Is that what you do? I call it toadying, sir!"

"Explain your meaning, sir!"

"Did we ever see you playing the ranterish prig at Whitehall? I seem to recall you weren't above playing the infatuated fool when the Duchess of Cleveland called you to her bed! And now, suddenly, you're the model of restraint, aren't you, pure as snow! Pah! You think of nothing but your own preferment!"

The two men glared at each other. There was a dangerous silence.

John Prynce coughed. "No, but Beaupree," he intervened, returning to the earlier subject. "Do you really think it was the honorable thing to do—to encourage a young lady of good family..."

"A young *la*-dy of good *fa-m*ily!" mimicked Henry, turning on him. He was now thoroughly irritated. "'S-truth, you have been living among these frogs for too long, my friend. Those Frenchified expressions of yours!"

"Frenchified? Who here is Frenchified, sirs?" inquired the Duke of Monmouth, their commander, who had just stepped out of his tent.

"Lord knows we have enough frogs in our midst." He drew an oversized handkerchief out of his coat sleeve and wafted it lazily in the air. "Do not forget we are here to wave the English flag, gentlemen! Else what will His Majesty our dear Papa say?" He pirouetted full circle, making sure all eyes were on him. "We cannot have any turncoats in our own ranks, sirs! No no! We'll rout the Frenchies out! We'll have 'em run the gantelope! We'll make them ride the wooden horse!"

"It was just Prynce here, sir," smirked Churchill, "our esteemed surgeon."

"Indeed," said Monmouth. He turned away, and shelved his little joke. If the man had been one of his favorites, he would have had some fun with him. But chirurgeons were beneath his notice, and this John Prynce was a strange rogue anyway. What was it Watson had told him about him again? That he had been a successful field officer in Portugal, and at Dunkirk. But for some reason the fellow had willingly given up his military command to serve as an amputator. Monmouth could not understand why any Englishman would give up the glory of battle for such a paltry post. Lost his nerve, probably. And unlike the other officers crowded around Monmouth, this Prynce was not exactly what you would call a courtier. Indeed, he had remained here in Courtrai all through the winter, with the troops, while Monmouth and his braves regaled their friends back in Whitehall with stories of the previous season's campaign. The only reason the man's presence was tolerated at all at these staff briefings was in deference to his lineage—he was a kinsman of that great wit, the Earl of Rochester—and to his past gallantry on the battlefield.

"Gentlemen! I have news!" he announced.

"An attack!" exclaimed Churchill, always the most eager.

"Not yet, sir!" smiled Monmouth. "Not yet. But it seems our uncle Louis is expected here forthwith. His mistress has had her whelp. We shall soon be on the march, gentlemen, *causa belli, iter bellicosum,* don't you know."

Despite all the fawning and scraping around him, the duke seemed to possess an endless need to reaffirm his royal connections, which only served to remind everyone that he was the English king's illegitimate son.

"When, sir?" asked Beaupree.

"Ah, that I cannot tell you yet," said Monmouth. He turned to his most senior officers. "Sir Thomas. My Lord Duras," he ordered. "Sir Harry. You too, Vernon. Please be so good as to step inside."

John leaned back against a tree-stump, aware of the sudden silence. For the other junior officers had gone quiet, struggling, as he knew they must, with the conflicting emotions of excited anticipation and unexpected dread.

34

THE MARCH

The entire army was on the move, a rolling river of lurching humanity, and Bessie and Lucinda two tiny drops in its wake.

Most of the cavalry, with the king and his entourage, had gone on ahead. The infantry (well drilled by Captain Martinet, who had lost his life in the previous summer's campaign but whose influence was still felt) proceeded at an orderly pace, six abreast. Next came the big guns, some of them so heavy that they required eight horses apiece to draw them; the wagons with the ammunitions and stores; and then, pell-mell, the officers' carriages, the mules loaded with baggage, and the camp-followers with their carts and goats and mules. The entire army, stretched out like this, measured several miles from end to end. If the vanguard took a shortcut through a field, the soft brown earth was packed to granite ruts by the time the last carts had passed. With trampled crops, polluted ponds and ruined orchards in its wake, the army cut a swath of destruction through the gentle countryside like hungry moths in an angora pullover.

Cornet Stickling had negotiated a place for Bessie and Lucinda in one of the carriages. It was owned by a French officer, the Marquis de la Faience, and was packed with a portion of the marquis' campaign furnishings—a pair of silver candelabra, brocade hangings for his tent, a large polished-silver mirror, two casks of brandy and a rolled-up carpet. There were besides these several boxes and trunks lashed to the roof and onto the back, leaving very little room for passengers. But the two women were too grateful to mind the discomfort.

"Mind you, I could have gone on foot," said Lucinda, gazing out the window at the phalanx of women struggling with large bundles on their backs, some of them loaded down with infants as well, "but you'd never have kept up, Bess."

Bessie shook her head. "I'm glad we have the carriage, pet. Look at those poor souls. I would that we could help them. It's a wonder they put up with this. I wonder why they don't stay home."

"Profit. Or else survival," said Lucinda succinctly, and Bessie once again wondered how and where her lamb could have picked up so much unpleasant wisdom, so fast.

During the march, camp was an abbreviated affair. There was no time to erect tents or build huts, so the soldiers slept where they sank to the ground in exhaustion. There was no fraternizing now between troops and camp followers: a warning had been issued that any woman who came too close to the army proper whilst on the march would be drummed out of camp. Fires were kept to a minimum because of the munitions' proximity, and the ovens, which took six hours to assemble, were functional just twice a week. And so the troops had to make do with rations of rock-hard bread, whatever water or ale they could carry in their own canteens, and male companionship.

Bessie and Lucinda tried sleeping inside the carriage on the first night, but it was so cramped and uncomfortable that they decided to spend the following night outdoors, as did most of their traveling companions. As long as the competition for the soldiers' attentions and money was suspended, the baggage-train people were a much friendlier lot, enjoying the camaraderie that comes of being embarked on a communal adventure. Perfect strangers shared food and huddled close for warmth. Seated in circles around their allotted fires, the camp followers sang sad songs, told tall tales, traded gimcracks, puffed at their pipes, picked each other over for lice, and stared into the swelling-ebbing embers until their eyeballs stung.

Word had already got out that Bessie knew something of physic, and she dealt very kindly with the first requests for help, explaining as best she could (her French consisting of very loud English, slowly articulated and accompanied by flamboyant gestures) that she had not yet had the time to amass a stock of basic ingredients, but giving out comforting advice nonetheless.

Lucinda found herself gravitating toward the fanciest French whores. She sat down just outside their exclusive circle, craning her neck to see what they were up to, trying to overhear their conversation. The whores fascinated her: they were so glamorous, and seemed so self-assured. They showed their teeth when they laughed, and they often laughed raucously, or derisively. They lent each other powders and pomatums, tried on each other's patches, and showed off trinkets they had stolen or received as gifts.

Occasionally one of them would catch Lucinda's gaze, and look away coldly, or turn her back. There were whispers and cackles of laughter. Lucinda knew that she did not belong in their world, that she shouldn't even desire to belong there. They were harlots, after all, and she was a lady. And yet how she wished she could be a part of that seductive coterie, even if it was just as an observer...

There was one whore who intrigued her even more than the rest; she found herself staring furtively at her. Indeed, this woman attracted many stares. She was African, as brown as the freshly tilled soil. Lucinda had seen a blackamoor child once, the pet of a lady who had visited the manor years ago; but never before had she seen anything as exotic as this.

The African woman stood almost a head taller than the other women, and her voice was low, foreign and musical. Her dark skin made a startling contrast to the whites of her eyes and the brilliant round teeth she hid behind her pink palms when she laughed. It was the woman's extraordinary gait, however, that intrigued Lucinda most. She wished she could walk like that, so liltingly insolent, so alluringly untouchable. The woman kept her torso perfectly still, the shoulders back, the neck elongated. There was no bounce, no movement up and down; just a sideways sway, the hips and rump pivoting smoothly around the immobile waist. It was this beautiful bearing, this regal gliding, with the lowered eyelids and the pouting lower lip, Lucinda decided, that gave the impression of a supremely confident being, a woman who knew exactly where she was going...

"Stop!" she therefore shouted to their driver, "*Arrêtez!*" when they passed what was unmistakably the African woman huddled in a ditch, spattered with mud, her head hidden in her lap. It was the fourth day of the march, and the rain was beating down mercilessly on the sodden baggage train.

Lucinda jumped down from the carriage and knelt by the woman's cowering form. She began shaking her. "*Madame!*" she urged her. "*Madame!* You can't stay here! Get up! *Levez-vous! Levez-vous donc!*"

"Not so rough, pet!" said Bessie, who had climbed out of the carriage behind Lucinda. "She doesn't understand what you are saying, she's half dead, poor thing. Let's just lift her into the carriage. Here! Armand!" She gesticulated at the coachman. "Help! *Ici!* Come!"

Assisted by the reluctant Armand, they managed to drag the sick woman into the carriage.

"Look at her!" clucked Bessie, "She's as weak as a kitten. Give her a little breathing room. Help me untie her bundle, lamb."

"Bessie, look!" gasped Lucinda. The bundle tied to the woman's hip, in a sling, had given a little cry. Lucinda carefully peeled away the cloth, revealing a tiny curly head.

"A baby!" exclaimed Bessie. "Oh, my, what a precious little thing!"

"It's all right. *Nous ne vous voulons pas de mal*, we won't hurt you," Lucinda soothed the woman, who was struggling to grab the baby out of Bessie's arms. Her eyes were bloodshot and wild. The red-rimmed lower lids seemed turned inside out.

"Here. There's your baby. There. Isn't that better?" They looked on tenderly as the exhausted mother clutched the child to her chest.

"*Je vous en prie, mesdames!*" came Armand's voice through the window, "Please! *On ne peut pas rester ici, voyons!* We'll lose our place, *de dieu...*"

"Oh, Armand," chided Lucinda, "Don't fret! *Ne faites pas cette tête!* We're going, we're going!" She jumped down from the carriage, and slapped one of the horses on the rump. "*Alley-hop!*" To Bessie, she shouted, "I'll walk alongside, there's no room for all four of us in there."

That night, for the first time, Lucinda had a sense of belonging. The carriage was now surrounded by some of the very women who had given

Lucinda the cold shoulder before. It seemed almost as if they were glad of this opportunity to break the ice. They expressed concern for the sick Zéfine (for that was her name), and nodded appreciatively as Lucinda translated Bessie's diagnosis of their colleague's condition.

"Tell them we'll have her ride in our carriage until she is stronger," Bessie said. "A body has to rest after giving birth, that's all there is to it. She was simply spent. The fever will pass."

"Bess, they're asking, aren't you going to bleed her?" translated Lucinda.

"That won't be necessary," said Bessie firmly.

"But, they say, how can you expect her to get better if you don't rid her of the bad blood?"

"Tell them to trust me," Bessie sighed.

Lucinda turned back to her new friends, and suggested they leave the patient in Bessie's capable hands.

"If you need anything, Bessie, just wave. We're going to sit over there, by the campfire," she announced happily.

The French army marched brazenly into the heart of the Spanish Netherlands. No one, said Louis, could accuse him of being the first to break the Peace of Aix-la-Chapelle. Had not the Spanish governor done so, when in December he had ridden to the assistance of the Prince of Orange at the siege of Charleroi?

Following the river Schelde, the army soon came upon the city of Ghent, which girded itself for an attack. But the army did not slow down, and the citizens of Ghent breathed a sigh of relief as Louis marched his men on toward Brussels. Brussels anxiously mobilized its troops.

But Louis did not stop at Brussels either (except to taste the local sturgeon, which he pronounced superb), nor did he continue north, as expected, toward Breda. Instead, the army swept suddenly east, and before the Dutch realized what was happening, the French were encamped outside Maastricht, the well-defended fortress Louis had passed by the previous year as not worth the effort.

This time, he decided, it was indeed worth the effort. In fact, it was the perfect target—this southernmost outpost of that annoying little republic calling itself the United Provinces of the Netherlands. He sent Marshalls Turenne and Condé east, up the Rhine, to hold off the Austrians and the Swedes. Maastricht was to be the king's own triumph, a prize he refused, for once, to share with the generals who tended to hog the glory for themselves. Maastricht would be a feather—nay, a magnificent ostrich *plume*—in his cap, and it was just the sort of place where a siege could be staged as *théâtre*, with the court and the ladies watching their Louis play the role of conquering hero.

As soon as the surrounding countryside was swept clear of enemy troops, the French court duly arrived and established itself in the neighboring village of Kerkum, overlooking the encamped army, which was already at work digging trenches and building earthworks.

The common camp followers were allotted a field behind the encampment of the Duc d'Orléans, on the far side of the River Meuse. A temporary bridge was to be hauled into place to link the two banks; in the meantime, people were ferried across in boats.

Bessie had just finished giving directions to the soldier who had come to help her put up the tent when Lucinda came bounding in.

"Lamb! What in the world have you done to yourself!" Bessie exclaimed in horror.

"What, Bess? Don't you like it? Don't I look pretty?"

"Pretty! Lord! You look like a..."

"Oh Bess, stop it. You don't know anything about it. It's what the ladies of the court wear."

"I don't care how those French trollops dress! I will not have you looking like that! I won't have it! Take that indecent thing off at once! Where did you get that...that get-up?"

"Blanchette lent it to me. And the petticoat is Trude's. I think it's very nice of them. *I* like it!" Lucinda twirled around, at a safe distance from Bessie.

"And what is that on your face? Oh, lamb, you don't need paint! And that patch—really, it makes you..."

"I do need it! I have a pimple on my chin, that's why I have the patch. So that it won't show."

"Do you really think an ugly black patch looks better than a little blemish? Pet!"

"Please, Bess! I want to look special, for Henry!"

"Special? You look special, all right, lamb, but it's not..."

"Madam?" It was the helpful soldier, who had stuck his head around the tent flap. "Must be going now. My lady requested that I escort her to the officers' camp..."

"Coming!" exclaimed Lucinda, and tripped out after him, while all Bessie could do was slap her palms against her cheeks and shake her head from side to side.

Lucinda was back in the tent within an hour. Her eyes were red. Tears had left streaks in the thick white powder on her cheeks. She had ripped the patch off her chin, and the pimple had begun to bleed.

"He sent me away!" she wailed at the tut-tutting Bessie. "He said I must wait until he sends for me! That I have no business coming to his tent unless he sends for me!"

"Oh, but lamb..." Bessie began.

"You were right!" she sobbed, "He didn't like the way I looked. He was angry. He hated it. He hates me!"

"Now, now," Bessie crooned, rubbing her shoulder blades, "Calm down, pet, there's a dear. Don't cry. Just a lovers' tiff. You'll both have forgotten all about it tomorrow."

But Lucinda wasn't sure she would ever forget the coldness in Henry's eyes, the way he had barred the entrance to his tent, and the shadow of someone else moving about inside.

35

AMENDS

The second meeting between John Prynce and Bessie was more amicable than the first.

"Mistress—Goose?" inquired the surgeon, as he stepped into her tent.

"May I help you?" said she, equally polite. She recognized him: he was the unpleasant man who'd mistaken the two of them for a whore and bawd when they had first arrived. But she took in the hesitant tone of voice and the hat clasped courteously to the chest.

"Yes indeed," he said. He looked around the claustrophobic tent. To his disappointment, the younger woman wasn't there. He bowed. "John Prynce, chirurgeon to the Royal English, ma'am."

"Well now!" said Bessie. He had a fine look about him, this Mr. Prynce, she decided: weather-tanned skin under an indifferent peruke, but gentle, attentive, youthful eyes.

"Yes," he said. "Uh—"

"Yes?" said Bess.

"Well, it has come to my attention, ma'am, that..."

"One moment please, sir." Bessie held her hand up commandingly, and leaned forward, addressing someone behind her visitor's back. "Gunner Donnelly! Come in, dear!" To Prynce, she said, "Pray excuse me, sir. This will not take long."

"Of course!" muttered John, stepping back to make way for the interloper. It was one of Bessie's patients, a Yorkshire artilleryman.

He watched in silence as she deftly cut away a bandage and examined the wound, dabbed at it with something, and bound it up again. "There!" she beamed. "Soon you'll be right as rain, hale as hail, hearty as a hurricane."

The gunner stammered his thanks, and, standing up, bumped his head on a kettle hanging from the tent pole. Some spoons and other utensils hanging next to the swinging kettle clanged like a chorus of protesting bells. "Now then, look after yourself!" she clucked, ushering him out, "We can't keep binding you up, can we, we'll be running out of linen at this rate!"

They were alone again, and Bessie turned to her visitor. "Now, sir," she said formally, "how may I help you?"

"What did you use?" John countered her question with another.

"Use?"

"Just now. To dress the wound."

"Oh, just a little vinegar. And an egg."

"A chicken egg?"

"Any egg will do. Duck, goose, robin. The white only. It helps to close the wound, you see."

"I see."

"You can save the yolk for a pudding."

"Indeed."

"It's much kinder than burning," she said defensively.

"Madam, I am no advocate of cauterization," he said.

"Of course I am not a physician," Bessie admitted.

"So I understand."

"But I'll have naught to do with witchcraft, either."

"I did not..."

She squared her shoulders. "All my remedies are simple common sense, sir, cures I have found to work well. There's no magic in it at all."

"Of course not, I never..."

"I just find it simpler, sometimes, to act mysterious and let them think what they will."

"I see." He smiled. "You delude your patients into believing their cure comes from a higher authority."

Her hands went up to her throat in alarm. "Please—sir," she faltered, "I swear to you I mean no harm. I..."

"Harm! My dear lady, I did not come here to accuse you. Black magic, witchcraft, it's all nonsense, as far as I'm concerned."

"Oh," said Bessie uncertainly.

"Of course. Please believe me. No, madam, I am here merely to satisfy the curiosity your fame has roused in me."

"My fame?" asked Bessie.

"Yes indeed, ma'am. There are those who take great delight in informing me of your achievements. They say you cured Maréchal Poltron and some others of the fever, and I saw for myself that you did such an excellent job on the Welshman with the cannonball-wound that there was no need to amputate..."

"Sir!" exclaimed Bessie modestly. "It was the Lord's will, He..."

"I came here in person," John continued, "to extend my sincerest compliments. And to..." His gaze started wandering again, as if the pitch of the tent's roof and the spiders scurrying back and forth on the oilcloth were of the greatest interest, "...to say how much I regret my erstwhile gross error regarding yourself and the other lady."

"Oh, that!" exclaimed Bessie generously. "That was nothing, really. Please think nothing of it, sir!"

"No, no, I wish to make amends."

"It really is not necessary."

"To yourself and, well, the other lady."

Bessie could not help dimpling with pleasure. She laid a hand on the surgeon's arm. "Please, sir, consider it done."

"Well, all right, but..."

"I assure you."

Reluctantly he backed toward the tent flap. There he hesitated again.

"Not to worry, I will tell her of your visit and your sentiment."

"Excellent," he said, and bowed. Then turned and strode back toward the river.

"Up! Come on, madam," barked Henry, "Out! That's enough, out you go, up and away."

Lucinda sat up and looked around, her face creased with lingering sleep, her hair disheveled. The tent was dark. "But it isn't even morning yet!" she complained.

"That is so," said Henry, grunting as he squeezed himself into his breeches. "But it is not too early for the king. He has announced his intent to inspect the siege works every morning. At daybreak. And my Lord Monmouth at his side, of course. It won't do not to be there."

"But," said Lucinda, rolling off the field bed and hurriedly dressing herself, "you said if there was a chance to see the king, you would let me come. Please? You promised!"

"Certainly not."

"But you did, you promised!"

"Did I?"

"Remember? I swore I wouldn't run over here unless I was sent for, and in return you promised that you..."

"I may have done," he said, holding out his arms for her to pin his ribbons on his sleeve. "But not the trenches."

"A promise is a promise! And besides, I know the ladies of the court are permitted to come and look. Didn't you hear that Mme de Fripon and that other lady, Countess Tabeauparler, went yesterday, and were almost fired upon?"

"That is exactly why women should not be allowed. They attract too much attention."

"I won't attract attention! I'm sensible enough not to wave a parasol about! And I'm not afraid, as long as I am with you."

"All right then," he said, to shut her up. "But just this once!"

"Just this once, Henry," she promised happily, untangling her shawl. She congratulated herself on her wiles, her ability to sway him. Everything was fine between them again, as Bessie had predicted. There had been four nighttime encounters in a row, and the captain had been appreciative.

Henry glanced at her. "But Gad, you are a sorry sight, wench," he sighed. "You can't come with me looking like that."

"Just give me a moment," she said, and, without bothering with a comb or mirror, pulled the matted hair back into a coil at the nape of her neck, stuffing it into a net she withdrew from her pocket. "That better?" she asked, sticking some hairpins into the pile.

Henry could not suppress a grin. The woolly strands escaping all about her head gave her a wanton look. The others would have no doubt about what Henry had been up to. He patted her on the rump.

"Out, out you go, then," he said, indulgently holding the tent flap open for her.

Sébastien de Vauban, King Louis' master tactician, the engineer upon whose expertise the entire siege hinged, was pacing nervously up and down inside the first parallel—the main trench closest to the French camp, which was to serve as supply avenue to the trenches zigzagging toward the citadel proper. Maastricht's fortifications presented a formidable challenge to the besieging force: five hornworks, a moat, and a great number of demi-lunes protecting the city walls. The fortress was manned by six thousand enemy troops.

Vauban's sappers—the men who did most of the digging—were drawn up in formation in anticipation of the king's arrival. They had been waiting for an hour and a half, and there was still no sign of His Majesty. Anxiously Vauban made some quick calculations in his head, altering some numbers and modifying the schedule for completion he was to present to the king. Every minute spent waiting was a minute wasted. He wadded his hands into fists, but discreetly, and smiled at the generals who had formed a circle around him.

"Vauban! My man!" It was the English duke—Monmouth, the English king's bastard son, the one Louis had put in command of the important Brussels Gate. A command of that size was usually reserved for more experienced favorites. Vauban hoped the king knew what he was doing. He bowed low—he had but a vague notion of this foreigner's position in the court hierarchy, but Vauban, lowly engineer that he was, found it safer to bow to any officer in this troop. Never had he seen a campaign with so many courtiers, such fops, such *minets,* such beribboned dukes and counts and princes! The place was swarming with them. It would be a miracle, a true miracle, if he managed to get the job done with so many amateurs getting in the way, countermanding orders, making nuisances of themselves. And they even brought their womenfolk! Yesterday a gaggle of court ladies had shown up in the trenches, causing a near-riot among his men. As luck would have it, the Dutch defenders had chosen that moment to show some mettle, and a couple of cannonballs had come harmlessly whizzing overhead. The ladies had not seen the need to prolong their adventure any longer, and had withdrawn all a-twitter over their narrow escape. What put Vauban in mind of this now was a very attractive young piece hovering in the background, behind the foreigners.

"Monsieur," he said, bowing his head to listen respectfully to the duke's questions about the width and positioning of the trenches in the area of the western *glacis*. He could not help stealing another glance at the little wench, however. She was not one of your court ladies, he could tell: she was not weighed down with the jewels and powders and wigs that made the others look like stuffed dolls. This one was more to his liking, a pretty, fresh little person, the kind a man could relate to.

Before he could answer the English duke's questions, however, there was a commotion: the king had finally arrived! Vauban scuttled back to his post, and spent the next twenty minutes mopping his brow, obsequiously defending his plans from a multi-pronged attack indiscriminately leveled at him by the top generals, whose incessant jockeying for position threatened to sabotage Vauban's entire operation.

"Well!" said the king at last. As soon as he opened his mouth, everyone else fell silent. "Very well, Vauban." The king pursed his thin upper lip in a semi-amused expression. There was a grateful response of pleased nods, expressions of agreement, and sighs of approval all around.

The monarch held up his hand. You could have heard a pin drop. He cleared his throat. "Well then. Very well. Continue, continue!" he said gravely, slapping the palm of his left hand with the buskin gloves in his right.

This was the signal for everyone to start bowing again, and soon the king was leading his retinue out of the clammy ditch.

When it was finally safe to straighten up, there was yet another interruption.

"Monsieur!" A red coat lined with yellow—one of the English officers. The fellow who had brought the young woman, he saw. "Henry

Beaupree, Monmouth's Regiment of Horse, at your service. May one have a moment of your time?"

"*Mais certainement,*" said Vauban. What else could he say? At least the fellow had the good sense to carry an honest French name, *Beaupré*. And the little baggage with him was certainly worth a closer look.

In his halting French, Henry began outlining a crafty plan he had dreamed up, of digging a false trench, a trench that led to nowhere, and luring the enemy into it, leaving the abandoned fort wide open to an assault. Vauban listened respectfully to this nonsense (he could barely understand this foreigner anyway, where did these people learn their French? This one's accent was *un scandale*), and when the Englishman was done, he nodded thoughtfully. "*Très intéressant,*" he said, "*Oui, oui, très intéressant,* very interesting, *tout à fait.*" Then he took him by the elbow and made him turn around so that his back was to the wench. "*Combien?*" he mouthed confidentially.

"*Combien?* How many?" repeated Henry, astounded that the great man should not only take the time to listen to his plan but, indeed, ask him what sort of manpower he would need to carry it out. Suppose Henry's plan was adopted by Vauban! He'd like to see the look on Churchill's face!

"*Pour la petite,*" Vauban said, nudging him, "The little one. How much?"

Startled, Henry looked over his shoulder at Lucinda, who was trying very hard not to let on that she could overhear this exchange.

"Ah!" he laughed. "The little one! No, I regret, Monsieur, but that one is not for sale."

Ah no, they never were, for Vauban. That's what stunk around here. The precious beribboned boys sucked up to him when they needed him, but did they ever come through for him when he needed something from them? Never. The thought of sharing a little morsel with someone like old Vauban made them puke into their scented handkerchiefs.

"*Bien. Bien!*" he exclaimed. He had already wasted so much time. "*Veuillez m'excuser...*"

He made Lucinda think of a crab as he scurried away sideways, his wig slapping at his cheeks, his face florid, one arm akimbo, his broad body bent double over the other arm, bowing in the fashion of the court.

36

SUCH TINY FEET

"*Ah, quels petits petons!* Such tiny little feet!"

Lucinda stared at the beaded slippers in her lap. She was sitting around the campfire with her new friends. Henry had not sent for her tonight. He had not sent for her the previous night either. Or the night before that. Her slippers had just been passed all around the circle, after Blanchette, who'd asked to borrow them, discovered they were too small for her feet, and challenged the others to try them on. There were clownish contortions and screams of laughter: no one else could get the slippers on.

"Just wait until you've had a couple of brats, my dear," sighed Geneviève Culelvaye, who was herself big with child. "It splays the feet."

"I met a Chinawoman, once," said Zéfine. "And she had the most precious little feet. It was so bad she couldn't walk normally, she could only hobble."

"They bind the feet," nodded Madame Bézée. "From the time they are very young. The Orientals, they spit on the woman with the big feet."

"It's fortunate, then, that we're not in China!" giggled Henriette. "Or none of us would have any customers, save Lucinda!"

"Henriette!" Zéfine admonished her. "You *know* Lucinda's officer is not a customer, he's her *lover*. She's a lady!"

"Not much of a lover, is he," sniffed Henriette, "keeping her waiting like this, with not a word..."

Lucinda hung her head.

Zéfine grabbed her hands and gave them a consoling squeeze, as a discussion began about Lucinda's predicament.

"Englishmen tire more easily, you know," said Blanchette wisely. "They have less endurance than our men. Your Frenchman, now, he'd just keep going, wouldn't he, he wouldn't even know he was tired. No he wouldn't. But your Englishman, he is smart, that one, he knows his limits, he knows he must save his strength for battle."

The others voiced their agreement.

"Well..." Lucinda defended her lover uncertainly, "It's not—I mean he always seems to have enough..."

"It's not at all unusual, *chérie*," clucked Mme Bézée, "for a man to conserve his powers on the eve of war."

"And the king keeps them all very busy, of course," said another. "Poor things."

Lucinda nodded, because she didn't want them to think she didn't share their compassion for the men and their silly war games. Secretly, however, she knew that Henry's silence was something different. It meant—it *had* to mean—that he was struggling with a weighty decision, a long-overdue declaration of true love.

Yes, as soon as it finally dawned on him that he was smitten, he would send for her, he would fall to his knees and beg her for forgiveness—nay, beg for her hand in marriage. And of course she would forgive him and say yes, although perhaps with a bit less alacrity than if it had taken him less time to get there; for she was starting to lose patience with him. She wished that he would conform a little more readily to the lover of her fantasies. All this recalcitrance was beginning to cool her own ardor somewhat.

She caught Henriette and Sabine—two of the highest-paid camp followers, who, although not fine enough to be considered courtesans, did count some courtiers among their clientele—exchanging a look. They were sisters, pouting bosom-buddies, and had a way of making you feel uneasy, shut out.

"*What*?" she said defiantly.

"Oh, nothing," they said. But in their faces you could read a thousand condolences.

Lieutenant Prynce paid Bessie another visit that week.

Bessie put her hands to her mouth, her eyes twinkling. "Sir, you have missed her again, I'm afraid. She is not here."

"Ah—you mean—the other lady..." he stammered.

"The lady. My mistress."

"Indeed, yes. But you are mistaken. It is *you* I came to see." He laughed, crushed that she should have spotted his disappointment.

"To see me?"

"Yes."

"Well!" said Bessie.

"I..."

She noticed that he had a habit of shutting his eyes a second before speaking, as one who stutters, although his speech was fluent enough. There was just enough hesitation to convey an earnestness, a desire to be sincere, that was rather endearing.

"I have a proposition to make to you, ma'am."

"A proposition!" Bessie repeated.

"Indeed." He looked around, and spotted a pile of folded blankets. He looked at her quizzically.

"Of course," said Bessie. "Please, sir. Sit down."

"Thank you. You see, it occurred to me that, since you seem to have some success in healing the sick and wounded—"

"I do," she said modestly.

"And I have made it my calling to do the same..."

His eyes strayed to a pile of neatly folded linens and lace. Next to it a basket of gay ribbons with a pair of embroidered slippers resting on top captured his attention.

Bessie coughed. He turned back to her guiltily. "I just thought—I was hoping, you see, that—"

"Yes?" said Bessie.

"That we might join forces. You and I."

"Oh!" Bessie exclaimed.

"If there is to be an assault, and it is my understanding that it is not far off, then we may expect a great number of casualties. And I thought, I could use your assistance..."

"Oh!" breathed Bessie again. She was flattered.

"The remuneration would not be great, of course, but I would see what I could do..."

"I know you would," she said quickly.

"Fine then!" said John, getting to his feet. "Then you agree?"

"Well..." said Bessie. She hesitated.

There was a silence. John sat down again uncertainly. "How might I persuade you?"

"I have one condition."

"Oh?"

"Yes. And I'm afraid...well, I'm afraid it may anger you."

"Madam. Please know how respectful I am of your ability. Do not be afraid of angering me."

"Well, sir, there are certain things I like to do *my* way. It's a little different from what you surgeons are used to."

"I am aware of that. That is precisely why I have come to you. I should like to learn from you."

"But then you'll...I fear I may be accused of satanic ways—"

"My dear lady! Of course not!" laughed John.

"If we are to work together, I will want to—well, do it my way, you see..."

John got up and squatted down before her. He was so close to her that she caught a whiff of his smell—a sober, candid odor of liniment, onions and blood. "That is what I wish, too. If your methods are better than mine, and I suspect that some of them may be, then I must be your pupil."

"Oh!" said Bessie, delighted. "Well, in that case, I agree."

37

OF FROGS AND ENGLISHMEN

Young women will sometimes go to any length to make their dreams come true. Take, for instance, the belief that if a fair damsel kisses a frog, hey presto, the frog will turn into a handsome prince. Who wouldn't want to give it a whirl? Many are tempted to try it—surreptitiously, of course, just as an experiment.

Before you go rushing down to the pond, however, be warned. For it is also said that touching a frog will give you warts.

Which isn't the only trick those great pranksters, Fate and Fortune, have in store for damsels who pin their hopes on old wives' tales.

As a young boy, John Prynce always loved to fix things. His tutors had despaired of teaching him anything useful, because instead of applying himself to his Latin, fencing or dancing lessons, he frittered away his time tinkering with broken spits, timepieces, or wagon wheels. Nothing made him so happy as to tackle something lads of his class would not normally attempt: he enjoyed building a fire in the hearth before the maid had a chance to do so, assisting the grooms in the birthing of a foal, or helping a carpenter mend a leaky roof. It should have come as no surprise to his disapproving relatives, then, that despite a comfortable legacy from his father, making it unnecessary for him to earn a living, he chose for himself a pastime that resembled—scandalously—a career.

It was some years, however, before he found his vocation. As a hot-headed adolescent, he had killed a rival in a duel, an act for which he suffered deep remorse, and which was to mark him for the rest of his life. His relatives fortunately managed to spare him from the gallows by buying him a commission in Sir John Reynolds' troop, at that time bound for Dunkirk to fight under the command of France's General Turenne. In Dunkirk the young cornet had witnessed the decimation of the English force, not in battle, but in the unhealthy damp and unsanitary privations of a winter in Mardyke. Three years later, when the English monarchy was restored and King Charles decided to let his army cut its teeth on a prize at a safe distance from Whitehall, John had volunteered for service with the Portuguese Brigade. It was in Portugal that he saw his first active service, and was struck not by the glory of war, but the gore. After watching several of his closest comrades bleed or suppurate to death, he became acquainted with a Swiss barber who was having some success in stemming the bleeding of amputated limbs. The man's method was to ligature the cut blood vessels, instead of the more accepted practice of cauterizing the wound with boiling oil, which, despite the imposing agony it caused, seemed to save few lives. John was sufficiently impressed to apprentice himself to the Swiss barber, having resolved to dedicate himself to tending to the wounded as a way of atoning for his youthful offense. Upon mastering the ligaturing technique, he spent the next several years touring Europe's medical institutions, supplementing his barber-surgeon's skills with a thorough grounding in anatomy (cutting up cadavers), comparative anatomy (dissecting birds, toads and other animals), pathology (memorizing the symptoms of a multitude of deadly and sadly incurable diseases), and the Latin he had eschewed as a boy.

"I decided," he told Bessie, "that it was better to save lives than to take them."

"So it is," agreed Bessie. She sighed. "I wish your colleagues would see it that way too."

"We all have the best of intentions, ma'am," he protested.

"Of course, of course! I mean no offense..."

"And now," he went on, "where were we? Ah yes, you were about to give me the ingredients of your styptic."

"My recipe to stop the bleeding? Well, just a pinch of lime, a dash of vinegar, a drop of arsenic. And alumroot, finely ground. To bind it, the egg white I told you of before."

"Yes, I have heard tell of the alum. You have found it efficacious?"

"If you wish to stop the bleeding, yes. If you believe in encouraging it, as most of your physicians do, then not."

"There is a time for flushing out the blood," he said stiffly, "and there is a time for stemming it."

Bessie pursed her lips. "I think you might find that giving your patient some strong wine or broth to drink—I can give you my recipe—does a body a world more good than lancing or cupping."

"Ah! Confortantia, of course, are a boon—"

Bessie looked puzzled.

"Tonics, ma'am. Such as the broth you describe."

"Yes," said Bessie.

"I am curious to hear your recipe."

"Well. I might take some leaves of rosemary..." Bessie began. Seeing him nod encouragement, she went on, "...singe them over a flame, and let them steep in the broth for four and twenty hours. Then I'll take a hunk of stale bread, with a good touch of the mold growing on't—"

"Mold? Why not fresh, ma'am?"

"It is the recipe, sir," she said, pursing her lips. "I cannot say why."

"Well, why not! If it was newt's tongue, perhaps, or bat's wing, I might be forgiven for drawing the wrong conclusion..."

Bessie looked at him in alarm, but his face had broken into a roguish grin, and her heart softened. She was just beginning to understand the gentleman's difficult sense of humor.

Before she could go on, the tent flaps parted. A water nymph burst in, strings of wet vegetation dripping from her hair.

"Bessie! What have we here? *You,* entertaining an officer in our tent? Oh fie, fie, fie!"

It was Lucinda, damp and apple-cheeked from a dip in the river. She couldn't wait to tell Bessie about the afternoon's activity. It had been such fun! They'd all gone to bathe in the river, and Zéfine had caught a frog, and then Blanchette and the others had made her kiss it, because, they said, if you kissed a frog, you would be married within the year. At first she had protested, squealing that she would never do such a thing, but in the end, persuaded by all the flattering attention, she had entered into the spirit of thing. She'd screwed up her nose and planted a kiss on the slimy creature's back, and then they had all petted her and made a fuss over her, and presented her with a bridal garland of water lilies for her head.

"Oh pet!" scolded Bessie, "This is Lieutenant..."

"Prynce. John Prynce, at your service, ma'am," stammered the lieutenant, bowing.

Lucinda, startled, recognized him. "Sir!" she said. She ripped the garland out of her wet hair and made a face at Bessie, who shrugged apologetically.

"I have been plying your companion, dear lady," John said hastily, "for her medicinal secrets."

"Aha," said Lucinda laconically.

"Yes." He laughed, trying to coax a smile out of her, "And I am unable to decide which name best suits her: Panakeia, Hygeia or Iaso."

Both women looked blank. John kicked himself. They'd think he was being pompous; when he most wanted to sound charming and glib. He tried to explain, which only made it worse.

"Panakeia, Hygeia and Iaso were the daughters of Aesculapius..."

"Ah." Lucinda was already looking bored; Bessie, anxiously confused.

"Aesculapius was the father of medicine," he went on hurriedly, "a Greek." He had no choice but to continue, lamely: "Zeus killed him. With a thunderbolt, because he was a mortal, and he was treading on the gods' toes—"

"The Lord God's toes," Bessie repeated, nodding devoutly.

"No, I meant the *Greek* gods..." He gave up when he saw Lucinda starting to back out of the tent. "I do trust," he interrupted himself, too loudly and too quickly, "that, uh, good mother Goose has conveyed to you my most sincere apologies?"

"She has," said Lucinda coldly. "But don't let me keep you. I leave you to your learned talk."

"Lucinda! Lamb!" exclaimed Bessie, but the lamb had already escaped.

* * *

"*That* wasn't very kind," she said to Lucinda later, when they were alone.

"Ha! Was it kind of him to take me for a whore?"

"No, pet, but it was an honest mistake, and he regrets it now."

"Why did he come here anyway?" She'd found it satisfying to see that fine-looking man squirm. Lucinda was used to put-downs; but to have the author of one of those insults beg her forgiveness! It was a novel sensation.

"He is coming to me for advice."

"I hope you haven't given him any."

"I have. He'll be the better healer for it." Bessie, sighing, inspected the backs of her stubby hands. "Poor souls—I mean your learned physicians and such. They've so much of their learning from books and cadavers, they haven't time to pay attention to the living. They treat the sick with remedies of death."

"I always thought you despised physicians," said Lucinda.

"I don't despise them, pet! No! I just think they are ignorant," said Bessie. "They can't help it. They don't know any better."

"And you do!" said Lucinda, smiling.

"There are some things I know, and some things I don't," said Bessie. "And the things I don't know, I know which they are. And I don't tamper with them."

"And the things you do know?"

"I know that if you tell someone he is going to die, he will most certainly die. I know that if you let him watch his life-blood drip into a barber's cup, he will lose strength and hope. I know— "She paused.

"What?" asked Lucinda dutifully.

"Never mind."

There were some things that any good midwife knew from experience, but you didn't blab about it, in case people decided you were a charlatan, or worse. For instance, Bessie always muttered that earnest little ditty to herself before a birth—a prayer of sorts, it was, even though it was the most dreadful gibberish, she was sure. She couldn't explain why she did this, but old Biddy Mudlin, to whom she had been apprenticed, had taught it to her. Biddy also used to wash her hands—of all things!—at a lying-in, even furtively using some spirits to clean under her fingernails, and Bessie had taken this habit over from her too. It was the sort of old-wives' quackery that the physicians abhorred. But whether it was the prayer or the washing or simple blind luck, the childbed fever that killed so many new mothers seldom visited her patients. Bessie wondered what this Mr. Prynce, who seemed refreshingly broad-minded, would make of it.

She turned her attention back to Lucinda. "I'll fix you something nice for your supper. Corporal Billen's wife traded me a mutton hash for my best cordial."

"I'm not hungry, Bess."

Six days had passed, and not a word from Henry. She had just found out he was seen strolling about the camp that very morning, hale and well.

"Has the captain...?"

"No!" Lucinda said bluntly. "Not yet."

"He is certainly—very busy, isn't he?" said Bessie gently.

"Oh, what do you know of it!" she exclaimed, tossing her head. "You don't understand a *thing*!"

"No I don't," Bessie sighed.

The siegeworks were coming along apace. The main network of ditches was almost dug, with only the final assault saps left to go, and Vauban was able to promise the king that the trenches would be ready for a full attack in less than a week. Even the most war-hardened musketeers had to admit that this was the most sophisticated siege operation ever staged. With Vauban's meticulous attention to detail, no one doubted that once the trenches were opened, the Dutch were done for.

Again the Duke of Monmouth summoned his coterie to his tent.

"Gentlemen!" he said. "It appears, sirs, an assault is not far off!"

There was a cheer of bravura.

"Are we ready, sirs, to storm the citadel?"

There was another roar of assent.

"Do we desire the victory to be ours?"

"Aarhh!"

"Shall we show these frogs what an Englishman's mettle is?"

"Rrrhh! Rrrhh!" the officers roared.

"Very good," said Monmouth, hushing them. "We are all agreed the glory by rights ought to be ours. Now we must ensure that the final attack will take place on our watch, not the frogman's."

A rotation system was in effect, under which Monmouth shared with four French major-generals the daily command of the trenches at the Brussels Gate. Thus each general had to wait four days for his turn, relieving his predecessor in the trenches at dusk of the fifth.

"But my liege!" said Sir Thomas Armstrong. "Surely the French king will want the prize to be yours. Why, otherwise, would he have given you the top command? He is so very fond of you— "

"Indeed," said Monmouth, smiling at the dazzling ring he was wearing on his left hand, a reward from Louis to his young nephew for the valor he had displayed in the previous season's campaign, "we have reason to believe that he is. But that does not solve our problem. We cannot be seen to curry favor, or to pull rank, gentlemen. After all, who is to say that de la Fieuiliad, de la Rochfort, de Lorge, or even de Rohanez are not as deserving of the honor as we are?"

There were murmurs of protest. Captain Churchill stumbled forward and fell to his knees. "Sir! I would give my life..." he choked.

Monmouth looked pleased. "Rise, dear heart! Rise!" he chided, extending his hand.

The sight of that gloved hand under Churchill's elbow was too much for Henry.

"We should *all* gladly give our lives," he snapped. "Every last man among us. But surely we could *try* to come up with a more practical solution?"

The Duke turned to him. "Ah, Beaupree! Did you have something in mind then?"

"Indeed I do, sir." Henry was forced to do some quick thinking. "There is a way..." he said, stalling.

"Let's hear it, then!" said Churchill, dusting his knees. "Let's hear it from Captain Beaupree, our *master* tactician."

Goaded by the sarcasm in his rival's voice, inspiration struck Henry at last. He said quietly, "I have some influence, sir, of a personal nature, with Vauban. I believe there may be a way to arrange the timing suitably."

"Some influence with Vauban? You, Beaupree? How so?" said Monmouth.

"Please, sir, may we discuss this privately, in your tent?"

38

THE FEN-JADE'S FEATHER

"Bess! Bessie!"

"What is it, lamb?"

"Cornet Stickling is here. Henry has sent for me!"

"Oh pet! I told you..."

"Help me into this gown, please Bess! Oh, and where are those new ribbons..."

"Stand still, lamb, let me lace you up. There! Bless you, you look a treat. There's really no need for paint—"

"Just a little powder...? You see? You see! I *knew* he would!"

To tell the truth, Lucinda was laying it on a bit thick—she was not as excited as she was pretending to be. Her feelings for the captain had cooled considerably in the past couple of weeks. But it was unthinkable not to go at this point. Henry had sent for her, after all! And tonight might very well be the night when her patience was finally rewarded, when he declared himself and plighted his troth. Perhaps her friends had been right after all about kissing that frog. She had invested so much in this man—not just time and effort, but her innocence, her bankable virtue—that it was inconceivable not to see it through to a profitable end.

She piled her hair on top of her head. "Do you mind if I go?" she asked guiltily, remembering her promise to help Bessie tonight.

"Not at all, lamb. Lieutenant Prynce and I have some matters to attend to anyway."

Lucinda felt a pang of envy. Turning around, she took a hairpin out of her mouth.

"You two are quite the pair," she teased, sticking the pin into her topknot. "Has he insulted you lately?"

"Not at all!" protested Bessie. "I wish you would let bygones be bygones, lamb. I like him. I like him very much."

"That's clear," sniffed Lucinda.

"And so would you, if you gave yourself half a chance."

"Oh yes?" said Lucinda, twisting a ringlet around her finger.

"Yes you would. He is a good man, a thousand times better..."

"Than who?"

"Oh, never mind. He's a good man, that's all. He has a heart."

"Oh, I see!" teased Lucinda. "How nice! Well, good luck with capturing that poor man's heart, Bess!"

"Oh lamb!" Bessie exclaimed, shaking her head. Because that wasn't what she'd meant at all, and Lucinda knew it too.

Henry, who was standing outside his tent, dismissed Cornet Stickling, and without wasting time took Lucinda inside for a tumble on his field bed.

That done, he let Lucinda nestle her head on his shoulder, and drew his arms around her. "Missed me, then?" he asked.

Lucinda looked up at him. "Henry!" she sighed. "Of course I did! It has been so long!"

Henry sighed. "There has been much to attend to, pippin. This is serious business, you know. But once all this is over, and the citadel taken..."

He did not elaborate, or commit himself any further.

There was an interval of silence, during which Henry dozed off for a few moments while Lucinda groped for words, suddenly remembering the sly insinuating looks of Henriette and Sabine. "But," she finally guessed, playing with his chest hairs and feeling her heart knocking in her chest, "I heard that you had a visit from some—some other women. Here in your tent."

His eyes snapped open. "You heard that, did you? Who told you?"

"The—women. Told me."

"Ah," said Henry slowly. "They told you. Well, I can explain..."

But he did not explain; instead, he tried to distract her by nuzzling her neck.

"I wish you would," she whispered.

"Wish I would what?" came his voice from somewhere beneath her hair. "Explain."

He sat up, aggrieved. "I see now," he said severely, "that whereas I had hoped my lady was longing for me every minute we were apart, she has deemed fit to exercise a suspicious nature which I must say I am most astonished to..."

"No!" exclaimed Lucinda hastily. "Oh, Henry, forgive me, I did not mean to imply..."

"No, no, I must confess the whole lurid episode, of course. Else your little mind will jump to all sorts of nasty conclusions, and we can't have that, can we?" Clamping her chin between his thumb and middle finger, he jiggled her jaw playfully. "Can we!" he teased. But she could not summon the required smile. She looked down.

He let go, sighing. She could tell that he was very disappointed in her.

"The women—strumpets—were summoned for a spot of entertainment. As an officer it is one's obligation to provide such...divertissements for one's superiors from time to time. I can scarce expect you to understand. I find it very distasteful myself. But surely you appreciate that one has a position to uphold. Else one stands to be trampled upon by every upstart trying to make an impression..."

He sounded so bitter that Lucinda felt contrite. Of course there were so many expectations of you if you were a man, expectations hard enough to live up to without this kind of petty rebuke from her! "I'm sorry!" she said again. "Please! Forgive me. I had no right..."

He sighed again. But she could tell he was mollified. "You had every right," he said. "You had every right, my turtle-dove, my juicy little vixen, my dainty baggage."

"Wenching again, Beaupree?" Churchill sneered. The English officers had just been treated to a touching farewell scene between Lucinda and the captain.

Henry did not deign to reply, but, brushing past Churchill, made his way to Monmouth's tent and was announced without delay.

"I wonder what his so-called plan is all about," muttered Churchill.

"My Lord Monmouth is certainly taking it seriously enough," said Sir Thomas Armstrong. "*And* I understand it has everything to do with the wenching you disapprove of so heartily."

"Ah?" said Churchill. "How so?"

"I understand," smirked Sir Thomas, "that our Vauban has taken a fancy to Beaupree's little English baggage."

"Ha!" exclaimed Churchill. "A bawd, our Beaupree! I would not put it past him!"

"Wait a minute!" protested John Prynce. "You don't mean to say they would compromise a lady..."

"Ah, but the lady is already compromised, as we know," said Edmund Mayne with a laugh.

"No!" said Prynce. "Surely they would not..."

At this moment Monmouth came strolling out of his tent, his hand on Henry's shoulder.

Churchill stepped forward. "So!" he said. "What do I hear, my lord! The secret's out, you know. You cannot hide it from us any longer."

"What secret is that, sirrah?" asked the duke.

"Why, Beaupree's little *cunt*-trivance, of course! Sir Thomas tells me that you'll have us license lickerishness!"

Monmouth looked baffled.

"What the captain is alluding to, your lordship," explained Vernon, his secretary, smoothly, "is Vauban's er—weakness for the fair sex..."

"Ah yes, ha!" laughed Monmouth. "Cunt-trivance! Contrivance! Ah yes, very good, sir, very good!"

"What is it exactly," asked Beaupree smoothly, his face a fraction too close to Churchill's, "that you object to, fondest?"

"I? Nothing!" said Churchill quickly, "No, no, I think it is an excellent plan, a most amusing plan! No, but our learned friend here, Mister Prynce, has been raising objections..."

"What *is* it with you, Prynce?" exclaimed Beaupree, turning on him. "Can't you ever take a joke?"

"A lady's honor is scarcely a joke, sir," said Prynce stiffly.

"Oh, spare me!" groaned Beaupree.

"I can't believe that this humorless fellow claims a kinship with our dear Lord Rochester!" Churchill put in.

"Yes, what's the matter, Prynce?" Monmouth said. "How did you come to be such a prude?"

"What I object to, my lord," said John, looking around for an ally, "is the apparent disregard for the consequences of...such a course of action, for the young lady in question. Consider her feelings. She is to my knowledge no common whore, and..."

"Of course not! That is what's so rich!" exclaimed Beaupree. "In lending her to him I shall be doing Vauban a great favor, a favor the old goat doesn't deserve!"

"What my esteemed colleague means," Churchill explained gravely to the surgeon, "is that, God willing, she will not teach the good Seigneur de Vauban any...*French*, if you understand my drift."

"Yes, Prynce," smirked Beaupree. "To put it in your own cousin Rochester's immortal words:

I send for my whore, when for fear of the clap,
I dally about her, and spew in her lap."

This witticism found an appreciative audience. "Yes! Yes! That's very good!" the duke laughed, dabbing at his eye with his handkerchief. "Ho, ho! Very good indeed!"

"Or how about this one?" shouted Beaupree,

"'Tis known the fringe of the fen-jade's feather
Oft harbors pestilential weather.
Since I durst not risk a pox i' the south,
I migrated up north, and came in her mouth—"

"Oh, that's good, that's good, that's even better!" guffawed Monmouth. "Ha ha! Dear Rochester, I miss him. What a wit!"

"Actually," coughed Beaupree modestly, "That was not Rochester's."

"Oh no?"

"No, it is mine..."

"You amaze me, sir!" said Monmouth, still chuckling. "I had no idea you were a poet! You must recite more for us, forthwith!"

"My lord," said Beaupree with a smirk, which Churchill was certain was aimed at him.

Damp morning, reeking of earth and dung. Puffs of mist clung to the ground in the distance; the muffled silence was interrupted every so often by the indignant clatter of drops shaken loose by the wind. Lucinda had found Bessie and Zéfine seated side by side on a hummock overlooking the camp. Bessie was showing the African woman the English way to swaddle a baby. Zéfine seemed unusually quiet, and Lucinda noticed a blackened puffiness around her jaw and neck.

Bessie too had surely noticed the bruises, but she was smiling comfortingly at the young mother.

"What a lovely, lovely boy," she cooed. "Tell Josephine, pet."

"*Qu'il est adorable,*" she translated. The baby was light-skinned but had a flared nose and frizzy hair. The novel combination fascinated her.

Zéfine smiled quietly. She traced the baby's cheek with her finger, then faltered, and suddenly gathered him up in a passionate hug.

"*Nous-deux et moi?*" she whispered into his hair, "*Nous-deux et moi.*"

"Us two and me?" said Bessie. "Is that what she's saying, pet?"

"Mmm," Lucinda assented.

They both looked away, toward the river, because the emotion was overwhelming; because it made Bessie remember the time when Lucinda had been a helpless infant in her arms; because for the first time in her life the possibility of that kind of love stirred inside Lucinda; because there was nothing else to say.

"Bessie!" Lucinda said suddenly. "Isn't that your good friend, Mr. Prynce?" He was striding up the hill towards them.

"Don't go—please stay, pet!" Bessie pleaded quickly. "It would be uncivil of you to..."

But Lucinda made no move to leave. She even smiled at him coolly as he approached.

"Ladies..." He made a formal little bow. Bessie and Zéfine got to their feet. Lucinda remained seated, nonchalant.

"A lovely day, isn't it, Mister Prynce?" Bessie said.

"Indeed," he said, looking at Lucinda. There was an awkward pause.

"This is Josephine," Bessie explained, "and her little one, Noé."

John nodded, not taking his eyes off Lucinda.

"So..." Lucinda said, gathering up her skirts, "no doubt you two have matters to attend to..."

"No!" he barked. Bessie and Lucinda stared at him. "I mean, please—stay. It is you I have come to see."

"Me?" said Lucinda.

"Yes. I have a matter of some urgency to convey to you."

"Oh?"

"I do not wish to distress you, ma'am, but I must warn you."

"Of what?"

"There is a plan—a plot afoot..."

"Well?" she prompted him, looking at Bessie, then back at him.

"Concerning your own person."

"Concerning me? What sort of plot would that be, sir?"

He had grabbed the hilt of his sword and was jiggling it nervously in its sheath. "There is talk that—that you will be—er—traded, to Monsieur de Vauban, in return for his favoring the Duke of Monmouth in the matter of the timing of the assault on the citadel."

"I don't understand..." said Lucinda. Bessie just stared, open-mouthed.

"Forgive me. What I mean is that..." He coughed uncomfortably. "That Vauban has requested you as his prize."

"His prize!" Lucinda scoffed. "That crab of a man! What in God's name would I do with him?"

"It is not what you would do with him, ma'am. It is what he would do with *you* that concerns me."

"Why—this is nonsense! Henry would never allow it. Have you told him of it?"

John threw a look of appeal at Bessie. "I am sorry ma'am. Believe me, I am chagrined to be the bearer of such tidings. But—" His eyes closed helplessly for an instant—"I understand the idea came from Captain Beaupree."

"No! *The captain?* How do you mean, the captain!" Lucinda forced laugh. "The captain would never do such a thing!" She whirled around at Bessie. "Did you hear what your *friend* just said?" she cried, and, gathering her skirts, ran down the hill.

Bessie stared after her, then turned around to face John, her hands reproachfully on her wide hips.

He raised his hands helplessly. "It is the truth, madam," he said. The left hand fell to his side; the right one set to rubbing his nose sheepishly. "I felt it was my duty…"

39

DRAGON'S CLAW

The trenches were opened on June 17. The sappers now ceded their places to the foot soldiers, who took up position within striking range of the fortress. There was one setback, however: heavy downpours had filled the trenches with rain. The drenched troops sat hunched behind their muddy parapets with water up to their waists. But the earthworks were holding up well, and despite some perfunctory shelling by the defenders' artillery, casualties were negligible.

Four days later Henry sent for Lucinda again. Monmouth's troops had just been relieved by General de Lorge and his men, and after twenty-four hours of misery in the pouring rain, Henry was in a foul mood.

"Help me get out of these sopping things," he groused at Lucinda. "I'm near death, wench."

"Near death!" exclaimed Lucinda. She sank to her knees and began tugging at his boots.

"Aarrgh...!" he growled, and kicked her away. "You're no help at all, jade!" He tore the boots off himself and flung them across the tent.

Lucinda, who had landed on her backside, picked herself up and, trying to hide her mortification, began rubbing at the muddy footprint on her gown.

"May we...?" It was Lewis and Edward Watson, Lord Rockingham's sons, and their cousin Francis, the duke's aide-de-camp.

"By all means!" said Henry, suddenly gracious. He waved at some stools piled behind the field bed, and his visitors pulled them up to the table. Then he turned to Lucinda, and muttered, "Go, fetch Stickling, and tell him to bring some brandy."

When she returned to the tent with the subaltern and the brandy,

Henry's mood had lightened considerably. He even smiled at her, with an "Ah! There you are, my sweet!"

The other three turned to stare at her, grinning.

Lucinda blushed, and stood uncertainly just inside the tent flap.

"Come in! By all means, wench!" Henry said heartily, waving her closer. When she was near enough, he drew her onto his lap, with her back to him. Lucinda had no choice but to sit there foolishly on display, Henry's hands resting lightly on her breasts, while the men discussed the day's work.

"It's too bad, too bad," said Edward Watson, shaking his head. "To get within thirty paces of the counterscarp, and then to be thwarted!"

"The duke is furious," said Francis. "And very, very disappointed. Although you would never know it to look at him, of course, dear prince! He was certain he could have made a lodgment quite easily, you know."

"How long do you think it will take to complete the new sap-works the king has ordered?" asked Henry.

"Two days, four days, a week...It's hard to tell," said Francis. There was a silence.

"We were so close! If only the French king weren't so lily-livered!" complained Henry.

"No, in my opinion, he is right," put in Lewis Watson. "We all know the Dutch have mines littering the place; they could easily have blown our troops to hell. He was right to halt the attempt."

"Pish! I think we could have taken the counterscarp," said Henry, toying with Lucinda's sleeve. "I agree with the duke: the Dutch have staked everything upon those mines, but once they are played, they have played their last card."

"But think of the casualties..." protested Lewis.

"A few lives sacrificed for the good of all," said Francis. "Come, man, whether it is today or one month hence, there will be casualties. Besides, what's a few men, compared with the glory that should be ours?"

"And still will be," said Henry grimly.

Lucinda blushed, unhappily, for suddenly all the men's eyes were on her.

* * *

"Monsieur de Vauban? Why him?" asked Lucinda anxiously. "*Why* does he wish to see me?"

"He does not wish to see you, *per se*," Henry smiled; "he wishes to see me, and I am inviting you to come along. Why, I thought you would be pleased!"

"Thank you," stammered Lucinda, "but, actually, I should get back. I must..."

"No excuses!" laughed Henry. He pinned her waist between his arms, and swung her first this way, then that. "What is it, pigeon? Don't you want to be seen with me?"

"Well, I...I just don't think it's my place..." she stammered.

"Your place! Ah, baggage!" he said. "If only you knew!" He looked into her eyes tenderly, charmingly. "And if I were to tell you that it *was* your place, and that you must not refuse me? Why—what am I to think? Am I to think that if I had a mind to ask something of you—any small favor, really—I should be rejected by you, hard-hearted little minx that you are?"

"No! Henry! No!" she exclaimed. "Of course not..."

"Well then!" he said, and pushed her out of the tent.

Later, after they returned from Vauban's tent, Henry was in a fine mood.

"Aahh!" he exclaimed, pulling her close. "My delightful filly! I have grown very fond of you, you know."

Lucinda rubbed her eyes.

"I do believe that you made quite an impression on those frogs," he said.

"Oh, really," she said, and sniffed.

"What is it?" he asked defensively.

"Oh, I don't know," she said. "But. I don't like to be...paraded."

"Paraded? Is that what I was doing, parading you? Oh my cozy baggage, is that what you think I was doing? I was doing nothing of the sort, I assure you."

"No?"

"No. Of course not. The idea!"

"What were you whispering about, the two of you, all that time?"

"None of your business. Men's business. Strategy, that sort of thing. Vauban has taken me into his confidence."

"Then what has it got to do with me?"

"I have already told you, nothing!"

"How do you think it makes me feel, having to stand there awkwardly, uselessly, and that Frenchman throwing me looks..."

"What looks? Oh come, Lucinda, surely you are imagining..."

"It's not just my imagination."

"No?"

"No."

"How is that, vixen?"

"I heard a rumor."

"She heard a rumor! Yet again! Well, well!"

"Yes. I heard...I heard I was to be traded, to Vauban."

Without missing a beat, he replied, "You heard that, did you? Who told you?"

"It doesn't matter who told me."

"I insist on knowing who told you."

"I insist on being told the truth."

"The truth? Ha! The truth, my pretty miss? Well, the truth is that Vauban has taken a fancy to you."

"Ah!" she said sullenly.

"Yes indeed, and you ought to be flattered. He is a great man, a very great man..."

"Yes, a great, ugly old man."

"Oh come, my turtledove. If he enjoys having a gander, where's the harm? Don't you want to help me in my endeavors? As for this rumor about being 'traded'—whatever that means—it's all nonsense. I truly wish you would tell me who told you such a pack of lies."

On her way up from the pontoon bridge across the river, she spotted Bessie kneeling under a large awning. As she drew near, she saw what she was doing: washing a corpse. There were two more bodies waiting to be packed up and tidily dispatched to their final resting place.

"Bessie!" she said.

Bessie turned around. "Not now, lamb, I'm busy. Go on back to the tent, pet. This is no sight for a young lady."

"No, I want to help," she said, gazing at the sorry spectacle. "There must be something I can do!"

"There is plenty to do," said a voice in her ear. She spun around. It was the surgeon John Prynce, with blood up to his elbows. He made a rather grim picture.

"Oh, hello," she said quickly. "Well, put me to work, then." She looked at him defiantly. He knew nothing of it, of course, but she had not betrayed him. She had not betrayed him to Henry. She had refused to give Henry the name of the man who had brought her the rumor about Vauban. The Lord knew she had no good reason to be nice to this Mr. Prynce, but she had protected him nonetheless. "What should I do?"

"This way," he said, and led her to the other side of the open tent, where a chorus of soft moaning and high-pitched wailing greeted her ears. The wounded, the amputated, the freshly maimed, the blinded and deafened. There were only a dozen or so, lying bandaged around a glowing brazier, but to the stunned Lucinda it looked like a horde writhing in hell. "Just do what you can to make them comfortable," the surgeon instructed her. "They need to be kept warm. And give them something to drink—there is a bottle of brandy over there, and some ale. Try to keep their spirits up. Make them believe they'll feel better tomorrow."

"But..." she began. But he had already gone back to help Bessie with the corpses.

To her own surprise, Lucinda proved to be rather good at tending to the casualties—the less severely injured ones, at any rate. At Bessie's urging, her talent for sketching was resurrected, and proved a useful icebreaker. She was soon much in demand as a portraitist; some soldiers even swore that their suffering was worth it just for the satisfaction of having a likeness of themselves, on a scrap of parchment, to keep.

"They can be so affectionate, so grateful," she told Bessie, "it breaks your heart, doesn't it?"

"It breaks your heart," Bessie agreed. "But have you told the captain that you are working here now?"

"Why should I?"

"Well, how will they find you, if he sends someone to fetch you?"

"I don't care. Let him come and look for me himself," she said lightly.

"Aha!" said Bessie. Her lamb was finally beginning to play the game the way Bessie felt it should be played.

As it turned out, it was several days before anyone came looking for Lucinda, because the siege had taken a serious turn and the officers, even when not engaged in active duty, spent the greater part of the day at their observation posts, following the progress of the sappers digging their way closer to the fortress walls. The evenings were taken up with strategy sessions; this was not the time for wenching.

In the meantime Lucinda was learning from Bessie how to change a bandage and cleanse a wound, how to talk to an amputee in a manner designed to raise his spirits, or, if that proved impossible, to cheerfully ignore his understandable ill-humor. She even overcame her natural recoil at the constant presence of vomit, putrefaction and excrement. Bessie did not mind the stench; Lieutenant Prynce did not mind it; then why should she?

She found herself watching, out of the corner of her eye, Lieutenant Prynce's incessant activity, his firmness, his deftness, his professional geniality. It pleased her very much to see him in action, although she found it necessary to hide this from him. He had insulted her, after all, not once, but twice: first in mistaking her for a whore, the second time in implying that her lover was a pander willing to trade her to another. But the sting of those insults was fading in the filtered light of the infirmary tent, where he walked like an angel, a savior, and everyone looked up to him. She imagined that he too was sneaking covert glances at her: but every time she peeked, he seemed intent on his work. The tables were slowly turning: the more she admired him, the shyer and more tongue-tied she was in his presence. The shyer she was, the more comfortable he grew with her, ragging her easily as if she were a younger sister, winking at her when he did happen to catch her eye.

Bessie saw the change. At least, she thought she detected it. She could not resist testing her hypothesis.

"Mister Prynce thinks very highly of you, you know, pet," she said as they were walking back to their tent one night. She noted that her comment made Lucinda blush.

"Really? Why? What did he say?" she asked.

"What I just said, lamb."

"No, really, what were his exact words?"

Bessie smiled, and told her, word for word.

When they arrived at the infirmary tent early the next morning, Lieutenant Prynce was waiting for them. "There is not much for you to do today. It would be best if you went back to your tent and rested. I do not want to overwork you."

"Oh we aren't tired!" beamed Lucinda. "Are we, Bess?"

He could not help smiling back. But, composing his face, he went on gravely, "All the same, I think it would be best."

Bessie's hands went up to her mouth. "You think the main assault is imminent, that is what you mean, isn't it?"

"I am sorry, ladies. I am not at liberty to…"

"Come, lamb," said Bessie, tugging at the disappointed Lucinda's arm. "Let's do as Mister Prynce says."

"I am happy to report, Sire," Vauban said to his sovereign late that afternoon, "that the new sap network will be completed before nightfall."

"We may go ahead, then?" asked the king.

"His Majesty may go ahead."

"Well then! Very well!" The king looked as excited as a child. "Alert the Duc d'Orléans and Général Montal. And send the Duke of Monmouth to us, with whichever of his generals has the watch."

"I believe it is the English duke himself tonight, Sire."

"Young James! Well then! Well done, Sébastien. Well done. He shall have our own Regiment of Foot," he said generously, "under the Marquis de Montbrun. That should give him a sufficient force, should it not?"

"I trust that it will, Sire, but…"

"Well?"

"I hope, Sire, that this, er, young person, the duke, will be able to live up to the immense trust His Majesty has invested in him…"

"Always the cautious one, my dear Vauban, always so careful! But no, no, we are sure that he will do very well! *And* he shall have some fine things to say about us when he writes home to our cousin his dear papa, *n'est-ce pas!*"

"No doubt, Sire. No doubt."

"Very well. Excellent. Indeed." The king tapped his fine upper lip thoughtfully. "Now. Let us see. As commander in chief, it behooves us, naturally, to consider every eventuality. Naturally. Does it not, my man. But of course. You must never forget this, Vauban. It is our duty. Yes indeed. And so perhaps—yes, perhaps, in addition, we'll give him our musketeers. The Royal Musketeers. Ah! Most suitable indeed. What say you to our little plan, Vauban? With Captain d'Artagnan at his side, the duke cannot go wrong. Brilliant! Do we not have the solution at our very fingertips, as ever? Our d'Artagnan will keep an eye on that English rapscallion, will he not!"

"An excellent plan, Sire." Vauban bowed low.

"Very well then. We are agreed. In three hours we give the command."

Lucinda's daydreams had grown a bit muddled of late. Instead of focusing on the happy moment when Henry at last realized how much he loved her and made her his wife, the fantasies once again featured the faceless hero who used to rescue her from the tedium of her childhood in the days before she'd met Henry.

She leaned back against a tent pole and closed her eyes, drifting into a reverie.

They were galloping away across an arid flatland; behind them, a drag-on was bellowing its death-roar. The monster was pinned to the ground by a pike speared through the heart. For a few brief moments more she was flooded with relief. But then...

"No, no!" she shuddered. "It is too late! Look!" And she peeled back her left sleeve to reveal, where her hand should have been...a gnarled, green, scaly claw.

Her rescuer sucked in his breath. For a moment he faltered. He looked down into her despairing eyes, then back to the revolting claw. She closed her eyes, and longed for death.

But suddenly she felt his touch. He was picking up the claw—he picked it up as if it were a velvet glove!—and held it gently to his cheek. "It doesn't matter," he whispered. "Nothing matters— nothing except that I have you now, and will never let you go..."

"Lamb, what's the matter?" came Bessie's concerned voice.

To her chagrin, Lucinda realized that real tears were rolling down her cheeks.

"Nothing!" She quickly wiped the tears away. "I was just feeling a little—homesick, that's all," she improvised.

"Homesick!" exclaimed Bessie.

Fortunately there was an interruption. They heard a loud explosion, followed by a rattle of gunfire.

"The attack!" shouted Lucinda, and ran outside. And, indeed, she could make out, in the distance across the river, the trenches crammed with lines of red and blue, and great puffs of white smoke, or dust—it was hard to tell in the half-light—all along the base of the citadel.

"That's it, pet!" shouted Bessie, hitching her skirts up to make running easier. "Come along, let's go! Lieutenant Prynce will be needing us!"

40

THE ASSAULT

The English rapscallion, as King Louis called him, acquitted himself well that night. His objectives—an escarpment and a demi-lune at the foot of the citadel—were neatly captured from the Dutch in a daring full-frontal assault. By late that night, the situation was well in hand, new trenches were being dug up to the very walls of the fortress, and Monmouth and his braves were jubilant about a job well done.

The Dutch did not give up without a fight, however. At daybreak the duke was awakened with the news that the defenders had managed to spring one of their mines, killing fifty of his men. Within a couple of hours the demi-lune was back in Dutch hands.

At Monmouth's command post, no one could agree on what to do next. Obviously, the demi-lune had to be retaken—it was either that, lose face, or, worse, be made a laughing-stock. The survivors of General Montbrun's troop, including the English pike men and grenadiers, were trapped by enemy fire. The duke sent word to the king that he needed reinforcements—he had only the king's own Royal Musketeers left in reserve—but his message was intercepted by the Duc d'Orléans, the king's brother, who felt that enough had been done for the English upstart and conveniently forgot to pass on the request.

Thirty minutes went by with no response from the king, and the Dutch were merrily digging in. Monmouth was sulking on his field bed, which had been set up in the open air. "Look at those bastards!" exclaimed Sir Thomas, who was peering at the fort through Monmouth's glass, "Just look at them! They're throwing up earth left and right like so many moles! Soon it'll be damned-near impossible to get at them!"

"Right!" said Monmouth, reluctantly pulling himself to his feet. The officers looked at him gratefully. "Right!" he said with a little more enthusiasm, holding out his elbows so that his equerry could buckle his breastplate under his armpits. "Gentlemen! The king is not in a mind to send us the reinforcements we need. But we shan't let victory escape us. No, gentlemen! We shall do it ourselves. Arm yourselves! For England!"

"For England!" cheered the English cavalry officers and courtiers who formed Monmouth's inner circle.

"Well now, Sir Thomas!" the duke prodded his most trusted adviser, who was picking his nose hesitantly. "What say you to my noble plan?"

"Most noble! Most noble!" Sir Thomas said. "Er—we'll need covering fire, of course, my lord," he prompted. "Perhaps d'Artagnan..."

"D'Artagnan!" the duke shouted. "Here, man, old fellow! Order your reserves. Be ready to cover us with your fire. You know what to do. Watch us retake that demi-lune!"

"Certainly, your Excellency," said d'Artagnan with a grin. This English duke was turning out to be made of finer mettle than he'd thought. You did not often meet a lieutenant-general willing to lead the men out himself. Whistling, d'Artagnan strolled down to the trenches, calling his men.

"Are we ready, gentlemen?" the duke asked, setting his hat at a rakish angle.

"Ready!" the English band shouted, affecting as much nonchalant enthusiasm as they could muster.

They found d'Artagnan waiting for them at the narrow entrance to the third parallel. He bowed. "Just give me a moment, sir, to reorder the musketeers. The groin will hold no more than two abreast..."

"To hell with the groin!" shouted Monmouth. "Follow me!" Sword in hand, he leaped up the slippery bank of the trench and swung himself over the parapet. Without looking back to see if he was being followed, he sloshed across the open field. The English officers jostled one another in their desire to follow as close on his heels as possible; the surprised musketeers had no choice but to follow. The sound of Monmouth's incongruously cheerful "*Allons, camarades!*" over the din made them press on.

Now they were within fifty paces of the demi-lune. The Dutch had thrown up a barricade blocking their path.

"Please, my lord, wait! *Attendez!*" It was d'Artagnan, puffing. It was not easy for him to catch up with the lithe young Englishman.

"Well, d'Artagnan? I haven't all day," the duke snapped.

"Let us retreat to the trenches, my lord. It is a trap. The enemy can pick us off one by one as we pass this place."

"Oh, come now, d'Artagnan. Are you afraid? Must I," said the duke severely, "show you Frenchmen what valor is? Forward!"

"No, wait, my lord!" shouted d'Artagnan. "Let me go first, in that case. I insist..."

He pushed past Monmouth and ran at the barricade, head first. A bullet happened to come traveling with some velocity from the opposite direction and hit a bull's eye. D'Artagnan's brains spattered the barricade, and his body, in its fall, knocked down a few of the stakes.

For a moment, Monmouth was stunned. Then he turned to the open-mouthed troops. "Follow me!" he shouted, and dashed forward through the narrow opening, stepping over d'Artagnan's body. And follow him they did—although not without paying a heavy price for their obedience. At least half of their number fell to keep the old musketeer company, face-down in the mud.

After some very heavy hand-to-hand fighting, the survivors finally regained control of the demi-lune, and held it until reinforcements arrived. The French now had a firm foothold in the citadel, and even the defenders themselves could see that this meant the beginning of the end for the beleaguered fort. The troops under Monmouth's command had suffered almost two thousand casualties, but, putting that aside, all agreed that the English king's bastard son had done a perfectly outstanding job.

Outside the infirmary tent overflowing with wounded men, Lucinda looked around helplessly. She didn't even know where to start. Numbly she started dabbing at a gushing wound with some lint dipped in Bessie's famous ointment.

"Not that way! Here! Make room!" It was Lieutenant Prynce, pushing her out of the way. She stepped back hastily. Her eyes stung. She had made a fool of herself! Now he wouldn't like her any more.

But he was oblivious, intent on applying a tourniquet to the injured man's arm.

Someone grabbed her ankle. *"Espèce d'ordure!"* she heard, *"Ordure, crapule, putain, putain!"* and then, piteously, *"Maman, maman!"* She bent down to pry the bloody hand from her leg. The man had only half a face. The other half was a gory mess. An eye was hanging by a clotted string down his cheek. "I'm sorry," she stammered, "I'll just..." and fled, tripping over bodies on the ground and upsetting a bucket with something heavy and glistening in it—she hoped it wasn't what she thought it might be, a human leg.

Shaking, she knelt down behind a chaplain who was administering last rites to two men at once. A woman in the next row—she thought she recognized one of the French sutlers—was trying to undo the buttons of a gurgling man's coat. She was having a hard time of it, because the blood washing out of his throat made the buttons slippery, and she was cursing under her breath.

"Let me help—" Lucinda began.

The woman scowled at her. "Get away from me. *Allez-vous-en!* There's plenty for everyone!"

"Oh, excuse me," muttered Lucinda. She now noticed the woman had a bundle of coats—fancy ones, with gold braid and ribbon—on the ground beside her and that there were three or four silver officers' gorgets strung around her neck. She started backing away from her.

"Well, well! The baggage everyone's looking for!" It was Captain John Churchill, nursing an injured hand. His pain made him extremely irritable. "What are *you* doing here?"

"I...I..." stammered Lucinda.

"Where's your pander then?" he sneered.

"Pander!" she repeated.

"Your swain, my *dear.*"

"Is he..."

"I don't know what's become of him. I do know his men are looking for you, however."

"Oh God!" Lucinda had been so busy that she had not given a thought to Henry for hours. He was wounded, or unconscious, or worse! She would never forgive herself...

She ran over to Bessie's side. "Bess, I have to go. I must find Henry..."

Bessie waved her away. "Go, pet," she said. The girl was just getting in the way at this point.

Lucinda raced up the slope toward the English enclave. She was choking on tears. Henry, Henry...She would never, never forgive herself!

But Henry was fine. He had received not so much as a scratch in the fighting. He was changing out of his mud-stained clothes when Cornet Stickling announced her.

"Ah!" he said. "She's been found! Finally! Where have you been, baggage? I never expected you to be so elusive..." He signaled to the cornet, who bowed and slipped away.

"Oh, Henry," she sobbed, running towards him with outstretched arms. "You're unharmed! I was so afraid—I thought you might be dead..."

"I might have been," he said, stepping back out of her reach and fastidiously raising his elbows into the air, "I had some narrow escapes, I can tell you. No, no, not now! Woman, your hands! I'll *kill* you if you get any of that on my clean shirt." She looked at her hands. They were striped with drying blood. "Come now, Lucinda, don't pout. Sit there while I get dressed."

Obediently she sat down in a corner. She wiped her hands on one of the blankets. Her heart was still pounding. Something was wrong. The tent had been tidied up and there were candles blazing everywhere, although it wasn't quite dark yet. All of Henry's plate was set out on a side table, heaped with fruit and delicacies. The decanter was full.

Henry was soon dressed, but took his time adjusting his periwig. Lucinda's pride prevented her from going to him until he made amends for his coldness. So she just sat there for a while, ignored.

"Captain, sir, his Lordship the Duke of Monmouth..."

Monmouth pushed past the cornet into the tent. He smiled broadly. Henry smiled broadly. The duke's cheeks seemed flushed. Henry's seemed flushed too. For a moment the duke just stood there. Then he took two strides toward Henry. Together, the two men took up a lot of space. They were larger than life. They never took their blazing eyes off each other. They were oblivious of Lucinda in her corner.

Monmouth stretched out a hand to Henry, who clasped it in both of his, then, holding on, sank to his knees and bowed his head.

"My lord!" he said, his voice choked with emotion. "Never in my life have I witnessed such bravery, such leadership..."

"Ah, Beaupree," the duke murmured, "Enough! On your feet! You know I could not have done it without the likes of you."

Humbly, Henry got to his feet. "It was spectacular," he said, shaking his head. "My lord—you have my undying loyalty."

"I must confess that I am pleased, Beaupree. I am very pleased." The duke flashed him another generous smile. "I wish I could do something to show you how very pleased I am. I pray that Fortune will reward me one day in a manner that will allow me to favor my most loyal followers, and I give you my word..."

"My lord!" A flush of delight spread over Henry's face, and he bowed again, his face very close to his general's shoulder. The intimacy was so intense that Lucinda felt a wave of panic.

She coughed.

Both men turned to stare at her. Their faces fell.

"To the business at hand, then," said the duke stiffly. "I see the wench has been found."

"Indeed," agreed Henry. "There she is."

"Come here, jade," the duke ordered. He turned to Henry. "You have informed her of her duty?"

"Of course, my lord," he said, avoiding Lucinda's eyes.

"Well." Monmouth raised an eyebrow. "I am afraid you will have to go with her, to apologize for the delay." He undid two buttons of his tight coat before sitting down in Henry's campaign chair. "But don't be long."

"*What is* my duty?" Lucinda whispered fiercely as Henry pulled her out of the tent. She didn't care if the duke heard her and she betrayed Henry's little lie. She was furious. She tried to wriggle out of his grasp.

"No you don't!" he said.

"Ouch! Henry! Let me go!" she complained, frightened now. "Where are we going?" She was afraid she might already know the answer.

"I believe you know where we are going," he said lightly.

"To Vauban? To *Vauban?* Then it's true...?"

"Oh, Lucinda," he said, and put his arm around her shoulder. With the other hand he did not let go of her wrist, however. "Do this for me, won't you? And don't make a fuss. It's not so much to ask..."

"Not so much to ask!" she sobbed.

He stopped in the middle of the path, and turned to face her. He tried to coax a smile out of her. "Ah, pippin, please don't take it so hard! We all have our duty. I have mine, and you have yours."

She shook her arm to release his grip, but he did not let go. "Sleeping with Vauban is *not* my duty!"

"Well, you don't have to *sleep* with him, my sweet," he cajoled. "Just—do to him what you do to me sometimes. That will please him, and I'm sure he won't keep you."

"No! Never!"

"Oh, but you must."

"I tell you no!"

He pulled her close to him. She wrenched her face around, away from him, accidentally biting her tongue. Her mouth was flooded with a metallic taste.

"Lucinda, my little filly," came his voice in her ear. "You know that I would do anything for you. You know that, don't you? Just do this little thing for me. You love me, don't you? You do, I know you do, and I know you will do this for me. Won't you!"

She stamped her foot on his boot.

He laughed. "I promise you, I'll make it up to you."

She tried to knee him in the groin, but he held her away, still laughing.

"Make it up to me!" Anger pinched her vocal cords so that the words came out as an infuriated squeak. "How? What exactly is this 'promise' I hear so much about?"

"How do you mean, vixen?"

"Are you saying you'll marry me?"

That made him stop laughing.

"*Ma-arry* you!" he said slowly. "Marry you?"

He snorted, as if he could suddenly see the humor in it. "Well. Why not?"

He made it sound as if it were the most far-fetched thing in the world: a thing that had never occurred to him before.

Through tent walls she could see a shadow play of men drinking, men slapping each other on the back, large vague shadows and small cleanly defined shadows circling each other in a menacing dance. Suddenly she felt very weak, very small. Empty, worthless. She let him pull her along without a struggle.

"All right, I promise," came a soothing, slightly exasperated voice from high above her. "I'll do it, baggage, I'll—I'll marry you, if that's what it takes."

It was pitch-black when she stumbled out of Vauban's tent. Most of the men had turned in for the night. She heard voices behind her, a group of soldiers heading for some leisure activity across the river. They were noisily boastful and heavy-footed. Lucinda slunk back into the shadows between two tents, and waited until they had passed. She had no right to be there as a woman, alone and unaccompanied.

She heard the defiant bells of Maastricht's carillon coldly sounding the hour. Every noise made her start: the pop-pop of lone muskets answering each other, a horse whinnying dismally in the distance. A nightmare moon grimaced at her, its mouth horribly open. It had only half a face.

A light inside the infirmary tent made it glow like a beacon. She pushed her way through the frayed flaps of the low-hanging roof. There was calm here now, the chaos of the afternoon ordered and tamed. The dead had been carted away; the living were for the most part bandaged and neatly bedded. Bessie and John Prynce were seated by the brazier.

Her knees wobbled, and she clutched one of the poles. Her head throbbed with the sudden light, and she had to close her eyes.

"Pet!" Now Bessie was beside her. "What's the matter? What's happened?" Through a rainbow haze made by Bessie's hair, she could see Lieutenant Prynce sauntering closer, looking concerned and unduly kind.

It was this undeserved kindness that made the tears come. She had a good cry into Bessie's shoulder.

"What is it?" John hissed to Bessie.

"I don't know, she'll have to tell us," said Bessie, helpless. "Come, now, pet, can't you tell us what happened? Are you hurt?"

Lucinda waved a hand at John, but could not look at him directly. "You were right, sir, and I apologize for not believing you..." she managed at last.

The surgeon's face went white. "Vauban...!" he said.

"What happened?" cried Bessie, "Tell us!"

"Nothing happened," she said. "Nothing happened!" And she started laughing hysterically, through the tears.

When Lucinda and Henry reached Vauban's tent, they were told he had stepped out for a moment. Henry hurriedly entrusted Lucinda to Vauban's assistant, Jean Gonflé, with a message of apology for the delay.

"You are not going to *leave* me here!" she cried, as it dawned on her that he was about to do just that.

"Oh come, darling." He winked at her—"We agreed!"

"No!" she pleaded, "We did not agree! Please! Henry! I can't..."

"Oh yes you can!" he chuckled playfully, and turned to the Frenchman. "Women. They never know what they want, do they. This one just extracted a promise from me to *marry* her! To honor and obey!"

The assistant made a clucking noise. His prim little mouth pouted the barest of polite smiles as he watched the clownish antics the Englishman was putting on for his benefit. Henry's hand was clasped above his head, as if holding a rope, head hung over to one side, tongue lolling, eyes popping out of his head. He straightened when he caught sight of Lucinda's reddening eyes, and said, "All the same, sir, I advise you to keep an eye on her and not let her out of your sight."

"Henry!" she shrieked. But he was gone.

Lucinda tried to size up Vauban's assistant from beneath lowered lids. Jean Gonflé was a small, neatly muscled man with a sparse moustache and finely honed beard. His expression was not one of sympathy.

It was more of a leer. She started sidling toward the tent opening. He clicked his tongue, leaned forward and grabbed her shoulder. Firmly, he led her to a chair and pushed her down into it. Then he walked to the table, picked up a goblet in one hand and a carafe in the other, and held them up at her questioningly. She shook her head and shrank back into her chair. They did not speak. He evidently thought she spoke no French, and she did not feel like disabusing him.

After a few minutes of staring at her derisively, the assistant remembered that he had other duties, and called for a guard, a burly fellow who breathed noisily through his mouth and smelled pungently of garlic.

A lifetime later—the assistant had come in a few times to check on her, Lucinda's foot had fallen asleep, she had gone through her entire stock of favorite daydreams, as well as a number of plans for warding off Vauban (including falling into a dead faint, melting his heart with her imprecations, dazzling him with her beauty and her virtue, or escaping by butting him with her head and knocking him down) the man himself walked in. He glanced at Lucinda, shook his head disapprovingly, and sank into the campaign chair next to a brazier that had been lit for him.

He did not speak. He lowered his head into his hands, as if it was very heavy (and Lucinda, noting its size, imagined it must be heavier than your average head).

Lucinda stood up. She felt it was incumbent on her to say something.

"*Monsieur?*" she began.

He looked at her dully. She could now see that his eyes were bloodshot and teary.

"*Que voulez-vous, madame!*" he said disdainfully. "What do you want?"

"Please," she said, uttering the words she had been rehearsing for the past two hours, "I—I believe there has been a misunderstanding ..."

"My prize, eh!" he said bitterly. "My English prize. Yes indeed." He sat up, and gave her a withering look-over. Then he turned, and spat onto the ground behind him. "The devil—it's my prize from the devil. I sold the lives of my dearest comrades—for a piece of foreign tail! Well, madam, I have no appetite for you now. No appetite at all."

"But..." Lucinda tried.

He stood up. His eyes were cold. "*But? But? Madame!* But God has punished me, don't you see! What an idiot I was, trusting that English bastard fool who thinks only of his own glory! Who flaunts the rules, who could care less about carefully laid plans..." He was shouting at Lucinda now, and she was cowering guiltily. "What did you think we built those trenches for, eh? Did you think we did it just to give ourselves something to do? For a lark? No, madam, it was to save lives. To save French lives, I should say, because apparently you English don't worry too much about that sort of thing. God directs *us* to spill as little blood as necessary, madame. I had it all planned. And then that fop Monmouth"—he spat the English name out so vehemently that his lips were flecked with foam—"he goes and wrecks everything, two thousand lost, including my own Paul and the greatest warrior of all, d'Artagnan..." He threw himself into his chair and began to moan, hunched over the table strewn with parchments, "Forgive me, *nom de Dieu,* name of God, sacred Mother of God, forgive me, forgive me..."

"Well..." said Lucinda hesitantly, looking over her shoulder. "In that case..." she whispered, and started backing toward the entrance.

"That's right, garbage, out, out! *Oui, c'est ça, va-t'en—putain, espèce d'ordure,* you English whore!" he screeched after her.

John was staring at her with a strange look on his face as she finished telling them of Henry's betrayal and Vauban's humiliating (although welcome) rejection. "So you see," she finished lamely, "nothing really happened, in the end..." and felt the tears well up in her aching eyes again.

"Oh, pet," said Bessie. "Pet, pet, pet, when will you ever learn..."

John cleared his throat. The women both looked up at him. He paused a few long moments, his eyes closed, before speaking. "I am to blame, madam," he finally said quietly. "Once again in my unforgivable doltishness I have done you an injustice. You see, your reaction to my warning led me to believe that this—danger was of no concern to you, that you were willing..."

"That I was *willing*...!"

John hung his head. "I do not mean it as a reproach, madam. I see now that I was mistaken. I only mean—I only meant to explain to you why I was remiss in shielding you from this great insult. Knowing what I know now, I cannot forgive myself. My failure to protect you—it is unpardonable."

"No, no!" whispered Lucinda, her voice cracking. "You mustn't blame yourself! You tried to warn me, but I would not listen!"

He was looking at her cautiously. There was a disconcerting silence. She realized that perhaps she hadn't said enough. She started babbling. "I was a fool, and I believed Captain Beaupree—I mean, I wanted to believe him. I...I kept hoping...but I see now that I cannot. I was wrong about him. He is a scoundrel, a villain. I'll never believe anything he says again. I know that now—" Her sentence was left dangling dangerously in mid-air.

Their eyes locked for a few moments until suddenly they realized they were gazing unguardedly. Both looked away, embarrassed.

"Well. What *I* believe," Bessie jumped in brightly, "is that it is late, and you are very upset, pet, and very tired, and you probably haven't eaten a thing." She turned to the surgeon. "I think it would be best if you took her back to our tent, sir. I mean, if you wouldn't mind. I'll sit up with these poor souls tonight. You need your rest."

"Oh, but I cannot let you..." he began half-heartedly.

"I assure you. An old woman needs less sleep than you young people." She beamed at them. "Go on, now, dears. There's that suet pudding I made yesterday, lamb, it's in the box under our shifts, and half a ham."

"Ah, a suet pudding!" said John. "It does sound appealing..."

"Go. You deserve it," she ordered.

Overcome by Bessie's determination, the reluctant pair shuffled out of the tent.

They walked silently side by side down to the water and across the pontoon bridge. On the other side, Lucinda stopped him.

"I can find my way to the tent from here," she said shyly, "thank you. I do not need an escort. You needn't bother..."

"I won't hear of it! No, no, I promised mother Goose."

"But I tell you it isn't necessary." Her heart was heavy as lead. She was sure he had seen through Bessie's little ploy to throw them together, and braced herself for yet another rejection.

Instead, she felt the warmth of a hand groping for hers.

"Madam..."

"Lucinda."

"Lucinda." He breathed it like a sigh of relief. He held her hand gingerly. She held her arm out stiffly, trying to control the trembling, her muscles immediately aching with this attempt at nonchalance. "I—I was looking forward to some of that suet pudding, actually."

"Oh!" she said. "Well, in that case..."

He kept her hand in his all the way up the hill, neither of them acknowledging the electrifying intimacy of it.

She finally disengaged herself awkwardly when they arrived at the tent. "Let me find some light..." she said, her voice sounding like a fog-horn in the blackness. She stumbled about, not quite knowing what she was doing. In the end it was he who found the tinderbox, and lit a candle.

"You are trembling!" he said. "Here, let me light the brazier for you." She stared at the back of his head, amazed at his practicality. "Now come and sit down here," he said. He shook out one of the blankets and folded it around her shoulders. Instead of withdrawing, his arm remained where it was, gentle on her back. She shuddered violently, and he drew her closer to him.

That was how they sat for a long time, she shuddering occasionally and he pulling her closer every time.

"The pudding!" she exclaimed at one point.

"The pudding can wait," he said.

41

POT OF GOLD

The sensation is that of falling, falling, plummeting, the bowels leapfrogging over the bursting heart as the body plunges down, down, into thin air.

This, by the way, is why it is called "Falling in love".

"Hold me, hold me," she whispered into John's shoulder. She caught herself, and pressed her lips together. She hoped that he hadn't heard her. At the same time she hoped that he had.

He leaned back on the pile of blankets, pulling her with him so that they were now lying stretched out on the floor. This allowed her to nestle even closer to him, her forehead touching his chin, her profile pressed into his neck.

"Hush, try to sleep now, you must rest," he murmured. But he betrayed the sentiment by shifting again and holding her even more tightly than before. She wriggled closer too—she could not get enough of this thawing warmth. Her skin tingled, needing touch, more touch. Her heart was beating with hard knocks in her chest. She felt his chest contracting and expanding, expanding and contracting, and she heard and felt his breath, heavy now, in and on her ear.

He disengaged his hand from her elbow, slid it up along her upper arm toward her armpit, then slowly squeezed it tight again. Both paid rapt attention for a few moments to that large hand spanning her arm. It seemed a symbol of a new reality, a reality that involved nothing but just the two of them.

She could no longer ignore the hardness pointing through the layers of skirts against her thighs. A little flutter of fear gripped her heart—no, not fear. It was joy, it was excitement. Her legs relaxed a little. The hardness responded, pressing closer.

"John," she groaned, "we mustn't..."

But she belied her words by burying her head even deeper into the hollow of his neck, gulping in the humid air hovering there.

"No, we mustn't," he agreed, and, exhaling heavily through his nose, started stroking her back.

She could not help giving in to the melting feeling. Just a minute or so more of this, she promised herself. Then she would push him away. Gradually, every tense muscle in her body relaxed; the more relaxed, the more pliable her body, increasing the surface area available for closeness. Bit by bit, he gathered her up.

Lucinda, panting now, had to come up for fresh air. She lifted her face from his neck and found his nose, his eyes, his mouth, waiting. Their noses touched, rubbed, slid past each other as their mouths connected. Hesitantly at first, each took, then gave a kiss in turn, back and forth, forth and back. It is hard to say which of them first broke this courteous reciprocation, but all at once—and, it seemed, simultaneously—all restraint was thrown to the wind, and her lips and tongue, engorged with warm blood, were swept up in a rollicking dance with his.

Again she had a guilty impulse to stop before it was too late.

"John," she broke off, sighing, "John! We are forgetting ourselves. This was not the idea..."

But he did not, he could not, relax his hold on her. His mouth was set in a slack expression incapable, at this moment, of human utterance. His wide, faraway pupils and flat glassy stare betrayed his absolute, determined desire. That look sent a shudder of ecstasy shooting through her vessels and she gave herself up to the same overpowering, helpless sense of urgency.

They did not undress; there was nothing so deliberate about what was happening to them. Their clothes somehow got pushed aside in the places that mattered as their damp bodies adjusted to each other involuntarily.

And so it was that the delirious, the wonderful, the inevitable came to pass. Like two magnets drawn together across an invisible force field, with shifts of position almost imperceptible, these two could not help, in the end, slipping smoothly, oh so smoothly—comfortably, oh so comfortably!—into an interlocking hold, home at last.

"Oh," she gasped. Her face was no longer turned up to his but buried once more in his clavicle. How to describe the feeling? She was not, as when she lay with Henry, attacked, invaded, importuned: she was, of her own volition, clutching at him, drawing him deep, deeper into the very core of her being. Her other senses—sight, smell, sound—were rendered void and it was touch, only burning, glowing touch, that mattered. He moved—just once—and "Oh!" she gasped again.

A rhythm started. They began, in unison, to move, tentatively at first, gently, hesitantly, bashfully, even. But after only a little of this—it can't have been more than, say, a minute—a groan escaped him, and, as if goaded by some new demonic force, he had to pause, to gather up some pent-up force. With a shudder of anticipation, she felt him brace his feet deliberately against the floor. And now the rhythm started again, but bolder this time—syncopated—wilder...

She stopped. "Stop!" she said, "Stop, please, we can't..."

But the words came out sounding like sobs of gladness stuck in her throat, and almost immediately, by mutual consent, they took up again where they'd left off, too far gone now to think of the consequences.

When it was over, they lay immobile for a long time.

It was John who moved first. He needed to shift his arm, which was beginning to fall asleep under the weight of her head. "Mmmm," he murmured.

She turned her head and looked up at him. Tears were drying on her cheeks.

"John John John oh John," she said, pointlessly but poetically.

His hand was immersed in the hair above her neck. He twisted his fingers into the tangle, and gave it a proprietary tug.

"Ouch," she laughed. And the next instant, remembering the gravity of their situation, "*Now* what are we to do?" she demanded, her nose pressed to his nose, her eyes flashing mockingly.

It was clear to them that the act that had just been completed had been committed not in the name of ordinary lust. No, it had been, in all its glory, that elusive goal each of us hopes to find one day: the pot of gold at the end of the rainbow, the taste of heaven, the absolute-ultimate merger; in other words, true, reciprocal love. At the magic moment, despite everything else they had to pay attention to, they found the strength to gaze deeply into each other's eyes, and call out the other's name, brokenly. That, as everyone knows, is the stamp, the seal, the prearranged signal that love, true love, is at work, not to be confused with that other, less noble sport.

"*Now* what?" she repeated, nudging his chin with her nose.

He moaned. It was hard for him to break the perfect silence; to surrender to the foolishness of words.

"Now what?" he finally grunted, blissfully. "Us. We two. You. Me. You and me. For ever."

Even though they resonated warmly in her ear, the cryptic words seemed to come from very far away. With her eyelids half-closed, it was exactly like floating in one of her dreams. Ah, but she was awake, and the words were real! There was more: "I have loved you—from the moment I first laid eyes on you. I have hated Beaupree since the moment I understood you were his."

The mention of Henry made her sit up in alarm. "Henry! If he finds out—he'll kill you! A—a duel! Won't he? Oh please, I don't want you to, to—"

"No, no," he soothed her. "There will be no duel. After what he did to you...And we are brothers, comrades-at-arms. There is a code of honor. His Majesty has strictly forbidden any duels among the officers. I am certain we can come to an understanding..."

To himself, he was grimly going over the numbers required to buy Beaupree off. The rogue always needed money. Surely his proprietary interest in the woman he considered his mistress—the thought made John grit his teeth with fury—could be snuffed with an adequate bribe. John had ten thousand pistoles stashed away in his tent; and if that wouldn't do it, he could always cash some bills being held for him in Paris.

John's confidence filtered through to Lucinda. She could trust him, he was not just placating her. He could make everything come out all right. She was so happy. So very, very happy. And John. It was John. It had been John all along, the hero of her dreams. How astonishing. How perfect. She dozed off in his arms, exhaustion winning the day.

She did not sleep for long, however, for John could not resist stroking her, exploring intimately those aspects of her that were now his to discover, and his ruminations soon woke her up.

"Hello," she said shyly.

"Well hello to you," he smiled, and went back to his grazing.

It wasn't long before he took her again; and she partook of him, equally.

And that, in a nutshell, says it all.

42

THE PUMPKIN

A beautiful coach, all made of the purest Venetian glass, a lovely crystal bubble of a thing, starts to roll downhill, slowly at first. Somewhere close by a loud clock begins to strike: ONE—TWO—THREE! Inside, the two passengers, with a thrill, realize what that sound means—FIVE—SIX—SEVEN!—as they are swept away in the runaway carriage, faster, faster, knowing full well what is about to happen, but powerless to stop it—NINE!—TEN!—ELEVEN! They look at each other in horror, amazement and rapture—

TWELVE!

The coach explodes into a thousand pieces, and they bump to a grinding stop. For a few moments, dazed, they lie on the ground, lifeless. Slowly they open their eyes. Behold! There is their coach, a few feet away from them, in the ditch. Only it has changed into a pumpkin again, a humble pumpkin, smashed in the mud. Sad, deflated, they turn and look at each other. There is mud there too, on the chin, cheek and forehead...but there is something else as well. It is a flash of light, the sparkle of a single tear, in the other's eye.

And then hope returns. For it is suddenly clear that no matter how bleak things may seem now, that pumpkin, or one just like it, is capable of turning itself into a magic coach again, and take them on many another joy-ride to many another glittering ball.

To sum up, then: this was no ordinary night. It was a night without end, a night without time, a night that was doing everything in its power to prolong the ecstasy, to draw itself out elastically, to behave as if there were no tomorrow and love were never-ending. Every time Lucinda and John dozed off (and doze off they did), it wasn't long before the night would prod them, sending a message (a barking dog, a braying mule, a mosquito humming in their ears) to remind them that the warm flesh intertwined with theirs was a treasure too precious to be used for so common a pastime as sleep; and so they would shake off their drowsiness and continue their relentless exploration of each other.

Over the ham and the suet pudding (the best they had ever tasted, they decided), John and Lucinda found time to tell each other their innermost secrets, and here was the most miraculous thing of all: they discovered that no matter what the subject, their views were identical down to the last detail, so that it grew almost embarrassing to have to exclaim with delight and a mouth full of food, time and time again, "So do I!" Or, "Isn't it?" Or, "I know just what you mean!"

It was now clear to Lucinda that for the first time in her life she had stumbled upon another human being who was of like mind in every respect, and who was therefore just as smart and wonderful as she was. Is that not the best thing about love—that, given the license to adore someone else, you can see yourself so becomingly reflected in another's lovestruck eyes?

"Have you ever felt like this before?" she asked. She knew, of course, that it was unlikely for a man of John's age never to have lain with another woman, but it was nevertheless critical that she be the only serious, the only *true* object of his passion.

"No, of course not," he reassured her. "Although I thought I was in love with someone once. I was completely obsessed. You remind me very much of her."

"Oh?" A tiny pang of jealousy started whetting its blade on her heartstrings. "Who was she?"

"It was a long time ago. She was my betrothed."

"You...your wife?" she asked, alarmed.

"No!" he said quickly. "No, Please don't think I...I should explain. The marriage had been arranged, but it never took place."

"Ah," sighed Lucinda, relieved.

"It was only when she ran off with another man that I realized how much I wanted her."

She cradled his head in her arms and started rubbing his back, the way Bessie used to, when she needed comforting. She noted that there was hair on his shoulders, where Henry had none. It gave her an inexplicably satisfying thrill. But she felt his heaviness, and tried to focus on his confession. She felt his disappointment as if it were her own. She was well acquainted with the sting of unrequited love, after all. "She was mad not to want you," she crooned.

"I wasn't much of a prize," he said bitterly. "She was absolutely right. I was a dolt. I did her a great disservice. A great injustice."

There was a long silence. Lucinda's curiosity finally got the better of her self-control, however.

"I want to know everything about you," she whispered into his buttery hair. "Please tell me about this—this maid who broke your heart."

He shrugged. "I'm afraid it was I who broke hers."

He glanced up and saw the stricken expression on her face.

"I'm sorry. I'd rather not. It's not a pretty story..."

"I understand," Lucinda said quietly. She was just starting to find out that losing your heart is only the beginning; that there can be so much more to lose as well.

Daybreak, when it finally came, found them sitting in the opening of the tent, watching a gaudily backlit sky arrange and rearrange its implausible colors along the horizon. A chirpy chorus of delirious birdsong hailed the dawning of a brand new world. Lucinda felt a little drained by all this perfection. John was telling her which parts of her anatomy he found the most appealing, and his hand rested on one of the places he had so described.

"So—your betrothed, what did she look like?" she interrupted him, lightly. She couldn't help it.

He grunted. "You are not going to let that rest, are you?" he said.

"You don't have to tell me," she said quickly.

He stared into the distance. "She looked—well, she looked a bit like you."

"Like me?"

"It struck me when we first met, the resemblance. But you—you're much prettier."

"Oh."

"And she was never real to me. Believe me. She was just a lovely idea that was promised to me. I had only seen her twice. I was very young, a mere boy. And a hothead. It wasn't love. It was jealousy. Of the other man, I mean."

"Well," she said, "if it wasn't really love, there's no reason not to tell me about her, is there?"

He sighed. After a pause, he said, "Yes. I must tell you. But it is something I am not very proud of. I don't want you to think badly of me."

"I would never, ever think badly of you!" she cried.

He shook his head, frowning apologetically. "It was an error of my youth—I was a different person then."

Lucinda snuggled against him. She understood his motivation for wanting to appear faultless to her. Of not wanting to shatter the image of perfection. But nothing, *nothing* John had done in his youth could ever dismay her. He was perfect. She just wanted to be able to dismiss this rival from the scene, that was all. She wanted to hear her described; draw her own comparisons; then lay her to rest.

"Tell me. Please?"

"All right. I was not even sixteen. My relatives arranged it because, as I told you, my parents died when I was very young. They said it would be a very good match; she came from a wealthy family, and had a good portion. She was pretty..."—he stroked Lucinda's curls—"I liked the idea of being married to her. But she was just a child, and it was decided that we would wait until she was of an age to decide for herself."

"And then?"

"And then—well, the next thing, she had—given herself to another."

"She married someone else?"

"No. Worse. Her parents were against it. She just ran off with him. Bolted."

"Oh, John," she sighed, sharing his mortification. She grabbed his hand, but he pulled it away and stood up, stretching self-consciously. He stood in the tent opening, gazing out at the stirring camp.

"That wasn't the end of it. I was in a rage. I thought I was the laughingstock of the county. I could think of nothing else. I paid a man—a spy—to find out where they had gone. Eventually he tracked them down for me. I went there and found them. Challenged him to a duel."

He glanced over at Lucinda. She put all her heart into a wry, encouraging smile. He turned away again and closed his eyes a moment.

"I never meant to kill him. I wanted to draw blood, *my* blood, I wanted her to see me bleeding, I wanted her to take pity on me. But that isn't how it turned out." His voice was so hoarse that she had to strain to hear him. "Suddenly—I saw him lying on the ground, gored by my sword..."

"Oh, John!" Her heart ached for him.

He laughed bitterly. "Of course she wouldn't have anything to do with me. She couldn't stop screaming. She was great with child. *His* child. I was so ashamed, so sorry for what I had done. The shock brought on her pains. I'm ashamed that I did not stay—It was my turn to bolt. I could not face having to answer for what I had done. "

At the end of his story, they were both quiet. Very quiet. Lucinda's mouth was dry. She hated that Jezebel who had hurt him so much. John was well rid of her.

And yet...Why did the story sound so familiar? Something about it was a little close to home. She found herself asking,

"What happened to her?"

"I don't know. I had to flee. I left money for my rival's burial, and for a midwife for his lady. I ran off and joined the army, in France. It was quite a few years before it was safe for me to return to England. I did try to contact her family then, but they were no help. They'd disowned her, you see."

Lucinda said nothing. It was John who broke the silence. "It was then that I vowed never to take a life again. That was my penance: to save lives instead. I apprenticed myself to a barber-surgeon. And here I am."

Lucinda's head was spinning.

"What was her name?" Her voice sounded muffled inside her head.

"Her name?" He turned around and knelt down by her side. "What does it matter?"

"I'd just like to know her name."

"Olivia. Lady Olivia Steppys."

Click.

Click.

Click.

Lucinda's heart snapped shut, one segment at a time. She could observe, as from a great distance, her happiness extinguishing itself in slow motion. With enormous dignity, like a sheet of burning paper crumpling majestically into ashes.

"Lucinda."

He was leaning over her, an uncertain grin on his face. Was she teasing him? She had gone so quiet, all of a sudden.

She looked up, and tried to smile. She felt unbearable pity for him, for both of them.

He could not make out her mood. He tried to get his hands under her arms, which she held rigidly by her side, to tickle her.

She neither laughed nor protested. She stood up, and pulled her cloak tightly around herself.

"I must go down to the river now, to wash," she managed.

"What's the matter? I'll come with you."

"No. Go see to the wounded. I will come by later," she lied.

And she made her way carefully, purposefully, down to the river.

43

A MISCARRIAGE OF FATE

Maastricht capitulated a week later, and as soon as the king was bored with inspecting and showing off his new prize, the camp began to break up.

"What now, lamb?" said Bessie.

"What, Bess?"

"We can't stay here moping. Everyone is leaving. It's time to go home."

"Home?"

"Lamb. I know you are upset, I know you are suffering. But please—don't make it harder than it is. I think it's for the best. There is enough money left for our passage."

"Whatever you want. I don't care."

Bessie sighed, and began tidying up the tent. Her lamb had been sunk in a sullen stupor for days, and she was not snapping out of it. Bessie was glad, of course, that Lucinda had finally come to her senses about Captain Beaupree. Although the final indignity was that the poor girl had been robbed of the pleasure of letting him know it, since Henry had apparently decided, quite on his own, to deprive himself of her company. There had been no summons, no apology, no acknowledgement of any kind. Once, snarling at Bessie to leave her alone, Lucinda had hinted that there had been a last-ditch marriage proposal the night of the assault, but Bessie found this hard to believe. In any case, even if it was true and the subject of marriage had indeed come up, the captain evidently now preferred to forget that it had ever happened.

But that fiasco was overshadowed by something far more upsetting. Bessie truly didn't know whom to feel sorrier for, her poor lamb or that poor Mister Prynce, who was flapping around the infirmary like a freshly beheaded chicken, poor soul, getting in the way and scaring away the patients.

Twice, three times that awful day last week he had returned to their tent looking for Lucinda, and had left with increasing bewilderment when an apologetic Bessie had had to turn him away. At that point Lucinda had not yet told her what had happened, but Bessie knew there was something very, very wrong. She had been able to wring it out of the girl in the end.

Sitting in a corner that night, peeling carrots, she'd watched Lucinda groom her hair vacantly, methodically, like a cat.

"It is strange, isn't it," Bessie had begun, lightly, "how one's humors can change so quickly —"

Lucinda gave an exasperated sigh, irritably acknowledging that Bessie was starting to probe.

"Just the other morning, for instance, Lieutenant Prynce seemed so elated—well, I have never seen him like that. He was fairly bursting out of his skin."

"Ha!"

"And next thing I know, he comes looking for you and you make me send him away, pale as a peahen, a lost soul."

"Perhaps he is a lost soul. Or a peahen."

Bessie started slicing the carrots with her knife, deftly, against her thumb. The slices plopped into her apron. "Pet. If anything has happened between you two—perhaps you will tell me, so that I'll know what to say to him. I mean, if he didn't behave like a gentleman, I'll—"

Lucinda snickered bitterly. "Oh, he behaved like a gentleman, all right!"

"Well, whatever he did to you, I should like to know. I don't know what to say to him. Consider my position."

"All right," shouted Lucinda. "All *right*! You should know that..."—a harsh growl emerged from her throat—"I *hate* him. And so should you."

"You hate him! Lamb! If you'd said you hated the captain, I'd quite understand. But why *him*?"

"I hate him even more than I hate the captain!"

"Lord! What did he *do*?"

"I des*pise* him. He is my mortal enemy."

"Come, lamb, it can't be as bad as that! What did he do to you? Tell me!"

"He killed my father." She said it almost flippantly.

Bessie laughed. "He killed your father! Lamb! Why do you say these things? You know your father is long dead..."

"That's what I mean. John—Lieutenant Prynce. Killed him."

"You don't mean..."

"Is it so hard to understand?" yelled Lucinda. "I found out that your dear Mister Prynce is the man who was once my mother's betrothed. He told me so himself. The rejected suitor who killed my father, *you* know, in a duel, just before I was born."

"Oh!"

There was a long, aghast silence.

"Does he know?" Bessie said at last.

"What?"

"That you are the offspring of—"

"No. *I'm* not going to tell him!"

"Oh, pet!"

"The funniest thing is," said Lucinda mirthlessly, "that I thought I had finally found the one, the only man I could ever—"

"Lamb! Don't think that! You'll see, you are so young yet, and there are so many herring in the sea..."

Lucinda's outraged snort cut short that familiar line of reasoning.

After Bessie informed him of the fortuitous prenatal connection between Lucinda and himself, John no longer came looking for Lucinda. He did go looking for Beaupree, and spat in his face, and was called out, and met him and his second early the next morning in a lonely hollow on the other side of Kerkum, and received a flesh wound in the thigh just moments before the duel was broken up by the Duke of Monmouth, who arrived on the scene in the nick of the time. (Since there had been some stalling on Beaupree's part, we cannot blame Prynce for suspecting his adversary of being responsible for the breach of secrecy). After being forced to listen to a stern lecture and made to give his adversary a sullen embrace, he was ordered to pay him two thousand pistoles and a silver platter in reparation. Finally he was allowed to hobble back to the infirmary tent.

It was Bessie who bound up his leg. Nothing was said between them, but it was clear from the way she shook her head, and the tenderness with which she attended him, that she was hoping he would pull himself together.

He tried, he really did try, but it was hard, because of the bitterness of the blow fate had dealt him, exacerbated by the great quantity of liquor that was finding its way down his numb gullet and befuddling his aching brain. In truth, as he confided to a fellow drunk at one of the canteens, he was afraid that the minute his hands stopped shaking he might very well have to pick up his barber's tools, slice open his own chest and cleanly amputate the ice-cold heart that was surely growing gangrenous in there.

Slouching around the partially dismantled camp, he would suddenly bray with laughter at his preposterous predicament. His true love was the daughter of the maid who had spurned him; her father, the youth he had foolishly killed in a duel! But instead of joining in the laughter, the people just looked away. They did not jeer at him. They did not seem to notice what a buffoon he'd become. A massive, *massive* miscarriage of fate had befallen him, and yet it had created not a stir, not a whisper. No one pointed at him, no one gossiped, no one sniggered. He suddenly grew furious. He lunged at a soldier who, instead of paying attention, stood polishing a bayonet. The man backed away politely. John sat down heavily in the dust and buried his face in his knees. Life was one catastrophic farce. That's what it was about, wasn't it? It was about being given a glimpse of paradise, and having the gates slammed shut in your face. And then to have your friends mutter, *Ah well, that's life, old man,* and with unseemly alacrity avoid your depressing company altogether. The joke of it was that you couldn't blame anyone else, because it was all your own damned fault...

He found himself being drawn back to the infirmary in the end, not because he cared now who lived or died, but because Bessie might be there, and Bessie was his one link to the angel who now, rightfully, abhorred him.

"Mister Prynce," she said, "Mister Prynce. Let me take another look at that wound of yours. That's it, sit down here."

He did as he was told.

"The camp is moving on," came her soothing voice, "and we should be moving on too."

"Indeed," he said.

"Yes, I am taking my young lady back to England, sir. We'll follow the wagons headed north, to Utrecht, and then make our way to the coast from there. I think that's best, don't you?"

"Yes," he said woodenly.

"If it is any consolation," she said, "she is taking it very hard too."

"A consolation? Not really," he replied in a voice creaking with despair.

44

BODEGRAVEN AND ZWAMMERDAM

The French offensive against Holland had begun in 1672, one year before Bessie and Lucinda joined Louis XIV's massive wagon train. Louis had succeeded in crossing the Rhine with his army that year, and had found only negligible resistance in his sweep toward Amsterdam.

However, the Dutch, with their backs against the wall and the French invader on their doorstep, had had one last card up their sleeve. They cut the dikes and opened the sluices to let in the sea, flooding the low-lying countryside from the Zuyderzee on one side to the North Sea on the other. This simple measure had stopped the mighty conqueror in his tracks. There had been nothing for it but to retire to Paris for the winter, and hope for a hearty freeze.

It was a mild winter. The troops Louis left behind at Utrecht under the command of General Luxembourg took out their frustration on the towns and villages on the south side of the watery divide. They were allowed to run wild that winter, raping, murdering and pillaging everywhere they went. The villages of Bodegraven and Zwammerdam were burned to the ground.

It was to supply this same General Luxembourg in Utrecht that a portion of the baggage train was now being sent north from Maastricht. The rest of the baggage trundled off in the opposite direction with the main army, headed for Westphalia.

On the second night of the northbound caravan's march, they bivouacked outside Weert. Bessie was stirring a communal broth over an open fire.

"What's in the pot, Missis?" asked Goodbody O'Day, a sturdy Irish war widow and part-time bawd who could drink any man under the table and was in charge of some of the packhorses.

Bessie's eyes twinkled. "Eels. The ditches are swimming with them here." She proudly drew a long, lugubrious specimen out of the pot, to show her.

Suddenly Lucinda felt ill. She tried to stand up straight, but doubled over instead on a wave of nausea, and vomited heavily onto the ground.

"Lamb! What's come over you?" Bessie exclaimed, patting her between the shoulder blades. When the heaving had stopped, she cleaned the girl's face with a corner of her apron.

"I don't know, something I ate, I expect," Lucinda mumbled, wiping her bespattered slippers on the grass.

Bessie kept a close watch on her that night and the next day. Finally, observing Lucinda reeling from another bout behind some bushes, she grabbed her by the hands.

"How long have you been feeling like this, pet?"

"Oh, I'm sure it'll go away. I just feel a little queasy, lately."

"I see. And when did the blood last come?"

"The blood? You mean my terms?"

"Yes."

"I don't know. A few weeks ago, I think."

Bessie folded her arms and looked at her severely. "You may be with child, pet. I shouldn't wonder, with all your carrying on..."

"With child!" Lucinda was aghast. "But..."

What she was thinking was surely she had suffered enough.

It took some courage to ask the next question.

"Bessie," she said at last—they were camped outside Zaltbommel, less than two days' journey from Utrecht; the troops had already marched on ahead—"if, as you say, I am with child..."

"Oh," said Bessie, "we're not certain of that yet, lamb."

"But say that I *am* with child. How—how will I know who the father is?"

Bessie gave her a keen look. Either Lucinda was pretending to be more naïve than Bessie imagined, or Bessie's guess about what had passed that night between her pet and Lieutenant Prynce was about to be confirmed.

"Well, pet," she began. "It all depends."

"Depends? On what?"

"It depends," she said carefully, "on who bedded you when it was conceived."

"Oh," said Lucinda.

"Yes. If, for instance, your—uh, paramour were Captain Beaupree, then it would be his child."

"What if there was someone else—as well?"

"If there was someone else as well, then we should never know for sure," said Bessie firmly. She folded her arms across her chest and pursed her lips.

"Oh, Lord." Lucinda hauled herself to her feet.

"Where are you going now, lamb!"

"A little walk, if that's all right with *you*!" she spat out.

"Don't go far, lamb," Bessie pleaded, suddenly anxious. She regretted having shown her disapproval like that. "Please, pet. I don't like it when you wander off by yourself in these foreign parts."

Grimacing wanly, Lucinda brought out a withering, "Ah, Bess—still worried I might be set upon by pirates or Frenchmen?" and hobbled off toward a copse in the distance.

Despite her expertise in the healing arts, Bessie was not possessed of a well-rounded education. She knew less than nothing of astronomy, alchemy or Greek, and had no patience with politics, geography or world events. (Bear in mind that she did not have a husband to inform her.) If you had asked Bessie what this huge army was up to in the United Provinces, she would have been at a loss to explain it to you. Not that she differed much in this respect from the majority of soldiers, or even some generals, taking part in King Louis XIV's magnificent campaigns. All they knew was that there was a living to be made, there were orders to be followed, and that their betters must have good reasons to pick the fights they did.

Which is why, when Bessie found herself suddenly seized by the hair and poked in the ribs by a group of wild-eyed people brandishing axes and pitchforks with the guttural battle cry *Bodegraven en Zwammerdam! Bodegraven en Zwammerdam, Bodegraven en Zwammerdam!* her last conscious thought on this earth was that she had no *idea* what they were shouting about.

45

THE HERO

Writers of fiction, of all people, have no right to question the veracity of history books. After all, historians are tasked with giving nothing but the facts, whereas fiction bestows on the writer the license to throw away those facts and simply invent. Beware, however, of putting all your faith in the work of the scholars, no matter how thorough, credible, and authoritative they may seem.

Take the rape of Bodegraven and Zwammerdam, for instance. You will be hard pressed to find even a single reference to this incident in any French history book. Which is understandable, from a French point of view, since it would surely take some of the shine off France's glorious past to dwell unnecessarily on a macabre episode in which the entire civilian populations of two small Dutch towns were unspeakably raped, mutilated, tortured, burned and otherwise annihilated by bored French troops serving under General Luxembourg in the winter of 1672.

Dutch historians, on the other hand, have been less willing to let bygones be bygones. In the Netherlands, "Bodegraven en Zwammerdam" is a dirge that is memorized by conscientious schoolchildren to this day.

As for the retaliation by the local Dutch populace—the massacre of one hundred and fifty camp followers of Louis XIV's army outside the town of Zaltbommel the following summer—you will find no mention of it in any history book whatsoever, neither French nor Dutch. Nor, digging through the records or documents of the period, are you likely to come across a single contemporaneous reference to that tragedy, other than a complaint sent by General

Luxembourg to Louvain, France's war minister, that the supplies
he was expecting never arrived because the baggage was burnt by a
rebellious mob.

You see now how important it is to read between the lines.

It is time to return to our hero—although "hero" is a label not to be tossed off so lightly. There are plenty of so-called "heroes" in literature, sadly, who never perform even a single heroic deed! No, a *true* hero, the sort implied here, earns his stripes by the way he handles the most extreme, ultimate challenge. It is when physical hardships have sapped the last ounce of remaining strength, when the goal seems utterly out of reach, in other words, when any ordinary mortal would have long given up, that the true hero finds the will to make a last stand, to spit in the witch's eye, to cut his way through the forest of thorns, to climb the burning stairs to the attic, or make one last charge at the dragon.

Whether John Prynce can be called a true hero or not is a matter of conjecture. A man certainly can't be excused from heroic duty because he chooses to drown his sorrow in his cups. But, lurching on horseback around the neatly pine-forested ridges of the Ardennes, our Prynce did eventually regain his sobriety. Or, rather, sobriety hit him squarely between the eyes in the form of a single, devastating thought: in letting Lucinda slip away, he had just made the second most unforgivable mistake of his life.

Being a hero of sorts, he knew what he had to do.

He wheeled his horse around.

It took him three days and two nights of straight riding to catch up with the northbound baggage train. It wasn't until the third day, however, that he came into the truly flat, hollow land that gives Holland its name: a grid-landscape of perfectly symmetrical fields separated from one another by drainage ditches clotted with pond scum, punctuated here and there by some pollarded willows, a windmill, a bridge, a thatched farmhouse, or a herd of well-behaved cows peacefully grazing,

A smear of white shimmered along the horizon. John sat up and peered blearily into the distance. What in God's holy name was *that*?

Less than an hour later he found himself trotting alongside fields strangely draped in white as far as the eye could see. He seemed to have entered a stark, desert landscape, an ocean of white. Ghostly sheets everywhere, held down at their corners by stones, lazily rippling and bulging in the breeze. There was an awful tidiness about the scene. The whiteness reflected the sunlight sharply, and John had to tilt his hat low over his eyes against the glare. Despite the sun on his back, he suddenly felt cold.

The warm earth was laid to rest, wrapped in a shroud.

A farmer's wife who sold him a jug of buttermilk and some bread and cheese giggled at his worried face. She pointed out the mounds of untreated linens, and the large vats of lye these were soaking in before being spread out in the sun. She showed him the bolts and bundles neatly packed into hampers, ready to be shipped out. Her own apron was a dazzling white and billowed with every gust of wind, like a sail.

But her cheery explanation of that region's bleaching industry did not dispel John's eerie sense of foreboding.

On a clear afternoon in a land short on mountains, hills, ridges, crags or other topographical obstacles, a traveller leaving one town can often see clear to the next, and even beyond that, to the town or village behind it. Leaving Kerkdrie now, John spotted the tower of Zaltbommel in the distance, and, rising from the level horizon behind it, a column of black smoke reaching to the clouds. There was no reason to start shaking with a dreadful premonition, or to suspect the smoke, miles away, had anything to do with anybody he knew; yet John was unable to shake the conviction that something terrible had happened to his one true love.

And indeed, spurring his horse to a gallop, passing through the town of Zaltbommel at an impatient trot, then galloping out again at full speed, his horse lathered with foam, his own skull prickling with sweat, coming closer to the smoke, closer, and then spying a horribly mutilated woman—not Lucinda, thank God!—one of her legs half hacked off, her breasts amputated, her mouth slashed from cheek to cheek, lying dead in the middle of the road, his worst fears were confirmed. The smoke, he now saw, came from a heap of smoldering wagons. He left his nervous horse tied to a tree and made his way to what was left of the camp on foot.

Blood and gore all around; piles of bodies, piles of brutal, gruesome bodies. One woman had been decapitated and hung upside down, her legs spread wide; the head was balanced with macabre humor in her crotch.

There was a terrible stench of burning flesh. It was impossible to shut it out. It insinuated itself evilly into the sinuses and made the eyes water. John found himself retching, and retching again, and fighting the urge to run away, to bury the scene deep in his nightmares.

But he could not. He must not. He had to find Lucinda. He wiped his mouth, and steeled himself. He started to sort, methodically, through the piles of corpses.

It was Bessie he found first, lying on the ground pop-eyed and spread-eagled, a pitchfork through her chest. Averting his own streaming eyes, he reached out and numbly closed hers.

This could not be. He was not awake. What was going on here? Where were the local people? Why had they not come to help, or, at the very least, to gawk? Was there no one alive, then, but him?

He had come too late. There was nothing for him to do now. It occurred to him that he ought to say a prayer for Bessie. For all of them… but—God!—the enormity of it! It was overwhelming. It was too much to expect of him! The feelings were wrong, too. He should be feeling pity for these poor souls, not this awful, this dire disgust. As if it was *their* shame. A brutal indignity they should have been able to forestall: a disgrace they ought never to have permitted…

He felt himself teetering on the edge. No safety net below. Emptiness all around. Blank, glaring, howling, unfathomable space. No limits, no end. Cut loose from all the fables we make up to comfort ourselves—the walls, the roofs, the blankets, the cozy corners. (Human beings are basically good, life is good, people do not, cannot behave like this. Death, rape, violence, evil—I know of it, I have heard of it, but it is not for me, it is something that happens, to be sure, but not to me and mine. At least, not here, not now, not any more, not yet!)

He was floundering in a bottomless pit. The abyss was rummaging around in his soul. It was pulling out all the stops in his head and booming out a fugue of doom.

He had to pull himself together, to focus on one thing at a time. One thing, dead or alive. What was it? Her. He must find her. He must call her. He must know if...

But to find Lucinda, he had to confront the terror again. The belching, lethargic horror of being too late. How was he ever to know her? The bodies in the wagons were for the most part burnt beyond recognition.

Under a charred wagon wheel, something winked at him in the sun. He knelt down. He picked it up. He bowed his throbbing head. A little mule, covered in ashes. An embroidered slipper.

Lucinda had shown him a pair of glass-beaded slippers, that night in her tent. Her legacy from her mother, she had said. Yes, he was sure that he recognized it! The beading was incomplete, around the heel. What had she told him again? That her mother had died before finishing it, or some such thing. Lucinda's mother—but there was another horror snapping at his heels—

What were the odds of Olivia, she who had rejected him for another, turning out to be the mother of his one true love? And, worse—had he not wanted to punish Olivia, at the time, for her falseness? Admit it, he had. He had! But not like this. Never! God! It was another horror that did not bear thinking about, another horror to rend black holes in his broken soul! He let go of the slipper in a sudden panic, as if it was a burning coal, a murder weapon, some dead, revolting thing.

Something tapped him gently on the back. He spun around, staggering to his feet. A charred human limb, dangling from a mass of burnt flesh, swayed in the breeze. He almost lost his balance, and reeled backwards.

Then he heard a high-pitched cry. A weak little mewl. Gratefully he turned in the direction of the sound. Sticking out from beneath a heap of bodies, he spied the long dusky legs of the African woman. Lucinda's friend. Zéfine.

Desperately he dug through the corpses. There was something warm in there. Alive. He pulled it out.

John stared at the infant. The infant looked back at him uncompromisingly. It blinked its large liquid eyes at him. A perfectly formed bubble emerged from its soft lips. John held his breath.

A gust of wind on its damp head made it startle. It stiffened and threw its little palms heavenwards, in horror.

Instinctively, John drew the little bundle close to his chest and started making clucking noises. The baby relaxed, and began to butt its face against the third button of John's coat.

Fortified by the infant's admirable reflexes, John took a deep breath and strode back to the place where he had found the slipper.

It was impossible to extract any useful information from the sullen burghers of Zaltbommel. No one had seen what happened. No one knew who was responsible. Nobody really cared to know what had happened to that French filth, if he really wanted to know the truth. Nobody knew who had stolen the packhorses and the stores. People suggested darkly that John should quiz the French general, the whores' paymaster, the one they called Luxembourg, who was quartered in Utrecht and was eating them all out of house and home.

John stayed around long enough to organize—and finance—the digging of a mass grave. The innkeeper's wife sold him a pewter horn with a sponge teat wrapped in linen, for feeding the child. She charged him two pistoles for it. Then, perhaps to atone for robbing him blind, she waddled over to him in the spotless taproom with a tankard of boiled cow's milk. Suddenly putting on a great show of motherly concern, she shook her head and tut-tutted sadly over "de poor liddle sing".

John had not the slightest inclination to leave the poor little thing with her.

46

LOST

"*Goed zo! Nog een hapje!*"

Lucinda tasted something warm; something liquid dribbled onto her chin. She peeled one of her eyelids open, painfully. There was a spoon in front of her; grasping it, a gnarled red hand. Her trembling eyelid sank shut again. It felt much safer that way.

It was pitch black when she awoke a second time. She could hear herself breathing, and it occurred to her that she was alive. She would remain calm no matter what. There was a blanket covering her. She was lying on some sort of lumpy mattress, with her icy feet sticking out. She tried sitting up. There was a smell of stale cooked cabbage. She heard someone snoring not too far away. There was some grating horror, something abominable…Severely, she shut it out of her mind. Gravity pulled down her head and shoulders, and she succumbed again.

A stench of manure lay heavily on the air, and a discord of cackling and crowing told her that it was morning. She raised her head. An old face, crosshatched, smiled at her and addressed her in guttural gibberish. She shook her head, and tried to listen, to focus on the woman's gestures to make some sense of the words.

Now an old man squeezed in through the narrow doorway. He was shaking his woolly head angrily, pointing at her. She sat up. He gestured at her to follow him. The old woman protested, and instead pulled her over to a table with a steaming bowl of porridge. The woman pushed her husband out of the way so that Lucinda could sit down, and she fell on the food hungrily, ignoring the quarrel behind her.

When she had finished, the old woman smiled at her again. *"Lekker?"* she was asking. "Very good," said Lucinda, watching the old man climb shakily up on a stool. Muttering, he stretched his bent frame as far as it would go, reaching for something balanced across the rafters. It was an oar. He hauled it down, stepped off the stool, carried it, bowlegged, over to the door, leaned it against the lintel, adjusted it so that it would balance, watched it for a few seconds to make sure it would not fall, marched resolutely back to the stool, climbed up again and reached for its twin, almost lost his balance, growled some lengthy expletive, reached up again and captured the uncooperative implement, lowered it to the ground, leaned on it heavily to let himself down and, regaining his balance, looked around with an air of defiance, as if he challenged anyone to do it as well as he had.

The old woman was saying something to Lucinda, and touched her cheek. Sadly, she pointed to the door and waved her hand. Lucinda got up and followed the old man who, with the oars under his arms, was stumbling down to the canal where a little wooden boat was tied up to a pole. She turned. "Thank you!" she cried.

"Dank U!" the old woman said, nodding, to show that she had understood.

When she had climbed into the boat, the old man started pointing and gesturing, grunting and puffing. She looked around, confused. Impatiently, he grabbed her by the hair and yanked her head down so that she was forced to lie at his feet. "Ouch!" she complained, but she did not move. For with a rush of heart-stopping fear, she remembered what had happened the day before, and understood what he meant. She mustn't show her face. It was dangerous. Humbly, she remained prostrate on the slimy bottom of the boat, and entrusted herself to him.

The peasant punted the length of the canal and then, where the canal turned into a river, rowed upstream along the bank for a couple of miles. Finally he pulled into a stand of rushes, and prodded her shoulder. She sat up. He pointed in the direction of the bank. She stepped out into the shallow water, her bare feet squelching in the mud.

"Dank U!" she cried, as she scrambled up the bank.

He shrugged, and backed out into the river.

* * *

"One more step. And another..."

She had begun talking to herself. Muttering under her breath like a madwoman was somehow helping her keep herself together. And at least talking to herself in her mother tongue afforded her a small measure of fluency in this country where she was otherwise a foreign object of scorn, tongue-tied, dumb, and rejected.

Even after days of this, begging had not lost its shame. Never, *never* would she get used to it. Each time she summoned the courage to ask, she steeled herself for rejection, or, worse, grudging generosity invariably delivered with a judgmental sneer. She couldn't blame them: she too had always assumed that beggars were cheaters, liars and thieves. She used to think beggars capable of pretending misery—even capable of amputating a limb—just in order to make a very nice living preying on decent folk. That was before she had experienced the hunger pains that made a starving person desperate enough to brave any amount of contempt.

"Nou? Wat wil je?" asked a suspicious farmer's wife, peering out of the top half of her door at Lucinda.

She held out her hands, cupped.

Now the woman became distracted, staring past Lucinda's shoulder as if she didn't exist. Turning her back, she busied herself in her kitchen, slinging pails around, yelling something at the children, shouting orders at a lazy boy sweeping the yard.

Lucinda did not budge. It took all the effort she possessed to keep herself erect, her head humbly bowed. Every so often the farmer's wife would glance in her direction, only to see her still standing there. The woman made herself even busier, lifting a heavy sack of flour with a groan, retying her apron more securely, kicking a dog out of the way. Finally, as if it could wait no longer, she started breaking eggs into a bowl.

Lucinda let out a sigh.

"Hier!" Without warning, the woman threw an egg at Lucinda's head. But the girl was alert as a dog. She caught it deftly in mid-air.

"Dank U," she said, and shuffled off. She didn't have enough self-control to wait until she was out of sight before cramming the egg into her mouth and sucking out the raw ooze to the last drop.

As Lucinda drew nearer to Amsterdam, the farms became more prosperous and the people even less compassionate. But she had heard that Amsterdam was a fine city, full of rich, generous merchants. If she could make it to Amsterdam, then perhaps the rasping hollow in her belly would be filled, the unaccustomed heaviness would go away, and the nightmare darkness would lift. It was a goal, and in the absence of any other possible purpose or hope of rescue, she plodded on.

PART
THREE

47

A VIRGIN

If you think there is a chance you could lose your way in the dark and impenetrable forest, you must devise a way to leave a trail behind.

But bear in mind that the birds will eat your breadcrumbs, the wind will scatter your blazes, the rain will wash away the chalk marks, and time will erase most promises.

"Prynce! Dear fellow!"

John looked up from the *Gazette* he was reading and saw Samuel Wynde, a friend of his youth. He stood up, and inclined his head.

"Wynde," he mumbled reluctantly. "Allow me to offer you a coffee."

"Never touch the stuff, old boy! The humors, you know. One is too much afflicted with the choler as it is."

Prynce smiled politely.

"Fellow! A bottle of claret over here!" bellowed Wynde. "More coffee for my friend!"

Prynce resumed his seat at the long coffee house table, and folded the paper.

"Well, man! Where have you been hiding? It has been years! I had heard—your cousin Rochester told me—you were with my Lord Monmouth at Maastricht in '73, when he had his Glorious Victory."

"Ah yes, that glorious victory," said John mildly.

"Did you go to the re-enactment of the siege at Windsor? Quite the spectacle!"

"No, I can't say that I did," said John.

"I must say the duke cut a dashing figure. So handsome, isn't he! And His Majesty so very proud of him. He will very soon be declared the Heir, you know. I have it on the very best authority..."

"That will be very nice for him," said John, taking a sip of his coffee.

"I am intimate with Sir Thomas Armstrong and some of the others. They keep me informed. They'll tell me anything I want to know."

"Quite."

"Dear old Prynce. But we never see you at court! Where the devil have you been hiding, old boy? Not still playing the quack, are you?"

"I'm afraid I am," said John. "Actually, I have opened a lying-in hospital, in St. Giles, for poor women..."

"Fancy that," exclaimed Wynde, biting back a yawn. He craned his head to look around the coffee-house. Suddenly he jumped out of his seat. "My lord!" he called out. "Excuse me, old boy, but I must pay my respects."

"By all means," said John, picking up his *Gazette*.

A short while later, a triumphantly sweating Samuel was at his elbow again. He was putting on his gloves.

"Lord Dunnover has done me the honor of inviting me to see the new pictures he acquired on his Grand Tour," he said. "Will you come? I hear they are wonderful, quite lewd, especially the Italians."

"Thank you, but I don't think I—"said John.

Wynde pulled him to his reluctant feet. "Come! Let me introduce you to Lord Dunnover! You will be amused! You will be entertained! You will mingle with the better sort of people for once! It will do you good!"

"In truth," John protested, "I truly..." But he allowed Wynde to drag him reluctantly out the door.

The better sort of people had never been very much to John Prynce's liking. The better sort of people were epitomized, for him, by his kinsman John, Earl of Rochester, formerly darling of the court, who for some years had been wasting his considerable poetic talent on increasingly vituperative and pornographic doggerel, and whose alcoholic posturing and imbecilic escapades had finally earned him the distinction of being the only member of King Charles' licentious court to be banished from it at least three times.

John had had to go to his cousin for permission to spend—"squander!" his lordship had guffawed—his personal inheritance on his pet project, the maternity hospital in St. Giles. Lord Rochester had been sober enough that morning to appreciate the idea of his dour relative playing quack to the masses.

"By all means!" he had roared. "And what do these worthy mothers come up with, in payment?" He winked at John with a leer. "That's a nice little business, I warrant," he slurped, "why seek out the bawds of Dog & Bitch Yard if you can get all you want for free, eh?"

It is difficult to be a man of principle in an age of meager morality. John did not consider himself a saint, nor was he a religious man; his actions were inspired simply by a very clear idea of what was right. It was his lot, however, to live in a world ruled by people who were more interested in appearances than in substance; a world in which worth was measured uniquely in wealth, and where talent, honesty, great deeds or worthy causes were generally regarded—if they were unprofitable—as just so much of a waste of time.

"Mother Marfidy!" he shouted when he arrived back at his lodgings that evening. He threw himself into a chair and tore off his boots.

"Sir? What is it?" The nurse came in, running. It wasn't like Master to shout. Perhaps he was sick. His eyes looked unnaturally bright.

"Bring me Noé, Nurse," he panted. "Bring me the boy."

"At once, sir!" she said.

John started pacing up and down the room, a room suddenly too small to contain him. He stopped, stooped over the fire and stoked it with exaggerated gestures, as if to rid himself of excess energy.

"Here we are then. Here's the little man." The nurse came in again, carrying the little boy blinking his eyes at the light.

"Ah! There he is!" John held out his arms, and Noé let himself fall into them sideways.

"Noé," John said excitedly. "We are going away. We are going on a journey..."

"A journey!" exclaimed Nurse Marfidy. "Really!"

He turned to her. "Please pack whatever you need for him. And for yourself as well. We leave for the Continent tomorrow. I wish to take the child."

"Certainly, sir," said the nurse. "But, sir! Have you—have you any...?"

She could not finish her question, because with his free hand he had grabbed her by the startled arm and started prancing around her solemnly, as if she were his partner in a minuet.

"Wool...? Yes, sir, yes, sir," he hummed into the delighted boy's ear. "Three bags full."

He had lingered a few paces behind Samuel Wynde and the rest of Lord Dunnover's entourage as they oohed and aahed over the new paintings—lavish jobs, brimming with allegory and heaving breasts. They were not to John's taste, and he did not feel the need to chime in. He was wondering how soon he could make his escape when he spotted her.

Lucinda.

It was her face. Her eyes. Her clavicle. The angle of the jaw.

He gasped.

Lord Dunnover turned from the large canvas he had been showing Wynde.

"Ah. I see your friend prefers the Dutch. I am not so partial to them myself. Rather dull, aren't they, compared to the Italians? One likes to see a little flesh."

"I like this one," John managed. "I like it very much indeed."

"Madonna and Child, my lord?" It was Wynde who hazarded this guess. "Very nice."

"It's by one of those Hollanders—" Lord snapped his fingers. "Come, Pruett!"

"Arent Dirrekzoon Prul," Pruett, an earnest little man in a black coat, supplied in a nasal voice.

"Prul," his lordship informed his guests gravely. "He is the next Rubens, gentlemen. I have it on the highest authority."

Lucinda was draped in greenish gauze and satin, gazing down in a resigned sort of way at the babe in her arms. She was sitting in a dark room; a window behind her let in a faint light, which left a glint on her cheek and the child's forehead. The painting was a little flat, a little conventional, yet very tender.

Tears sprang to John's eyes. It was Lucinda, it must be. Or else—or else it was her double, someone who looked devilishly like her. But... the likeness, now that he looked more closely, was not exactly...What was it that was different? The painter had failed to make her look desirable. Although she was certainly beautiful. But he had failed to capture Lucinda's challenge, her coyness, the awkward, girlish determination to have an effect on you. This woman was oblivious of the observer. She was forcing you to look at the infant in her arms, as if that stiff little bundle (the artist was not very good at children: the head was too small, its proportions all wrong) were the only thing worth looking at in this whole world.

"I have an Announcement too," bragged Lord Dunnover. "Found it in Rome. I'll show it to you. It has a much better Virgin than this one."

"I—I should like to buy it from you," John blurted out. "I must have it. Whatever the cost."

Lord Dunnover stared at him in amazement for a few moments, then examined his painting more closely, through his glass.

"Sir!" he said grandly at last, "My pictures are not for sale." His eyes traced the cut of John's coat, up and down. "Besides, I do not think that you, sir, could afford it."

48

THE CUSTOMER

Arent Dirrekzoon Prul lived on Amsterdam's Sint-Antoniebree Street, in a narrow townhouse with tall windows and vertiginous stairs. John was shown up these by a sturdy blonde maid with red cheeks and chafed elbows, who scaled the narrow treads as nimbly as a mountain goat.

On the landing she opened the door to a long, high-ceilinged room. There were two chairs pulled up to a table covered with a Turkey rug, and a curtained bed built into the wall. It was chilly in the room. The tiled stove was not lit.

Standing in the center of the room was a paunchy middle-aged man in a velvet dressing-gown. He wore a green velvet cap on his balding head. He spread out his arms in a sign of welcome.

"Ah! *Goed zo, Dieneke! Een klant!*"

"Pardon me, I..."

"An *English* customer! Good, so! Monseigneur...?"

"Prynce, John Prynce," he muttered.

The painter waved his stubby hand at the maid, who left and closed the door behind her. "Delighted! And you are making de whole tour, or just our liddle country?"

"Just Amsterdam," John began.

"You haf come to de right place! You like Amsterdam? You like art? We haf fery good art here, whatefer you like..."

"I saw one of your pictures at Lord Dunnover's, and I..."

"You heard off me! Dear sir! You like my paintings! Dear sir! Fine, so!"

Arent turned and opened a little door built into the woodwork surrounding the bed. He started pulling out rolled-up canvases by the handful.

"You like still-lifes? Sea scapes? An portrret?"

"Actually, Lord Dunnover had a Madonna, and I..."

"Rrrelidgious subdjects! Good so, sir!"

He started unrolling some of the canvases, shaking his head and tossing half a dozen into a corner. "Ha! Here, so!" he exclaimed at last. "King Dafid and Goliat!"

"Actually..." John began.

"Wait! You will like my Jezebel, vat de defil did I do wis her..."

"No, that's not..."

"You don't like de Old Testament? A Christus, den?"

"I was thinking more along the lines of—perhaps you have a picture similar to the one I saw, the Mother and Child..."

Arent flung the canvas he had been holding onto the bed. "Of course. Wan mom-*ent*, please." He left the room, yelled something to Dieneke, and came back in, beaming.

The two men stood facing each other awkwardly for a few moments.

"Zo! You like our liddle country, de Younited Provincies?" asked the painter, still smiling professionally from ear to ear.

"Very much," said John politely. He coughed. "The streets are so clean," he added.

"Yes, yes, ower ladies, dey don't like de durt," Arent chuckled.

The door was pushed open, revealing Dieneke's broad hip. She backed into the room dragging a large canvas in a heavy frame.

"Dis is de kind of sing you are looking for," stated Arent.

"Yes indeed," breathed John.

Another Virgin. Another woodenly drawn baby. Another gentle, attentive Lucinda.

"He is ferry good, yes. But he is already sold. He is for Antonijn Verkoop, you have hurd of him maybe? But you *must* have hurd of him! He is a very big man, an important man you know, his business is cloth and lace! He is a very good customer of mine. But of course it is no problem, *Monseigneur*. I make anoder wan, very quick."

"Using the same model?" John ventured.

"De model?" said Arent. "You mean de Maria. Yes of course, I use de same wan." He smiled broadly. "Dat's my *vrouwtje*. My liddle wife."

49

BEAUTY ASLEEP

Picture a room in some remote tower. There is a bed, and on that bed lies a woman. Her hair is spread out on the pillow like the points of the zodiac. Her eyes are closed; she shows no sign of life. She seems entranced; in modern parlance, comatose.

Be not deceived: this sleeping beauty is not a woman under the influence. There is not a bottle, not a needle, not a spinning wheel in sight.

She is merely the victim of one of life's more insidious jokes.

Just a short time ago—oh, but it seems like a hundred years!— she was a fair maiden, vain, heartless and carefree. Everybody called her darling. A few princes even fought over her. She felt like a million doubloons.

So what happened?

It's only that it's all over now. It's only that somebody finally won her hand, and she is now a wife and mother. And she is exhausted all the time, her waist has grown flabby, no one pays any attention to her anymore, and she believes she has become invisible.

No wonder she finds it hard to get up in the morning.

"You must understand that I am married now. I am his wife," said Lucinda severely. She would not look at him. The painting had not lied: there was something different about her. This Lucinda was torpid, remote. Her look of utter shock upon seeing John had given way to sullen aloofness. Arent, seeing her fierce blush, had immediately realized they knew each other. He'd backed out of the room and shut the door softly behind him.

"I know, but..."

"You know nothing!" snapped Lucinda. "Nothing!"

"No, but..." he began disconsolately.

The infant in her lap had started making impatient noises, and she now reached down and began unlacing the chemise under her fur-trimmed vest. John watched in horrified fascination as she reached in and drew out an engorged breast webbed with blue. Deftly pinching the darkened nipple between her third and fourth finger, she guided it into the child's mouth.

"What makes you think you can come here making demands of me?" she continued spitefully. She refused to look at him. "After what you did! And after...after all this time!"

"But..."

"I am a mother now. I have two children—" She broke off suddenly, still gazing intently at the baby's bonneted head.

He saw a breach in her defenses.

"Lucinda! Please!! I realized immediately I shouldn't have let you go...I tried to... I wanted to find you... but I thought you were dead!"

"Ha!" she exclaimed, tossing her head. The gesture reminded him of the old Lucinda.

He stood up. "Listen to me, Lucinda. I know what happened to Bessie and the rest of the baggage train. I was there. I went back to look for you. I came too late. I saw—with my own eyes. I could not find you in the rubble, so I thought..."

Her voice was almost a growl. "If you had truly tried to find me, if what you say is true..."

"It *is* true! "

"Really!" she said derisively.

"I'll prove it to you!" He strode towards the door, furious now.

"Where are you going?" she asked.

"To fetch my proof!" he stormed.

"Oh, but..." she began, but he had already slammed the door behind him.

* * *

An hour later he was back, with Noé.

"What's this?" said Lucinda.

"My proof," he said.

"I don't understand," said Lucinda.

"This is Zéfine's child. I found him in her arms. I have been raising him as my own," he said shortly.

For the first time Lucinda seemed at a loss for words, and he saw an opening at last, a chance to slash his way through the forest of thorns she had built up around herself. "You were there, weren't you?" he burst out reproachfully. "Why didn't *you* find him? Noé? He was still alive."

She looked at him openmouthed, and spread her hands on her lap nervously. "I didn't know...I had no idea!" she faltered. "I assumed—I supposed he was dead too."

John suddenly felt foolish. Her face was ashen. Her fingers were tightly woven around her handkerchief.

"Of course," he said quickly. "It was wrong to reproach you. It must have been—you must have been terrified..."

She made an impatient gesture with her hand. "I had wandered off somewhere, before the attack came. I heard the screams. I hid in a ditch. Then, when—they—had left, I went back, but when I saw..."

"Please!" John interrupted her. "You needn't..."

She kicked something out from under her skirts. It was a copper-lined box glowing with embers, a foot-warmer. She snapped open her fan, and started fanning herself. "I must have assumed the baby was dead too. It never crossed my mind. I don't remember exactly what I did. I ran, I just kept running. A peasant found me lying in his field, and must have carried me to his cottage. His wife was kind, but the man made me leave. I begged my way to Amsterdam. I even...They don't allow beggars here, you know. They put me in a home for indigent women. I was put to work. Then, because I..." Suddenly she stopped.

"Yes?" he asked.

"When they saw I was with child, a lady, one of the regentesses of the home, took me in as her servant. Arent was painting her portrait. He asked me to sit for him. As his model. Before I had the child..."

She stopped again, and glanced toward the door.

"Before you had the child—"

"He—he offered to take me in. To marry me. I was very grateful. Am very grateful to him, I mean."

"I see," said John.

"He is a good husband." She said it defensively.

"I am sure that he is," said John.

"And he is letting me paint, too. I am learning quite a bit, in fact."

"That's very nice for you. I am happy for you both."

Lucinda gave a short, bitter laugh. John said nothing more. He put all his energy into willing her to look up, to acknowledge the agony in his eyes, to relieve the leaden ache in his groin.

From a nearby clock tower came the sound of a simple little tune played on crystal-clear chimes. It sliced through the dreadful silence like a hacksaw. "I never thought," she said, "that I'd ever see you again."

"I have never stopped thinking about you," he brought out woodenly.

"No?" she asked.

"No." He cleared his throat. "I have prayed to heaven that you might forgive me for—for my crime. Against your mother, against your father. Against you."

"Ah. That," she said flatly. "I don't think of it as a crime, now."

"No?" he said.

"I think of it more as...fate."

"Fate?"

"Things just never turn out right for me," she said. She was looking squarely at him at last. "It wasn't meant to be."

John hung his head.

"I am sorry. You have come all this way. But I hope you will understand that I cannot..."

He did not want to hear her say it. "Actually," he said, and fumbled in his pocket. "I really just wanted to return this."

Out of his pocket he drew the glass-beaded slipper.

"My slipper!" she exclaimed. "Where did you get it?"

He took a few steps forward, and placed it cautiously in her lap. "I found it among—er, the remains," he said. He stepped back. Suddenly he did not know what to do with his curiously hovering hands. He clasped them sternly behind his back. "It's what made me think you were dead."

"I see," she said. For a long moment she stared at the slipper, her head bowed. Then, abruptly, she threw it back at him. He just managed to catch it. "I don't want it," she said tightly. "What in Heaven's name made you think I would have any use for it?"

"Right, then," he said. He crumpled the slipper up in an aching fist. He inclined his head, and started backing toward the door.

She remained immobile in her chair. But she raised her hand just as he was about to disappear.

"The boy—you may leave him here. I will take care of him."

"Thank you. But he stays with me. I will not be parted from him. As I told you, I am raising him as my son."

Outside, on the landing, Noé was playing with a curly-headed little girl. He refused to leave, and in the end John was forced to pick him up and carry him down the stairs kicking and screaming.

She was seething, seething! She wanted to kick something. She wanted to smash the water jug on the floor, but restrained herself, because she did not want to have to explain it to Arent.

How *dare* that man come here and confront her like that? How *could* he! He had no *idea* what she had been through, no idea at all! From where she was sitting, she was not doing badly at all. To have pulled herself out of the mire, painfully, inch by inch, into a perfectly respectable life, only to have this specter from her past march unscathed into her parlor, acting all judgmental about the choices she had been forced to make...The injustice of it! *He* didn't know what it was like to be pregnant and penniless. To have that weight in your belly demanding to be fed, and no means of feeding it! To be forced to beg, to steal, to agree to sell your body, even, to some lecherous low-life, for a crust of bread! Hell, he had no idea how much she had suffered. And then the indignity of being taken in by a bunch of self-righteous matrons in the charitable home, who took delight in scrubbing, de-lousing and lecturing her, and then being put to work cleaning out fireplaces and stove chambers (wasn't that her lot in life—to wind up as a cindersweep wherever she went?) under the supervision of a gaggle of loud, bossy Dutchwomen with standards twice as exacting as Aunt Arabella's! Good God! What did he want? What did he expect? That she would wait for him to show up—three years too late? Ha!

"Lu-sinneke?" Arent stuck his head around the door.

She started, guiltily. She had no idea how long she had been sitting there. It was already getting dark, and she was supposed to be preparing the fish stew.

"Sorry, Arent," she said. "I must have forgotten the time..."

"No matter, no matter!" he said jovially. "My little Sinneke, you made us a good sale today. You deserve a kiss!"

Hovering over her, he nuzzled her ear with his fleshy lips. She recoiled a bit from the sour, tobacco-and-gin smell.

"I knew him, from before..." she confessed.

"I could tell!" he said heartily. He winked at her. "I charged him thirty-five florins for the Madonna! In advance! I knew whatever I asked, he'd pay!" he crowed.

She stared at him stonily.

"Ah, come, wifey! Don't give me that look! I'm sorry! But I know what I married, don't I! About your, uh—past, which we don't talk about. So, then!"

"It is not what you think at all!" she began vehemently.

"I'm not saying, am I? I'm not making accusations, treasuretrove. All's forgiven and forgotten, and we don't speak of it. Cuddlebunnikins. Come on! Wifeykins, my sweetiechild."

She let herself be cajoled into a reluctant kiss.

50

AWAKENING

A purgatory of feelings, feelings that had been lulled to sleep for three years. Feelings buried in forty months of survival, of bad dreams, of obligations and gratitude, of focusing on her deliverers, of focusing on her babies. Suddenly, from one day to the next, she found herself awake, Sleeping Beauty rudely kissed by a new reality. She rubbed her eyes. Where was she? What had happened? What were these children, this husband, making demands, constantly making demands of her? Helping themselves to her body, her feelings, sucking her dry? How could she have been so proud, so in love with these little bundles of flesh? Suddenly she looked on them with loathing.

"Your milk will dry up," said Dieneke sternly.

"You do it, then!" she snapped. "I'm not a cow!"

"I would if I could, you know I would," said Dieneke mournfully, and carried the screaming baby out of the room.

For some reason this unsatisfactory exchange made Lucinda think of Bessie. And thinking of Bessie sparked even more anguish. She started shivering. It was cold in here, and her back ached. Arent was always so stingy with the firewood. And Dieneke wouldn't listen to her, only to the master. She'd have to do it herself, as usual. She stormed downstairs and gathered a bundle in her apron. She started staggering up the stairs. Lord! Her legs felt like jelly! She had to sit down halfway up. The logs made an awful clatter as they rolled down to the bottom. From the kitchen came a cry of alarm from Dieneke, and a great howling from the children. Weakly, Lucinda started wailing too.

* * *

Her illness lasted over a month. At first she had been bled daily, but the barber refused to come back after she threw the bedpan at him. At last she was beginning to recover her strength.

"Come, Missus," said Dieneke. "Shall I bring you your needlework? Some coal and paper? Busy hands make a light heart, you know."

"I'm thinking, Dieneke," Lucinda said. "Leave me alone."

"Thinking!" scoffed Dieneke. "*Thinking* won't mend a broken jug, Missus!"

Lucinda shrugged. What did Dieneke know. The only thoughts in Dieneke's head were recipes for pancakes and floor polish. And Lucinda had been preoccupied with domestic matters for far too long as well. For the first time since she had made her home here, she was allowing herself to indulge in some serious reveries. About love, about being rescued.

She tried to revive the faceless heroes of her childhood fantasies. But it was impossible. John's face and body were integral to this dream.

Which led her to reconsider her anger. Of course she was angry at John! She was furious with him. It was her duty to be so; he was her father's murderer, after all. John was the culprit responsible for the calamity that was Lucinda's life. Wasn't he?

She closed the door on that thought, and opened another, tentatively. But...she argued in his defense. What if...her heart started beating faster; the door opened a little wider. What if John too had been wronged? He had been scorned by her mother, after all, and humiliated by her father. Any man would have been upset, in his place. And surely he had not intended to kill anyone! There had been a duel, and these things happened. John had lived to regret it. He rued the day he had found the runaways and allowed his anger to get the better of him. To atone for a deed he deemed unforgivable, he had given up rank and prestige. He had traded in his sword for a surgeon's knife.

How could her mother have been so foolish, so unwise to reject John, anyway? How could she not have recognized how lucky she was to have been promised to such a man?

Lucinda realized, with a start, that it wasn't John she was angry at.

Her mother had abandoned her. She had selfishly only thought of her own happiness. Her mother had cast a spell over not one, but two men who wanted her. Her poor, dead mother, that misty, idealized, tragic creature she had always worshipped, was suddenly revealed to be something quite different. A rival!

As for her father, she suddenly found herself unable to muster any great sympathy for him, either. In stealing another man's betrothed, he had really been no better than a thief. Of course she wished that her father had not been killed in that duel. Any daughter would. But what then? If John had not killed her father—oh God, better not to think of it, but really— the roles might have been reversed, and her father might have slain John! And where did that leave Lucinda?

Where in God's name did that leave her?

She fussed over the children, deeply guilty about her lengthy withdrawal.

Liesbet, the eldest, had her arms in a stranglehold about Lucinda's neck, making it hard for her mother to finish feeding Arentje. "Mama," boomed Liesbet in her ear, "Mamaatje, why are you sad?"

"Sad?" she said, prying Liesbet's hands off her throat. "No—sad? No, what makes you think that, treasure?"

Liesbet tried to push her little brother off Lucinda's lap and drew a line above her mother's eyebrows with a stubby finger. "Be happy!" she ordered.

"I *am* happy. You make me happy, child," Lucinda clucked obediently. There was no doubt left in her mind who the child's father was. She had a grave way about her, and had John's habit of closing her eyes a moment before bringing out a thought. She hugged the little girl tightly, and buried her face in her neck.

"Hey! Lemme go!" Liesbet protested, wriggling free.

Dieneke walked in just in time to see the struggle. She folded her arms. "Too much oil snuffs the flame," she said dryly.

"The pot criticizes the kettle," retorted Lucinda, "for being black."

She congratulated herself on having enough Dutch to parry and thrust with her fault-finding servant.

* * *

Once the baby was weaned, Lucinda began spending more time in the studio. Arent had an apprentice, one Karel Klek, a chubby youth whose singular lack of talent would not be tolerated in a more successful artist's studio. But Karel managed to make himself useful mixing paints, cleaning brushes and priming panels, and his cheery disposition made his artistic shortcomings forgivable.

"Oh, Missus!" Karel said admiringly one morning, watching Lucinda put the finishing touches to a canvas, a still life of flowers and butterflies, "It's good! It's pretty good!"

"You think so, Kareltje?" Lucinda said, smiling. She stretched, reaching out to the vase in front of her and running the tips of her fingers apologetically along the drooping petals. Just a week ago the flowers had been fresh and glorious; now that she was done with them, they were sad and wilted.

"I bet even a picture dealer couldn't tell that was painted by a woman," Karel said proudly.

"Really!" she scoffed.

"I believe it, Missus, I do!" said Karel.

"What do you believe, knave?" asked Arent, who had just come in.

"I was just telling Missus that you couldn't tell that painting was done by a woman," Karel told him.

"Ho! Speak for yourself, boy!" Arent guffawed. He stood before Lucinda's painting, tilted his head sideways, and took two steps back. "But that's not bad, not bad at all!" he puffed. "Good so, Sienneke, my girl! Very good! I see that buying the flowers wasn't such a waste of money after all! I still say you should have done some studies first." Turning to Karel, he said, "Haven't I told you a hundred times you should never begin a picture without working it out first? But I'll grant it, this one hasn't turned out bad! I can get at least eight florins for that!"

Lucinda bowed her head, to hide a pleased grin. She felt Arent's hand on her shoulder. "Soon we'll have her working on some of my commissions!" Arent speculated. He began nuzzling her neck, and she had to slap a probing hand away from her lap.

He stood up straight. "I am a lucky man, Karel," he boasted. "Why, who else do we know who has such a pretty *vrouwtje* who breeds him a healthy son, keeps a clean house, and is even starting to bring home some of the bacon as well?"

Lucinda had no idea how her paintings happened. She did not have a plan; she did not work the composition out beforehand, as Arent was telling her to do. What she did was stare at the empty canvas before her and just DRINK it in, filling her mind to the top with that blankness, while allowing everything else in her head to trickle out like sand in an hourglass. Only when her mind was properly empty of reason did she reach for her brush. Then she would start painting, her unblinking eyes riveted on the subject like a boat tied up to the dock, the fumes of the paints lapping at her nose, the whole spectrum of possibilities dancing like motes of light around her head. Blindly, the brush reached out to touch a glistening mound of umber on the palette. Oops—it had picked up a smudge of white on the side by mistake! No matter: the resulting smear lit up the edge of the tankard with what was probably just the right glint of light. She could not stop to correct it anyway: she had to paint on, on, driven by the overwhelming urge to see the picture emerge in front of her; to give it life.

Weariness finally overtook her, and she had to close her burning eyes. When she opened them again, it was like waking from a trance. She gaped at the painting in front of her. Who had done that? Had *she*? Really? But how?

She kept staring at the picture she had just completed until the colors bled into one another in the greying light. All it needed now was the flourish of Arent's signature, in the lower right-hand corner. She gave a happy sigh. In her imagination, John Prynce was standing behind her, thunderstruck. "I never knew you were so talented," he whispered, awed...

"What in damnation are you doing, wife? It's already past suppertime! Dieneke is all in a stew, she says you didn't buy any cabbage, you know I can't bear my *stamppot* without cabbage..."

"Sorry, Arent! I was just coming..."

"Too late, woman, too late. I won't eat that shit, you know I won't. I'm off to the *Hound*. At least there I'll get something decent to eat."

Lucinda ran after him. "I'm sorry! But why didn't Dieneke tell me? She went to market herself this morning!"

"You know not to bother me with your women's problems," barked Arent. "Your quarrels with your servant are no concern of mine."

"Wait! I finished another painting! You know, the grapes and the tankard!"

"I told you," came his voice from the stairs, "I like to be lenient. I like to see you do what makes you happy. But enough is enough. A wife who neglects her husband is the devil's dam!"

51

PUSS IN BOOTS

Some say that a woman is very like a cat. On the surface she may appear most tractable and domesticated, but deep down she is the most fiercely independent and ornery of beings. Such a woman, if she is resolved to make something of herself, is well advised to pull on some leather boots or other alluring footgear, and stride boldly into the world to find herself a master. Depending on her wit and determination, it is not impossible for such a woman to capture all that her heart desires, while remaining, in the eyes of the world, the most docile of pussycats.

It is true that this scheme usually means that her master reaps all the credit for her hard work.

But is this not a small price to pay for half a kingdom?

Lucinda was now spending more time in the studio than her spouse, for Arent was able to sell her paintings almost as fast as she turned them out, leaving him at liberty to spend his waking hours in the *Hound*.

He had begun coaching Lucinda in the art of the tavern scene, a genre popular with Amsterdam's well-to-do merchants. The trick to these was to cram them with entertaining details—lewd old men pawing buxom maidens, bawds counting money, drunkards, dogs, naughty children, and oodles of glistening oysters. Lucinda had turned out half a dozen of these, and they were proving to be even more profitable than the careful still lifes of her early apprenticeship.

"What's this?" Arent grumbled one morning, returning from a lengthy session out back, in the privy. He scratched his head and yawned.

"I didn't tell you to do a portrait, did I?"

"Oh, it's not really a portrait," said Lucinda quickly. "It's just that I had been sketching Liesbet, and I thought it would make such a pretty picture..."

"There's not much of a market for children these days," Arent said sourly.

"No, it's something to keep..."

"And I see you've used some of the good linen too. I wish you'd think of the cost, you could have used the burlap, couldn't you? I wish you had asked me first."

"I'm sorry. I wanted to practice painting faces, you know I rarely have the chance—"

"Wifey. We have been over that a hundred times. Haven't we? I can't let you do faces because the customers wouldn't like it. Whoever heard of having his likeness painted by a woman? I let you do the backgrounds and the clothes. Isn't that enough?"

"Of course it is, Arent," she said. "I just..."

"Oh, come here and give your old hubby a kiss. Liesbetje, run along and play."

After a short conjugal interlude, Arent left her to her painting, and to her reveries.

Lucinda had given the matter much thought, and she had almost made up her mind. Sooner or later, she would—possibly—no, probably—have to tell Liesbet who her real father was. It would be a terrible thing to do to Arent, of course, Arent who had been so generous with them, who had never shown Liesbet the slightest prejudice. But there it was: Arent was not the real father, and Lucinda felt she owed her daughter the truth. Not now, perhaps, but when she was a little older. She bit her lip. How thrilled Liesbet would be, to know she was the offspring not of an artistic commoner, but of an aristocratic man of science! Not that Arent wasn't a wonderful, kindhearted man; but there was his drinking, and his gluttony, and his oafishness to consider. Lucinda knew that any maiden, given a choice, prefers to have a gentleman for a sire.

And did she not owe the truth to John Prynce? Somewhere on earth there lived a child of his flesh and blood, and he did not know it! It was too bad that Liesbet was a girl, not a boy, but Lucinda trusted that John was broadminded enough not to let the child's gender detract from his joy in knowing himself to be a father.

Yes, it was right to imperil her own position—think of the scandal! Arent might throw her out!—for her child. As a mother, she had no other option.

"Go, my daughter," she imagined herself whispering to Liesbet. *"That gentleman there is your father. Go to him, and kiss his hand."*

The girl went softly to him, and did as she was told. He looked up, startled. "Why—what is this?" he began. Then he spotted Lucinda standing just inside the doorway. "You!" he exclaimed sternly. "What are you doing here?"

"What is it, John?" asked an elegant lady stepping out of the shadows. "Who are these women?"

Lucinda stammered, "Forgive me, my lady. But please do not send away this maiden. She is your husband's child. I humbly implore you to accept her as your own."

"But..." he said. "But I had no idea! If I had known...if only you had let me know..."

She bowed her head. "Please," she whispered, "Please! Do not make it harder for all of us. I will leave you now..."

Liesbet dropped her father's hand and stretched both arms imploringly toward Lucinda. "No, Mama! Don't go!" she cried. Turning back to her father, she entreated, "The cruel Dutchman has turned her out! She has not a penny to her name! She has sacrificed everything! She'll wind up in the poorhouse! She'll be buried in a pauper's grave!"

But already Lucinda was running, already she was fleeing that house, down a long, polished marble staircase, slipping, tripping, losing a slipper in her headlong flight—

She heard Dieneke clumping up the stairs. Hastily she wiped away a tear.

"What is it, Dieneke?" she exclaimed when she saw the maid's glum, reddened face.

"Miep Stol next door's been taken with the pox," said Dieneke, "and they say there's a dozen people dead of it already, in Haarlem."

"Come, Dieneke! Every time there's bad news, you act as if it's the end of the world! Come, cheer up, silly! Nothing's going to happen!"

But of all contagions, the worst by far is fear, and Dieneke's fear reached out and caught Lucinda by the throat.

If it was your fate to live in the seventeenth century and no member of your family had ever succumbed to the plague or the smallpox, you would consider yourself fortunate indeed. The reality was that gross, unnatural, horrific death lurked around every corner, and if it did not pounce this time, it would surely get you on the next round.

The smallpox epidemic in question took Liesbet, Karel Klek, and Arent Prul.

When it was all over, only the baby, Dieneke and Lucinda were left.

52

PENELOPE

Trudging home one afternoon along a towpath with her son, Lucinda stopped when she reached the outlying hovels of the city. She turned around to drink in one last time the open landscape she had been sketching.

A flock of birds silhouetted against the twilit sky came wavering towards them. Seconds later the air above them was filled with a flapping, squealing ferment. Arentje whooped with delight and waved his little arms in the air. For a few moments he and his mother watched the birds swooping and gliding, now almost standing still, then, as if of one mind, skimming up and away again.

Lucinda envied them their sense of purpose, the aggressive certainty of their dance. She tried to make out if it was one bird that set the pace while the rest followed; but singling out a leader was impossible. A bird that was out in front on one round was just as likely to fall back and bring up the rear the next. Then how to explain this supernatural precision? Were the birds able to read each other's minds, or were they dancing to some celestial rhythm she would never be able to hear?

She sighed. "Come," she said to her son, and took his hand. "Dieneke will have supper waiting. Bacon pancakes tonight!"

She turned and slowly picked her way along the bewildering road.

Lying in bed awake, listening to Arentje and Dieneke's breathing—the three of them now shared the parlor's cupboard-bed—Lucinda tried to shake off the demons that visited her every night, smothering her like the hot featherbed. Her throat was tight; her tears were gone. What now? What should she do? What was the right thing to do? What did God wish her to do?

Surely, in taking her daughter and her husband from her, God had sent one last message. But what did it mean? Did it mean that she was being punished for having had disloyal thoughts about Arent? Or for having used Liesbet's parentage as an excuse for those disloyal thoughts? Or was it that she had yearned for freedom, and this was the price one paid for freedom? It was like the fable of the woodcutter wife's foolish three wishes: no matter what you wished for, you were worse off, in the end, than before. It was a lesson in humility. A lesson in accepting one's fate.

She got out of bed, moving slowly, like an old woman. She lit a candle, tiptoed out of the room and into the studio. There she sat down heavily before the canvas she had been working on since Easter. It was a lavish still life, for the French ambassador. He had sent her the props for it—a silver charger, a damask cloth, outrageously expensive flowers, including two exquisitely striped tulips. He had told her it was all hers to keep. She was supposed to be impressed. She frowned at the painting. She did not like it. It was too safe, too rich, too removed from real life. What it needed was something to remind her client of the vanity of earthly possessions. A common, tousled dandelion. No—an ant, a worm, some...vermin. A cockroach! Yes! She had just the place for it, too: slithering sideways up the slick, shiny silver. Her face broke into a wicked grin.

In the two years since Arent' Prul's death, her reputation had grown. She had even begun to sign her paintings with her own name, and, to her surprise, no one had objected. On the contrary, people seemed to enjoy the novelty. There was far more interest in her paintings now that it was known that they were the work of a pretty, exotic young widow, and not her deceased husband.

The French ambassador was quite taken with her, and was trying to persuade her to move to Paris, where he said she would be a sensation. She didn't know if she wanted to be a sensation. What she wanted was to have her Liesbet back, that was what she wanted!

But the idea of leaving Amsterdam had begun to appeal to her. After all, what was there for her here? What was she *doing* here? Years of grief, of loneliness, of longing, of waiting—but for what? Even with all the debts paid, there was plenty of money left, enough to send some of her neighbors sniffing around with unwelcome offers of marriage. She had been fending them off with the plea that she was still in mourning, but time was running out for that excuse.

She walked to the back of the room, and pulled out a large painting that she kept hidden under a sheet. Something fell off a shelf and onto the floor. She picked it up and stared at it. That old thing! She had forgotten all about it. It was Liesbetje's half-finished portrait. It was a good likeness, especially around the eyes. Arent had caught her working on it one day, and she had guiltily put it aside. For what Arent hadn't known then, was that she had begun the portrait with the foolish notion that she might some day send it to John Prynce...

Liesbet's likeness stared at her solemnly. With an unsteady finger Lucinda traced the outline of the unresponsive little cheek.

Trembling, she turned to the other painting. It was large—larger than anything she had ever done. She propped the stretcher up on the table, where the moonlight caught it so that she could make out the familiar shapes.

It was a history painting, a painting that told a classical tale. It gave her a thrill every time she looked at it. How shocked Arent would have been! It was of a scope far beyond what he would ever have allowed her to tackle. Poor Arent had not had much success with his own history paintings. One hung, ignored, on the back wall of the *Hound*. Another had been cut into quarters, the canvas reused for more profitable vignettes. Paintings with classical subjects were expensive to produce because they took up a great deal of time, and Arent's sort of client would never dream of commissioning one. To paint one without any money down was tantamount to tossing florins out the window. But Lucinda was now free to do as she liked.

The painting showed a woman at a loom, one arm leaning on the frame, the other stretched out behind her, as if she had just completed a pass with the shuttle. In her lap lay a loose coil of yarn of the same flaxen color as the hair cascading down her back. To the left was an open doorway through which you could see some male faces spying on the woman.

In the background, over her other shoulder, was a portico leading to a dark and turbulent sea breaking on jagged cliffs, and, very faintly, a tattered ship struggling along on the horizon. It was her favorite story, the story of Penelope, that paragon of domesticity, waiting for her husband Odysseus to return home from the wars; outwitting her suitors, never giving up hope, clinging to the belief that patience and constancy would some day be rewarded.

For a long time she stood there, drinking it in. She remembered the desperation with which she had begun it, just days after Liesbet, Arent and Karel were laid to rest.

She had wanted to smother the entire canvas in the thick paint, the way a mother needs to wrap a crying child in the soft warm body of her consolation.

"You know, Missus, I was talking to Maria Verklapper, and she thinks you really ought to hurry up and get married again soon—"

"Dieneke. Please!"

"She thinks it's asking for trouble. She says everyone's talking about you."

"They don't know a thing about me, Dieneke."

"No, Missus. But they—there's talk."

"Ha! Such as...?"

"Such as? Well, such as, everyone thinks Liesbet weren't Master's child."

"It's none of their business. It's none of yours, either."

"Of course not. Sorry. I'm sorry, Missus."

"That's all right, Dieneke."

"Still, Missus..."

"What now, Dieneke!"

"It's just, they don't understand why you don't pick someone nice, like Joop de Gijn or Johannes Stoer, you know, then there would be no reason for no more talk..."

Lucinda did not lose her temper. She understood that there was no malice intended. Her neighbors were all good, kind people, who had only her best interests at heart.

But she longed to get away, she longed for a place that was less comfortable, less cozy, less spotless. She longed for a vile, vast, chaotic place where nobody knew her business. And she also had to get away from the bells, that maddening carillon outside her window, it was driving her insane—

Ah, my darling Augustine, Augustine, Augustine
Ah, my darling Augustine
Everything gone.

The children used to dance to that ditty, holding hands. Such solid grace they had. Such unquestioning acceptance of their own existence. She could see Liesbet hauling her little brother around and pulling him down on the final *"gone,"* landing hard on their bottoms, shouting with glee.

Her voice sounded reedy, forced. "I'm leaving, anyway. I have made up my mind. As soon as the house is sold."

"Yes, but, Missus—"

"Are you coming or not?"

"But, *Paris*!"

"Yes, Paris."

"I don't know—"

"You don't have to come. I am giving you a choice."

"I've never been away from home, Missus…"

"I know. It is not an easy decision to make. I understand that."

"I'm not used to foreigners."

"Well, suit yourself." She turned, and looked out the window. The bells, mercifully, had stopped, but the shrill vibrations still lingered.

"Missus!"

"Yes, Dieneke."

"Maybe I will."

"You'll come?"

"Maybe I will. That's what I said."

"You don't have to."

"I know that."

* * *

Not long after this, the house in Amsterdam was sold, and Lucinda moved to Paris with her son and her maidservant. With the help of the French ambassador, she was able to find suitable lodgings, and they were soon settled comfortably in one of the city's more fashionable neighborhoods.

As it turned out, Lucinda was indeed a sensation in Paris, albeit a minor one. In a very short space of time she had more portrait commissions than she could handle. This was in part because she had a fresh, candid approach to portraiture that the French found intriguing; but also because she was young, and attractive, and society immediately ruled her irresistible, and once society had ruled such a thing, nothing would do but to have oneself driven to the Rue Saint Louis and to have oneself painted by *la petite Anglaise,* the little Englishwoman, herself.

53

A CARRIAGE

In Paris it did not take Lucinda long to find out that if you are blessed with some measure of wealth or fame, you will have people falling all over themselves in their eagerness to do you special favors. Therefore, although Lucinda was paid handsomely for her portraits, and so for the first time in her life felt perfectly capable of seeing to her own affairs, she now found herself overwhelmed with advice and offers of assistance. She did find this rather ironic, since when she had been starving and destitute, and could have used a little help, none had been forthcoming. She understood, however, that it was best to accept such favors gracefully, on the understanding that the goal was as much to gratify the donor, and make him feel important, as to do her a good turn.

It was thus that in a very short space of time Lucinda had gained an apartment in a most desirable location, all sorts of intriguing invitations, and a client list of truly impressive proportions.

One of her most persistent benefactors was the Marquis de Quelquonque, who had decided to make it his mission to transform the rather provincial but talented little foreigner into a star of Paris society. Naturally—to be blunt about it—the marquis did have ulterior motives in doing so: he was tiring of one of his current mistresses, and thought that Madame Sunderland, with just a little polishing, might make a perfectly satisfactory substitute.

Madame Sunderland had just turned down the marquis' offer to procure for her, at a very reasonable price, an *equipage* which had until recently belonged to a penurious Polish princess.

"A carriage—no, no, I go out so rarely, *Monsieur le Marquis*," she demurred, "it would be a waste."

"But Madame must be seen in public more often!" he said. "All Paris ought to be granted a glimpse of such...*simple* charms!" His right eyebrow shot up as he looked her up and down, not altogether approvingly.

Lucinda tucked a strand of stray hair behind her ear, then folded her paint-smudged hands in her lap. "Sir!" she said. "You flatter me. Forgive me. I really don't think...you see, I must needs devote myself to my work..."

"As you wish!" he stated coolly. "Madame will think it over, of course."

"Certainly," she said.

"And now," said the marquis, getting to his feet, "before I take my leave, I have just one other small boon to ask of Madame, and I trust Madame will not refuse me there."

"I do hope not!" she murmured.

"I have taken the liberty of recommending Madame to the Superintendent of the Royal Buildings. This gentleman has expressed an interest in having his portrait done. I pray that Madame will not turn him away. His name is Charles Perrault. He is not a nobleman, you understand, but Madame will find him a most valuable patron nonetheless. He is Minister Colbert's right-hand man, and wields a certain influence. He is a member of the *Académie*, and has been entrusted, moreover, with refurbishing the state rooms of the Palace of Versailles. He is always looking for painters and sculptors."

"Marquis!" stammered Lucinda. "You are too good!"

"This is what they always tell one," said the marquis, patting his elaborate peruke. "Madame is by no means the first to say it, but I do not lie to Madame when I tell her I am not, I am veritably not *that* good!"

There were no daydreams anymore, her daydreams were gone. Taking their place were the night dreams—unflattering, unhinging self-recriminations that stole into her mind in the dead of night. They replayed for her the most shameful moments of her life. Her feeble, giggly attempts to ward off Uncle Edmund. Her idiotic misjudgment of Henry's affections. Her failure to speak up for herself when Vauban took her for a common whore. The humiliations of beggardom and the pauper's institution. Marrying Arent not for love, but for a better life. The anger and pride that had made her turn her back on what may have been her one and only chance at love...

But one nightmare loomed more horribly than all the others; one in particular haunted her mercilessly, and she dreaded falling asleep because of it.

In this dream she was standing outside Arent's room, leaning against the wall. She had to lean because her knees were knocking together like two bowling pins. Dieneke was shouting at her. "The Master! Missus! Oh Missus, Missus, help him. Help us! What are we to do?" But she was paralyzed, pinned to the wall, glued to the floor, unable to move, unable to make her shaking legs carry her over the threshold into that room where a horribly blistered Arent lay screaming.

In the end it had been Dieneke who had stayed with him, Dieneke who had nursed him, and Dieneke who had washed and wrapped the ravaged body and carried it gently down to the death wagon.

Waking up in a sweat, she tried to focus on the time, a little later, when her darling, her Liesbet, was smitten in turn—her courage had not failed her then! How she had toiled over her, how she had wept, how she had kissed her and hugged her and slobbered over that little body, drinking in her pain, not caring for her own safety, praying, imploring death to take her if that would save her child! No, there was nothing more she could have done for Liesbet. But what had she done for Arent, what had she done to save Thomas, what about Bessie, Zéfine, or the rest of the camp followers...?

This was the reason she could no longer find solace in the world of daydreams. She had lost her own untainted self. Never again would she be the pure, unblemished innocent—the brave young heroine her dream scenarios required.

That world was now barred to her forever.

Lucinda had discovered that the most effective way to capture a sitter's personality was to engage the client in conversation during the prelimi-

nary sketching. It was the secret of her success. Unlike the more traditional portraiture, which showed fashionable people frozen in haughty
poses, Madame Sunderland turned out animated likenesses that caught
her subjects gesticulating or on the verge of speaking, often revealing
some vulnerability as well as whatever warmth or charm they possessed.

In the Superintendent of Royal Buildings and Works recommend-
ed to her by the marquis, Lucinda found an uncommonly unglamor-
ous subject, endowed with a swagged chin, heavy paunch and garnet
complexion. But after a rather awkward first interview, she discovered
in him a refreshing gruffness and keenness of mind that made him, in
her opinion, the most satisfying subject she had painted to date. By the
second sitting they had dropped the conventions of polite conversation
and were so deeply engrossed in discourse that they were dismayed when
Dieneke knocked on the door with the news that Lucinda's next subject
was tapping her foot in the front parlor.

Never before had Lucinda found such an excellent sounding board
for her unschooled ideas on art, and she was astonished that this important, learned Frenchman should be genuinely interested in her own
history, or that he liked to talk about the very subjects that were close to
her own heart.

But, some may object, isn't this just another example of the deception
of the flesh, which so often persuades us that we have found a soul mate
when it is in fact the other kind of mating that's intended? Certainly, it
cannot be denied that Superintendent Perrault enjoyed Lucinda's company as much for her looks as for her talents and conversation; however,
he never gave any hint that he might have improper intentions. Indeed, he
often spoke openly, lovingly even, of his dear departed wife and his four
young children—this in refreshing contrast to the marquis, who breezed
through his courtship of Lucinda without ever letting on that he had a wife
who was still very much alive, in addition to not one, but two troublesome
mistresses. In any case, Lucinda eagerly looked forward to the superintendent's visits. Even though she could not always agree with him, he brought
her a tidy, optimistic view of the world, which not only helped to place her
failures in a more positive light, but also reminded her strongly of Bessie.

"You sound like my old nurse," she told him wistfully. "She was always telling me to look on the bright side."

"Is it not right to wish for a happy ending?" he asked. "You speak as if your life were over. You are resigned to your lot, you say. But you are so young yet! I may be more advanced in years than you, but I wake every morning inspired by all there is yet to achieve."

"Ah?" asked Lucinda.

"Yes, Madame, I do not look back. I have faith in the future, in all that is to come. We are in the modern century, *nom de Dieu* (Madame will forgive me), the century of progress, of new and exciting inventions! I have not the time to dwell on the past!"

"I don't dwell on..." Lucinda began, then stopped. She realized that her thoughts were indeed mostly on the wretched past. She was not inclined to give herself anything to look forward to.

"For instance," he went on, "at present we are looking into diverting the course of the Loire, so that it will flow past the palace at Versailles. Won't it be grand, for the king some day to be able to behold that majestic river from his royal apartments? How fortunate we are to serve a monarch who possesses such vision! It will solve the water problem too, since the plans call for Versailles to have far more working fountains than it has today, and the flow is not sufficient even now."

She could not help laughing. "So you are able to move rivers? What next? Mountains?"

"Indeed. Nothing is impossible. Although the Loire, I grant you, does present a fair bit of difficulty. I have sent out my surveyors to take its level in various locations, and my engineers advise me there may not be sufficient incline for the scheme to be workable. However, all is not lost; for we have already succeeding in diverting the waters of the Seine for the fountains, and the Eure is another exccllent candidate."

Lucinda pondered on that a while. "I wish I could believe, as you do," she finally said, putting down her brush, "that I could move rivers. That there was nothing I couldn't do."

"Yes! We live in an age, Madame, unprecedented in the history of man. We have the greatest minds in the world, men of science, the arts and architecture, all engaged in carrying out the wishes of our monarch, the Apollo of our time. We are truly blessed to live in such an age. If that is not reason to rejoice, what is?"

The Marquis de Quelquonque was most persuasive, and in the end Lucinda had to give in, and found herself the owner of an open carriage and two horses, a coachman, a footman, and a groom. This rash acquisition also forced her to move, because the apartment in the Rue Saint Louis had neither stable nor servants' quarters. Her new home, which the marquis assured her she would come to love as much as the old one, was a rambling mansion near the Palais-Royal.

"Oh, Missus!" said Dieneke. "How are we ever going to make *this* cozy? All these rooms! I'll need more help. It's much too much for us to manage!"

Lucinda looked around the cavernous reception rooms. She sighed. She had known from the start the carriage was a mistake. When was she ever going to learn to say no, to stop trying to be nice and please others, and follow her own instincts instead?

"I am sure we'll be very comfortable here," she said defensively. "And when in Paris, do as the Parisians do. What I mean, Dieneke, is that you really don't have to polish the place from top to bottom, as you did at home. No one here notices."

Dieneke sniffed. She had already told Missus how she felt about the appalling housekeeping standards of the French. She took a cloth out of her apron pocket, and started rubbing furiously at a tarnished doorknob.

Lucinda's very first client and friend in Paris had been the French ambassador's sister, Marie-Lise, Countess Bienmaline. It was she who had provided Lucinda with an entrée into Paris's high society. She was enchanted with her portrait, in which Lucinda had depicted the countess seated pensively at a desk, an open book at her elbow. Marie-Lise was a widow some years older than Lucinda, enviably elegant and world-wise; she belonged to a group of influential ladies who devoted themselves to intellectual and artistic pursuits, and were tolerant enough to take the talented foreigner under their wing.

It was the countess whom Lucinda first told of her dilemma. "This move will ruin me," she confessed. "Even if I were to start charging twice as much for my pictures, I would never have the funds to pay for all this."

The countess shook her head. "Then why not get rid of the carriage, and let me find you a smaller place?"

"Oh, but," she said reluctantly, "I really don't want the marquis to take offence, he has been so kind…"

"Ah! The marquis! Tell me, my dear, has he offered to help you to meet your expenses?"

"Actually, he has," she said, "He has offered to pay for it all, but of course I could not accept…"

"Clever man! Of course he has!"

"What do you mean, Countess?" she asked.

"Don't you see, my dear? It is one of the oldest tricks in the book."

"It is?"

"Just think. What is his motive in encouraging you to incur expenses you are not able to meet?"

"Oh. You mean…I might have to accept his offer, and then…"

"And then, out of gratitude, of course, one must needs surrender—" The countess mimed her point by lifting her dainty feet off the floor as if she were about to fall backward, legs spread in a most unladylike posture.

"I see!" Lucinda said. She laughed shamefacedly. "What a fool I am!"

The countess patted Lucinda's hand. "We are all fools, *chère*, until we learn to play the game. And then, of course, we are known as scheming bitches."

54

BELLE OF THE BALL

Now that she had a carriage, she felt obliged to use it. She ventured out timidly at first, making short excursions to the Tuileries or Boulevard du Temple. She did not know what to make of the French. On the one hand, there was the hostile indifference that branded her an interloper in a very closed society. On the other hand, there was genuine interest in her as an artist; her status as an ambassadress of culture opened doors that would be barred to her otherwise.

She even found herself attending, one night, a lavish *bal masqué* given by her first patron, the ambassador to the United Provinces of the Netherlands, to mark his return to Paris.

"I couldn't possibly go," she had said to the countess, showing her the engraved invitation, "but it was very kind of your brother to invite me."

"Oh, but you must!" exclaimed Marie-Lise. "You do have so much to learn, don't you! One does not refuse one's patron, *ma chère*!"

Lucinda, embarrassed, stammered, "But...I don't know what I would wear."

"What do you mean?" said the countess. "A ball gown, of course!"

"That is, you see," said Lucinda, "I am not equipped..."

"Ah! I understand! But that is no problem, my dear. I will send you my dressmaker. Leave it to me. He is the best couturier there is. He is a wizard! I shall instruct him to fashion you a gown that will make heads turn. You will be irresistible!"

And indeed, inspecting herself in the looking glass a fortnight later, swishing her billowing gown from side to side, she barely recognized herself. She did look magnificent. The soft blue silk was woven through with silver thread. When she moved, the skirts rippled like water. At the last minute the countess had sent over a set of satin sleeve-ribbons, a pair of fat pearl earrings, and an embroidered mask on an ivory wand. Nervously, she thought of the expense. If Arent were alive, he would have a fit! But as her coach swept up to the ambassador's magnificent *hôtel*, she could not suppress a rush of triumph. If only her scornful cousins in Dorset could see her now!

A pair of liveried footmen bowed low as they helped her out of the carriage. As she climbed the staircase, her gown swept the treads behind her like a monarch's train. She sensed, but was careful not to acknowledge, the approving stares.

At the top of the steps she hesitated, but the people pressing from behind pushed her forward, over the threshold and into the fray. The air inside the ballroom was humid, thick with candle smoke and perspiration. She almost gagged. There was no time to look around and admire the sumptuous, glittering décor, for she was immediately accosted by a masked stranger and swept up in the dance. Although her memory of Monsieur Piétain's lessons was a little rusty, she managed to finesse her way through a Branlé, a Gavotte and a Minuet before breaking free, breathless. Burying her hands in her skirt to prevent them from being grabbed again, she backed away from the dancers, and sidled over to the tall windows at the far end of the room. Her palms were wet with her partners' sweat. She wiped them on her gown and peered out into the dark.

Through the undulating glass, some rollicking figures swam into view. She recognized them with a shock. There was Liesbet, swinging her little brother around! And Bessie hovering behind them. And Thomas, and Arent. Behind them she spotted Zéfine, Blanchette and Karel Klek, bowing, stepping and twirling.

Nothing made sense anymore. What had she done to deserve this? What made her, suddenly, the center of attention? It was a nightmare! Already, reflected in the glass, she could make out a masked figure bearing down upon her. The Marquis de Quelquonque, no doubt (she recognized his unctuous gait), determined to lead her back to the dance. When all she wished for—the only thing she truly wanted—was to be out there in the dark with her ghosts, who shut her out in this dreadful light. And excluded her so ruthlessly, so heartlessly, from their ineffable secrets and unearthly delights.

When Superintendent Perrault arrived for his portrait sitting the following afternoon, he found her in a subdued mood.

"I understand," he said, "that Madame created quite a stir last night, at the ambassador's ball."

"I did?" she asked as she adjusted the drape of the backdrop.

"Indeed. All Paris wants to know the identity of the pretty newcomer who made such a stir, and then left so abruptly. I am inclined to think that it was you. "

"I suppose it was. I left before the midnight banquet."

"But why?"

"I was weary." His eyebrows went up. "And not at all hungry," she added.

"But everyone said you were the belle of the ball!" he exclaimed, shaking his head. "To leave before midnight—it is simply unheard of!"

She shrugged. "In that case I shan't attend any more balls," she said.

"Ah, but Madame! To be honored by society, to be hailed as a beauty, is that not what every lady of good family most desires?"

She gave a short laugh. "'Of good family'? *Moi?*"

"My dear lady! But I understood that...your grandfather was an earl, was he not?"

"He was. But that does not mean that my family was good. At least, they were not good to me. There was a question about my birth. I was not considered worthy, in their eyes."

"I see," he said, embarrassed.

"I was shunned," she went on, dabbing her brush on the palette more forcefully than necessary. "And, later, beaten. Put to work, you know, sweeping cinders, scrubbing floors, feeding hogs."

"Madame!" he exclaimed.

She shook her head, appalled at having confessed to such a shameful past. She wished she could take it back. "Please—Let us talk no more of it."

"As you wish." There was a pause. It was Perrault who broke the silence. "For one so young," he said, "Madame has certainly had her share of misfortune."

"I suppose I was born under an unlucky star," she said. "I was cursed at birth."

"Ah, but not entirely…"

"Cursed at birth," she said stubbornly. "A despised, unwanted orphan."

"Perhaps, but not entirely unwanted. Not many orphans, after all, are blessed with such a devoted *marraine* to watch over them. Are they!"

Startled, she looked up. "A godmother? How do you mean?"

"That very pleasant person you have told me of, that good person who raised you—"

"Ah, you mean Bessie! But…"

"Indeed. Genuine, devoted love, such as you tell me *la mère l'Oie*, mother Goose, gave you, it is a precious gift! One might say that you were born under a *lucky* star!"

Lucinda felt the tears well up. "I never considered how precious it was—her love—when she was alive. I was always longing for something else. Something better. Something, I don't know, grander. And now it's too late."

"Too late? But it is never too late!"

Swallowing hard, she said, "It is easier to have no expectations."

"No, no, Madame must never give up hope! When God sends us trials, He is but testing our mettle and our virtue! The greater the misfortune we are made to bear, the more certain our reward!"

"Do you really think so?"

"Absolutely!" he shouted, flinging an arm in the air, which caused his wig to flop sideways, upsetting her carefully arranged composition. "These trials exist only to teach us a lesson. As long as we remain good and pure of heart, Madame, we must trust that our wishes will some day come true."

Despite some skepticism, Lucinda could not dismiss Monsieur Perrault's assurances out of hand. It was as if in teaching her the pleasures of grand (and often preposterous) generalization, he were showing her a way to sweep away her own, quite individual, pain.

If the glamour of the ballroom was not to her liking, Lucinda did find plenty to like in the more intimate, although no less glamorous, space of Madame de Galantine's salon. It was the countess who had introduced her to this lively gathering of Parisian wives, widows and courtesans. Lucinda was immediately smitten. These women, who were dressed tastefully, if less expensively than the court ladies, were extremely outspoken. They reminded her of her friends from the baggage train, except that instead of French whores' crude jokes, the conversation here was of a more genteel variety. At first she was content to just sit and listen, for the learned talk of poetry, politics and philosophy went quite over her head. But when she discovered that the ladies also enjoyed banter and gossip, she began to join in, timidly at first, but later more boldly, as she began to understand the underlying wit, especially as it pertained to men.

"Have you heard about that *poulle*, that chicken, who now declares that we are the equals of men?" demanded Marie Vaudage, the actress. "How did the poor creature ever get such a bizarre idea?"

"Ah, *chère*, you mean François Poullain, that one?" said Thérèse Patromal, the buxom wife of a prominent lawyer. "One hears he is advised not to show his face in Paris."

"Indeed, he had better lie low," said Madame de Galantine. "He proposes that it makes no difference what sex one is. That a woman can be educated just like a man." She gave a bitter laugh.

Madame Pernod sighed. "Ah, how many times must we hear that argument? I am sick of it! Let us talk of other things." She started fanning herself energetically.

Marie Vaudage turned to Lucinda. "They mock us, dear Madame."

"Who?" asked Lucinda, baffled.

"The men. Yes. The dramatists and poets and such."

"But why do they mock us?" asked Lucinda.

"For having opinions, naturally!" pouted Madame Patromal.

"They think," explained the countess, "that if they let us have our say, their entire little world will come tumbling down."

"Ah yes. The sky will fall! Let us therefore prattle away, and let us have nothing more to do with men," Madame de Galantine declared.

"Oh, but..." said Lucinda. She stopped. She wasn't sure if Madame de Galantine was being serious. She was beginning to understand that in this company, you were supposed to say the opposite of what you meant.

"No, no, continue!" ordered her hostess. "We speak our minds here, Madame. You must not be shy."

"Uh...I have no opinions on the matter, really," said Lucinda lamely.

"But you do! You certainly do," exclaimed Countess Bienmaline. "I have heard you opine on a number of matters, precious." Turning to the others, she said, "And Madame has excellent taste in men."

"Do tell, who?"

"The Marquis de Quelquonque..."

The ladies groaned.

"Oh, I really don't..." Lucinda began.

"No, no, my dear, we are just teasing," the countess explained. To the ladies, she said, "Monsieur Perrault is her friend."

"Ah! Which one? The one who designed the colonnade of the Louvre, Claude?"

"No, the younger brother. The one who attends Minister Colbert."

"Ah, Charles, *that* one! But he is a perfectly charming fellow! And a poet, too."

"Poor man. His wife passed away but lately—"

"Yes, Marie Guichon. Pretty thing, so sad."

"A man of means, they say; and a widower to boot!"

"I assure you," said Lucinda quickly, "that I am not...I have no interest in..."

"Of course not, my dear!" laughed the countess. "'It is understood." She turned to the others, and chided, "When I said friend, I did not mean *friend*."

Lucinda was blushing. "A poet? It does not surprise me. Mr. Perrault possesses a fine spirit."

"Indeed he does. We thought his *Dialogue between Love and Friendship* was exquisite, don't you remember, Marie?"

"Ah yes, so precious!" said Mademoiselle Vaudage, "Let me see if I can recall the last verse." She jumped to her feet, and, taking a theatrical stance, declaimed:

"...Adieu, my sister; for there is so much for me to do.
There are lovers to punish, and others to recompense;
and above all I must attend to Iris, who is about to depart for the ball,
where I must help her to conquer every honest person's heart,
and oblige all assembled there to admit
she is both the most beautiful and most amiable lady in all the world."

There was a smattering of applause. "Divine!" sighed Madame Pernod.

"Very good, very good," said Madame de Galantine. "We must invite Monsieur Perrault to one of our gatherings. Although one hears that he is a very busy man."

55

THE LABYRINTH

If you had to place a bet on who would win the race, the tortoise or the hare, you would be a fool to give the tortoise even the ghost of a chance. Do not be misled, however. The tortoise may be a patient plodder, and the hare surpassing fleet of foot; but you must not forget that haste is the enemy of perfection, perfect is the enemy of good, and in a just world, slow and steady wins the day.

Of all the people Lucinda had met in Paris, the Superintendent of Royal Buildings and Works was the only one to express a genuine interest in her personal history. Feigning a tactful reluctance to probe, he managed to draw most of it out of her in the end. With some restrictions, naturally. Monsieur Perrault was therefore left with the impression that although Lucinda's virtue had oftentimes been assailed, it had not been surrendered until her wedding night.

She blushed, having just finished telling him about Uncle Edmund's unwelcome advances. "It is not a pretty tale."

"I am sorry, Madame, for your pain. The path of righteousness never runs straight."

She bit her lip. "But why? I mean, if our intentions are good, why must we suffer?"

"That, Madame, is one of life's great questions." He scratched his moustache with a stubby finger. "Take, for instance, *Peau-d'âne...*"

"*Peau-d'âne?*"

"Ah, but you *must* know that story! Did your *marraine* not tell it to you? It's the one about the princess who is so beautiful that her father the king, a widower who wishes to remarry, can find no woman more suitable for his bed than his own flesh and blood! You do not know it, *alors*?"

Lucinda shook her head.

"But let me tell it to you then! Well. In order to prevent this unnatural marriage, which is, naturally, odious to her, the princess flees the palace in disguise—hiding her beauty beneath a magic donkey's skin. This is the origin of the name, you see. Peau d'âne. Ass's Skin. What hardships she suffers you cannot imagine! She ends up a lowly drudge, reviled by all."

Lucinda stared at him. "But it wasn't her fault!"

"Ah, you are too impatient! You must wait for the moral! Well, a prince happens by her hovel one day, and catches a glimpse of her lovely visage beneath the foul ass's skin. The vision preys on his mind, but none will believe that the poor mad creature is actually a dazzling beauty. The prince falls ill, he is sick with love; in his delirium, he asks for a cake to be baked by the despised maidservant. As she is preparing the cake, her ring slips from her finger into the batter. When the prince eats the cake, he bites on the ring, and announces forthwith that he will take in marriage none but the hand that fits the ring..."

"Don't tell me," she interrupted. "The ring fits no one's finger except..."

"Except Peau-d'âne's," he concluded. He sighed contentedly. "I have always liked that story. Don't you?"

"Yes, but," she protested, "I don't see—I don't see why he waited until he found the ring, I mean, if he loved her, why didn't he just go to her? Why did she have to *prove* anything? Why does the heroine always have to prove herself?"

"It is the story, Madame," he said, a little hurt.

"It's a good story," she granted. "But it is only a story."

"A story with a moral," he corrected her.

"Which is...?" she asked.

"But I am surprised that you don't see it! The moral, Madame, is that virtue, and above all its female manifestation—patience—will be rewarded in the end."

Lucinda started fanning herself. "If patience were all that's..." she began.

He did not let her finish. "Permit me to remark, Madame, that the ladies at court are very fond of that story."

"Well," she said, "then it must be an excellent story." She smiled at him, content to drop the subject. But she stored it in her mind as a topic she might bring up the next time she attended Madame de Galantine's salon.

Upon taking his leave, Monsieur Perrault said that it would give him immense pleasure if she would accord him the honor of showing Madame and her son the Labyrinth of Versailles. "There you will see manifested," he said, "what I mean when I speak of 'morals.'"

Five days later Lucinda's carriage drew up to an ornate gate deep within the gardens of Versailles. Superintendent Perrault opened the door and, with a bow, assisted mother and son as they climbed out. "Welcome to the Labyrinth," he said proudly. "Behold!"

They gazed up at the two statues Mr. Perrault was pointing to—two figures perched on pedestals outside the gate. He began addressing them in a loud voice a bit more pedantic than usual; Lucinda noticed that a huddle of perfumed courtiers was within earshot.

"The gentleman you see depicted here, with his writing scroll," he said, waving at the right-hand statue, "is, of course, Aesop, the author of the Fables."

Lucinda and Arentje turned to stare at Aesop, an ugly old man.

"And here, on the left, behold the lovely Cupid, with a spool of thread," he said. "Can you tell me what it signifies?"

Lucinda raised her palms shoulder-high. Arentje lustily shook his head.

"It means that in order to thread one's way through love's labyrinth, one needs not only heart, but brains."

They were aware of giggles and whispers coming from the courtiers. Stiffly ignoring them, Perrault took out a bundle of keys, and unlocked the gate with a sweeping gesture. "Come. Follow me."

The Labyrinth was a network of allées cut through a maze of tall hedges. At each intersection stood a fountain depicting one of the fables. Brightly painted lead sculptures of animals arranged in pairs—serpents and foxes, roosters and porcupines, hares and tortoises—spewed water at one another in elegant arcs, setting off trickling water melodies. Never in her life had Lucinda seen anything like it. She felt she had stepped into a world of enchantment. Breathlessly she rushed after Arentje, who was galloping from one fountain to the next. Perrault came lumbering along behind.

"Now, now, children," Perrault panted, "no need for such haste!"

Arentje was clambering up a shell-encrusted basin, stretching his little hand to touch the jet of water spraying from a stork's beak. "No, Arentje, come down!" she scolded, catching him by the hem of his doublet. "You'll get drenched!"

"Let him play," said Perrault indulgently. "It is in play that children learn, Madame. That is the function of this maze. It was built for the edification of the dauphin."

"The dauphin!" said Lucinda. "Goodness! Arentje, be careful, or we'll be accused of harming the property of the king! Monsieur Perrault, are we truly permitted...?"

He waved his hand. "It gives me great pleasure to bring young people to this place. It was my idea, you know, my fantasy. You might say that I was the designer."

Lucinda shook her head. "You are a man of many talents, Monsieur Perrault. Are the verses likewise yours?" There was a plaque beside each fountain with a quatrain describing the fable represented there.

"Sadly, no. The inscriptions were made by Monsieur de Benserade. I had wanted to commission Monsieur de la Fontaine to compose them, but he has fallen out of favor with the king," said Perrault. "It did fall on me to write the morals, however. They are collected in this little volume." He withdrew a slender book bound in red and gold leather from somewhere inside his coat, and offered it to her with a bow. "It would do me an immense pleasure if Madame would read it. There she will find some edifying morals, I hope."

Leafing through the booklet later in her studio, Lucinda did not see much of a connection between the squabbling animals and Perrault's "morals," which were mainly pithy quips about the power of love and the phenomenon of female beauty, of both the inner and outward kind.

All this male attention, no matter how unwelcome, was having an effect on her. The numbness that had descended on her after the attack on the baggage train had begun to wear off. She was emerging from a long stupor, and from the conviction that her life was over. An unsettling awareness of herself as a desirable woman was taking hold, and she felt her body's secret longings reassert themselves, resulting in hot nights and torrid dreams.

John.

She found herself addressing him in her mind as if he were physically present. His face, the way he stood with his chin thrust forward, intent and grave— she could almost smell his scent, feel the weight of his strong hand, heavy on her neck. She wanted to share every thought with him, every insight, every sunset, every dotted landscape.

Sometimes, she told him in sudden rush of excitement, it's like little pieces of paradise raining down. Fragments of paradise, perfect drops of distilled truth, bouncing off your eyelashes, nose and outstretched tongue.

In this frame of mind it was easy to pretend it was John, and not kind, pompous Superintendent Perrault, who stepped back and admired her paintings, and told her she was beautiful.

The countess, whose life was one endless round of divertissements, persuaded her to attend the theatre with her the next week.

"But what if I don't like it?" Lucinda protested, as she climbed into the carriage.

This made Marie-Lise laugh heartily. "Whoever heard of anyone not liking the *Comédie*?" she exclaimed. "Really, my dear! It is *the* place to be seen. Trust me!"

It turned out that Lucinda was spellbound by the play, in which a beautiful queen spurned one nice young king who loved her, and pined for another, who would not marry her. She felt very sad for poor Bérénice, but it was hard to follow the story because the countess kept nudging her and pointing out swains in the audience.

"Shhh!" she whispered, a little irritably. "What is it now?"

"My dear," said Marie-Lise, "I *am* sorry! But you are so amusing! You really are caught up in the play, aren't you! You want to lower your wrap a little, my dear, one doesn't want to look like a *bourgeoise*, does one. I just wanted to tell you that Prince Fainéant was looking our way. Over there, by the pillar."

Lucinda adjusted her wrap to reveal her décolleté, and obediently turned her head to look for the prince. But her eye was caught instead by a neat little man in the throng below their balcony staring at her angrily, as if he were trying to put a name to the face.

She knew that man.

She kept her composure. She turned back to Marie-Lise, and said quietly, "Will you forgive me, dear Countess, for not staying? I have such a headache."

"But I am bored too! This fellow Racine is really too much. Really! His play is not very amusing, not amusing at all. Let's go!" decided the countess.

As she was gathering up her belongings, Lucinda caught sight of the lady in the next box, whose fan had gone up to her mouth in dismay. She had to turn for one last look. Poor Bérénice was staggering offstage, dangerously waving a dagger.

"Well?" complained the countess. "Are you coming, or not?"

When she was home, Lucinda decided she would keep her excursions to an absolute minimum. She could not afford to run into Vauban's assistant, or anyone else who might recognize her as a camp follower, again.

"I came across one of Madame's former acquaintances the other day," the marquis informed her on his next visit.

"Oh?" asked Lucinda.

"Jean Gonflé. He remembers you well."

"Jean Gonflé?" she repeated. "I do not think..."

"Yes, yes, he said he knew you from Maastricht. Said you were a great friend of his mentor, the Seigneur de Vauban."

She busied herself with her paints, and refused to look up at him.

"You do not deny it then."

"Deny it? Deny what?" she bristled. "I have met the Seigneur de Vauban. As for this other person, I have no idea, no."

"Monsieur Gonflé saw you at the *Comédie*. He thought the connection might interest me."

"I do not see how it could interest you, Marquis," she said icily. She rose. "And now, you must pardon me, I have a client waiting."

He lingered over her hand as he took his leave. "Madame need have no fear," he breathed, his slick moustache brushing her knuckles. "Madame must be assured that her secrets are always safe with me."

56

PATIENCE

The Superintendent of Buildings was very pleased with his portrait, which was completed in a matter of weeks, but he was reluctant to give up his pleasant visits to the Rue Saint Honoré. He had also gathered that his young English friend was having some financial difficulties, and it was for this reason that he mentioned he was looking for pictures for the walls of a newly-completed salon in the Palace of Versailles.

"Oh—you mean," she stammered, "you mean—for His Majesty?"

"My portrait, it is very handsome," he replied, "and your still-lifes, they are exquisite. I am sure that the king will find your work as admirable as I do, and perhaps we can find the perfect little niche somewhere..."

"But," she blurted out, "...but I can also do big pictures—you know..."

"Big pictures? From such a petite woman?" he teased.

"Wait here!" she cried, and ran out of the room.

She rang for Dieneke and asked her to bring up the painting of Penelope and the suitors.

He examined it gravely. "*You* did this?" he asked, after a long pause.

"It is mine," she admitted cautiously.

"But it is excellent!" he exclaimed. "But you are a genius!"

"Oh, I don't know..." she demurred.

"Certainly. Homer, is it not?"

"Yes, I believe," she said.

"The Odyssey. Naturally! One can see that. It is the lady Penelope at her loom." He made himself comfortable on a chair and began explaining her picture to her. "Your painting illustrates, Madame, the point I was making about life and art. Like Penelope and her tapestry, the artist takes the most eventful threads of life, you see Madame, and weaves them just so, to create a story. But life itself is infinite and immutable, whereas in art it is controlled, rewritten, constantly unraveled and put together again. Is it not? Art reveals the patterns. Art takes life and makes it legend. This is what your painting says to me."

"It does?" said Lucinda. She snorted. She found the whole business so futile sometimes—here she was, trying to convey a world of solitude, a world of silence and private meaning, only to have to listen to other people's glib and noisy interpretations.

"I am quite serious, Madame," he pouted. "Why do you laugh?"

"I am sorry, Monsieur. But, I mean—*your* life may be a legend, but mine is not."

"You are mistaken, Madame! On the contrary! Why, from what you have told me of your life so far, it is quite an extraordinary little history!"

"A fiasco, you mean!" she said grimly, although still smiling. "An unmitigated disaster, I should say."

"A disaster? Madame! I regret that you think that! Because surely there is no need to think it is a disaster!"

"Oh, no?"

"I mean that it is never too late to turn one's life around. In your case—see what you have achieved!" He waved at the ornate furnishings. "You have managed to pick yourself up out of the gutter. Thanks to your courage, your beauty, your resilience, and your natural talent, of course, you have built up quite a nice little position..."

"I don't care for any of that," she said sullenly. "All I care for is what I have lost."

"What is lost may also be retrieved. At least, repaired. Evidently."

She leaned back in her chair, and started fanning her cheeks with a paint-rag. "Not so evidently! Not evidently at all! I have made a dreadful mess of things..."

"Never, Madame! Let me put it this way. We are in charge of our own story. It is up to us to find the story, you see Madame, and trim away the extraneous matter, just as a sculptor chisels at a stone to reveal his sculpture. Your life, Madame, contains the bones of a good story, an excellent story, a story to be proud of. But I am certain of it! All that remains is for you to recognize it. And of course you must find a fitting ending. Your story lacks a proper ending, that is all."

"An ending!" she said darkly. "You want an ending? Ha! What about death? Isn't that an ending?" She crumpled the rag and threw it into a corner of the room. "Don't think I haven't given it any thought."

He raised his beetling brow. "Death is an ending, yes, certainly," he said carefully. "But taking one's own life—to escape from one's story by ruthlessly imposing the ending—that is not the answer. Surely! One is searching, you see, not for an escape, but for a satisfying conclusion. Which of these do you think a premature death would achieve? An escape, or a satisfying end? And where would be the moral? *That* is the real question."

There was a silence while she mulled this over. The Superintendent, humming, made a great show of examining her Penelope painting, so that she could dry her eyes discreetly.

"My fantasies," she finally confessed, "usually end with a rescue. A bold hero galloping up in the nick of time, to save me and to make me his."

"Well then! There's your ending!" he smiled, mopping his brow. He sat down heavily on a chair against the wall.

"But that doesn't happen in real life. It doesn't happen to me. It will never happen to me now."

"Are you certain of that?"

"Of course!" She added with a hollow chuckle, "Actually, someone *almost* came to my rescue, once, or at least he said he tried. But of course it came to naught."

"Ah. You must tell me." She detected a whiff of jealousy. "Who was he? Have I heard about this personage yet?"

Lucinda decided it was time to put an end to the conversation, which was giving her the jitters. She stretched as if she was suddenly very tired, and yawned, "So I just sit and wait for my hero to show up? And wait, and wait? Like Penelope?"

His laugh sounded forced. "Or the patient Griseldis! Or the beauty in the dormant forest, who waited a hundred years for her prince to come. Ah, Madame! But that is not real life! Such things take place only in fairy tales."

She looked so crestfallen that he hastened to inject some levity. "I mean to say, Madame, that in real life, unlike Griseldis, our Parisian ladies haven't a grain of patience. So that it is their husbands who are obliged to practice the art of patience in their stead."

Lucinda finally smiled. "Then perhaps I would do well to acquire a patient husband."

"Madame..." He blushed crimson. "Ah...But you would make me the happiest of men..."

"No, no," she said quickly. "Dear me, that wasn't what I meant at all. I hope you understand. Although it is so very kind of you—"

"Ah, no, of course not," he said, looking away in embarrassment. "Please forgive me..." He started towards the door, and Lucinda rang the bell for Dieneke.

He turned back. "But allow me one last piece of advice before I take my leave, Madame. You need not follow in the footsteps of Penelope, or the patient Griseldis, or the dormant beauty. You need not wait passively for your prince to show up. There are other, more practical ways to give your story a happy ending, you know."

The maid stuck her head around the door. "Dieneke," Lucinda said to her in Dutch, "Monsieur Perrault is leaving. Will you please bring him his cane?"

57

THE FACE THAT LAUNCHED
A THOUSAND SHIPS

In order to rescue his young friend from her financial troubles, Superintendent Charles Perrault talked his boss, Minister Colbert, into commissioning a large painting from her for Versailles.

"The king's preference, naturally, is for battle scenes, and such," the superintendent informed her, "especially in commemoration of his glorious victories."

"Ah," said Lucinda, without much enthusiasm.

They were interrupted by Arentje, who stormed into the room clamoring for a story. Perrault smiled, and bowed low to the boy.

"Certainly I will tell you a story, as soon as I have finished my business with your lovely *Maman*, my dear Marquis de Carabas." It was a nickname that never failed to make Arentje squeal with laughter.

"Promise!" he threatened.

"Promised, *cher Marquis*."

Perrault turned back to the boy's mother.

"As I was saying, the king's victories. Yes, and since you were present at the conquest of Maastricht, that was mentioned as a possibility..."

Lucinda crossed her arms and patted her elbows nervously.

"But—and please excuse me if I was mistaken—I did remind the minister that such a picture might not be suited to the female sensibility."

"You are not wrong," she said gratefully. "Battles? Carnage? I don't think I would do a very good job of it."

"A pity. But it is very understandable, Madame. Believe me, we are mindful of your frailty. But," he went on, pulling at his lip, "I did have another idea. Might you be willing to part with your excellent painting of Penelope and the suitors?"

She hesitated. "I am very attached to that one, Monsieur."

"My thought was that that painting might appeal to His Majesty if you were to make a companion piece for it."

"A companion piece?"

"You see, Madame, your picture tells but half the story."

"Oh. You mean Odysseus' homecoming..."

"No, not that. The husband's homecoming, it is already nicely implied in your painting. Your painting shows the redemption—the penance. What we need now is what went before: the perdition, the root cause..."

"Root cause?"

"Tell me, Madame, why did Penelope's husband leave her behind in Ithaca?"

"Because of the war. The Trojan War. But..."

"Indeed, and what started this famous war?"

"I don't know...I suppose it was when Helen..." she began.

"Helen! You are correct. It was she."

Lucinda laughed. "I didn't mean that she, on her own, started the war, that's absurd..."

"It is not absurd, Madame. Call her Eve, call her Helen, or by any other name—search for the woman, and you will find the seed, the root, the germ of the corruption. This is the nature of woman, is it not? Your sex is weak and peace-loving by nature, yet you drive men to do terrible things."

"Ah!" she commented.

"Indeed. I think the king would be most pleased to have, for his private rooms, the abduction of Helen of Greece by Paris of Troy."

She thought it over. "I could do that," she said. A picture was starting to form in her mind: a composition of a swooning woman swept up into the strong arms of a warrior on a rearing white horse. "Yes!" she said, with growing enthusiasm, "I *think* I could do that."

"I do not doubt it, Madame," he said. "And I can assure you the remuneration, for the two pictures, will be most handsome."

"Thank you! *Thank* you! I'll start on it at once!"

"It is important to make it the same size as the other one," he cautioned. "And one other thing…"

"Yes?"

"Madame…let me put this as delicately as I can. Your Penelope, she is very beautiful, but her beauty, it is…subdued. As is necessary, of course, to illustrate her extraordinary modesty and virtue," he added hastily. "However, when it comes to painting Helen, I think a different approach may be in order."

"Oh?" she said.

"Yes, especially if His Majesty is to approve the paintings. It would be best to emphasize, if you will forgive me, a certain voluptuous quality…"

"I understand," said Lucinda. "Don't worry. I know exactly what you mean."

She started the new picture that same day, and worked on it feverishly, interrupted only by the marquis, who was now in the habit of calling on her daily.

"I am afraid Madame will be angry with me for drawing her away from her work," he simpered.

"Not at all, Monsieur," she said reluctantly. "It is always a pleasure…"

"The pleasure is mine, Madame, all mine!" he swaggered, and put out a hand to touch her hair. She backed away from him quickly. "Do forgive me, but I could not resist!" he laughed. "The blue paint, it is so… becoming!"

She swung around to inspect herself in the mirror. The hair over her left ear was indeed tipped with blue. She tried scraping some of it off with her fingernails.

He cleared his throat to make her turn around again. "Madame must promise me one thing," he demanded.

"Sir?"

"She must promise me that when I make her mine, she will give up this foolish pastime. A Frenchman likes his mistresses painted on the lip and cheek, Madame, but not upon the *coiffure*. You must admit that it is a little bizarre!"

She refused to smile back. He intercepted a quick angry glance in the direction of her studio. Her lack of further response emphatically discouraged further conversation.

The marquis sighed loudly, then flung himself down on a bench, burying his nose in the crook of his arm.

Still she said nothing, not a word of encouragement or penitence. After a few moments, he came up for air, his swarthy face flushed.

"You cannot understand, Madame, how I suffer. Believe me! If I did not suffer so, I should not importune you like this."

"It goes without saying," she said.

He shot her a look of indignation. "You have no heart, Madame!" he implored.

She did not respond.

He rose, and adjusted the cuffs of his sleeve with dignity. "But Madame must also understand," he went on casually, "that one's patience has its limits. We should both be sorry, should we not, if this painful craving I possess for Madame pushed me to the brink, and I should let slip some gross indiscretion about her past..."

Lucinda patted her cheeks, which were now rather flushed, but gave no other indication that his words had ruffled her. "If," she suggested, "the marquis will allow me to fulfill this one obligation to the king, I think he will find that once it is done, his suit will receive the attention it deserves."

"Indeed?"

"I assure you."

"Ah!" he chortled triumphantly. "Madame has no idea how happy these words make me!" He came toward her, arms outstretched. She stepped back discreetly.

"But Monsieur le Marquis must understand that his kind attentions," she continued, "are of such a distracting nature, that it is difficult to complete my work..."

His arms fell to his sides. "I see," he pouted.

"If the marquis will permit me to continue without constant interruption," Lucinda went on with a desperate smile of encouragement, "my picture will most assuredly be finished in record time."

"In that case, one must leave Madame to her labors."

As soon as the coast was clear, Lucinda jumped up and made for the studio where poor Dieneke was in all likelihood catching a chill.

Dieneke had been more than flattered when her mistress had asked her to pose for another painting.

"This time, you are the most beautiful woman in the world," Lucinda told her, "the face that launched a thousand ships, you know!"

"Oh, Missus!" giggled Dieneke. "How ever will you manage that?"

"You'll see," Lucinda promised.

And in fact, with just a little artistic license, it was not hard to transform the varicose-veined, heavy-hipped Dieneke into a swooning, voluptuous blonde. "A silk purse from a sow's ear," Dieneke scoffed.

"Oh come, Dieneke!" Lucinda chided. "You mustn't put yourself down! You really are very pretty!"

Dieneke shrugged. "I don't think you'll find many men as agrees with you, Missus."

"Oh, but Arent did, didn't he?" she said.

Dieneke sat bolt upright, upsetting the composition. Lucinda held up a warning hand, but it was too late. The carefully draped folds slid off Dieneke to the floor in a heap.

"I'm sorry..." Dieneke stumbled.

"Never mind! I'll just do it again Sit still."

As she was rearranging Dieneke's veils, she noticed that the maid was trembling. Carefully, she said, "I am sorry that I upset you, Dieneke. I didn't mean to."

"That's all right, Missus," Dieneke mumbled. She started sniffling.

Lucinda walked back to her easel. Nonchalantly, she said, "Didn't you think I knew about you and Arent?"

"You *knew*—about me and Master?" gasped Dieneke.

"Of course. I've known—oh, a long time. For ever."

"Oh!" said Dieneke miserably.

"I found some canvases in the shed, and it was evident it was you…"

"But believe me, Missus, he only took me as a model before…"

"Before he married me. I know that, Dieneke. And I don't blame you. I really don't. In fact, I blame myself. After all, you were there first…"

"Missus!" the maid shrieked. "But you should have thrown me out… You should *still* throw me out!"

"Why should I?"

Dieneke was sobbing too loudly, now, to reply.

"For the longest time, I couldn't understand what made you stay," whispered Lucinda, her throat tightening. "But now I think I know." She was crying too. "You loved him, didn't you," she said.

Dieneke shook her head vehemently.

"Yes you did. Even with no hope…"

Dieneke moaned.

Lucinda found herself kneeling on the floor in front of Dieneke, and holding out her arms to her.

There they remained, hugging and sobbing, until they heard Arentje's bright voice calling out to them.

She worked at the painting in a mad fever, stopping only when the twilight turned to blackness, rising from her bed in the middle of the night to be sure to catch the very first rays of morning light. In six and a half weeks it was done. She had completed the painting in record time.

She frowned at it. She hoped they would like it at court. She herself could not bear to look at it anymore. She was ashamed that she had accepted the commission, even though without it she could not pay her debts or leave Paris. Somehow she felt that this painting violated her integrity. The paint was not quite dry, but she could not wait to get it out of her house, and the other one too. She sent word to the ministry that the pictures were ready.

The very next morning Lucinda received a message from the marquis.

"*To the Delicious Object of my Sighs,*" it read. "*One hears the king is to have his pictures today. Tomorrow the trembling organ that is my heart, Madame, claims that other prize, far too long awaited.*"

She showed it to the countess.

"Oh, dear!" said Marie-Lise.

"I need your help, *Contesse,*" said Lucinda.

58

THE LAST LAUGH

The Dutch serving woman showed the marquis into the blue salon. He noted approvingly that a carafe and some refreshments were set out on the sideboard.

"Madame says she'll be with you shortly," said the woman in her execrable accent. The marquis nodded curtly. He resolved to speak to Madame about this lumpish maid of hers again. He could not understand why Madame was so stubborn on this issue. He might have to take it upon himself to arrange for a more acceptable replacement.

After pacing about loudly to let Madame know he had arrived, he tiptoed to the double doors on the far side of the room, which he guessed led to her chamber. There was no sound from within. Stealthily, he turned the knob and peeked in. Indeed, there was the canopy of a bed. The room was empty. He slipped inside. Madame must be in her private closet, for he noticed a thin line of light outlining a door on the other side of the bed.

He patted the silky coverlet, and decided to make himself comfortable. He loosened the elaborate bow of his cravat, and unwound it from around his neck. Next he unbuckled his belt and hung it, carefully, so the rapier would not slip out, over the back of a chair. He eased his shoulders out of his tight-fitting coat and unbuttoned the brocade vest underneath, releasing the girdle containing his corpulence. The beribboned shoes were kicked off next, and he rolled down the stockings carefully so as not to disturb the preventive bandage he wore around his right leg, which was prone to the gout.

Ah, that was better! He inspected his moustache in the looking glass, and adjusted its curvature a little above his lip. His shirt was open, and he was gratified to perceive some chest hairs protruding in manly fashion.

He sat down at the foot of the bed, and considered. He did not wish to shock the young lady, but surely they were both too sophisticated (given what the man Gonflé had told him about her) to play games. Better to be forthright, and not indulge in pretense. So off came the shirt, and, with admirable dexterity, the breeches were rapidly unbuttoned.

It was when he was trying to ease the breeches down over the bulky bandage on his leg and ankle without tearing the delicate silk, that he heard voices in the outer room. Female voices. Not one, but several.

Hastily he stood up, but, hobbled by the tight garment around his knees, lost his balance and landed on the parquet with a crash.

"Marquis?" Lucinda's voice called gaily. "Are you in here?"

"One moment Madame..." he began, but it was too late.

"Oh!" she exclaimed, from the doorway. "Oh, pardon me, I did not expect..."

"What did you not expect, *chère*?" came a voice behind her, and "Oh!"— another exclamation of horror, this one from Countess Bienmaline.

Now there were squeals of concern for the countess, who had fainted gracefully in the open doorway, and in less than a moment the sprawling marquis was the object of scrutiny of at least half a dozen ladies, all exclaiming "Oh!" in various keys and levels of outrage, with the most strident vociferation issuing from the lips of the mistress the marquis had but recently jilted, who was also of the party.

"*Mesdames*...Ladies, my apologies, I..." he began, pulling down some of the bed coverings in a fumbling attempt to cover his privates.

There was an appalled silence for a second or two.

"Please..." said Lucinda, "please...! I'm so sorry...Please, by all means do not rise on our account, Marquis."

The ladies turned to each other wide-eyed and hand-upon-mouth; then there was an explosion of mirth at the apt phrasing.

"Please do not...*rise*, Monsieur!" sputtered Madame Patromal, a short, buxom brunette, heaving with delight.

"Not on *our* account, sir!" choked another—he recognized the actress Marie Vaudage—who was holding on to her friend's shoulders for support.

"Stop!" thundered the marquis.

The ladies stopped laughing, arrested by the authority of his voice.

"This is a very regrettable situation, ladies," he panted, "but please hear me out. It...it is a misunderstanding. Allow me to explain. Your hostess is not the virtuous lady you take her to be!"

"No?" said la Vaudage. "But..."

"Let me finish! Madame was but recently a common camp follower of His Majesty's army, if you must know the truth."

"But you are a *monster*, Marquis!" clucked the countess, who had made a remarkable recovery. She turned to Lucinda. "He is a monster, my dear," she informed her friend, patting her hand.

"I have proof! Ladies, if you turn this into a scandal, if you insist on making me a laughing-stock, you'll oblige me to tell the *tout-monde* that Madame is a tart who has made good under false pretenses, and..."

"You rat! Who's going to believe you!" sputtered Madame Sansfaçon, his erstwhile mistress.

"You must try to see it from our perspective. I mean, even you cannot deny that Madame is fully clothed, and you, Marquis, are not," the countess pointed out helpfully.

"Let's escort him outside and have the neighborhood bear witness!" suggested Madame Patromal.

"*Bare* witness, you mean, my dear Bouqinette!" whooped Madame Sansfaçon, and that set them all off again.

Lucinda had been watching the scene as if it had nothing to do with her. Now she stepped into the bedchamber, and held up a hand, waiting for the laughter to subside.

"Thank you," she said quietly. "Ladies, friends, I appreciate your... enthusiasm. But now allow me to have a private word with the marquis."

"But *chère*!" protested the countess. "I thought..."

"Please. It is enough."

"*Chère*!" exclaimed the countess. "Are you feeling *sorry* for him now?"

"Of course not!" said Lucinda defensively. "But...I think we need not take this any further." Ignoring the questioning looks, she squared her chin and went on: "If you would just take the ladies into my studio, *Contesse*, and wait for me there..."

"But you do realize, don't you," the countess protested, "that if you dismiss your witnesses, you give this gentleman a free hand? He will be at liberty to say anything he likes about you, and without witnesses, there is no one to contradict him!"

"I know it, Contesse," said Lucinda. "Trust me."

Marie-Lise threw up her hands. "As you wish, *chère*," she said. "I hope you know what you are doing."

By the time they were alone the marquis had managed to pull up his breeches and, clutching at a bedpost, heaved himself to his feet.

"She is correct," he coughed, his color beginning to return to normal, "I shall tell the world that you are a whore, Madame, and give out gratis to all who will listen every last detail of your wild gyrations in the sack."

She was quiet.

"Unless, of course," he went on, somewhat encouraged, "Madame granted me freely what I most desired, and saw the advisability of per-suading her friends to hold their tongues about this unfortunate little episode..."

Still she said nothing.

"In which case, of course, Madame should be certain that I would defend her honor to the point of risking my life..."

"Oh, that will not be necessary," said Lucinda, staring at the ceiling.

"What? Ah, I see it now!" he panted, his face growing dark. "I am outfoxed! It's that upstart Perrault, is it not! Madame has been receiving Monsieur Perrault; *oui*, I have my informants. And to think that I made the introduction, *voyons*! Who would have thought the knave would have the audacity to sabotage me! Ah, the lecher, oh, villain..."

"Monsieur Perrault is an honorable man, I assure you. He has never tried to assail my virtue, nor has he tried to impugn me, as you have."

"But Madame!" he pleaded wetly, for he was at the same time trying to button his vest and the effort entailed a protruding tongue. "To im-pugn you was not my intent! I only wished to claim what was rightfully mine! You gave me to understand..."

"Marquis," said Lucinda. "I have given you nothing to understand."

"No?" he objected. "You..."

"Hear me out."

"Well?" grumbled the marquis, smoothing his coat flaps.

"I do not need to be persuaded that I mean the opposite of what I am saying. I assure you that I mean it."

"Say it, then!" snapped the marquis, arranging his cravat.

"*Cher* Marquis," said Lucinda, folding her hands carefully, "I have never had the slightest desire to be seduced by you. Even if you took me by force, I would not feel a speck of gratitude. I know that you will find this hard to believe, but I am quite happy not to be your mistress. Nor any man's toy, for that matter." She held up her hand, for he was about to interrupt her. "Nor do I need a man to defend my honor, as the marquis has so generously offered."

"Pah! Madame prefers to be regarded by the world as a slut, then!" the marquis sneered.

"Ever since I reached womanhood," Lucinda said with dignity, "the world to which you refer has seen fit to regard me as a slut, a useless piece of baggage. The world sees what it wants to see, Marquis. And I never knew what to do about it. But I am strengthened, Sir, by the knowledge that there are some who see me as I truly am, and who do not despise me."

"Aha!" said the marquis. "Well then, I see that Madame chooses to be branded a lewd minx. And if she is happy with that fate..."

"It is time," said Lucinda severely, "for me to take fate into my own hands."

"Madame must face the consequences, then," said the marquis.

"Then I must. I confess," she went on, "that I am grateful to you for one thing, Marquis."

"Indeed!" he said.

"Yes, I am grateful to you for showing me that wanting to be liked, not wanting to give offense, has been my greatest weakness."

"But weakness, Madame, is becoming in a woman! It is this obstinacy you display that is unseemly!"

"If it is obstinacy, then let me stand by it."

"Very well, Madame," he scowled, for he could not see the point of continuing this discussion.

"One more thing before you leave. I shall ask the countess and her friends to be discreet. As for my own reputation, I leave that entirely up to you."

"Madame is too good," said the marquis, somewhat mollified. "But Madame must also understand that she plays a dangerous game," he warned, slinking over her hand one final time as he took his leave.

Ruefully, she reflected that the marquis had no idea how tame this little game seemed to her now, compared to the fearful quest upon which she was about to embark.

The king found his new pictures sufficiently intriguing to demand to see the artist and her delightful model. Unfortunately, at the time of the unveiling, the artist and her model had already departed for England. The lady had some urgent business to attend to in her native land, according to Superintendent Perrault. And that, decided Minister Colbert, was probably just as well. He was certain that his aide had had something to do with the little painter's hasty departure; he suspected that there was more to their relationship than the rogue would let on. If she was indeed his mistress, Perrault would be reluctant, naturally, to share her, or her model, with His Majesty; and who could blame him?

"Do you mean to tell us, Perrault," Colbert whispered, "that these rumors we hear are without foundation, that any resemblance in the paintings to any member of the court is fortuitous?"

"Pure chance, dear Minister, pure chance!" chortled Perrault.

Gravely, Colbert inspected the canvases once again. The composition of the second painting was excellent, the expressions noble yet ecstatic, the naked flesh appetizingly flushed, and the leopard skin slung about Paris's shoulder exquisitely detailed.

He turned back to the first painting. He would keep this to himself of course, but he was almost certain that the artist had tampered with it since Perrault had first shown it to him. Not only was this Penelope considerably more tousled and alluring than he remembered, but there was also no denying that the most prominent of the suitors lurking behind her, an evil-looking villain, showed an uncommon resemblance to the Marquis de Quelquonque.

59

THE SLIPPER

In the stagecoach, Lucinda tried to make her mind go blank, to banish the imaginary scenarios from her head. There would be no more daydreaming from now on; she had sworn never again to be misled by her own fantasies. Dieneke was dozing next to her, with Arentje snuggled between them.

She gazed out the window at the English countryside. It had been so long since she had left that she was struck by how different from the Continent it looked. Compact, closely grazed hills. No bristling forests. No sweeping vistas. No vast skies. Everything more muted. A difference not only in the greener light, but in the trees themselves. In France the trees grew tall and vertical, carefully spaced out along the avenues like sentries endlessly saluting. Here in England they were rounder, densely symmetrical, set back from and quite unconnected to the road that snaked through the hedgerows like an earthworm slithering across the soil. The snug scale of it felt reassuring, familiar. Her skull prickled. She was coming home.

In London a hackney coach drove them to the Hospital for Women in St. Giles. There she was given the address of Mr. Prynce, in Lincoln's Inn Fields.

The house was a modest affair, low to the ground. It looked more like a series of linked cottages than a grand abode. An elderly woman answered the door.

Lucinda stammered her name.

"Wait here," she was told.

She remained out on the front stoop until she heard footsteps on the stairs inside.

Stepping out of the bright daylight into the gloom of the hall, she blinked. All she could see was a fuzzy outline of a man. She hesitated, waiting for her eyes to adjust.

"Lucinda." The voice sounded mocking, not at all surprised.

"John! Am I...?"

"Too late?" A bitter laugh. "I'm still here. As you can see."

"I mean, you..."

"Yes. I have been waiting for you."

"Oh. But...how..."

"I knew you were on your way."

"You *knew*?"

"I have my spies. I have made it my business to keep track of you. In Amsterdam, you know, and then in Paris."

"Really!"

"I was informed the Dutchman was dead..."

"Oh!"

"Yes."

"But, if you *knew!*" Her knees were starting to tremble. "Then why—"

"Why what?"

"Why did you not come for me...?"

He tilted his head up at the sun streaming in through the fanlight over her head. He cleared his throat, began again, this time with somewhat less irritation. "— I think...I suppose I wanted *you* to come looking for *me*."

"But..."

"You gave me no reason to hope."

"No, I suppose not."

"Not even the slightest."

"Well, but here I am."

"Yes, so you are."

The ensuing silence between them was so deep that she could feel her heart sinking into it as in a quicksand. She wanted to turn around and run away from the disappointing reality of this, back to the relative smoothness and ease of her fantasies. But her feet were heavily planted on the hallway floor. She took a step forward. His features finally swam into focus. He looked as awkward and unhappy as she felt. She did not remember him looking so—well, ordinary. He seemed smaller. Sadder. Grayer, balder.

He hung his head. "My life has been nothing—without you."

She took a deep breath. "But what happened to Noé?" she asked.

"He's upstairs. A big boy now."

She nodded. "That's good. I—I hope you will let me see him."

"Of course. And your own little ones..."

"Just Arentje," she said. She had to blink. "Liesbet died —."

"Oh, of course, I'd heard," he said stiffly. "I am sorry for your loss."

Her ribs ached with tension. Where was the warm, generous resonance in his voice that she had imagined so often? His voice was resentfully creaky. He was so insecure! Surely it wasn't all her fault?

"Well!" She forced herself to smile, although her eyes were wet. As if this really was very amusing.

"Remember your slipper?" he suddenly blurted out, to cover up the awkwardness.

"Of course!"

"I still have it. I—I kept it..."

"You *kept* it?"

"You may think me foolishly sentimental, but I could not..."

"Not at all!" she said hurriedly. "Please! Show it to me!"

It was a great relief to them both that he could turn away for a few moments in order to tug open a large oak chest.

"Ah! Here it is!" he exulted, swaggering slightly, as if she hadn't really believed him.

It was a pitiful little thing: dirty, worn, scuffed. But the glass beads still glittered as brightly as ever.

More for his sake than her own, she clasped her hands together, and breathed, "You *have* kept it! Let me try it on!"

"You don't have to, I mean, don't think I—I..." he stuttered, stung by the artificiality of her enthusiasm.

"No, really, I want to!" she said, gamely pulling up a chair that stood sentry next to the door.

He handed her the slipper with a gesture of reverence. Without further ado she kicked off her dusty shoe, revealing a sagging, rather grubby stocking. Hastily, to cover it up, she jammed the slipper onto her foot.

The wool of the stocking was much too bulky for the narrow little mule. She grabbed the stocking by the toes and pulled it off in one impatient motion. The sight of her naked foot was too much for John, who turned his head away. Lucinda quickly pointed her toes and curled her foot inwards, like a claw, before inserting it once more into the forlorn little shoe. But still it was too snug. She yanked at the recalcitrant leather. As hard as she tugged, she could not wedge her toes in.

She slumped back in the chair.

"See?" she said. "It doesn't fit!"

"It doesn't fit?" he repeated. "No, I...that can't be! Here, let me try it!"

He knelt down before her, and proceeded to cram her foot into the soft leather with a determination that bordered on despair.

"It's no use!" she laughed. She kicked her foot to shake him off. But she too felt like crying. "It isn't even close! My feet have spread!" And then, "Stop it! Let go, John! You can't make it fit!"

He sat back on his haunches. He swallowed. He looked at the piece of leather in his hand, grown dark with significance, invested with such a store of romanticized love. He opened his mouth as if to say something, but nothing came out. He brought his elbow up and swiped at his brow helplessly with the back of his arm, like a disconsolate child.

That gesture, unaccountably, affected Lucinda like a punch in the stomach. It made her suck in her breath with a gasp.

He looked up at her, startled.

For the first time since her arrival, he really looked at her. Stared at her boldly. Tried to make out what she really was; to see how he could make this dejected, flat-footed woman conform to the dainty, ethereal image he had of her in his mind.

Lucinda returned his stare, and she, too, saw reality. Not the strong, invincible hero of her imagination, but something else, something entirely new—or, rather, something that had always been a part of him, but that she had not chosen to see before.

It was an aura of regret; a fear of life as great as her own; a vulnerability that demanded, compelled, her deepest tenderness.

Cautiously, she leaned forward and held out her cold hands.

He looked at them in surprise; then with a groan clasped them in his.

And, wondrous to relate, at that touch the fire began to glow again, first mildly sparking in their fingertips, but spreading rapidly past the elbows into the chest, and finally, as they fell gratefully into each other's arms, turning into the wild conflagration they both remembered, that licked their bones and seared their loins and fed upon their innards.

BIOGRAPHY AND MYTHOLOGY

Names marked with an asterisk (*) are real historical characters

Noé Prynce became an apothecary and a physician. His exotic dark looks earned him the reputation of having supernatural healing powers, and this stood him in good stead when he took over from his father as chief physician of the Mother Goose Hospital for Women in St. Giles in 1698.

Arent Arentzn. Prul the Younger became a painter like his father and mother before him, and enjoyed some popularity as a court portraitist. Since he was not in the habit of signing his pictures, no painting in existence today can be authoritatively attributed to him.

Lady Clarissa eventually regained the power of speech. Unfortunately, the harmony of her marriage was never restored. After her husband, **Sir Edmund Nayerdell**, succumbed to a fatal apoplexy, Lady Clarissa converted to Papism so that she might enter a convent in France. She never mastered the French language, but that was not a problem, since the order of nuns she joined was a silent one.

Sarah Nayerdell married a very rich man, became the mistress of a mansion not very different from her childhood home, and developed a passion for whist and a taste for Barbadoes waters before she was out of her twenties.

Robert Steppys, Second Earl of Hempstead, enjoyed a brief period of happiness and some popularity with the ladies once his skin cleared up. Unfortunately, he was stricken with small-pox just a few years later, which he survived, but left his face more marred than before. He never married and spent a fortune on building an extravagant new church (never completed) in the heart of Bitterbury.

James, Duke of Monmouth*, tried in 1685 to wrest the English throne from his uncle, King James the Second, in a popular uprising known as Monmouth's Rebellion. The coup attempt failed, and Monmouth was executed as a traitor. Monmouth's Dutch cousin **William of Orange***, on the other hand, had no trouble ousting his unpopular father-in-law from the English throne (the same King James—you see what a dysfunctional family this was!) a few years later. King William and Queen Mary are today chiefly remembered for lending their names to a style of furniture.

John Churchill* pursued his military and political ambitions with great gusto, earning a title and considerable wealth in the process. As the Duke of Marlborough, he was the commander who eventually outfoxed and defeated Louis XIV at Blenheim, Malplaquet and Oudenaarde. His exploits inspired his great-great-great-great-great-great-great-grandson Winston, who took on another great dictator in the twentieth century.

Henry Beaupree never made it very far in the army hierarchy, because, it was said, he had earned the enmity of some very influential people. In 1685 he threw in his lot with the Duke of Monmouth. He escaped execution after the battle of Sedgemoor by turning informant, only to die two years later in a debtor's prison.

The health of the poet **John Wilmot, Earl of Rochester*** deteriorated precipitously in the last two years of his life. He spent the months leading up to his death in devout repentance and earnest repudiation of his former debauched life. He was 32 years old.

The fame of the **Chevalier d'Artagnan***, the commander of Louis XIV's musketeers killed during the siege of Maastricht, was revived two centuries after his death by the writer Alexandre Dumas, who turned him into the hero of one of the most popular novels of all time.

Sébastien le Prestre de Vauban* is remembered by historians as the man who perfected the art of siege warfare and invented the socket bayonet. He had the reputation of being a very tenderhearted man. In his will he made generous provisions for four women besides his wife, all of whom had borne him children.

Dieneke Huizen lived to a ripe old age. She became rich in her dotage from a floor polish called *The Dutch Maid's Secret,* which she sold in penny-bottles from a barrow in London's Leather Lane.

Marie-Lise, Countess Bienmaline, enjoyed the reputation of being a patroness of the arts, and in later years her salon was attended by the most prominent thinkers of her day. She has been cited by some scholars as one of the models for Molière's *Femmes Savantes,* but that is patently absurd, since she was lauded by her many admirers as captivatingly shallow and refreshingly empty-headed.

Jean-Baptiste Colbert* was King Louis XIV's Minister of Finances, and Charles Perrault's boss. His innovations included the royal manufactories of mirror glass, and the royal tapestries works at Gobelin. Under his rule, merchants and craftsmen whose work was deemed unsatisfactory were sent to the pillory.

Charles Perrault* died in 1703 confident that he would be remembered for his influence in the arts, architecture and literature. He was justifiably proud of his intellectual exploits—the great dispute with Boileau known as the Quarrel of the Ancients and the Moderns for instance, or the controversial "Vindication of Women" (*Apologie des Femmes,* published in 1694).

He would perhaps have been mortified to learn that his immortality was in fact assured by a simple little book of folk tales, *The Tales of*

Mother Goose, which was published shortly before his death. Of these tales, one in particular stood out, and became a hit with children the world over.

It was titled *L'Histoire de Cendrillon, ou la Petite Pantoufle de Verre: The History of Cinderella, or the Little Glass Slipper.*

Lucinda Sunderland never produced another great classical painting in the mold of *Penelope and the Suitors* or *The Abduction of Helen.* All that is left to us of her later work is a handful of quiet domestic scenes. Very little more is known about her life. What we do know is that Sunderland and the surgeon **John Prynce** lived out their lives as man and wife, and that at least three more children were born from their union.

Some might say, then, that they lived happily ever after.

A word of caution, however. No matter how appealing this happily-ever-after ending may be, we must be extremely careful in applying it. For to be perfectly frank, such a baldly optimistic prognosis is plausible only in daydreams, or in fairy tales.

ABOUT THE AUTHOR

Hester Velmans is a novelist and translator of literary fiction. She grew up in Amsterdam, New York, Paris, Geneva and London, and now lives in Western Massachusetts. *SLIPPER* is her first novel for adults. For more, visit her website: www.hestervelmans.com.

CPSIA information can be obtained
at www.ICGtesting.com
Printed in the USA
BVHW04s1939040618
518174BV00001B/148/P